Stealing Pike's Peak

Stealing Pike's Peak

Gabe Galambos

9-19-01

Bob—
Thanks for your
help with the upcoming book.
Hope you enjoy this one.

Gabe Galambos

Writers Club Press
San Jose New York Lincoln Shanghai

Stealing Pike's Peak

All Rights Reserved © 2000 by Gabe Galambos

No part of this book may be reproduced or transmitted in any form or by
any means, graphic, electronic, or mechanical, including photocopying,
recording, taping, or by any information storage retrieval system,
without the permission in writing from the publisher.

Writers Club Press
an imprint of iUniverse.com, Inc.

For information address:
iUniverse.com, Inc.
620 North 48th Street, Suite 201
Lincoln, NE 68504-3467
www.iuniverse.com

This is a work of fiction. Any reference to true events, locales,
organizations, or characters are presented in a fictitious
manner to enhance the novel's sense of reality.

ISBN: 0-595-13681-8

Printed in the United States of America

To my parents,
with gratitude.

Prologue

---

*A*ugust, Manhattan

Ibrahim Husseini stared.

And stared again, his dark eyes fixed on the photograph in the book, so caught by the image that others who waded around him at the Bestseller section of Barnes and Noble seemed to disappear.

Until now it had been just another day, one wasted by the detailed drudgery of his job at the small accounting firm near Fifth and 18th. His life had not always been so misdirected. There had been a time, before the vast ocean—*this cursed America*—when what he did mattered. The cruel ocean tossed him about, at times submerging him, and he had feared he might drown, along with the pitiful refuse awash in his midst.

But now, comforting himself with a cup of hazelnut coffee before the subway ride home to Brooklyn, Husseini sensed there may yet be a way to save himself. He concentrated ever harder on the photograph in the middle of *Pike's Peak*. In the three years since coming to America, he had become enamored with the strategy and brutality of American football. In New York especially, the book about Jets quarterback Zach Pike was hot, and he hadn't been able to resist skimming through it.

The photo before him was a moment in time, a split second, captured and captioned: **Family and friends mug with Zach following a game of touch, Falmouth, Cape Cod, summer 1985. In Back: sister Liz,**

Ma and Pa Pike, brothers Teddy and Sam. In Front: Zach, Meg Symes, Zvi Langer.

Oh, how happy they were! The All-American family: blond bikini-clad daughter, giant redwood sons, a loving mother, a proud father.

Zach clutched a football, his lanky fourteen year old frame and youthful exuberance firmly anchored by Papa Pike's large hands on his shoulders. The tank-topped girl in the middle, Meg, mischievously tickled her two flanking friends. But it was on this boy, Zvi Langer, that Husseini mainly focused.

There was something about those sharp, sparkling eyes, the dimples framing a toothy smile, the expectant look. That beastly look!

Suddenly Husseini reached out to a shelf for support. A cascade of books crashed to the floor. He barked an embarrassed laugh, swallowed it. And as he bent over to pick up the books, horrific images exploded before his eyes.

Desperate hands instinctively reaching up to remnants of a bloody throat, futile in that it no longer supported a wavering head. Over and over, in rapid-fire sequence, the image flashed, until it slowed to a final frame and faded away.

After he'd put the last book back on the shelf, Husseini, cradling two copies of *Pike's Peak*, headed towards the check-out salesgirl.

"Please, I would very much like to purchase these two books. Please, these books."

"Why of course, sir," said the salesgirl, eyeing him curiously as she rang up the sale. "I hope you enjoy the books," she said.

"I am sure I will. Thank you very much."

Submerged in a wave of pedestrian traffic as he left the bookstore, Husseini imagined how excited Charlie Hammami, in London, would be to receive this treasure, this *gift from Allah.* He'd fed ex the second copy tomorrow morning, first thing.

Squinting into a bright late-day sun, he stroked a hand over his mouth, patted his mustache, and quickened his steps towards the subway station. He was impatient to get home and start reading.

A billowing wind suddenly careened between cavernous skyscrapers and pushed him along. And for just a moment Ibrahim Husseini could have sworn it was a *Hamsin*, a desert wind.

CHAPTER ONE

"So, ZZZaaCH, there you are on the Miami eighteen yard line, it's third down with four yards to go."

Joe Allen, Sunday night anchor of WNBC's Sports Wrap, lowered his wire-frame glasses and they settled in a customary spot almost on the tip of his nose. He inched forward and closer to his guest, disregarding any semblance of personal space.

"Eleven seconds remain on the clock," he whispered each word carefully, "a field goal ties it for you and forces an overtime. You win this game and you're in the playoffs. You lose, you go home."

The anchor shrugged his shoulders, threw apart his arms, dropped his notes, and with his trademark flair for the theatrical beseeched, "What were you thinking? What, praise be, *were you thinking?*"

Squirming slightly in the chair, Zach Pike laughed. "Call 911, there's a quarterback having a heart attack here, that's what I was thinking."

Then, settling himself, Zach continued. "With no time-outs left I was either throwing the ball into the ground, out of bounds, or into the end zone. I've always felt that if a game can be won in regulation time, it's imperative to do so. There's no fairness with overtime, there's just a coin flip to see which team gets the ball first. Since overtime is sudden-death we could have lost without a chance to do something with the ball."

"Let's roll the tape of the play. Describe it for us Zach, if you would."

As the Jets players scrambled up to the line of scrimmage, Zach's voice could be overheard. "It's strange really. A lot of times when faced with a big play, each facet of it seems to unravel in slow motion. It's a big advantage because that way I can size up the situation and hopefully make the right decision."

Zach cupped his hands around his mouth and yelled over the din of a hostile Miami crowd to the receiver on his left. Turning right, he gesticulated wildly to two wideouts. As he was about to bend behind the center, he wheeled around to his lone running back and twisted his right foot back and forth into the ground. On his first bark behind the center the ball was snapped into his awaiting hands.

As Zach glided into his backpedal, a blitzing middle linebacker dove between the center and guard when suddenly, right before the sack, the running back drove into the linebacker's legs, flipping him up in the air and downward head first.

Zach reared up, impervious to the crashing bodies all around him. He cocked his arm, feigned a throw to the sideline, and with a flick of his wrist launched a beautiful spiral which nestled softly into the outstretched arms of a streaking receiver in the far right corner of the end zone.

"And so there I am," Zach continued as the video showed him throwing up his arms and pumping his fist, "looking pretty relieved, let me tell you."

"Thanks for coming on with us, ZZZaaCH, despite the late hour. We know you've had a busy day. Can we book you again," teased Joe Allen, "after you win another MVP in the Super Bowl?"

"Tell you what! If we win another Super Bowl, MVP or not, I'll even host your show. How 'bout that?"

Joe Allen leaned back, lowered his wire frame glasses almost to the tip of his nose, his eyebrows arching over an incredulous gaze.

Standing by the camera crew, Brian Sullivan, the limo driver, marveled at how fortunate he was to have his job. Sure it was only part-time until he graduated in May from City College, but heck, it paid the bills and gave him the opportunity to meet people like Zach Pike.

After picking Zach up at the airport following the win down in Miami, Brian had brought him straight to the WNBC studio in Rockefeller Center.

"Where do you go to school? What's your major? Are you from the city?" Zach had wanted to know.

There was almost no talk about the big game itself. Brian had at first felt awed by the sports legend, but Zach put him totally at ease.

"Hey Brian, do you know how to get to Hempstead, Long Island?" Zach asked while putting on his goose-down parka.

Hah, Fancy-ville! "Sure." He smiled at Zach. "You're not the only celeb I've ever chauffeured."

"I'll be back in half an hour," Meg Symes told the attendant of the outdoor parking lot on Lexington Avenue. Then she closed the door of her red Toyota Camry.

She walked briskly past the Waldorf Astoria as crystal snowflakes drifted down and clung to her tartan shawl.

How surprised Zach would be to see her waiting for him. They would laugh, and Zach would lift her up to him and twirl her around until there was a dizzyingly long kiss. And then, once they were back at Zach's, they would snuggle before a crackling fire, sip some hot cider, and make love until falling asleep in an interwoven embrace.

She smiled to herself at the possibilities.

Fifth Avenue was an enchanted wonderland and Meg hardly knew where to go first. Peering into the festive Christmas windows of Saks Fifth Avenue, she glanced at her reflection and was surprised at just how radiantly happy she was. Since moving from San Francisco to New York almost a year ago, she had exchanged her fast-paced position in an advertising firm in the TransAmerica Pyramid building for one equally demanding on Broadway. The move had meant trading cable cars and hiking in Yosemite for roller blading in Central Park and wandering around the Met.

So the big difference—*hell, all the difference*—was in finally succumbing to Zach's persistent overtures that they renew an old high school romance. A romance that was doomed for no other reason other than its being a first one, a naive one, one that had misled them into thinking there would surely be others that were even better. There weren't.

She strolled down the Promenade and Channel Gardens, towards the huge eighty foot Christmas tree of Rockefeller Plaza, thinking back. It seemed to her she'd known Zach forever.

At first they'd been friends at elementary school. Then they, and a few others, were close friends in a high school cliquish way. Going steady followed in their junior and senior years, but then Zach went to Ann Arbor to play for the Wolverines, while she stayed in Boston and attended Boston College. They saw each other at breaks and every summer but their relationship was changing. They were caught up in new worlds, busy with new acquaintances.

At some point they'd become close friends once more.

Standing now in the warm aura of the Christmas tree, Meg felt utterly serene. The Tree's colorful lights and enchanting ornaments charmed her. And suddenly she found herself praying along with the nearby illuminated angels that she and Zach would always be as in love as the lone couple who, arms wound around each other, now glided off the ice skating rink below the imposing bronzed statue of Prometheus.

But now it was time to go meet him.

"Hey Brian, go deep," urged Zach as he scooped up a handful of fresh snow.

The limo driver and the N.F.L.quarterback had just said good night to WNBC's security guard and were goofing around on the snowy side street. Brian trotted fifteen yards and spun his torso in earnest anticipation of the bomb.

The snowball softly disintegrated above his head.

Brian stopped and, putting his hands on his hips, went limp in disappointment.

For a moment Zach thought it was just a big act. But Brian's wince and the way his face curled, and then fell, convinced him it wasn't.

"Sorry pal," shrugged Zach. "I hate this powdery shit."

Just then three men, seemingly out of nowhere, emerged from the white haze and stood directly in his path.

"Mr. Pike, we would be most honored to have your autograph," said the youngest and largest of the men as he thrust forward a pencil and notepad.

Zach hesitated. Unlike typical fans, these men were gray and humorless. Shark-like, they circled around him. An inner voice urged Zach to turn, to get away, to run.

He reasoned the voice away, dismissing it as foolishness. He took the pencil and pad and began signing.

Immediately, a crushing blow in the small of his back blindsided him, jolting him off his feet into the snow. The man who had asked for the autograph slammed on top of him and shoved a handkerchief doused with sweet pungent chloroform over his mouth and nose.

Struggling in the growing darkness, Zach noticed Brian suddenly pounce from behind. Brian tore at the man's hair. He ripped the man's face.

But a third man, one who stood a few feet away, knocked Brian aside with a swift kick to the head. The man whipped out a silencer fitted Ingram M-10 machine pistol, and in that instant Zach knew Brian's fight was over. Brian was about to die. The clip was emptied in a two second burst.

It was the dazed look on the faces of a couple, perhaps honeymooners, that Meg first noticed. They were staggering, clutching onto each other for support.

Looking past them she saw men dragging and pulling some poor soul into a black Jeep, all the while raining down furious blows upon him.

"No!" Meg shrieked as the realization smacked her with sickening certainty.

Within a heartbeat she was running, running, as hard as she could.

NO. Please God, NO!

The Jeep's tires squealed.

"Help!" Meg cried. "Won't somebody please help?" she pleaded.

The Jeep bolted away into the white night.

Meg frantically turned in every direction.

And as police sirens wailed louder and closer, Meg found herself cradling the head of a boy, his flesh and organs ripped apart, his blood melting through the film of snow on the ground.

Her tears fell softly over the boy's angelic face and into his open eyes. The eyes reflected bright Christmas tree lights and as Meg gazed, the lights began to spin and move wildly, some pulsating brighter, some fading away.

CHAPTER TWO

"*G*ood Morning! We have some horrifying news to report as our headline story." Matt Lauer made the announcement with studied gravity.

"At approximately 11:50 P.M., after appearing on New York's Sports Wrap program, New York Jet quarterback Zach Pike was abducted by several men who, eyewitnesses say, spirited him away in a waiting vehicle. The twenty-year-old limousine driver who accompanied Pike, identified as Brian Sullivan, was fatally wounded in a hail of gunfire. Police at this time say they have no leads as to Pike's whereabouts, TODAY, Monday, the eighteenth of December."

The instant the TODAY show jingle ended there was videotape of a disconsolate woman slumped over in the snow, police desperately working over a disfigured body, and people, crying and bewildered, pacing aimlessly about.

Lauer continued. "Camera crews were on the scene last night for this dramatic footage just moments after the incident. All this transpired right in front of our NBC affiliate in Rockefeller Center. We're going to go live to Katie Couric, who is out there now."

"Thank you, Matt. Police and the FBI have cordoned off the crime area from what is a rapidly growing throng of onlookers. People here are distressed, perplexed, and, most of all, furious over this terrible event. Behind me I think you can see Mobile Crime Unit Technicians marking with yellow chalk areas in which they've found any scrap of evidence. They're placing some findings into evidence bags right now.

"Standing next to me," Couric said with a turn to her left, "is Detective Billy Haynes of the New York Police Department. `Detective Haynes, what do you hope to find back there?`"

"Well, Katie, I'll tell you," said a hefty man in a gray three-piece suit. "Scene investigation is based on what forensic scientists like to call the *transfer of material* premise. When two entities come in contact with each other, material is transferred from one to the other." The accent was part New York, a lot Southern. "Now from what we've gathered, and from what witnesses have told us, there was quite a pitched battle here. Our Crime Lab will be able to examine serology and ballistics evidence, as well as hairs and fibers with microscopy trace. We'll send some substances to the Fingerprint Laser Unit."

"Katie," interrupted Lauer, "we're going to go live now to Brookline, Massachusetts, to the home of Zach Pike's parents. Family members and close friends have been arriving all through the night and continue to do so. I understand that Ben Pike, Zach's father, is about to read a prepared statement."

A grizzled but robust man, clad in a tweed sports coat despite the morning chill, approached a bouquet of outstretched microphones.

"On behalf of our entire family, I would like to express our sympathy to the family of Brian Sullivan. Our thoughts and prayers are with you. At this time we do not know who, or for that matter why, Zach was abducted last night. There has been no communication with those involved."

A tremor swept over Ben as he glanced up, and swallowed hard. "To those who have committed this crime, you are responsible for my son's well-being. Please—" His voice broke, then he went on. "You have nothing to gain by continuing to hold my son. I ask that you release him immediately. We have no further statements."

Turning to leave, Ben was hit with a barrage of questions from the assembled media.

"Should a ransom demand be made, how would you pay it?"

"Why do you think Zach was abducted?"

"Has Zach been involved in any shady dealings?"

Clearing his throat, Ben looked over the crowd with moist eyes.

"We understand you people in the media have a job to do. We can't stop you from maintaining a vigil around our house. But please—please—don't turn this into a circus! Respect our privacy during this difficult time."

Lauer straightened from a reflective pose as the camera swung onto him. "As you may know," he somberly said, "we were scheduled to bring you live satellite reports from famine-stricken Sudan. However, in light of breaking developments, we will continue to cover the Zach Pike story for the rest of the morning."

In Long Island City, by the foot of the Queensboro Bridge, four deliberate men were preparing to finish what had been an exhilarating few hours. They had come to an old General Electric factory that sat dormant, hidden among railroad yards and even older factories. There the get-away driver and the three assailants abandoned the Jeep, removed bloody clothes, and tended to a variety of cuts and abrasions.

Staring at their bound and gagged quarry, the culmination of the mandate they had received, the men became pensive.

"Yousef," said the eldest of the group, Sayid Abu Zaid, in a calm quiet voice, "I think it is time you gave the medicine."

A tall man cleaned his eyeglasses with a handkerchief and slowly walked forward. Zach Pike followed his every step beneath hooded, swollen eyes.

In Yousef Yassin's hand was a long syringe filled with a drug cocktail. While doing surgical rotations at Mount Sinai Hospital, anesthesiologists had talked about the powerful synergistic properties of the DART, a combination of versed for relaxation, glycopyrolate to slow secretions, and ketamine to stimulate respiration. He'd stolen a vial from the hospital for the occasion.

"Zach," assured Yousef with a pat on a bared shoulder, "this is some medication that will put you to sleep for a few hours." Wiping the intended area near the shoulder with an alcohol prep pad, Yousef drove the syringe home and prayed that the DART, a substantial amount considering Zach's 215 pounds, would not kill. There was always that risk with anesthetics, especially for one who would be unattended for so long.

Now the four men worked quickly, furiously. Vernon Compton-El, a black convert to Islam, and brawny Hassan Kamal carried Zach through a loading door and into a parked G.E. truck. In the truck was a large wooden crate. In the wooden crate there was a doorless and empty refrigerator.

As soon as Zach was hoisted up and lowered into the blanket-cushioned refrigerator, Yousef and Sayid threw two more blankets over him and then fitted a series of rubber belts over where the door had been. They picked up the top of the crate, hammered it shut. Words had been stamped on the lid:

DESTINATION: SUDAN
HUMANITARIAN AID
NOT FOR RESALE—NOT COMMERCIAL VALUE

"Brothers," said Sayid, "it is almost dawn. It is time to pray."

Kneeling on the ground, occasionally lying prostrate in total submission, the four recited the *Shahada*, the profession of faith.

"There is no god, but God, and Muhammad is his prophet."

In the thin light of daybreak the four embraced and went in separate directions.

Yousef, having long ago learned how to function despite sleepless nights, was off to the hospital to care for the sick, the elderly, and the dying.

Hassan, barely twenty years old, felt exhausted in his massive body. He was going home to sleep. At some point he would call in sick to the Middle Eastern specialty food shop where he worked.

The devout Sayid returned home to have breakfast with his wife. She would assume he spent another night studying the Koran in a Brooklyn storefront mosque.

As for Vernon Compton-El, he drove the G.E. truck down the Van Wyck Expressway. And his mind began to wander.

It seemed like just yesterday that the Afghan Refugee Center in Brooklyn sent him where all true believers gravitated in 1981, to battle the Soviets as a Mujaheddin *Holy Warrior,* in Afghanistan.

Those were heady days and Mujaheddin from all over the Islamic world were already in Afghanistan when Compton-El arrived. The CIA was there too. Supporting their appointed guerilla fighter, Gulbuddin Hekmatyar, the CIA set up boot camps and funneled three billion dollars his way. But Hekmatyar believed that terrorizing Allah's enemies applied not only to the Soviets, but to the Americans as well. Owing to the CIA's misreading of Hekmatyar, by the time Compton-El returned to the States he was ready to fight a Jihad Holy War against infidels wherever they might be. But by now he had a growing family to feed and a mortgage to pay. So he diligently went to work as a driver for G.E. thinking his soldiering days were behind him and that assuring his place in heaven would take place somewhere down the road.

How fortunate I am, mused Compton-El, *that the road is now, and that I am finally chosen to serve Allah.*

Compton-El guided his truck into JFK Airport and followed the signs towards the North Passenger Terminal, the principal cargo area for the famine relief flights.

"What ya got here pal?" yawned a security guard.

"Got me some refrigerators. For those poor folks in Africa." Compton-El stuck the export declaration out the driver's side window.

The guard took it, jotted down a few numbers on a security form, and wrote down the time as he glanced at his watch.

"My damn relief shift better show up soon," he said as he handed back the export declaration. "Well, have a good one."

A Southern Air Transport 747, swarming with hectic activity, had its sides and nose splayed open. Compton-El drove over to where some forklift operators were working and yelled, "Over here men!" He opened the back of the truck, then went to find the Airline Loadmaster.

A balding man whose leather jacket was zippered halfway up a colorful silk tie was standing near the wing of the plane with two other men, a UNICEF rep, and one from customs.

"Excuse me," Compton-El said. "You the Loadmaster?"

He nodded. "Name's Hutchinson. What can I do for you?"

Compton-El introduced himself, explained about the refrigerators and presented the export declaration and bill of lading. Then he walked back to his truck, emptied now by a cookie-sheet forklift of its contents, and drove off with a feeling of serenity: MISSION ACCOMPLISHED.

Hutchinson watched him go. He'd thought the man wouldn't show— it was just two hours from take off. Three days ago, he had been approached by a travel agency owner named Bahr, to expedite the on-off loading and balancing of a crate numbered 004JX bearing a refrigerator. If he made sure cargo handlers at JFK and Khartoum were careful with it, there would be a tidy sum, *baksheesh* he thought the Arabs called it, that would be deposited into his account. Once the crate was in Khartoum a health ministry official would clear it through customs and be responsible from there.

"A refrigerator, my ass," Hutchinson muttered to himself at the time, but the job seemed easy enough and the money was good, very good.

For the next two hours Hutchinson bounced around like a traffic cop directing ball bearing pallets of medical equipment, portable plastic latrines, and generators. He met the pilot, co-pilot, and navigator and wished them a good trip. And then he scrambled on board along with several young UNICEF workers who'd brought their sleeping bags, books, cards, and food.

Right before take-off Hutchinson walked over to crate 004JX and carefully inspected it. There were a couple of small holes on each side of the crate. He took a flashlight and strained to see inside. Much to his surprise, he thought he actually saw the white of a refrigerator. Lacking the ability to poke and pry further, he slapped the crate hard.

There was no sound, no reaction, no further insight forthcoming.

Resigned, Hutchinson shuffled to the jump seat behind the cockpit and fastened his seatbelt. Advance weather bulletins had predicted a bumpy ride.

CHAPTER THREE

"*I*'ve got a surprise for you Zvi," Dalia said. She smiled, a warm breeze ruffled her hair; a brilliant late December sun highlighted her blond curls.

"Is it a…puppy?"

"No silly," scolded Dalia, her hands hidden behind her arched rocking back. "I'll give you a hint. It has something to do with Chanukah."

"Oh! Well then, it must be my present. It's a bicycle, right?" Zvi's smile broadened.

"NO!" Dalia stretched her hands before her. "I'm going to have to tell you. It's a *sivivon*. To celebrate the victory of Judah the Maccabbee and the Jews over the Greek Syrians. Remember? I'll spin it for you."

Dalia squatted and adeptly spun the top, each side of which contained the first letter of the words she was exuberantly emphasizing.

"GREAT MIRACLE WAS HERE! GREAT MIRACLE WAS HERE!"

The top wobbled and came to rest with the letter *PAI*, for the word HERE, facing up.

"You know Dalia, in America and everywhere else outside of Israel, a *sivivon* is called a dreidel and children play with a dreidel that has the letter for the word THERE instead of HERE."

Dalia wrinkled her nose and tilted her head in deep thought.

"That's because the miracle, the victory, was here," explained Zvi, "in Israel, not in the Diaspora."

14

"I don't understand, Zvi. A miracle is good for everybody, every-where. It's good for here," she giggled while placing her hand on Zvi's heart. "And it's good for the belly, and your fingers, and toes." Her fin-gers darted here and there, tickling him.

Zvi laughed as Dalia abruptly turned and ran off to play with the other children.

It had been a busy day taking the children on this field trip to Tiberias, and Zvi wasn't sure who was having a better time, the children or himself. First he'd taken them to Hamat Tiberias, the national park with its trickling hot springs and spectacular fourth century A.D. mosaic synagogue floor. After that they'd gone to kibbutz Ginosar's musuem to see how a second temple period fishing boat had been retrieved intact from the muddy shores of the Sea of Galilee.

The children loved the boat ride over the shimmering blue of the Sea and they now dallied along a seaside Promenade, snacking on felafel and ice cream. Soon it would be time to return to kibbutz Ein Gev.

Whenever he was on break from his archaeology studies at Hebrew University in Jerusalem, Zvi loved returning to the kibbutz. It was more than just his mother's cooking or the opportunity to hang out with friends he had known since kibbutz nursery days.

For him it was a safe harbor from the heavy burdens of his life, a respite from the chronic siege of anxiety, even terror, that haunted his day.

Watching the children play catch along the Promenade, Zvi saw himself, and his friends, and what once was. Which reminded him: he'd better check Sunday's football results, see who'd won. Having lived in the States as a teenager, he still tried to follow the New England Patriots, his favorite team since their Super Bowl appearance in 1986, the year he returned to Israel. More than that, Zvi faithfully followed the exploits of his favorite player, Jet quarterback Zach Pike, who also happened to be his best friend.

Zvi pulled a late edition Jerusalem Post from his day pack and opened it to the second to last page. He found the paragraph on the

Pats' win, which confirmed their playoff spot as a wild card. Then his gaze settled on the blurb of the Jets victory. Zach had thrown three touchdowns, one coming for a winning strike as time expired. But there was something ominous about the last line notifying readers of a related story on page one.

It was a short Associated Press insert in bold type halfway down the right side of the page that must have come across at press time.

It was learned that New York Jet quarterback Zach Pike was abducted by unknown assailants at Rockefeller Plaza last night. Authorities do not know his location or his condition. A limousine driver at the scene was fatally shot.

Menacing possibilities suddenly spiraled all around Zvi, momentarily disorienting him.

"We're going now, children," he said calmly to the group. "Quickly, back to the kibbutz."

It was twenty-one kilometers to Ein Gev over the same route Zvi had covered just a week before in the Sea of Galilee Marathon. He'd run it on a whim. The course was flat, he was in good shape, and with half the kibbutz present to cheer him on, Zvi had finished in three hours, ten minutes. It had been exhilirating.

But now familiar bends in the road, clumps of palm trees, and kibbutz banana and date plantations were on the periphery. His focus was straight-ahead, in fast forward. Zvi turned the minibus left past a **WEL-COME TO EIN GEV** sign and deposited the children at the main house.

He burst through the front door where his mother was folding laundry, his eyes hot, his face stiff.

"Zvi, what is it?" she asked, holding a shirt to her heart. "What's wrong?"

"Zach's been kidnapped!" He handed her the newspaper.

"Your father's still at a Knesset meeting," she said, looking up from the article. Her face, as beautiful as ever, was drained of all color.

"There's some sort of no-confidence vote again. I'll reach him on his cell phone."

While his parents spoke Zvi dialed the Pike residence from his parents' bedroom. It was 3:10 P.M., which would make it 9:10 A.M. in Boston.

"Hello." The voice was soft and subdued

Zvi hesitated for a moment. "Is this the Pike's?"

"Yes. Who may I ask is calling?"

"Meggie, is that you?" Of course she'd be there, he realized.

This time the hesitation was from the other end.

"Zvi? Oh, Zvi it's so good to hear from you. You heard what happened? It's just awful around here. I came up this morning from New York to be with the family. Zach's mom is beside herself…."

"Meggie, settle down. Tell me exactly what happened."

Meg recounted the previous night's events as calmly as she could. Listening, Zvi half buried his head in the crook of his elbow.

"Zvi, are you okay?"

" I'm going to be flying in tomorrow. My parents will probably come too. It'll be alright Meggie, you'll see."

"Zvi. Hurry! Please hurry."

As Zvi left the kibbutz in his beat-up Renault, the old Roman fort of Susita, backed by the imposing brown wall of the Golan Heights, towered above him. The farmers and fisherman of Ein Gev had taken Susita from the Syrians in a surprise night attack in 1948's War of Independence. The battle won the Sea of Galilee for Israel. But until the 1967 Six Day War the Heights had remained in Syrian hands, enabling them to subject nearby Israeli settlements to artillery barrages. Driving now beneath the Heights, Zvi felt their loomimg presence.

With luck it would take him two hours to drive to Tel Aviv. He climbed past Mount Tabor, where the prophet and poet Deborah had once called an Israelite army under Barak to assemble and *fight from heaven,* then sped through the Jezre'el valley, site of epic battles, all the while agonizing over who would possibly want to hurt Zach. A thought took shape as he drove below *Har Megiddo*, Mount Megiddo, where St. John the Divine had foretold the ultimate Armageddon between the forces of good and evil would take place. By the time Zvi reached Netanya, on the Mediterranean, and made a beeline south to T.A., he had reached a disturbing conclusion: Nobody in their right mind would want to harm somebody like Zach. They must mean, through Zach, to obtain something or to harm somebody else.

Zvi parked the Renault just outside the partially walled military compound called the KIRYA in the heart of Tel Aviv. A serious looking serviceman of Sephardic origin studied Zvi's ordinary Reservist Booklet from his small security booth. An M-16 dangled from his shoulder.

"What's your business here?"

"I'm here to notify my unit that I'll be going out of the country," replied Zvi.

"What unit is that?"

"Intelligence."

A phone call cleared Zvi past the security booth. He walked into a military city of tan buildings and barracks and navigated his way through an intricate maze. After five minutes he came to a nondescript building, where several soldiers with brown Golani Brigade berets and Galil assault rifles were milling about.

A cute redheaded female soldier smiled and took Zvi's Reservist Booklet through an open window.

"How can I help you?"

"I need to see Chief of Staff Almog or Deputy Chief Lahav."

The redhead handed the Booklet to another soldier behind her who immediately disappeared with it.

After what seemed to be an inordinately long period she answered a phone call, nodded, and smiled again. "Major General Lahav's not in, but Lieutenant General Almog will see you."

Zvi was accompanied past several manned computer stations and down a stairway he had had occasion to descend before. He'd known either Chief of Staff Almog or Deputy Lahav would be in this late in the afternoon, but he was glad it was Almog.

"Zvika, I'm so happy to see you. How have you been?" A short, ruddy man who Zvi, at 5 feet 10, always seemed to tower over sprang from behind a cluttered desk. Almog greeted him with a warm smile and twinkling eyes. Almost at once his face changed.

"Zvika, what's wrong? What's the matter?"

Before Zvi could respond, Almog dragged him by the arm and coaxed him into a chair.

Belying the Chief of Staff's slight paunch and compassionate fatherly ways was an *Itur Haoz* courage medal pinned to his chest. Some of his accomplishments were almost public knowledge. In his day Almog had completed a dangerous rite of initiation by journeying on foot to the ancient Jordanian red rock city of Petra; helped overpower Black September terrorist hijackers aboard a Sabena jet in 1972; and directed an electronic jamming blanket from a Boeing 707 in a 1988 operation that wiped out el-Fatah head Abu Jihad. Rumors abounded in military circles about Almog's more secret feats.

"I'm flying to Boston tomorrow," Zvi said wearily. "A friend, a good friend, has been kidnapped. Apparently, nothing is known about his condition or the perpetrators."

"Zvika, I don't think that's a good idea. Do you think you can do more than the local police?"

"No, no. I'm not going because of that. Our whole family is very close to his. In fact, they are just like family to me. I want to be there for them."

Almog walked over to a carafe and poured two glasses of ice water. "You know," he said while handing a glass to Zvi, "you could have just called to let us know you were going out of the country."

Zvi raised the glass, poured the water down his dry throat. He quickly revised what he'd been going to say.

" I had things to do in Tel Aviv anyway." Zvi was not at all sure he was convincing. "Besides, I had to get out for awhile. I couldn't just stay still. You know?"

The Chief of Staff looked hurt that one of his best soldiers had inexplicably resolved to clam up. But he didn't pry any further.

"I understand. Just leave the particulars about where you'll be and when you expect to return with my secretary."

"Will do."

Almog squeezed a stubby hand on Zvi's shoulder. "Have a safe trip. I hope your friend is fine. Zvika, if there's anything I can do…."

"I know. Thanks."

It was 8:00 P.M. when Zvi finally returned home. His mother was scurrying about, frenetically racing with clothes-laden arms between the bedroom and three open suitcases in the living room. As usual Oded Langer was on the phone with Knesset cronies. He paced around the room, biting into a hot dog whenever the party at the other end of the line interrupted him. He still wore the same blue dress shirt and gray pants that he'd worn at work.

Zvi's father was a first generation Israeli-born *sabra,* a big deal when he was born in 1940 to parents who'd had the foresight to flee Hitler's Germany. Even now his hair was still jet black, his eyes focused and intense, his movements quick and emphatic—like Zvi's. People often said that the acorn didn't fall far from the tree. For many years Zvi hoped that the physical similarities were where comparison ended.

"Zvi, there's hot dogs and beans. I want you to eat something," Aviva ordered. "But first we have to light candles."

Eight colorful candles, and one *shamas* lighting candle, stood in a row by a window. The Langers were a secular family. Chanukah candle lighting and Passover seders were observed as a matter of custom. But as of late Zvi had begun attending Torah and Talmud classes at a Yeshiva in Jerusalem.

"Intellectual curiosity," was how he explained his new found religious interest. In fact, Zvi knew that what he sought was not sweeping religious enlightenment but rather answers, intense and personal answers. Who was he? Why did he have to be the one? What was to become of him?

Oded Langer once again delegated lighting the candles in favor of Zvi, who now donned a blue knit kippah.

"Blessed are You, Hashem our God, King of the universe, Who has wrought miracles for our forefathers, in those days, at this season.

"These lights we kindle upon the miracles, the wonders, the salvations, and the battles which you performed."

Mesmerized by the glowing candles, their flames flickering and reflected in the window glass, it seemed to Zvi that Zach was once again close by, partaking in his family's happiness as they sang all of *Maoz Tsur's* verses.

"O mighty Rock of my salvation,
   to praise You is a delight.
 Restore my House of prayer
   and there we will bring a thanksgiving offering.

 Troubles sated my soul,
   when with grief my strength was consumed.
 They had embittered my life with hardship,
   with the calf-like kingdom's bondage."

His mother's hand clasped his own and his father rubbed the back of his neck as they continued singing, making Zvi worry that his parents sensed his shivering, and shared his dread.

It's starting again; the madness is starting again.

"Bare your holy arm
   and hasten the End for salvation—

Avenge the vengeance of Your servant's blood
from the wicked nation.
For the triumph is too long delayed for us,
and there is no end to days of evil…"

The "Rrringg" roused Zvi from a twilight state. The day's news and the jitters over tomorrow morning's flight had already ruled out real sleep.

12:30 A.M.! Now what?

His father caught the phone at the start of the second sound.

"Itzik, I thought you wouldn't be able to get back to me before we fly to Boston."

Despite his father's muted voice, Zvi could hear every word from his adjacent bedroom.

"Yeah, I know it's been a long time."

Who would call so late just to catch up on old times?

"Let me just make certain; your line is secure, isn't it?"

Well, this wasn't going to be just idle chit-chat after all.

His father's next muffled words stabbed him with the same sort of pain as other words, of another time.

"We may have a problem here. Ben Pike's boy has been kidnapped!"

After a few moments the hurt subsided into numbness. And Zvi took solace in knowing that his father was at least thinking along the same lines as himself, alerting someone, the same way he should have but could not alert Chief of Staff Almog.

The numbness was calming, protective, therapeutic. It suddenly dawned on Zvi that perhaps he was in some sort of diffuse, subtle shock.

CHAPTER FOUR

$\mathcal{T}$he best thing that happened to Zach was that he kept passing out. The worst thing that happened was that his bouts of consciousness kept getting longer and longer.

Iinitially, Zach awakened to a loud humming sound and the definite sensation that he was moving; more to the point, that he was in transit. It hurt to think and it hurt all over. His arms and legs were paralyzed, his eyes, face and ribs throbbed in pain. His mouth felt grotesquely stretched inwards and he gasped for breath. He was being suffocated. Buried alive....

When Zach next came to he sensed he was in a motor vehicle of some kind. A horn honked, a motor stammered to a standstill and then revved up again, and there was occasional laughing and cursing in a language he could not understand. A faint smell of exhaust pipes and spicy cooking wafted in the air. With each bump in the road different fragments of what happened in Rockefeller Plaza jarred his mind: a snowball, a handkerchief in his face, a gunshot, and, strangely, what he thought was Meg's distant scream.

He now woke up with a start, a gasp escaping from his ungagged mouth. An unshaded light bulb suspended from the ceiling illuminated a white plastered cell. Save for a small barred window on a metal door, there was no link to the world outside. A small mirror dangled by a nail above a washbasin. Looking down Zach saw his legs were shackled in chains. Only a blanket seperated himself from a cool, hard floor. He shut his eyes tight and commanded himself to snap out of it, but when his eyes opened, the nightmare was still there.

Ahmed Mohammed ibn Sayid had grown up in the Gezira district that seperated the White and Blue Nile, along muddy banks from which, as a boy, he saw ebony, ivory, and gold merchants ply felucca sailing boats. By the age of nine he had astounded religious teachers by memorizing all the suras in the Koran. His eyes were large and sparkling; a birthmark dotted his right cheek; his lips were full and there was a good luck sign *falsa* appearing as a v-shaped gap between his front teeth. His neighbors on the river island of Abba claimed that he bore all the required characteristics, including proper lineage. He himself had always known that he possesed the religious zeal of a dervish and the charisma of a sheik—qualities that would surely one day guide him in restoring the faith to its original simplicity.

Ahmed Mohammed ibn Sayid was the "Anticipated One," the messiah, the next Mahdi.

Ahmed Mohammed ibn Sayid, his aide at his side, tingled with excitement as his personal bodyguard drove the Peugeot 504 down the wide colonial style Sharia el-Nil boulevard. The Blue Nile and Tuti island drifted by on his right and the People's Palace, Grand Hotel, and the Sudan National Museum flickered by in rapid succession on his left. The Peugeot would soon be leaving Khartoum for Omdurman, across the White Nile.

It had been four months since ibn Sayid was politely asked if he would be so kind as to take custody of a valuable package that would be arriving from America. It seemed a gentleman living in London called Charlie Hammami had received a tip from a former employee that a famous American sports hero could be most valuable.

Apparently, this man called Hammami, had at one time helped sponsor a trip to Algeria of prominent Egyptian cleric Abdul Ali Latif. After

Latif had delivered a rousing speech before members of the radically fundamentalist Algerian Islamic Salvation Front, he'd returned from the engagement to Hammami's palatial Algiers guesthouse where he was brutally mowed down. Hammami, embarrassed and disgraced, closed his Algiers residence and had to dismiss his Algiers employees. Despite eyewitness accounts and repeated scrutiny of closed circuit video that captured the incident, nothing could be done about it. Until possibly now.

The Peugeot swung past the rebuilt conical domed tomb of the 19th century Mahdi, the one ibn Sayid modeled his life after. "There is no god but Allah. And Mohammed is the prophet of Allah. And Ahmed Mohammed el Mahdi is the successor of Allah's prophet!"

Mahdi ibn Sayid closed his eyes in reverance. He knew the story well.

In 1882 the *Ansars*, the followers of the 19th century Mahdi, overwhelmed Egyptian armies commanded by British officer William Hicks. Fearing that garrisons would be cut off throughout Sudan by the growing Mahdi movement, Britain decided to dispatch General Charles "Chinese" Gordon to supervise the orderly evacuation of all foreigners from Sudan. Gordon had earned his nickname during the Second Foreign War in China in which he at times wore a yellow jacket and peacock feathered hat symbolizing his high rank in the Chinese army. In Britain he became even more popular when he fiercely opposed the thriving slave market in Africa.

Upon reaching Khartoum in 1884, Gordon determined he could not extricate the garrisons, nor would he abandon them. He and his men soon were under seige in Khartoum. Public outcry in Britain at last persuaded the government to send a relief force, a flying column, to save Gordon. The unit arrived two days late. Gordon's garrison had been slaughtered, his own decapitated head was brought to the Mahdi's tent and placed on a pole where it greeted the arriving British troops.

The Mahdi had successfully angered Queen Victoria, nearly over-throwing the British government in the process, and taken Europeans as his slaves. Spears, swords and barbaric fanaticism had triumphed over repeating rifles and artillery. The Mahdists kept control of the Sudan for over ten years. They expelled the "Turk," all those infedils and even Moslems alligning themselves with infedils, who plundered the land and tyrannically oppressed true Moslems. The Ansars also were disci-plined followers of the Mahdi's tariqa, or path of Islam, which he called simply "The Way." His doctrine emphasized a stricter, more literal adherence to the Koran's teachings.

In 1895 Sir Herbert Kitchener began executing a methodical plan to reconquer the Sudan just as Rudolf Slatin, an Austrian ambassador, escaped from prison after years of captivity. His stirring book, *Fire and Sword in the Sudan*, ignited British public opinion in favor of Kitchener's new military campaign. Kitchener constructed a railroad supply line across 550 kilometers of barren terrain from Wadi Halfa to Barbar in northern Sudan. From that point units of the Anglo-Egyptian Expeditionary Force marched and sailed 400 kilometers toward Omdurman. In 1897 the Mahdists threw their entire army of 60,000 men into a frontal assault. Their suits of mail, swords and shields were no match for Kitchener's western force. Over 11,000 Mahdists were killed, while Kitchener's losses amounted to 48 dead. Many of those losses were inflicted upon the 21st Lancers, one of whose young officers was Winston Churchill. Even though the Mahdi had long since died, Kitchener felt no qualms about leveling his tomb.

No matter how many times Mahdi ibn Sayid reflected upon the story, he always burned with anger.

The Mahdi was greeted now at the prison gates by warden Hassan, a brown complexioned man, product of the intermarriage between Arab and African that is so common in Sudan. Hassan was wearing a long flowing *jalabiyya* and a loosely wrapped *emmas* turban.

"*Kayf hallak?*" inquired the warden as they shook hands.

"*Kwayyis il Hamdulilliah,* fine, thanks be to god," beamed the Mahdi. "And you, is all *tamam?*"

"*Tamaaam,*" replied Hassan with a big smile. He leaned his head back for emphasis.

"I understand that the American arrived this morning."

"A Bedford truck brought him from Khartoum International. Permit me to show him to you."

They entered a large courtyard, above them manned watchtowers sat atop a high surrounding wall. Groups of prisoners, some wearing jalabiyyas, some wearing shirt and pants, squatted and dipped bread into common pots of fuul and fasooliya stewed beans. As was customary, they used their right hand for eating, their left being reserved for hygienic functions. They ate in silence, each trying to establish an invisible non-presence by only furtively glancing towards the Mahdi and Hassan.

"The crazies," laughed Hassan with a nod toward several men who talked to themselves and dragged their chained legs in no particular direction. "And this," he said while nodding at a row of white-washed buildings, "is where our political prisoners are kept. Our man is in this one."

A uniformed guard leaped to attention when the warden and his guests entered a dark bleak hallway.

"He's right through that barred window over there." Hassan directed the Mahdi in the proper direction with a flick of his eyes.

Zach lay on his side away from the cell's one window, his knees crunched towards his chest. His mind was so deeply withdrawn upon itself that he never heard the group come into the building. Nevertheless, a sixth sense informed him that he was being watched. He lifted and turned his head to see a man with a peculiar smile and a prominent gap between his front teeth. The man wore a skull-cap of palm straw. He said nothing, only stared as if amused, or impressed.

"Where am I? What am I doing here?" asked Zach as he raised himself to his full 6 foot three inch height. Starting towards the window, Zach looked at the man again and abruptly stopped. The man's smile had dissolved, in its place was a mouth agape. The pupils of the man's eyes momentarily dilated in fear. Then they narrowed into slits of loathing.

"How dare you approach me and treat me with such disrespect." The Mahdi's voice was controlled and even. "You are in Sudan. You are my prisoner. If your life means anything to you then you must never question me or my authority again."

The Mahdi backed away from the window and looked his bearded assistant in the eye. "Let the news go forth. Let them know of our demands."

He then focused hard upon warden Hassan. Nothing needed to be said. It was beneath him to have to direct retribution. Besides, Hassan knew his business only too well.

Hassan called for two armed guards and they joined him as he unlocked the metal door. Hassan withdrew from his belt a *curbash*, a hippopotamus hide whip. One of the guards pulled on Zach's leg chains, flinging him hard onto the floor.

The very first lash on Zach's back drew blood. His muscles spasmed. Zach was accustomed to the hammering and jarring pains of football, but the pain of the whip was different. It cut and burned its way into the mind, even as it branded the body.

The Mahdi understood the power of the whip and listened attentively in the hallway. The cruel subjugation made its victims beg for mercy even as pride and self worth were flayed away.

Whoosh, slap,____, whoosh, slap,____, whoosh, slap,____.

No screaming. No beseeching. No begging.

The Mahdi hurriedly left the dark hallway. He stepped outside and had to turn away, squinting, from the white-washed reflections of a bright sun.

Peter Jennings pursed his lips together and whistled softly as he scanned the Associated Press and United Press International reports. In fifteen minutes he would be going to air with the evening news.

"Holy shit! Holy shit!" he said under his breath.

David Brinkley, having stopped by the network to gather mail, came up to Peter's desk.

"Listen, Peter: Retirement be damned!" In his hands was a copy of the wire reports. "I want to go on tonight, for just a minute or so. There's something I have to say about this."

"Sure, David. Amazing stuff, this."

"Incredible, I'd say."

The floor director got the go-ahead over his headset. He waved his hand below the appropriate camera. Jennings gave a brief nod.

"Good evening. Our headline news is the disappearance of Zach Pike. In a developing story there is an unsubstantiated, but nevertheless plausible, lead as to Pike's abductors. The following declaration and list of demands just came over both Associated Press and United Press International wires.

'We, the Sudanese Ansar Army, are holding Zach Pike in our custody. He is safe and sound. However he will not be free until the following conditions are met.

1) Monies, in the amount of half a billion dollars, should be paid us.

2) All Islamic fundamentalist activists are to be released from Egyptian jails where, despite their innocence, they are being held.

3) All those being held in connection with the World Trade Center bombing are to be immediately freed. These include Sheik Omar Abdel Rahman, Mahmud Abouhalima, Siddig Ali, Clement Rodney Hampton-El, among others. In addition, all those being detained in connection with the July 1993 planned bombing of the United Nations and Holland and Lincoln tunnels are to be set free.

'We stongly urge you to satisfy these conditions as soon as possible.'"

Jennings leaned forward at his desk, his face earnest and sober, as he stared out of the screen straight, it seemed, at Meg.

"We are trying to follow this breaking development as best we can. We hope to have former U.S. ambassador to the Sudan, Gilford McKenzie, join us before the end of this broadcast. We also are establishing a line to our network middle east experts. Among other things we will try to find out more about this fundamentalist group in Sudan and why they would want to take somebody like Zach Pike. We will also try to find out just what an Ansar is. My colleague, David Brinkley, learned of all this just minutes ago, as did we all, and has a few words to say on the subject. David?"

Brinkley glanced down at a few scribbled notes. Meg leaned forward and closer to the television. She clenched and unclenched her hands.

"Until moments ago," Brinkley said in his stately manner, "what we thought we had here was a kidnapping of a twenty-nine-year old and the murder of a twenty-year-old college student. Terrible crimes certainly, but still somehow the types of horrible crimes that sadly do on occasion take place in this country. True, the twenty-nine-year-old happens to be a football superstar, which has meant a totally absorbed public and a salivating media. But, nevertheless, this was our own American calamity. In its own bizarre way it seemed like something we could fathom. We would be able to cope.

"And now this! If it's true, and AP and UPI usually are reliable sources. Are we really expected to release men convicted of blowing up our buildings, of killing and terrorizing our citizens, in order to try and save an innocent life? Or do we stick to our principles and judicial system, not negotiate, and sacrifice Zach Pike if need be? In the boldest terms, which weighs more; the sanctity of an individual or the good of the community?

"It seems we'd better brace ourselves for a gut-wrenching gut-check. But we'd better be careful, too. This dilemma could ultimately transform our collective national psyche. We could, in our anguish, become the hostage, trapped, with no real way out.

"We do have options, of course. One obvious one being capitulation, total or partial.

"Another option? Well, an innocent national treasure named Zach Pike was, it appears, somehow spirited away from his home, from his protector, the United States, and forcibly taken to a distant shore. That is arguably tantamount to a foreign entity making a declaration of war. And so the other option is to go ahead and fight to win back what is rightfully ours. But how do we fight, and against whom?

"Dilemma." David Brinkley gave a shake of his head, a breath of a sigh. "Back to you, Peter."

Meg could not believe it—she couldn't! She fell forward, hiding her face in her lap, and cried.

CHAPTER FIVE

*T*he press conference had been hastily arranged. Football beat writers knew their way around the New York Jets front office headquarters on the campus of Hofstra University in Hempstead, Long Island, but a horde of others did not.

Magazine, newspaper, radio, and television reporters descended upon the small school like piranhas in a feeding frenzy. There was gridlock at the school's entrance; a Manhattan style traffic jam by the Athletic Center. In the end one electric news gathering van followed another until every E.N.G. and every reporter was in place for the 10:00 P.M. start.

Johnny Ciampana, owner of the Jets, mashed the end of a Macanudo cigar. He shook his head slowly, his mouth twisted into a sneer.

"I can't believe I'm going to do this, Wally. This goes against everything I believe in, but what can I do?"

Wally Ostrovski thought Ciampana was going to be sick. As head coach, Ostrovski had known "Champagne" Johnny for five plus years and had never seen him squirm, let alone doubt himself before. Ciampana always wielded his self-confidence, toughness, and especially his instincts, as weapons to overcome any obstacle in his path. In the process he'd parlayed his skills into deals that had amassed him a fortune in commercial real estate. He earned his moniker long before he ever sipped champagne, or had champagne unceremoniously dumped on him, following Super Bowl wins.

"Wally boy, I like to think I treat everyone fairly, whether it be in business, player contracts......, anything. And when I'm right about something, if people try to muscle or extort something out of me, out of principle I never cave in. But these sons of bitches really got me. If I deal they win. It would always goad me but I guess I could live with it. The problem is that if I resort to being a hardass, we, the fans, Zach's family, we could all lose. *And I mean really lose."*

Ciampana blew his nose on a handkerchief that shook ever so slightly in his hand. "And that, well, I just couldn't live with."

The old man, resplendent in his custom fitted suit and red bow tie, clapped Ostrovski on the shoulder, then stood up. "Okay, let's go."

A trail of front office personnel somberly followed Ciampana out to a hushed gymnasium that now doubled as a press room. The only sound that could be heard was the whir and click of cameras. Facing Ciampana at the far back of the gym was a wall of giant picture posters of great moments in Jets history. In front of the wall was a jam-packed crowd and, scattered in its midst, Ciampana spotted forlorn Jets players everywhere he looked. Irv Goodman, co-captain and offensive tackle, had his eyes closed in prayer. "Earthquake" Hayes, his Pro-Bowl defensive tackle, looked teary-eyed. Joe Crockett, the team's multi-purpose running back, was bent over, wringing his hands.

"As you can well imagine, the news concerning Zach has stunned and saddened the entire Jets organization. I have not, as yet, had the opportunity to speak with those who are working on this case but I feel it's in Zach's best interests for the organization to step up—right now!" Ciampana hoped he was doing the right thing.

"The Jets, and myself, are prepared to evaluate and pursue the monetary demands of those who are holding Zach Pike. While this alone may not satisfy all of the items on their wish list, it is at least something we have some control over. We feel this is a good faith gesture. What we expect in return is the safe and speedy return of Zach. That is the foremost issue on our minds."

As Ciampana fielded questions one particular picture poster on the back wall seemed like a magnet, compelling him to look.

It was a blown-up photo from an AFC championship game against the Raiders. With Oakland leading 24-20 late in the game, the Jets faced a fourth down and one yard to go on the Raiders 15 yard line. Zach had pitched the ball to Joe Crockett who sprinted along with the entire offense to the right. The Raiders pursued and flowed to the right.

And then suddenly the moment that was captured in the picture: Crockett stopped, looked left, and lobbed a ball across the field to a wide open Zach who had swung out of the backfield. The Jets never had any intention of running right. It was a ruse, and one could almost see the faces of the Raiders players behind their facemasks as they helplessly realized they had been suckered.

It was then that Ciampana's voice trailed off and he stuck his hands in his pockets. The press conference, the ransom money, nothing was going to make any difference. Any difference at all.

The EL AL 747 was a bustling, self-contained miniaturization of the Israel it had departed from.

A group of orthodox Jewish men gathered into a *minyan* at the back of the jet for morning prayers. Harried stewardesses strained to keep their civility as they serviced a demanding populace that never seemed totally satisfied. Older tourists blocked aisles as they gabbed and shared notes of their travels with other senior citizens. Frazzled mothers changed diapers, breast fed, and rocked their wailing babies. And both pre-army and post-army youth dressed in sweatshirts and faded jeans laughed and confidently looked forward to overseas adventures.

Zvi Langer was by now ever so grateful that the onboard movie was finally beginning. He closed his eyes but didn't sleep. A familiar recollection was pushing its way to the fore—again. Zvi clenched the armrests and shoved his legs beneath the seat in front of him. But the memory chafed, and gnawed, and would not let go.

The Shayetet Fleet 13 missile boat, armed with Gabriel and Harpoon surface-to-surface projectiles, gently rolled up and down with each oncoming wave. Four cobra attack choppers on board groaned under the relentless motion. Below twenty soldiers of Sayeret Matkal, the elite reconnaisance unit of the general staff, silently waited for the all clear signal from two naval scuba commandos who had reached the Tizi—Ouzou beach.

"*Yala,* let's go," said the boat commander.

The soldiers, dressed like civilians, scrambled up and out to rubber dinghies that would race them to shore. A crescent moon shined just enough for Zvi to distinguish the spectacular mountain scenery of Tizi—Ouzou, some fifty kilometers east of Algiers.

Mossad agents waited beside three rented minibuses to drive members of the unit to their destination. While the Sayeret Matkal soldiers climbed into the minibuses, Kommando Hayami naval commandos secured a beachhead.

North of their position a Boeing 707, bearing civilian EL AL identification, maintained routine commercial contact with air traffic contollers in Barcelona. But on board the 707 were the director of A'man military intelligence, the Mossad director, and Deputy Chief of Staff Lahav. And aside from coordinating all ground, sea, and air activities involved with the operation, they were also ready to electronically disable most of the security communications around Algiers.

The minibuses rolled into a quiet hillside neighborhood and then diverged by the National Museum of Antiquities on Parc de la Liberte'. A hundred meters up the hill was the Palais du Peuple, the former residence of the French governor and Algerian head of state. In the distance, dominating the city skyline, Zvi could see the Martyr's Monument with its three huge stylised palm leaves sheltering an eternal flame.

Zvi glanced at his watch. By now a task force of four Sayeret Matkal Commandos would be jamming the telephone lines of the neighborhood by short circuiting a telephone junction box that had been seen during surveillance. Soon they would be setting up perimeter positions in the nearby Parc from which they could control any hostile traffic that would come their way. In the meantime, Zvi and his strike force impatiently waited, and worried.

The Israeli intelligence community, with the approval of the Prime Minister's Committee for Security and Foreign Affairs, had ordered the assasination of an Egyptian sheik. Abdul Ali Latif was becoming too dangerous. If Egypt, the most populous country in the Arab world, fell into the militant Islamist camp, the political psychology of the Mid East would change for the worst.

Egypt seemed incapable of cracking down on Latif's revived Jihad organization, the group behind the assasination of Anwar Sadat. Fear was escalating that Latif was a unifyer, a man that could rally even Egypt's other fundamentalists groups, the Islamic Brotherhood and Gama al Islamiya, under his sphere of influence.

Israel had to act. It could not carry out an operation in Egypt, with whom it maintained diplomatic relations. But here in Algeria to bolster support for other fundamentalists, Latif was deemed a vulnerable target. The suburban villa of his host, Charlie Hammami, would be taken by military forces augmenting the Mossad.

As the last light in the upstairs bedroom of the French style villa blinked off, commandos inside the two remaining minivans ran over in their minds one last time what they rehearsed so often in Israel. Split-second timing would be critical. It was 1:45 A.M. There was no more time for fear, only jittery anticipation.

The close bond Zvi felt—a bond implicit in special operations forces—made looking into the faces of his friends too unnerving. So he didn't look. But his other senses were wildly acute. He heard Uri's rapid and shallow breathing, picked up the scent of Erez's sharp tension, and felt Shmuel's steely bulk lightly lean upon him. In a matter of seconds silenced weapons with laser range finders and sights would crackle the still night.

The terminal assault began at precisely 1:50 A.M. Eight commandos burst out of the minibus parked down the street and began sprinting fifty meters towards a security cubicle by the villa's driveway. Thirty seconds later Zvi and his men scampered from the minibus parked on the other end of the street.

The other force immediately eliminated one sleeping guard in the cubicle and one that stood by the front door. They next tried to open the locked door but when they could not do so they placed a small amount of C-4 plastique over the crack of the door at latch level. A sandbag for tamping the charges through the door covered the plastique. Two Sayeret commandos lit a very short fuse of a blasting cap in the plastique and then dove for cover.

Ten seconds later Zvi's strike force flew through a gaping hole where the door had been without ever breaking stride. Uri and Erez began spraying Uzi machine guns into the foyer a moment before reaching it. Uri ducked inside to the left and began a pinning sweep from top right to bottom left. Erez crouched inside to the right and began a similar sweep, this time from top left to bottom right.

Right on their heels, Zvi and Shmuel charged through smoke and drifting debris and up a majestic semi-spiralling staircase, bounding up two, three, even four stairs at a time. Suddenly a light blazed on and, a moment later, horrible screams began resonating throughout the villa.

Zvi and Shmuel opened the door of the guest bedroom where Latif was spending the night. The Sheik was sitting upright in a canopied bed of satin sheets and fumbling with a pistol. As he lifted his head up to look at the door, a stream of bullets sent him reeling back towards the head of the bed. Tiny geysers of blood splashed all over the sheets.

Darting out of the Sheik's bedroom, Zvi and Shmuel ran out the door and right into a guard's line of fire. Zvi dove to the floor and returned fire. An instant later the guard's hands were clutching a vanishing neck, one that no longer supported a wobbling head.

"Let's get out of here!"

"Zvi, help me, help me!" Shmuel screamed. His guts bubbled to the surface of his stomach.

Hoisting Shmuel up in one motion Zvi used a fireman's carry as he leaped down the staircase. Halfway down he came across a villa employee who had pinned himself flat against the wall. The mustachioed man had witnessed the shoot-out at the top of the stairs and his white face reflected the traumatic sight.

"Please, don't kill me," he begged as Zvi raised his weapon.

Their dilated eyes met. They peered, unsure and suspicious. A second later Zvi continued hurtling down the stairs.

"*Shukran,* thank you," yelled the man as he slowly collapsed to the floor in relief.

"*Afwan,* you're welcome," answered Zvi.

The Sayeret forces were inside the villa for no more than one infernal minute. They sped away in their minibuses and decided not to try and make it all the way back to Tizi—Ouzou. There had been too much commotion and Algerian forces could be closing in. Twenty kilometers east of Algiers, on a lonely strip of sand, the cobra choppers picked them up to take them back to the missile boat while another one scooped up the naval commandos on the beach of Tizi—Ouzou.

"Excuse me," interrupted a stewardess, "but you're not looking well." Her reeking perfume clamored for his attention. "I just wanted to make sure you were all right."

"I'm fine, really. Thank you."

The stewardess smiled sweetly. "You're welcome," she said, still smiling. "Some juice?"

Taking the glass Zvi turned to see that his parents were safely sleeping just a row behind him. He mopped sweat from his forehead with a napkin and looked up at the movie screen. But his eyes focused at a spot far away. It was as if the screen were a finger held an inch away and right between his eyes; there, but transparent.

Zvi couldn't stop wondering, couldn't stop worrying. Had he been smiling at the Algiers villa employee when he said "you're welcome?" Had he in fact been smiling when he dove….and fired…*and killed?*

There was one thing Zvi knew for sure. He was crying on board the Cobra helicopter. Shmuel died en route to the missile boat.

CHAPTER SIX

*H*unched over an old metallic tank desk, Detective Billy Haynes pored over the Polaroid instants and then deftly swished another empty coffee cup into a wastepaper basket.

Twenty-five years before he and his young wife had moved to New York from Clarksville, Tennessee, drawn by the allure of the big city and the opportunities its crime element presented. Haynes began his career as a patrol officer but it didn't take long for his superiors to notice that he had the perceptiveness and imagination to be a detective. The force sent him to New York University to learn criminal justice and soon his wife started to be troubled by the long hours of his profession. She put her foot down saying, "Choose! It's either law enforcement or me!"

That was her big mistake.

Despite not having hot suppers waiting after a long day, despite long lonely nights where his companionship consisted of a t.v., cigarrettes, and a fifth of whiskey, he never truly regretted his decision. He simply loved what he did for a living.

After returning from the forensic autopsy at the medical examiner's office, Haynes had managed to get a couple of hours sleep at the Manhattan station, but now it was time to roll up his sleeves and get to work analyzing the evidence. The boys at the scientific investigative bureau had already completed an Absorbtion Elution antigen test for blood typing, found out under a stereoscope that yanked out hairs were both caucasian and negroid, preserved footprints in the snow with oil coating and casting material, and filed a ballistics report indicating those bullets which weren't destroyed or fragmented were 45 caliber, probably from an Ingram M-10. Unfortunately, there wasn't quality fingerprint evidence as gloves had been worn. A knit hat, a handkerchief doused with chloroform, and a pen and pad of paper had also been retrieved.

One witness Haynes had interviewed especially impressed him. He chuckled as he hummed the words to the Mel Tillis song, *"she's a tall glass of water, for a thirsty, thirsty man."* The thirsty—hell, lucky—man in this case was her boyfriend, Zach Pike. It figured. Wasn't that always the way it went?

Her mascara had run down her pink cheeks, her coat was drenched with Brian Sullivan's blood, and she was wet from the snow she had knelt in, but damned if she hadn't stood up straight and stuck out her chin. Despite everything Meg Symes had witnessed, she seemed nobly composed and courageous. A classy woman, that one.

But in the end, the best she could testify to was that there was one very large man, and two of average size, who had dragged Pike into a Jeep which immediately sped away. She could not distinguish any facial features.

Haynes picked up a photo from a 35 mm camera. On it was a feature that was likely to be the most important bit of evidence in this case. It was a picture of a knocked out incisor tooth from one of the culprits. An imprint in the top right corner of the photo read **Monday, December 18, 5:25 AM**. The tooth was perfectly preserved and was gold capped. A forensic odontologist had already informed him that the tooth belonged to somebody who had probably lived outside the United States since gold cappings were very rarely performed domestically on incisors. The odontologist also told Haynes that if a suspect were found he could determine if the tooth could be uniquely implanted into the suspect's dental space.

"Billy Bob, git your sorry ass over here." Precinct detective Walt Kennedy never let up ribbing Haynes in what he thought was a southern twang. "I think I got an informer on my line. Says it pertains to Zach Pike."

He took the receiver from Kennedy. "Detective Haynes here." He was out of breath, more from the excitement over a possible lead than the run to the phone.

"I think I may have some information regarding what happened in Rockefeller Plaza, but I don't want to give my name or come down to any police station." The voice was strained.

"I totally understand. You don't have to come in. But I'd very much like to meet you." Haynes thought fast. "Do you know King Kong Cookies? It's right below the Empire State Building."

The voice hesitated. "Yeah, I been there." The guy sounded youngish.

"Okay. I'll buy you some coffee, cookies, whatever you want. How bout we meet there in an hour, at say, 4:30?"

There was a second pause. "All right."

"I'll be wearing a blue winter coat. I've got grey hair and I'm kind of a big, rolypoly guy. My partner's also a big ole fella. He's young, probably about your age. How do we recognize you?"

"I'm in my early twenties. I'll be wearing a Jets cap."

"Right. One hour, Bud."

Haynes and Dave Torkilson, his partner, were grateful the caller was willing to meet them. But it was unclear as to whether the kid was looking to exchange information for payment, calling out of fear of imminent arrest, or if he was a good citizen informer. Haynes' guess—or anyway—hope, was that he was cooperating out of a sense of civic participation. Just in case Torkilson was able to quickly obtain a thousand dollars cash from the headquarters' coffers. He also put on a New York Giants cap.

A guy in a Jets cap, dark hair, was sitting by himself at a table far way from the cafe's revolving door entrance. As Haynes and Torkilson approached, the cops and the caller sized each other up.

"May we sit down?" Haynes asked politely.

"Sure." The informer was younger even than he sounded over the phone. After an uneasy silence a nervous smile lit up his face. "The Giants suck," he said, and Haynes instantly decided this was a good kid.

"I'm Billy Haynes," he said, smiling, "and this is Dave Torkilson. We really appreciate you meeting with us." Haynes swiveled his head, got the attention of a waitress.

"A coke and a big piece of that Bavarian for the Jets fan, a coffee and blueberry muffin for the Giants fan, and a coffee and bran muffin for me. I'm a Chicago Bears fan." He winked at the kid.

"My name's Danny."

"Okay Danny. Suppose you tell us why you wanted to meet us."

"I work at a restaurant in Brooklyn called the Oasis, an Arabic joint. About one o'clock this guy I know, Hassan Kamal, comes in for lunch. He looks like he's been in a war. His lip's all swollen and cut up, and he's got a big scratch running down his cheek. I ask him why he's not at work and he says, 'Rough night.' And then he smiles real funny, like he's up to no good. I don't really like Hassan but I keep talking with him. I asked him if he heard the news about Pike and then he laughed. 'Hear about it? I *know* about it.' And then he gets this stupid smile again."

Haynes nodded. If Danny's statements were true, Hassan Kamal had committed the most egregious of all mistakes, the mistake of a bumbling amateur: He talked too much. This was a real break, almost too easy, Haynes knew—but, hell—he, for one, was grateful to be lucky.

"Anything else, Danny?"

"No. By that point I had to go back to work." The young informer cracked his knuckles. "I just want you guys to know, I'm an Arab-American, and when another Moslem does something bad it hurts our whole community. But I am an American and this just seemed like the right thing to do." Danny then smiled mischievously. "I'm also a real big Zach Pike fan. Sure hope you find him soon."

"So do we Danny. So do we."

The reporters scarcely noticed the taxi pull up in front of the Georgian Colonial. There had been a steady flow of visitors all day long to the Pike residence, too many to count, and besides, the vigil seemed to pass quicker when cozying up to a hot thermos in a parked news van.

A large holiday wreath hung on the wooden front door, right below panes of stained glass. Like Ein Gev, this too was home. Even though the door was open a smidgen, Zvi rang the pipe organ doorbell.

"Aunt Aviva, Uncle Odie! Zvi. Thank you for coming." Sam Pike's broad arms easily enveloped the Langers. "Mom, Dad?" Sam yelled over a gathering of relatives, friends, and scrambling children. "Look who's here!"

Ben and Mary Pike excused themselves from company and made their way over to the entrance hall. Zvi was alarmed—they had grown so old. Tears rolled down Mary's face as she hugged Aviva. Still stout, she no longer looked strong. She would have to call on every bit of her Scottish fortitude to weather the current ordeal. Ben's face was bright red from drink. He briefly bear-hugged Oded and Zvi and tried to seem as upbeat as possible. But his moist blue eyes betrayed the trouble within.

Zvi hauled the suitcases to the top of the stairs, when he sensed someone running up behind him. A train of auburn hair swept around the bend as a lithe body flew toward him. Her long arms, and even longer legs, pumped in fluid unison. Even though Meg abruptly stopped a few feet from Zvi, her flushed face and wide open brown eyes seemed very close to him, magnified. Then she simply fell against him. Her fingers pulled at his shirt and her head hung on his shoulder.

"Meggie, I'm here now." Zvi stroked small circles over her back. "We'll see this through."

"Tell me," she whispered. "Tell me he'll be all right."

Zvi shifted uneasily. "Zach will be fine," he said softly. "You know *he's gifted.*"

Meg and Zvi laughed as they delicately seperated from each other. As a junior in high school Zach had been tabbed by one over-exuberant sports reporter as "the gifted one." Friends knew him better and for weeks they delighted in making Zach the butt of "O, GREAT GIFTED ONE" jokes.

"Zvi, it's been crazy. You can see what it's like here. I'm dying to get out for awhile."

"A walk would be good. Let's go."

They threw on coats, found gaps in the human obstacle course downstairs, and grabbed sandwiches as they slipped out the kitchen door. Crossing the backyard they avoided the media encampment by finding a familiar beaten path through shrubs and woods. The evening's polar air felt crisp and refreshing and the two old friends walked quickly so as to stay warm.

"I think often about Ayelet. I remember how she used to love to play hide and seek. I remember how we loved to braid each other's hair when-ever I baby sat." Meg sighed shakily. "How are your parents coping?"

"I marvel at how strong they are. Maybe that strength comes with age, I don't know. For me, well, it left a hole inside. Sometimes I think the hole can be seen even by little kids. Especially by little kids." Zvi thought for a moment about his tickling encounter with Dalia in Tiberias, the teasing affection he felt from her and the others.

Zvi's little sister, Ayelet, had died several years before when the car she was hitching home in from basic training spun out of control, and into an oncoming truck. Police said death was instantaneous. Jewish law dic-tated that she be buried the very next day but Ben, Mary, Zach, and Zach's sister Liz, did manage to arrive in Israel while the Langers were mourning and sitting their seven-day *Shivah*. Meg, who had been camp-ing at Crater Lake, was unable to fly to Israel but she was on the phone to Ein Gev half the night the moment she heard the news. Unexplicably, until Zvi's call yesterday, it had been the last time they had spoken. The last time that is, alone, without Zach being in on the conversation.

Zvi and Meg wound up standing in front of Brookline High and thoughts turned to happier moments.

"Remember April Fool's, the cafeteria," Meg said, grabbing Zvi's arm. Then her voice turned nasal. "Zach and Zvi, Zvi and Zach, Zach and Zvi." She cleared her throat. "We bring you, ZZ TOP."

The memory rose up: He and Zach were once again jumping onto a cafeteria table and rocking to the music. Their long fake beards flowed to the rhythm of their gyrations, their sunglasses reflected fluorescent cafeteria lights. They were so cool.

"She's got Le,egs," wailed Zvi. He turned back and forth as he made an imaginary guitar squeal. *"She knows how to use them."*

"The girl is alright," chipped in Meg as she reenacted her femme fatale bump and grind.

Zvi roared till he cried. "Stop it Meggie, you're killing me." He good-naturedly pushed her along. "Let's keep moving. I'm not used to this freezing weather."

The brown field in front of the high school, any field for that matter, was where Zvi had had some of his most joyous moments. At one time sports were Zvi's sole ticket to being accepted and respected.

When he'd first entered Mrs.Miller's seventh grade class nobody really knew what to make of the newcomer and his broken, accented English. But the moment they saw him play soccer and basketball, as soon as they tested him at gym and at recess, they knew this kid would fit in just fine. Zvi was as quick and as fast as the gazelle that his Hebrew name meant. But what really set him apart throughout that first year was his ability to joke and laugh even as he competed as fiercely as anybody in the school. Anybody, that is, except one individual.

Athletics were the domain of Zach Pike. He didn't play sports so much as he lived sports. Zach threw himself, body and soul, into every contest. His competetive instincts were so ferocious that he appeared intimidating to those who didn't know him very well. His aggressiveness naturally made everybody around him play harder. More by default than by choice, Zach Pike became a leader.

Stopping now at the field, Meg turned to him. "Tell me again about you and Zach, how you met."

Zvi gently kicked at a patch of snow, thinking back. "A week after I started at Runkle school, I was really feeling out of place. I had no friends and I really missed Ein Gev. There was this pick-up football game after school. After Zach and Eric Feinberg bucked up, we all lined up to be chosen. I stood at the far end, alone. I didn't really know what was going on and I definitely didn't know anything about football." Zvi shrugged.

"Then Zach, with his very first choice, walks over to me and drags me in front of everybody. 'I want him,' he says." Zvi grabbed Meg by the shoulders, looked hard into her eyes.

"Meggie, he could have picked anybody, but he went out of his way to show all the kids that I was okay with him." He let go of her, smiled.

"After the kickoff Zach says, 'This is a simple game. I throw the ball to you. You catch it. And then you run as fast as you can so these animals don't catch and eat you.' The whole game long I'm standing a few yards away from him after he gets the snap and instead of throwing downfield he pitches or tosses the ball to me. I don't want the animals to catch me so I run like a demon and manage to score a couple of times." They continued walking, leaning into the stiff wind with their collars turned up.

"It was always so easy for Zach. He was a natural. I don't think anybody can be surprised he became a star."

Meg tugged at his coat. "You're wrong Zvi. Zach had to work so damned hard all the time. You're the one for whom everything was so easy, whether it be sports, classes, anything! Zvi, you took to everything like a fish to water. Zach admired you, almost envied you, so much. He told me once that you were one in a million and I knew exactly what he meant. You were good at everything!"

Leaving the very field on which he'd captained the soccer team, Zvi considered Meg's remarks. Maybe she was right. Yet it seemed so unjust that Zach could excel at what he always wanted to do, while he himself was so good at what he did, without, it seemed, ever having made a conscious choice.

Where had all his dreams gone? What had gone so terribly wrong with his life anyhow?

Yellow ribbons hung on the doors and fences of the Pike's neighbors as Zvi and Meg hung onto each other, not believing *this* was actually happening. The lights burned warmly at home and Zvi, ashamed, redirected his thoughts from himself to Zach; specifically what he could possibly do for Zach. To what, he feared, he might have to do.

CHAPTER SEVEN

"*S*hit!"

There was no answer from behind the door of apartment 5C. The Office of the Chief of Detectives had deferred to Haynes' gut reaction to not waste time with surveillance and background checks. Time was of the essence in any murder case, but especially a high profile one, and a seemingly reliable tip from a good citizen informant was probable enough cause to move in quickly. But now Haynes and Torkilson would have to go to the magistrate and get search and arrest warrants.

As they exited the elevator a huge man carrying groceries walked past them. Haynes and Torkilson turned incredulously towards each other, each exchanging a look of "Did you see what I saw?"

"Hassan Kamal!"

The man reluctantly stopped and stood motionless. The detectives circled around. Kamal's eyes were glued to the floor. The young giant bore a perpetual five-o'clock shadow and a blooming scar and purplish lip contrasted strongly with his pasty complexion.

"I'm Detective Haynes and this is Detective Torkilson." They presented their identification. "We'd like to ask you some questions. Please come with us."

Kamal didn't know it, but he really had no choice in the matter. This was an arrest as far as the detectives were concerned and they would only release Kamal if questioning proved fruitless. If Kamal refused to cooperate they were simply going to arrest him, warrant or not. Haynes and Torkilson need not have worried; Kamal acquiesced with about as little fight as a sheep going to slaughter.

To Hassan Kamal the interview room at the station looked like a friendly business office, complete with a roll-arm sofa, coffee table, and fish tank. But after hearing the Miranda Warning and that the "interview" would be recorded on tape, Kamal decided the office was not such a nice place after all.

"Why weren't you at work today?" Haynes asked. He sat face-to-face with Kamal in a wing chair.

"I was tired. I was sick."

"Sick or tired?" Haynes put his hand on Kamal's forehead. "Funny, you don't have a temperature and you don't look sick. In fact, we know you felt good enough to go out for lunch today at the Oasis." Haynes leaned forward to closely examine Kamal's face.

"Tsssk, Tsssk. I'd hate to see what the other guy looks like." Haynes squeezed the suspect's beefy cheeks together and carefully lifted his battered lip. An incisor tooth was missing. "Suppose you tell us how this happened to you?"

Kamal was not bright enough to come up with a ready answer and he was unsophisticated regarding his rights, but he was afraid. He realized that he should not say anything. He clapped his arms across his chest.

Haynes knew the next few minutes were critical. If the suspect did not open up now, when he was so emotionally and psychologically off balance, valuable time would be lost. Sure, in the end he would talk, maybe even spill his guts out, but Haynes didn't want to wait even fifteen minutes more, let alone wait till the end.

"Son, you're in serious trouble here. Once convicted for murder and kidnapping, you will never, *ever*, see the light of day again. We have a gold-capped tooth, *your tooth*, in our possession. That tooth will be a perfect match for implantation into that space behind your lip. The pulp of that tooth will have your DNA markings." Haynes sat back and let his words sink in.

"Now, you can help us out, and in the process help yourself out, by simply answering our questions. And let me assure you, it's alot more pleasant to chat here than it is in Detective Torkilson's office." Kamal's eyes wandered frantically but Haynes shifted his head so as to maintain an unblinking eye-lock.

"Hassan, if you didn't pull the trigger on that boy Brian Sullivan in Rockeffeller Plaza, then you didn't really kill him, did you? Somebody else did. You don't have to throw your life away while the real killers go free."

Haynes leaned in now, his manner intimate, familiar. "If you tell me who those killers are, I promise I will go to the mat for you. I'll tell the district attorney how helpful you were. If you tell us who all those others are behind this stupid plan, if you turn state's evidence, it's possible that you will even be immune from prosecution." Haynes lit a cigarrette and whispered into Kamal's ear. "This opportunity is fleeting. *Grab it, Hassan!*"

Haynes leaned back and drew a long slow puff on the cigarrette. But his unflinching stare boxed Kamal further into the corner. Kamal searched up at the ceiling, down at the floor, into the detective's eyes, and ultimately up, down, and into his own mind's inclinations. The process seemed interminable.

"Detective Haynes," he muttered. He lifted his head, looked Haynes in the eye. "Here's what I know...."

"Zvi," Aviva called, "there you are. I have some egg nog for you. Remember how much you like it."

No matter how many times Zvi had circumnavigated the world, no matter that he was twenty-nine years old, his mother knew exactly how to innocently embarrass her son in front of friends and acquaintances he had not seen in years.

The egg nog was spiked and sprinkled with cinnamon. Scents of fruit cake, Baileys, and Kahlua filled the downstairs rooms. If it had not been for the one cataclysmic event which had brought them all together, Zvi felt they would all be having a very good time indeed.

A hubbub of news suddenly stilled the swirl of conversation: CNN was about to air a special bulletin. Everybody piled into the Pikes' enormous family room to view a big screen t.v. that had already been a listening post for hours.

"We have just received a video of Zach Pike that was circulated by the purported Sudanese Ansar Army. Let me caution you," warned Bernard Shaw, "that it is not easy to watch. It's probable that Zach Pike was under considerable duress at the time this was filmed."

The video was of poor quality. A bright sidelong beam illuminated half of Zach's face in ghastly light while the other half remained in ghostly shadow. Everyone in the room knew Zach well, but even so it was a struggle to recognize the one they loved so much. It was devastating how fast and how much someone could change.

His eyelids were monstrously enlarged. His face was swollen and bruised almost to the point of being unrecognizable. Zach sat ramrod straight, as if even the slightest movement would be excruciatingly painful. Aviva Langer and two other women abruptly escorted a distraught Mary Pike from the room. Oded Langer spoke in a continuous inaudible whisper to Ben, his face and body animated in his effort to encourage and comfort.

"I, Zach Pike, am being held by people who wish me no harm. They have assured me that I will be treated well." Zach's head repeatedly darted to the side from the prepared script before him, and then back.

"This is happening because righteous Moslems the world over have no other means by which to defend their faith and maintain those values they hold sacred." Zach's voice was flat. "How long must the faithful languish while the west, principally America, poisons Islamic souls and corrupts youthful minds? How long will her puppet, Egypt, fail to attend to the people's demands for justice and human dignity? How long will her other puppet, Israel, be permitted to grow as a cancer in the body before it is finally cut out? For my good, for your good, act immediately on the demands you have previously received. And maybe, *eeenchallah*, god willing, everything may yet work out for the best."

While others in the family room sat stunned into silence, Zvi was paradoxically buoyed by the video. He noticed the slightest twinge of a smile, almost a sneer really, when Zach tripped over the word *inchallah*. Zach also did not exhibit the type of profound resignation he had seen in the faces of some videotaped Israeli soldiers who had been captured. They had uniquely found ways of saying good-by and fixing themselves for deaths they knew were inevitable. Zach's eyes seemed to momentarily gleam when he concluded the text. He clearly expected to live.

"May I have your attention." Mary stood erect as she returned to the room. She had regained her public composure and had set aside her grieving for private moments.

"Some of you will be leaving tomorrow to return to your homes and your lives. I cannot tell you how much we appreciate your coming to be with us during these terrible moments. I think it is time we remember this miraculous season and not dwell solely on misfortune." She nodded to Liz who took a seat behind a Steinway Baby Grand that was next to a magnificent Christmas tree.

"Have yourself a merry little
Christmas; Let your heart be light

From now on our troubles will
be out of sight."

Concentric rings of friends closed in tight around the piano, and began to sing along, tremulously at first, then more heartily. A hand, Meg's hand, slipped into Zvi's.

"Here we are as in olden days
happy golden days of yore

Faithful friends who are dear to
us, gather near to us once more.

Through the years we all will be
together, If the Fates allow

Hang a shining star upon the highest bough.
And have yourself a merry little Christmas now."

At the end of the day, Billy Haynes knew he would crash. He would stumble home, disconnect the phone in his bedroom, kick off his shoes, and descend into oblivion. Immediately upon awakening, the Zach Pike case would once again be with him, *in him*; tweaking his brain, jangling his nerves.

But sleep was reserved for the future. Right now he was in overdrive. Kamal, as it turned out, did not know very much. He had never met two of the other perps before the Rockefeller Plaza incident. One, called Yousef, was apparently a doctor at Mount Sinai Hospital. The other, a black man named Vernon, was a driver for G.E. who had secured an old warehouse in Long Island City. There they had drugged Pike and put him into a refrigerator in a crate. The destination of the crate was Sudan. Kamal did know Sayid Abu Zaid, the one who recruited him and the others, from a mosque in Brooklyn that he sometimes attended.

Before doing anything else, Haynes contacted the FBI, apprising them of what he had just learned, and asking them to tap into the National Crime Information Center. The Center could check previous felony records. He also notified the office of the U.S. Attorney General in the Department of Justice, requesting names of wanted persons. Lastly, he called INTERPOL. Their National Central Bureau would fax international criminal history data and help in providing the location of suspects, should further international suspects be identified.

Within minutes detectives obtained search and arrest warrants. Sayid Abu Zaid was not at home but an exhaustive search did uncover an Ingram M-10. There was little doubt the barrel's lands, grooves, and left or right hand twist would fire a bullet that matched up perfectly with previously retrieved bullets. Gloves and an overcoat that still contained gunpowder carbon tracing evidence were also located. Officers were stationed at Abu Zaid's home to prevent his wife from making any calls, and to arrest him should he return.

The doctor, Yousef Yassin, was apprehended at the hospital. Tired and without the thought processes of a professional criminal, Yassin cracked under Haynes' strategy of focusing on the moral discrepancies between his sworn profession and the vicious crime he had committed. Other than details on the drugs he used, Yassin shed no new light on the case.

Vernon Compton-El's address was obtained from G.E. He was roused at his home, amid the crying of his wife and children, by a different detective team. By the time Haynes arrived back at the station the team had already drawn Compton-El's blood and hair samples and photographed and fingerprinted him. In addition, he'd been through a debasing strip search, ostensibly to identify scratch marks, a procedure fully permissable as long as it was not considered "shocking." He was ripe for questioning.

Although he'd appealed for an attorney, Compton-El kept blabbering away. "Abu Zaid told me once that Loadmaster, that Hutchinson guy, was contacted, my role was over. Everything would be okay. No arrests, no trouble. Nobody told me nothing like this was going to happen."

Still there was no Abu Zaid. Now that arrests were in progress, Haynes knew a suspect like Abu Zaid would have to be apprehended soon, before he caught wind of the arrests and escaped.

A detailed and specific arrest warrant was finally granted to nab Abu Zaid in the mosque where he frequently studied and prayed. Haynes had no qualms about seizing somebody at a house of worship. Yet, his detective's wariness caused him to dread the move. Should Abu Zaid resist arrest, reasonable force would make for an ugly scene and all kinds of questions would have to be answered. Careers could be jeopardized and civil lawsuits could be filed against him or his department. As it turned out, Haynes' concern was justified.

A *muezzin*, an *imam*, and a phalange of religious men shielded Abu Zaid from Haynes and his men. "You have no business here. Go away!"

"We have an arrest warrant for Sayid Abu Zaid. Please step aside."

"This is a mosque! You have no right to be here!" The outcry was becoming hysterical.

Suddenly a push was returned in kind by a young officer, and all hell broke loose. Police began dragging away elderly men who kicked and screamed hysterically. The most vociferous individuals were rounded up for booking.

Haynes could already see tomorrow's headlines: **POLICE RAID MOSQUE AND BRUTALIZE RELIGIOUS LEADERS.**

But screw the newspapers. Screw the press. Justice wasn't always convenient and tidy. Sometimes, if necessary, it had to be chased.

As police finally created order, Haynes spotted Abu Zaid in a far corner of the mosque. He was kneeling in prayer, his eyes closed in concentration, his hand cupped over an ear. Torkilson moved in for the arrest but Haynes waved him away. Seconds later, Abu Zaid stood up, turned toward Haynes, and submitted his outstretched arms.

Abu Zaid, unlike the others, proved to be a tough nut. He seemed to be detached from both the proceedings at the station and from questioning. Haynes reasoned with him, cajoled him, threatened him, and tried to portray the other perpetrators as his enemies. All the while precious time was slipping away.

At last Haynes, himself, simply couldn't take it any more. Seething rage scalded his face as he dismissed everybody but Abu Zaid from his office.

If not by reason, then by force.

Haynes whacked Abu Zaid in the back of the neck and then kicked the chair out from under him. After he half hoisted Abu Zaid up, Haynes then ran him hard into the wall, slamming his considerable weight against the crumpling man. A series of vicious kicks later, the beating complete, he forced Abu Zaid down into his chair.

Haynes felt a little bit better. He straightened out Abu Zaid's clothes and placed a cup of tea before him. Then he struggled to regain his own composure. After a couple of minutes his facial muscles relaxed and his face reverted back to its usual pale color.

"Now, Mr. Abu Zaid," his voice once again controlled, "please tell me who contacted you about organizing this group to kidnap Pike."

Perhaps it was respect for force. Perhaps, thought Haynes, it was like that interview he'd once seen of a Green Bay Packer player describing Vince Lombardi's coaching success: After being thoroughly put through the wringer and humiliated, one kind word or action made him want to run through a wall for Lombardi. Whatever it was, Abu Zaid began talking.

"A man named Tomas Bahr, a travel agency owner I know, said he was issued a *fatwa*, an Islamic advisory opinion that can be intrepreted as a directive, to get Zach Pike."

"Who issued it?"

"I don't know."

"Why was it issued?"

"I don't know. What I can tell you is that a *fatwa* is very serious." Abu Zaid then shot a most chilling look at Haynes. "If I were you, I would worry for Zach Pike."

Even though some guests were put up at the homes of neighbors, the huge house was still crammed with visitors. Aviva and Oded Langer slept on a sofa-bed in the den. Teddy Pike, his wife, and three kids bunked in his old room. The same went for Sam and Liz's families. Cousins and friends of the family found make-shift quarters in the living room and finished basement that Ben and his boys had long ago converted into a gym.

Somehow, Meg and Zvi wound up in Zach's old bedroom. It seemed only natural. There had been so many times, so many nights, they had slept over as teenagers, laughing and telling stories almost till daybreak.

In fact, even though Meg had lived in Brookline village, she practically grew up at the Pike's. Her father, as Meg described it, "took the long way home," when she was five years old. Her mother, saddled with three small children, first got fat and then got drunk. By the time Meg became friends with Zach in grade school, she had already half raised herself and two younger siblings, and in the process forged a gutsy independence which was often mistaken to be spunky insolence. But she only flourished when the Pikes showed her that it was possible to dream as well. Ben and Mary took Meg on family vacations and bought her better clothes. They even visited out-of-state prospective colleges with her until Meg finally decided to attend Boston College. More than anything, Zach's room, this house, always represented the world as it could be.

But now the room was hauntingly reminiscent of the past. It was as it had always been. A Patriots jersey signed by quarterback Steve Grogan hung on the wall over Zach's bed. A football autographed by Boston College great, Doug Flutie, sat on a night table. Celtics, Bruins, and Red Sox memorabilia were positioned with the utmost of care.

Zvi looked at some photographs that were wedged around a mirror over Zach's dresser. Several of the photos were from Zach's college days, but others were from earlier times.

And then Zvi discreetly saw in the reflection of the mirror an adjacent bathroom light go dim. Meg had changed into one of Zach's oversized Jets T-shirts and was now padding up, barefooted, behind him. He, himself, wore only a race top and running shorts. For a long while their eyes sadly settled on photo after photo: the three of them stuffing hamburgers into their faces at a barbecue; Zach and Zvi playing one-on-one basketball; Zach and Meg, arm-in-arm, about to go to the prom.

Then Zvi and Meg, by way of the mirror, looked at each other.

"Zvi. You said earlier this evening Zach would be fine. That everything would be okay."

"I'll make sure it is. I'm flying back to Israel tomorrow and I'll somehow find out what they know about this. I don't know precisely, but surely something can be done."

"What do you mean?"

"I can't explain exactly, not now at any rate. But I'm not just an archaeology student, Meggie. I can do things, and friends of mine in high places can do things. And they owe me, Meggie. They owe me."

Meg stared at Zvi in the mirror. At first glance he still looked as youthful and fun-loving as ever. But a furrow in his forehead and fine lines around pained eyes made Zvi appear, upon closer look, old beyond his years.

Meg was confused. The only thing she could cling to was Zvi's promise that he could do something. Zvi always was prodigiously capable. Yet she trembled slightly as she realized that the old, close friend next to her was someone she did not really know very well at all.

"Zvi, you also said earlier this evening that *we'd* see this through."

Zvi said nothing.

"I want to go with you to Israel. I feel so helpless here. The thought of being thousands of miles away from Zach, and away from you trying to find Zach, would make me crazy."

Again Zvi said nothing.

"Remember," said Meg as her blood coursed with victory, "he's my friend too."

Zvi tossed in a sleeping bag long after Meg sweetly breathed with sleep in Zach's bed. He understood that his silence was a sign of acquiescence;

a green light for Meg. What he did not understand was why he hadn't stopped, hadn't protested, Meg's intentions of accompanying him to Israel.

Just when sleep was about to overwhelm him, Zvi sprang to attention as a distant throb drew louder and louder. Zvi searched in the dark for the source even as the cadence got faster and drew closer. The throb seemed familiar but muffled, as if encased in a vault. Zvi held his breath and concentrated on pinpointing the source. It was very close now, beating in his ears, rushing all about him.

In him!

Zvi bolted upright and threw his hand over his chest as he felt—the passionate pulsing of his heart.

CHAPTER EIGHT

*P*resident Oliver Earl strode to the door seperating the Oval Office from his secretary's anteroom and motioned for three men to come in. He shook their hands formally and the men proceeded to exchange pleasantries with members of the National Security Council before taking their places in chairs opposite those of the President and Vice President. The members sat on a pair of facing, flanking sofas.

Lee Nunzio, executive assistant director of the FBI, had been called to the early morning emergency session by Oliver Earl personally. The two other men, Howard Jones, the CIA foreign service officer and current senior Middle East analyst, and Gilford McKenzie, former Ambassador to Sudan, had been invited by Lou Reed, the National Security Adviser.

"Gentlemen," the President began, "this was broadcast on CNN last night."

Earl was dressed in a dark blue suit and crimson tie. Nunzio felt he looked exceptionally grim. He knew the President would have personally viewed the video of Zach Pike numerous times. Nunzio also knew that Earl didn't care how many times members of his National Security Council had seen it; they were all going to witness the gripping, somber spectacle again.

"The barbaric abduction of an innocent American from U.S. soil and the terrorists' totally unacceptable ransom demands constitute a sufficient threat to national security for us to convene this morning."

The President clicked the remote to the console of television monitors Lyndon Johnson had had installed in the Oval Office in order to
simultaneously view network coverage of the Vietnam War. One of the
monitors began flickering the broadcast as all gathered around.

When the lights came back on, the President's face had changed from
ashen to nearly the same crimson as his tie. When he was sworn into the
Presidency, Earl had decided to use the *Resolute Desk* that the British
had had so beautifully carved as a gift in honor of the American arctic
rescue of the *HMS Resolute*. Several Presidents since Rutherford B.
Hayes had worked at the oak *Resolute* and the President had confided
that when he too was challenged by crisis, he hoped the desk would but-
tress his resolve to weather the crisis.

As Earl stepped out from behind the *Resolute* and led members of the
Council back to the facing sofas, he was still furious. The fundamentalists' actions were an affront to the office of the Presidency, an assault on
the sovereignty of the United States.

"Lee, could you fill us in on what the FBI knows and what it's doing?"

Nunzio, compact, with dark hair and a bureaucrat's impassive face,
tried to speak in an even voice. "N.Y.P.D. has arrested four men who
were actively involved in the Rockefeller Plaza incident. One of the men,
Sayid Abu Zaid, is an Egyptian who, like Sheik Omar Abdel Rahman,
illegally entered the U.S. via Sudan by lying to the Immigration and
Naturalization Service about his revolutionary activities. The Egyptian
Mukhabarat, their intelligence, have informed us that he was active with
the fundamentalist Gamaa al Islamiya movement."

Nunzio paused for a moment to finally inhale a calming breath. He
had hoped an early morning run and a brief walk down Pennsylvania
Avenue from the J. Edgar Hoover Building would be sufficiently relax-
ing. But being stared at now by the President, Vice President, the entire
Council—even a portrait of George Washington that hung over the
fireplace behind the President—was proving to be more daunting than
he thought it would be.

Nunzio started his FBI career twenty-four years earlier, right after college. At first he worked as an agent in Division Six, the criminal investigative division, and later he became a special agent in Division Five, the counterintelligence division. Dedication to duty and an ability to outwork anybody had catapulted him through the ranks, well beyond his modest expectations, and landed him here, in the inner sanctum. Soon he would succeed an aging FBI Director and become "*the man.*"

But for now all he wanted to do was get through this presentation. His eyes, scanning the room, found some humor in a Presidential seal that was woven into the rug just beyond his extended right leg. The American eagle that faced an olive branch was dispatching the words *e pluribus unum*, out of many, one, from its beak. How odd that a bald contortionist American eagle would spew out great Latin prose while he, the proud son of Italian immigrants, didn't know one word of the language of ancient Rome.

"Abu Zaid and Vernon Compton-El received CIA training in the mid 80's as Mujaheddin in Afghanistan," Nunzio continued, feeling more composed. "The other two, Yousef Yassin and Hassan Kamal, have no criminal history in the U.S., but neither do Abu Zaid or Compton-El for that matter. What's interesting is how incompetent these four actually were."

"What do you mean?" asked Lou Reed.

"Well, it's like the World Trade Center bombing and the planned attacks on the FBI building, tunnels, and United Nations. We can very easily catch those who are commiting the crime. They are a collection of criminally unsophisticated individuals who barely know each other and don't really know who is directing them. I don't mean to imply that they simply are fired up with political motivation and then randomly act. Rather, these people are directed from abroad to do something symbolically shocking, or get somebody. Then they manage to do it, following their own operational design. It's a tough situation, very hard to get a handle on."

"In the cold war days," Secretary of State Alfred Brown said, "Moscow would always protect rogue nations like Syria or Libya. These countries didn't much care if their hands were bloodstained and if their fingerprints were all over the deadly terror weapons at their disposal. Now terrorist nations do care, so their scheming is so loosely organized that those who commit crime on their behalf don't know who manages or finances them."

"That's right," Nunzio nodded his head. "Abu Zaid was told by an Arab-American businessman named Tomas Bahr to get Pike. He doesn't know why and he certainly doesn't care who spoke to Bahr. And as for money or financial backing, Abu Zaid and his ilk are so ideologically motivated, they don't care an awful lot about that either.

"Bahr meanwhile, even as the kidnapping is taking place, is on a plane to London. He vanishes once he gets there. Scotland Yard is researching this thing, but undoubtedly Bahr is taking refuge with the people overseas who came up with this idea. We've already issued a reward for information leading to further arrests. If you remember, a reward was instrumental in catching Ramzi Yousef, the mastermind behind the World Trade Center bombing, in Pakistan. But we can't really go too much further until we get Bahr."

"Unless, of course, we find Pike," Hurley Baker, Director of the CIA, pointed out. "Then we can work backwards, so to speak, by nabbing those holding Pike and discovering who had them hold Pike."

"That's another way of dissecting this thing," Nunzio agreed.

The problem-solving capability of the CIA always amazed Nunzio. Perhaps that was why his organization so often had disputes with them. While the FBI steadfastly followed one lead after another, the CIA had the wherewithal, the assets, to seize the crux of a problem and then surreptitiously, if necessary, pinpoint the *modus operandi*.

"I long ago froze assets to extremist groups and I've put new counter terror laws before Congress that expedite deportations and expand the usage of wire taps. What are you folks in the FBI going to do differently concerning this case?" the President asked.

"We're checking on charitable front organizations which still manage to funnel monies to fundamentalist groups. Perhaps that way we can pick up a trail," Nunzio said. "In addition, Siddig Ali, who after his arrest in connection with the bombings decided to plead guilty and help prosecutors, said that firearms training was taking place in Sheik Rahman's mosque and that explosives testing was taking place in camps like one near Harrisburg, Pennsylvania. We now know who instructed in those places and who some of the individuals were who participated in those training sessions. We are questioning them to see what they know." Nunzio took a deep breath. "We are also correcting an error we made a few years ago."

One reason Nunzio had advanced so far in the FBI was his ability to recognize a mistake, fess up to the mistake, and, most importantly, learn from the mistake. "After Rabbi Meir Kahane was assasinated in New York in 1990 by Sayid Abu Nosair, we failed to adequately translate and analyze material seized at his home. Had we done so at that time we would have learned that even then there was a call to bomb the World Trade Center. Now, even as we speak, there are agents working in close cooperation with Arabic experts from the Defense Department Language School, collecting and examining documents from the homes of the four men arrested and from the home of Tomas Bahr."

"If there's nothing further, Lee, then we'll hear now from Ambassador McKenzie." The President, in deference to McKenzie's advanced years and long service, maintained formal decorum with his brief introduction.

"Thank you, Mr. President." Gilford McKenzie, a distinguished look-ing war-horse, stood up to address the Council.

"There is a saying that God cried when he created Sudan. There is another saying that God laughed when he created Sudan." Several of the National Security Council attendees chuckled.

"Sudan is the largest country in Africa. For many years there has been a bitter civil war between the Moslem north and the Sudan People's Liberation Army in the south, which is comprised of Christians and adherents to indigenous African religions. Over 800,000 people have died in the past decade as a result of that war, primarily as a result of the famine the war created in the south and in refugee camps of the north." McKenzie paused and delicately cleared his throat.

"Five million people are now in imminent danger of starvation. Hence we have the international famine relief efforts now taking place. Why this predicament? Because the south won't accept *sharia* law that it feels the Moslem north is imposing upon them."

"Mr. Ambassador," interrupted the President, "can you explain for those who aren't clear about it just what *sharia* law is?"

"*Sharia* is a compilation of Islamic rules that govern dress, marriage, sex, education, politics, and justice. It seeks to substitute laws of man for those of god. The African south of Sudan feel that it is nothing short of a planned policy to exterminate their African nationalities."

McKenzie went on to explain that the Moslem north was now not only espousing fundamentalist Islam in their own country, but exporting a lethal brand of Islam abroad. Terrorist groups like the Popular Front for the Liberation of Palestine, the Palestinian Hamas, the Iranian backed Islamic Jihad, the banned Algerian Islamic Salvation Front, and Egypt's Gamaa al Islamiya all trained in Sudan. Sudan also sanctioned so called *spiritual education camps.* Some of them were run by a quasi-military force modeled after Iran's Revolutionary Guard and others by Iran's Quds Force, a secret army unit dedicated to exporting the Islamic revolution.

"The reason you are hearing so much about Iran," McKenzie concluded, "is that a marriage of sorts has taken place between the two countries. Shiite Iran sees Sudan as its first Sunni Muslim ally in the region. An important ally since Sudan borders Egypt and seven other countries, and lies in close proximity to Saudi Arabia and all that oil. Sudan, in turn, sees Iran as a cash cow for their poor country."

"These terrorist training camps you spoke of," Brown said, "plus possible complicity in the Trade Center bombing, has cost Sudan seventy-four million dollars in trade with the U.S. and forced us to place Sudan on the list of countries that support terrorism. In fact, two Sudanese United Nations officials were implicated in the failed U.N. bombing. Yet Sudan seems unfazed by all this. When we contacted them for assistance, they threw up their hands and said they knew nothing. What's your reading on this, Ambassador McKenzie?"

"It seems as if their government, the Revolutionary Command Council, has lost an internal struggle to the fundamentalist National Islamic Front party over the rate of Islamization. It is possible that the government doesn't know about Pike, but it's more likely that they are too afraid of the National Islamic Front party and Amir Kasawi, he's the NIF leader, to be of any use. One thing for sure, the National Islamic Front party knows. Events like the abduction of Pike simply don't happen without their knowledge."

"Thank you Mr. Ambassador." The President paused a few moments even after Gilford McKenzie sat down. He rubbed a hand slowly over his upper teeth while his eyes looked beyond the glass door and glass windows of the office.

"Mr. Jones," he said suddenly. "You're up."

Howard Jones, a spry towheaded man of sixty who still sported a boyish cowlick, leaped to his feet. A preacher's son, he'd adopted his father's Georgian Baptist zeal and directed it towards everything that was CIA. His very being embodied his father's fire and brimstone mannerisms, transforming his every talk, and his every walk, into high drama. Nunzio had always found Jones to be funny, and although Jones was often humorously impersonated, he was never derisively parodied. An exemplery foreign service record in North Africa, a sharp analytical approach to the Middle East, and sincere enthusiasm about his work protected him from that kind of ridicule.

"Proof!" Jones pounded the coffee table. "The CIA has proof that Sudan's United Nations ambassador was informed by the spiritual head of the National Islamic Front, Amir Kasawi himself, that even though those two implicated Sudanese U.N. officials had diplomatic cover they were to act as intelligence operatives. We photocopied a memorandum to that effect when we were investigating Sudanese complicity in the aborted U.N. bombing. Let me just at this point concur with Ambassador McKenzie that the National Islamic Front sooner or later is aware of everything that transpires in Sudan."

Jones rocked back and forth, and then continued. "Kasawi and the NIF, who are smart enough to pretend they're moderates, have a free hand in day-to-day internal security operations. They hold hundreds of political prisoners in ghost houses and in Khartoum's Kober prison."

"What do you mean by ghost houses?" Paul Calloway, the Secretary of Defense, asked.

"Ghost houses are former residences that the National Islamic Front has confiscated and turned into the most vile, infernal holes you can imagine. They are torture chambers, Sir! And God help the wretched soul who is thrown into them or into Kober Prison." Jones froze dramatically, facing in the direction of the Defense Secretary. He was working himself into one of his characteristic fits.

"Mr. Jones, we've been in touch with Egypt." Alfred Brown blessedly woke Jones up from his trance. "They are most interested in cooperating and sharing intelligence. They certainly have their share of fundamentalist terror directed at tourists and politicians. But for some time now they've seemed preoccupied with, almost paranoid about, Sudan."

Jones nodded. "For good reason. Egypt has its hands full managing various fundamentalist groups. These groups became popular by helping with food and blankets during crises like the 1992 earthquake, while the government came off as inept and unjust. But Sudan exacerbates

Egypt's situation. Egypt has become Sudan's short-term *raison detre.* Sudan is like a dagger at their back, infiltrating Egypt's southern provinces, Asyut for example, with its pulpit 'Islam is the Solution' dogma.'"

Jones paused for a moment and his creased, genial Will Rogers face lit up into a great big smile. "And as you all know, I know something about pulpits."

There was a round of mild laughter. "What are our HUMINT intelligence capabilities in Sudan?" asked the President after the laughter died down.

"Up until two years ago it was very very poor. Now, since our goof of erroneously bombing that baby milk factory we thought produced nerve gas, we've improved it so much it's just plain poor. We have a CIA chief, base chief really, over there but he is so closely watched he can't effectively meet with potential agents. Walk-ins are non-existent because everyone is petrified of being caught and thrown into ghost houses. Our chief spends most of his time just denying activities to the Sudanese government. The Defense attache' officer and our U.S. Information officer are also followed but fortunately Sudanese intelligence is operationally primitive, so we at times get snippets of information from them." Jones shrugged. "The CIA has found that collection is better using non-official cover assets, especially in hard target countries like Iran or Sudan, where official embassy cover doesn't exist or is virtually useless."

Jones went on to explain that a non official cover, or NOC, was usually a recent college grad recruited by the CIA to work for a U.S. company that does business overseas. While living a cover life as an engineer, banker, or export-import employee by day, the NOC would gather intelligence by night, during his off-hours. "The CIA's National Collections Branch has been carefully approaching CEO's to agree to this arrangement," Jones explained, "and CEO's who consent, out of patriotism, get a free employee out of the deal. The CIA's Covert Tax Branch has even worked out a system with the IRS to resolve the two W-2 forms the NOC gets every year. They get new names for CIA purposes, and there's a CIA staff person to handle NOC personal stuff like paying bills and so on, while they're living their cover life."

"I know this sounds exactly like the type of skullduggery the media always paints us of practicing," the Director of the CIA, Hurley Baker, acknowledged. "But it really is the only way we can effectively function in certain countries."

Nunzio, like all of the people gathered at the Oval Office, had heard previously about NOC's. But like some of them he was learning for the first time about just how elaborate NOC operations were. It was not really his place to start questioning, or offering opinions, about matters that did not involve the branch he served. He was, after all, an invitee to the National Security Council who was there to simply explain the FBI's role and view. However he was so stunned, so disturbed about CIA NOC activity, he couldn't stop himself.

"But these people have no diplomatic cover. If they're caught...."

Baker cut him off. "It's a very dangerous job."

The President cleared his throat, and Nunzio took it as a signal to let the matter drop. "Mr. Jones," the President said, "let's sum up. What is your professional opinion regarding the status of Zach Pike?"

"There are many competing fundamentalist bands in Sudan, as there are in Egypt, all of whom desperately want power. Kasawi's National Islamic Front in Khartoum has to placate the other bands. Someone like Zach Pike, who is valuable to them as a bargaining chip, would have to be placed in the custody of some person or organization these bands can all live with, a neutral party you might say. My best guess would be that this neutral party is so religious and devout that it doesn't concern itself with struggles over political power."

"Is it really plausible to believe that a religious group like that would not seek power? Could that kind of entity exist?" Lou Reed asked.

"In the world of mystical Islamic Sufism, which by its nature demands unswerving focus, that kind of group or individual could possibly exist.

The chance is, I'll admit, remote, human nature being what it is." Jones shrugged, smiled.

"I guess there's also a possibility that whoever's holding Pike is so inept or naive, maybe even literally insane, that the fundamentalist bands don't take him seriously. And there's one other thing." Jones edged forward in his chair. Nunzio, along with all the members of the Security Coucil, leaned forward.

"Our Behavioral Science Center in Langley has drawn up a psychological profile, a roadmap of behavior if you will, of how terrorist organizations operate. What drives these people is not the attainment of what we in the west would consider to be logical and substantive goals. The most basic of emotions, hate, jealousy, and revenge, makes them tick. We should know, as the terrorists already know, that even the release of their comrades in arms that we hold would not satisfy them. They don't even expect our compliance with their demands. They are looking for something else here. If they don't get what they're looking for they will hurt us, make no mistake about it, by killing Zach Pike. And even if they take hold of or achieve whatever it is they want, they may still kill Zach Pike. Or at the very least strike at us again, and very soon." Jones suddenly clutched at his tie and gazed heavenwards, then delivered his homily.

"For the most baneful of emotions are bottomless. In the final analysis, hate, jealousy, and revenge become not only the means, but ends unto their very selves."

The preacher would have been proud of his son.

As the meeting broke up, the President went over to Paul Calloway and Mac Streicher, Chairman of the Joint Chiefs of Staff. The two men were already gathering up their briefcases for the ride back to the Pentagon.

"I assume you'll be exploring what our options are." The President rested one hand on the gray-suited shoulder of his top civilian armed forces advisor and his other on the four star epaulet of his top military advisor. "But I want to say, now, before all of us are so caught up in this thing that taking five for a crap becomes our only escape, that I'm very grateful for your wise counsel."

"Ollie," Mark Handsman, the White House Chief of Staff interrupted him. "We've got to go. You've got a press conference."

The President slapped the shoulders of his military advisors. A moment later he was out of the Oval Office and striding away from the west wing towards the press room in the colonnade connecting the office wing to the residence. Lou Reed, his old hometown friend, and Mark Handsman, a recently acquired friend, struggled to keep pace with him as he spoke to them about the Pikes.

"You know, I spoke very early this morning with the kid's parents. Turns out his father's also a Battle of the Bulge veteran. For all I know, he could have been in a fox-hole a hundred yards away from me. At any other time it would have been a wonderful conversation. They're genuine salt-of-the-earth type of people. But I really didn't know what to say to them. Their boy's just had the crap beat out of him, and I had to keep reassuring them everything would be alright. *Damn it*, I don't know everything's going to be alright! And frankly I'm sick and tired of not being able to really speak my mind."

There was scarcely enough air to breathe in the press room. The White House Spokesman was addressing the media from a raised platform, a blue curtain with the White House logo as a backdrop. The President stood to the side, out of view of the media, and anticipated the questions that would be flung at him.

Would he strike at Sudan if it was learned that they had sponsored the abduction?

He would dance around that one.

Would he consider dealing with the fundamentalists?

NUTS!—what General A.C. McAuliffe replied to the ultimatum by the Germans at Bastogne during the Battle of the Bulge—is what he would want to say, but he wouldn't.

Why Zach Pike? Why was he taken?

Finally he would be able to give an honest and direct answer.

"I just don't know."

CHAPTER NINE

*T*he household was not yet quite awake, but it wasn't exactly asleep either. The long tumultuous night just past had left everyone too upset for that.

All night the footsteps of those who could not sleep sounded on the stairs as they found their way to the kitchen and, over a cup of tea or glass of milk, talked quietly among themselves about Zach. In the pre-dawn hours, an out-of-town family member trudged downstairs with his belongings for a lonely cab ride to the airport. And even now, as morning arrived, the stillness was occasionally punctuated by the whimper of a child who was having a nightmare, or by the sobbing of an adult who suddenly realized he was living one.

Oded meandered about the foyer while he waited for Ben to come downstairs. Neither man could sleep, but then again, it had been many years since either man had slept well anyways. With that in mind, they'd made plans the previous night to meet at 6:00 A.M. for one of their long walks. Back in the days when the Langers were neighbors of the Pikes, there always seemed to be so much to discuss during their walks—this morning more than ever.

Oded picked up a copy of Model Airplane News from the stack of mail on a round marble table. Ben's favorite diversion was flying small remote planes and the two neighbors had often put a plane through its paces at nearby parks. Both men understood the intracacies of flight,

Oded as a former major in the Israel Air Force, and Ben from his years of high tech engineering work for Lexington Labs. The difference was that Ben built a career out of his love for aeronautics, while Oded used his aviation background as a springboard into Israeli politics.

An occasional step creaked as Ben walked down the stairs. Despite his age he was still physically imposing. A square jaw and ruddy complexion, plus his burly frame, made him look like a tough old truck driver with whom one could down a few beers at a local pub. Yet his expressive sensitive eyes, and cultured voice, could also place him at the Boston Symphony. In fact, Ben could often be found at both venues, or at a town meeting, a charitable fund-raiser, or a defense systems symposium. He possessed a rare ability to talk to anyone, about anything, at anytime. But his most endearing quality was his capacity to listen and genuinely care. It was odd, then, that though he had so many friends, he had only one close friend.

Oded watched him put on his coat and momentarily stop to gaze at an old civil war photograph that hung among many treasured family photographs. It was a picture of Ben's great-grandfather, Zachary Hale Pike, a young officer of the Army of Northern Virginia, Lee's Army. Zach had an uncanny resemblance to his namesake. Their erect bearings exuded confident leadership but their self-effacing smiles were boyish and carefree.

Ben had distinct memories of his aged great-grandfather from his boyhood visits to the sprawling Richmond estate where he lived. But he couldn't ever summon any image of Zach as old, especially not now. He began shivering even before he and Oded stepped out into the cold.

They drove in silence for ten minutes and parked near Harvard Stadium, its Coliseum-like facade eerily conjuring visions of old epic struggles. After crossing the Charles River over Anderson Bridge, they turned right and walked along Memorial Drive. A gusty wind rolled over the frozen river and swirled up wisps of light snow. The bluster seemed at times to explode in their faces.

"Odie, this is just killing me," Ben said, his voice tight. "It's tearing me up inside. Zach is as pure as this snow. It wasn't supposed to be like this. Never in my worst dreams did I foresee anything like this."

Though Ben and Oded had children of the same age, they themselves now looked like a father and son engaging in deep discussion while out for a walk. Zach was born several years after his siblings, when Ben was already in his forties. Zach arrived at a time when life no longer seemed to stretch on forever, when the future and his ability to shape it did not appear as infallible as before, and when the past had begun to blur, even as elements of it acquired a sentimental glow. As a consequence, even though Ben loved all his children, Zach became his most precious.

The two old friends picked up speed as they marched together along a course they'd routinely covered many times before.

They'd first met soon after Zach and Zvi became friends. The two fathers came down to the Runkle School gym to watch their sons play an intramural basketball game. Both men had grown accustomed to watching their sons' athletic skills go unrivaled. So it came as a surprise when the boys absolutely took over the game for their respective teams. Back and forth they went at each other, Zach relentlessly pounding the boards for offensive rebounds, and Zvi driving past opponents for easy lay-ups.

"What's with that kid?" Ben asked Zach after the game.

"Who is that boy?" Oded asked Zvi.

Each boy introduced his friend to his father, and in the process introduced the fathers to each other.

There was much the two fathers had in common. But the reason they quickly became close friends was that they could talk so easily with each other.

Oded would spend an extended period of time attending the Kennedy School of Government at Harvard. After a distinguished air force career, he'd been encouraged by the state of Israel to train to be a political leader, and the Wexner-Israel Fellowship Program would be a great opportunity. There, among other things, he'd have the chance to meet Arab officials in a variety of Middle East Seminar Series.

"There's something very important I have to raise with you," Ben had said to Oded during a walk about two months after they'd become friends. "My engineering specialty at Lexington Labs concerns developing Remote Piloted Vehicles, RPV's. As you know from your military background, RPV's are cheap, pilotless, light aircraft that carry video cameras in order to perform reconnaissance work in enemy territory. The best part is they are guided by a ground-based pilot so that they can't get a human one killed."

"I'm familiar with them," Oded said. He was starting to feel apprehensive. "Israel has been experimenting with RPV's for years. At this time we are the world's foremost experts in the field. They have tremendous potential."

"Exactly! The Defense Resource Advisory Board decided RPV's were a weapon system worth developing and after an exhaustive Major System Acquisition Process our lab was contacted by the military. Unfortunately, there has been a lot of resistance by the Air Force and Navy over using them. Their pilots feel threatened. There still has been no push for production go-ahead. The Army keeps insisting on more and more Research and Development. Their latest wish is that the RPV weigh no more than 240 pounds so now we have to miniaturize all our components. The Army also wants the Aquila RPV to come with a truck and net to catch it if there is nowhere to land. These games are endless!"

"But won't the Defense Department insist that you start producing the RPV's, just override the hesitancy of the Army and Navy?" Oded asked.

"No. The Office of the Undersecretary of Defense for Research and Engineering is not capable of any critical independent advice. They long ago lost their clout."

"So what is it that you want Ben?"

"I've been issued a security clearance by the Department of Defense. That means I have access to classified information. And since I work on the RPV projects I have a bonafide need-to-know. Israel does have more experience with RPV's, but I'm absolutely certain technology I can get a hold of would be of tremendous value to Israel."

Oded's apprehension had widened into full blown dread. There were two gigantic problems with what Ben was proposing. First, Ben had become one of his best friends, even in this short period of time. Second, he himself had no diplomatic immunity.

Oded was shocked over Ben's willingness to commit espionage, to in effect become a spy for Israel. However his military background, a budding political career, and a curriculum base in International Security at the Kennedy School had made him sophisticated about intelligence operations.

He knew the Mossad would be very reluctant to run a spy in the United States because of intelligence cooperation agreements with the CIA. Only if the most professional trade-craft precautions were followed would they even consider it. But false-flag recruitement, letting Ben erroneously believe he was dealing with the intelligence service of another country, was out of the question because it was Ben himself who'd approached Israel.

And insisting Ben cooperate with the Mossad station of another country, so as not to risk compromise or embarrasment of a U.S.—based Mossad station and its operations, would also be difficult since at that particular point in time Ben rarely travelled, or had any reason to travel, abroad.

Oded was aware of another section of the Israeli intelligence community he felt might get involved. Lakam, the Defense Ministry's Office of Scientific Liaison, ran a bureau at the Israeli Embassy. Their past successes included persauding Swiss engineer Alfred Frauenknecht to supply blueprints of the French Mirage engine. Soon after Israel had adapted the technology in creating their own Kfir jet.

Oded flew down to New York and met Israel's science consul, Moshe Negbi. Negbi had worked for Israel Aircraft Industries and Oded had on many occasions compared notes with him on jet performance capabilities.

"A friend of mine," explained Oded, "an engineer specializing in the development of Remote Piloted Vehicles, wants to share classified information with Israel."

"Why?"

"He's frustrated by the turtle-like pace and lack of commitment to RPV's by the U.S military."

"Why does he want to work with us?" asked Negbi. "Why doesn't he go to the French or British?"

"He's fully aware that Israel is not only more advanced in RPV technology, but that we will also utilize RPV's in combat situations." After a pause, Oded continued. "He also says he is an ardent supporter of Israel."

"Why?" Moshe Negbi wondered aloud. Negbi was a child survivor of Dachau, a Bavarian concentration camp where he'd lost his parents and two younger brothers. His personal history had shaped his personality, and his psyche carried a healthy dose of skepticism and surprise towards gentiles who yearned to help Jews.

"I'm not sure why," Oded said to Negbi. "We've become close friends, but I still don't understand him very well."

"Listen. I'm going to have to go to the Ministry of Defense about this, discreetly of course. Assuming they let us proceed, we'll set up a way for Pike to start delivering blueprints and documents through this office. Then we'll assess the quality of the data."

"No." Oded didn't like the sound of that. "Ben Pike has assured me," he lied, "that he won't remove any physical evidence that could implicate him. All information will be passed on verbally—through me—someone he trusts." Oded held his breath, knowing that Negbi could balk right on the spot. But there was no way he was going to permit a friend to potentially incriminate himself by transfering secret documents.

The decision that he would act as an intermediary was not premiditated but spontaneous. In part he wanted to shield Ben from the clutches of an intelligence network. But, truthfully, in large part the decision was selfish. Oded's political career and influence would be enhanced if he remained involved in intelligence gathering. Perhaps one day the personal risk he was taking could be redeemed for a big favor, should he ever need it.

"This is unusual, to say the least," Negbi said. "And no disrespect intended, but can you act as an effective sounding board for Pike's high tech intelligence?"

"I know aeronautics, Moshe, and I understand how the military relies on air support." Oded rubbed his chin and broke out in a smile. "I'm actually the perfect man for this operation. I have the kind of memory that'll absorb everything Pike says, yet I can't be duped into giving him our RPV intelligence because I'm virtually ignorant about it. That's what you were getting at, isn't it?"

"I'm not sure how the big boys will react to this set up." Moshe Negbi was not amused. "Among other things they will want to know how much money to pay Pike. He will accept it, won't he?"

"The Pikes are very wealthy, primarily through inheritance. He isn't doing this for money. But sure, I'll ask him about reimbursement."

Oded recognized that doling out money and gifts was a classic technique of ensnaring an agent. Once an agent accepted them, he would be obligated to continue supplying information. Even more ominously for the agent, the intelligence network could point to money and gifts as proof of his cooperation, thereby finding a means to control him.

Oded never did ask Ben about accepting renumeration. He simply explained to Negbi and Lakam that Pike wasn't interested in it. But about that, as Oded suspected, he need not have been concerned. During the entire time that Ben provided valuable intelligence, he never once even hinted that he was interested in money.

What was his motive, then? Oded eventually realized that Ben was a throwback. He shared data and ideas for ideological and personal reasons. From an intelligence agent perspective, Ben did not fit into the milieu of the times. In many ways he was an anachronism. But his lofty motivations were timeless. It therefore came as no surprise to Oded that the man, Ben Pike, outlasted the stealth of Lakam, which disbanded after the Jonathan Pollard affair of the mid 80's.

Frail daylight seeped into the sky as Ben and Oded now took a left on Massachusetts Avenue and walked past the Massachusetts Institute of Technology. MIT was the reason the young and brilliant Ben Pike left Virginia after WWII. It was there that he first learned the physics and principles of flight.

Oded started to reminisce. "Back in 1973, when I was once young," he joked, "I was among the first pilots to be scrambled when the Yom Kippur War broke out. It was crazy. I would come back from a strike, slurp down a cup of coffee, make sure my plane was refueled and rearmed, and be back up in the air seven minutes later. We were abused to the max. But we had to keep getting back up there. In the first two hours of the war the Syrians blew up twenty-five Skyhawks and five Phantoms."

Oded ran over the facts for Ben, facts they both knew: that the most brutal of the Syrian missile sites were the SA-6, mobile enough to follow armor and infantry battalions, using a two-stage radar guidance system. When a jet would try to jam the radar on one of its frequencies, the missile would switch to the other. Upon nearing a target, the SA-6's heat-seeking homing device was activated. The SAM would slip in behind them and actually get into their tailpipes.

"Ben," Oded said, shaking his head, "a lot of jets fell into fireballs in the early stages of the war and there were precious few open parachutes to be seen." Even though he was now away from the wind tunnel of the Charles, he shuddered violently. He turned up his coat collar.

"We tried everything to eliminate those damn SA-6 sites. We did near vertical, almost suicidal, dives, released our bombs and radar seeking Shrike missiles, but the Syrians had set up an elaborate air-defense web. Other SA-6 missiles would find us. Then we tried dropping decoy flares so that the missiles' infrared sensors would guide it to the flare, away from us. But the missiles came at us in bursts and eventually hit us." He closed his eyes, remembering.

"But," Ben said, "in the end you prevailed."

"Right, but we never did find a solution to the SA-6. Then, a few years later, during the Lebanon incursion of June 1982, Israel's F-15 and F-16 jets shot down over 80 Syrian MIG's and destroyed 19 missile batteries without even losing a single jet. In December 1983, the U.S. Navy launched 28 aircraft against practically the same Syrian positions in the Bekaa Valley. Only 26 of the U.S. jets returned safely." Oded let the numbers sink in.

"Why the difference? You know the difference Ben! Israel made extensive use of RPV's, **your RPV's and the gadgetry you helped insert!**" RPV's, they both knew, that were equipped with video cameras, radar reflectors to decoy updated SA-8 missiles, and electronic equipment to locate SA-8 launchers for Israeli jets to destroy.

"You saved Israeli lives, Ben," Oded said quietly. "And the RPV's would have saved American ones too but the U.S. military didn't decide to use them until long after they saw what Israel could do with them."

Finally, starting in the mid-80's, the U.S. military became very interested in RPV's and ultimately used them in the Gulf War. Ben was among the leaders in advancing RPV technology. The Pioneer, an RPV based on a prototype Israel had utilized, flew at 15,000 feet, out of the range of small Iraqi antiaircraft weapons. It was almost impossible to hear from the ground and seemed like a mosquito on Iraqi radar. But it was not the only RPV that had reconnaissance success. The Army used a small RPV called a Pointer and the Marines carried exdrones for their advance into Kuwait. Artillery could see what the RPV saw and electronic gear aboard

Gabe Galambos 83

the RPV detected Iraqi radar for pilots to later destroy with antiradiation missiles. For all this, Ben was justly proud.

When they reached Harvard Square, the two men decided to duck into Au Bon Pain for breakfast. Even the long walk couldn't dispel the numbing cold or the numbing anxiety that lingered in their minds.

They found a table overlooking a large terrace and ordered coffee and croissants. In the spring and summer street musicians, jugglers, and chess players routinely entertained the tourists. At any other time of the year students would be hurrying by, but they were now on Christmas break. It seemed as if nothing was routine anymore. Oded stared at the barren scene, but it was what was not seen, what lurked on the periphery, that was closing in fast and scaring him half-to-death.

"You know, don't you Ben, that the FBI, media, you name it, is going to leave no stone unturned. Soon they will start asking, 'Why Zach Pike?' They'll speak with teammates, the owner of the Jets, past and current girlfriends, your kids, Mary, and you—*especially you*. They'll say to themselves, 'Hey, Zach Pike's old man has worked for years with confidential material for a defense contractor.' They'll notice that you've been to Israel several times in the past few years on behalf of Lexington Labs, working on cooperative bilateral programs. Nothing wrong with that. RPV's and Unmanned Aerial Vehicles, their payloads, and their ground stations were built in Israel, while testing and training took place in California, all per contract specifications. But they'll naturally wonder if Zach wasn't abducted in order to get back at you for working with Israel. And they'll keep digging deeper to see if you ever overstepped your bounds, whether here or in Israel, and helped Israel more than you were supposed to."

"I can take the heat and handle the inquiries," Ben said. He rubbed his massive hands together. "I got into this with my eyes wide open and I've never had a moment of regret. I've always believed one could only have regrets for things one did not do, but should have."

Oded said nothing. Suddenly Ben hunched over the table and looked uncharacteristically vulnerable and confused. "But I just don't understand it. This extremist Sudanese Ansar Army took Zach in order to get back at me for work I've done in Israel. But a lot of people work with Israel and have done so for many years. Why is this happening now, to me, and to my family? It would only make sense if the fundamentalists know the rest of the story—if they also know there's still so much more I plan on doing with Israel. And how would they know that?"

Ben buried his face in his hands. His anguish continued, muffled and subdued. "Then again, who says there has to be any connection here at all. Chance, a mysterious universal plan, God—call it what you want— but strange things sometime happen that have no logical explanation. Christ, I'm the scientist! And I've lived long enough, and seen enough, to know that much."

Oded stirred his coffee slowly, searching for the right way to say what he was so reluctant to utter. He rapped his spoon on the lip of his cup, moved aside his coffee and croissant, and planted both his hands on the table.

"Ben, please listen carefully. What I'm about to say, I beg you, must remain confidential." He paused and when he spoke again, his voice was lower, almost a murmur.

"Zvi is a prominent member of Israel's most secret military unit, a unit that frequently serves intelligence and their covert operations. Aviva and I are very proud of him. His job is not only risky, it's highly important. Aviva knows when he goes overseas it's for the unit, but she does not know details of what he does. As a member of the Knesset, as part of the inner circle, I'm privy to that kind of information. I also carry a certain amount of responsibility for the execution of those covert operations." He sighed heavily. There'd been times he'd hesitated, because it was Zvi he was sending into danger. But in the end he'd always done the right thing for Israel.

"Now you may be right in assuming Zach's in trouble because of your work for Israel. But there is also a chance that Zach is in danger because of his friendship with Zvi. I'm sure that's what Zvi's thinking right now."

Ben and Oded sat for a while, isolated, despondent, each absorbed with doubts over his own culpability in creating this terrible predicament.

Then, shattering the contemplative moment, Ben forcefully took hold of Oded's right hand and deliberately banged both their hands on the table.

"This is crazy. We can't eat ourselves up, Odie, constantly weighing our every action with every conceivable and distant consequence. If we did, we probably would be so crippled by fear and doubt that nothing would ever get done, and that's just too high a price. There are undoubtedly challenges we will still have to act upon. What you did, what I did, what Zvi did, were acts of conscience, in response to dilemmas that confronted us at the time."

"And what are the dilemmas of conscience," asked Oded bitterly, "that compelled you these last few years to continue nourishing Israel with your ideas for RPV's and Unmanned Aerial Vehicles? You helped enough before. Why couldn't you leave well enough alone?" He was verbalizing his own frustration that he couldn't protect Ben from members of Israeli intelligence he'd cooperated with during recent project development trips. Oded naturally wanted Israel to have access to the latest military high tech research, but not if it would jeopardize his good friend; not if his good friend would now be hounded by U.S. counterintelligence because of it.

"I'm sorry Ben," he said. "Sorry I ever brought up the whole thing."

"When Israel was being terrorized by Iraqi scuds in the Gulf War," explained Ben, "I realized it wasn't just because America had tied Israel's hands. It was because Israel really did not have any viable defense, Patriot missiles or not. All I kept thinking was what if these scuds were

ballistic missiles carrying chemical, biological, or even nuclear payloads?" He stared into space, then looked hard at Oded.

"Listen," he said. "I've been working on a project funded by the
Pentagon's Ballistic Missile Defense Organization to study a high-altitude, solar-powered UAV that will have boost phase intercept potential.
In other words, a UAV that can engage ballistic missiles early in their
flight, when their exhaust emissions are easily detectable by a narrow
infrared waveband that's great for low altitude resolution. Kinetic-kill,
hypervelocity rockets aboard the UAV fire before deployment of frac-
tioning payloads. With this kind of ability, any aggressor firing missiles
thinks twice knowing that lethal payloads could explode in their own
backyard." Ben's hands were clenched in excitement. His work had
always had this power to distract him from his sorrow.

" The key to this UAV, the Vulture, is that it's actually a platform, a
satellite, from which we can not only blow missiles up, but from which
it's possible to spy on enemy movements or even launch our own air-to-
surface missiles."

Ben's eyes were alight. He outlined the specs: the Vulture could fly for
several days with a 200 foot graphite, Mylar, and Stryrofoam epoxy
wingspan that had its weight distributed by actually being several small
planes connected together. It had an extremely light wing loading of
one half pound per square foot, better even than the four pound wing
loading of an eagle. Motors and several propellers provided propulsion
and they were powered by solar cells which by day electrolyzed water
into hydrogen and oxygen, and by night recombined the gases for elec-
tricity. The Vulture survived because it flew at over 65,000 feet, was
painted so as to reduce its infrared identification, and hauled decoys to
thwart radio frequency missiles. And if the Vulture was destroyed it
wouldn't matter very much, because it was relatively inexpensive and,
like all UAV's or RPV's, didn't carry a pilot.

"So why couldn't I leave well enough alone, you ask." Ben's voice was
growing louder. "Because despite the Pentagon's working with Israel's

defense ministry to a certain extent on this thing, the Pentagon and the services are not pushing this thing fast enough. There's not enough money allocated, there's not enough testing at Andrews and Edwards Air Force bases, and it's going to be years until we cut through the resistance, red-tape, and bullshit. It's the early days of the RPV's all over again, but this time I can't wait. I'm old! Hell, by now I should be retired and just playing with my grandkids!"

Oded listened with a mixture of admiration and bewilderment.

"Odie, I'm doing this for the same reason I assisted Israel in the first place. Your country, perhaps very soon, is going to need this terminal defense system, the Vulture. So I have confidence they'll produce it and use it. Maybe that'll spur the Pentagon to get its ass moving. Maybe it'll ultimately save American lives!"

Ben had worked himself up into a fury that, in part, did answer why he continued his involvement with Israel. But Oded found himself asking what Moshe Negbi had wondered so many years before. *"Why?"* Why this ardent support for Israel? And Oded remembered his own answer: *"I still don't understand him very well."*

Ben and Oded left Au Bon Pain and walked into Harvard Square. Everywhere they looked, towards the Coop, down Brattle Street, or especially into Out of Town News, the vista seemed so familiar and yet so treacherous.

Plastered on several magazines and international newspapers was the picture of Zach; captive, brutalized. It was all so cruel, so overwhelming, that it left Ben and Oded gasping for air as they hurried out.

Stumbling along, they came upon a monument near the Kennedy School of Government.

And so, my fellow Americans: ask not what your country can do for you—ask what you can do for your country.

My fellow citizens of the world: ask not what America will do for you, but what together we can do for the freedom of man.

John F. Kennedy
Inaugural Address January 20, 1961

They each read the quote silently and then, moved along by a relentless undercurrent, headed back over the Charles River, towards the car parked by Harvard Stadium.

CHAPTER TEN

*C*harlie Hammami reveled in happiness. He celebrated his lot in life.

"Allahu Akbar." God is great.

It wasn't just an adage, it was a truth Hammami wrapped himself in. The ingrained conviction sometimes led him in strange directions—for he had known difficult times—but the path always revealed itself to him in the end. On this day, at this point in his life, the path was level, almost obstacle-free, and the sun, *a glorious blessed sun*, at last shone brightly as he and his guest strolled about the Serpentine in London's Hyde Park.

"You look so different *Alec*. It's amazing what a pair of glasses and a toupee can do."

"Thank you for providing them. Thank you. Thank you. Thank you," said *Alec*. He squirmed in his newly fitted Harrod's suit and tried to maintain the proper gentlemanly carriage of one who would be so-named *Alec*.

Half a million. Half a million thank you's is what you really owe me, you pompous, coddled ass. Hammami indulged in a mental sneer as he thought about the payment required for Tomas Bahr to coordinate the abduction in New York.

In the Beirut of the early 1950's their positions and their destinies seemed the opposite of what they now were. Tomas was the rich kid, the Christian Arab kid who wore the best clothes, attended the best private schools, and lived in a grand hillside villa which overlooked the Mediterrenean.

Charlie was a poor Moslem kid whose family had fled Palestine with only the clothes on their back. He was educated on the streets and lived in a crowded tenement house with his nine brothers and sisters.

But Charlie was tough and he was smart. He regularly beat up Christian Arab kids for their money until one day a boy he was about to pummel made an intriguing proposal.

"Business! Let's do business."

"What do you mean?"

"This is the deal," explained the boy as he lay in a vulnerable prone position. "You leave me alone, and you work with me, and I'll get you into some real money."

Charlie sat down as the boy sat up.

"I have a small operation, an offshoot of my Uncle's business. My Uncle imports opium poppies from Turkey and it's real easy to sneak some away. Everyone I sell to loves eating and smoking the stuff. But sometimes I have a problem collecting money owed me, if you know what I mean. Listen, if you help recover from those kids who are running up a bill on me, I'll cut you into the action."

Charlie and the boy, Tomas, shook on it that same day. Charlie immediately recognized that this was his way out of squalor. This was to be the means of making a name for himself. This development could possibly provide him the tools by which he could one day exact revenge on the Jews and all those who helped Israel. Charlie swore to himself that he would work hard at becoming a success and that he would never forget how favorably God looked upon him.

"Allahu Akbar."

Over the years he learned everything he could about the drug business. Opium naturally led to heroin, and from there it was an easy progression to cocaine. Charlie made himself fabulously rich.

By contrast, Tomas squandered his opportunities and frittered away all the blessings he was born with. He lurched from one venture to another, and all along the way Charlie lent him money to get back on his feet again.

So when Charlie recently requested the favor of Tomas, and in return was confronted with an appeal for compensation, he was filled with contempt for his old business partner. He nevertheless decided to pay him. His request was that important.

"You did well, Alec. The cargo is safe. The same cannot be said for those you recruited in New York."

"Those idiots should have been more careful," shrugged Tomas without even stopping to consider their plight. He was more concerned with his own safety. Scotland Yard would be searching everywhere for him. He hoped his disguise, his new identification, and his worldly upbringing would be sufficient for him to pass for awhile as *Alec Livingston,* a high society gentleman.

"Alec, before we go back to my house, permit me to show you the Islamic treasures at the Victoria and Albert Museum. They're quite spectacular."

Charlie always showed his guests the Islamic collection at the nearby V & A. The jewelry, musical instruments, and crafts reflected a time of Islamic greatness. They were reminders of a golden era long before there was a Buckingham Palace and long before there was even a concept called America.

As they walked by his Victorian Knightsbridge mansion, Charlie cast an indifferent eye on his magnificent home in the middle of London. Indifferent, for he had grown to loathe not only England and the west, but the hollow emphasis they placed, and he himself regrettably had placed, on being wealthy. He found consolation in knowing that the riches he'd strived for his whole life at least granted him the power to shake the world. It gave him the ability to help Islam once again regain its preeminence. But first Islam would have to return to the fundamentalist doctrines that had once made it great.

And he had been doing his part in that endeavor when he sponsored Sheik Abdul Ali Latif to speak words of encouragement to members of the Algerian Islamic Salvation Front. But then an Israeli, *a Jew*, assasinated Latif in Algiers, *in his house*, and temporarily derailed his work, his dream, his good name. The humiliation tore at his heart until an old employee named Ibrahim Husseini notified him of a surprise finding. Suddenly he was jubilantly on the path once again.

Allahu Akbar.

"I know why you're doing this," interrupted Tomas, as if reading Charlie's mind, "but what if the Israeli doesn't come?"

"Alec, I know this is difficult for you to conceptualize, but such a notion as true friendship does exist. Your whole life, your every involvement with anybody, including myself, has always been based on selfishness. 'What can I get out of this deal?' Friendship is not a transaction where you weigh the costs versus the benefits! Friendship is benefits, benefits! It's what's called win, win! Costs and sacrifice don't enter into this at all!"

Tomas stood there looking nonplused. *Dimwit!* He never had understood the subtleties.

And never, not even when Charlie stood ready to strike him when they were boys, had Tomas ever cowered quite as much as he now did before his associate.

"I've read the football player's book," said Charlie as he struggled to regain his composure. "And from the glowing accounts I read about their common past, there is no doubt the footballer's friend will return. He must come back!"

Forty eight, forty nine, fifty.

Zach closed his eyes and lay motionless on the floor. Another set of push-ups, following a round of sit-ups, following a series of knee-bends.

Sometimes it helped to fixate on a crack on the ceiling. If he was lucky he could enter the universe of the crack and transport himself, away—to a football stadium, a loud throbbing stadium, packed with people who stood on their feet watching the Jets find a way to move down the field for a winning touchdown.

Zach would tap his shackled feet as he drifted into a back pedal, writhe his tender back as he twisted away from a sack, and blink his swollen eyes as he spotted a receiver down field. And then, after unleashing his mighty arm for a touchdown, he always spun out of the crack and crashed with a shock back into his cell.

Try as he might, and he did try hard, there simply were not enough diversions in an interminable day, nor enough dreams for a grueling night, to escape the questions, worries, and loneliness of his mind.

Why? Why is this happening to me? What must my family be going through? What, if anything, is being done? Does anyone even know where I am? What will become of me?

And then, invariably, tears would start as his longing for Meg rose up. He would see her beautiful face, hear her comforting voice, and feel her warm caress as she curled up beside him.

Oh Meg. Poor Meg.

Zach sat up and walked over on his knees to what remained of his dinner. His *shai bi-nana* was no longer warm, but the mint in the tea still filled some of the emptiness with its soothing aroma and sugary sweetness. Zach stared at his empty metal bowl and regretted scooping out all of his *fuul* beans with durra pita bread. He should have saved some.

All at once, even without looking up, Zach again sensed he was being watched by the peculiar smiling man with the gap between his front teeth. The man the guards called the Mahdi. Zach slowly lifted his eyes and saw the familiar large eyes and palm straw skull-cap.

"You asked me once why you were here. Do you remember?"

Remember? How can I forget, you ass-hole? You had your lackey flog half the skin off my back because of it.

"I've considered your question and have decided you are entitled to an answer."

Zach wrapped his arms around his knees and squeezed them up close.

"There is an old Arab proverb which says if a camel puts his nose into a tent, the body soon follows." Ahmed Mohammed ibn Sayid, the Mahdi, stared at him intently. Zach stared back.

"I grew up along the banks of the Nile, *Khawaja* Pike, on the island of Abba," he went on. "All my neighbors were fishermen. There we had another saying. 'If the hook is well baited, the fish will bite.' If we have the proper bait, if we can get the smelly hard-to-manage camel to poke his nose into the tent, we will soon have the entire camel." Zach raised his eyebrows and slowly moved his downturned head from side to side.

"Still confused *Khawaja* Pike? If it's any consolation the great Mahdi of the last century once wrote, 'Mahdiism is like time. No one understands its true nature but Allah the Almighty.'" And then with a laugh he was gone.

A madman! A raving loony tune!

Later that night Ishmael—or so Zach called him—a tall, painfully thin Arab guard of the nomadic Baggara tribes that have always been loyal to the Mahdiyya, brought Zach a glass of warm *laban* sweet milk. The *laban* sent Zach into an undulating, queasy sleep.

Later that night, Zach dreamt wildly.

It was hot and the sun was scorching the grass from green to brown. He was running and laughing, laughing and running. His bare feet skimmed across the grass.

It was summer! No school, vacation-time, and all around there was the wonderful expanse of nature. He was free. Free!

Somebody else was running alongside. Another boy. Smaller, even faster. He too was laughing.

"Quick, let's go up that tree," the boy said. "She won't find us there."

Up they went, higher and further. Almost to the very top. As soon as he would hoist the boy up to a branch, the boy would in turn pull him up to another level.

They sat precariously on the same limb. It was a long, dizzying way down.

The view was breathtaking. In the distance the blue ocean rolled its silver froth against the dunes of the Cape while sea gulls hovered above.

They spotted two men far below walking in their direction. They looked so funny in their colorful cruise wear shirts and baggy shorts. But they were so serious, absorbed in conversation.

"Shhh! They won't even know we're here," the boy chuckled.

"The performance reviews and evaluations are in." The familiar sounding voice drifted up to them. The words were crystal clear. "After seeing what Israel did with remote piloted vehicles, and after determining what the U.S. Navy could not do without them, I'm hearing the military will now finally find ways of employing RPV's."

"That's great. That's what you've always wanted."

"What it means though is that our relationship is changing. They're going to send me to Israel soon to work directly with contractors there. It'll be a short visit, but undoubtedly it'll be the first of many."

"If there's more joint project work, then there will be fewer secrets."

"That's not exactly the way it works. I'll be sent to find out how Israel used the RPV's and the U.S. in turn will put up more money to co-produce them. But the U.S. won't share all its intelligence. To a certain extent, Israel won't be getting all of the RPV classified information it needs. That's why I can continue to make a difference. Except now, it'll be from over there."

"You've been supplying confidential data and ideas through me for the past three years. Are you saying our set-up won't continue?"

"I don't know. If I have the opportunity to do it from Israel, with their experts and over actual RPV's, I think it'll be more effective."

"You don't have to do this anymore. You've woken up the U.S. military to the potential of RPV's and you've advanced, and can continue to advance, RPV research. You can just stop!"

"Thanks, but I can't just stop! There's more I have to do! You helped me get started as an agent and for that I'll always be grateful. I couldn't have done it without you."

The other boy began to dangerously teeter. The boy's face was white and the boy's eyeballs began swimming in their sockets.

A hand, his hand, reached up and grabbed the boy. Steadied him.

"It's okay," Zach told the boy as the two men walked away. "It's really kind of cool." But he didn't really believe it was.

"ZACK! ZVI! Stop fooling around. Let's get over to the beach already."

The girl was wearing a racy violet swim suit. She was blossoming into womanhood. And she was standing right below them.

"Where are you? Where are you?" she screamed.

"We're up here. Here we are Meggie," he answered as he guided the other boy, his shaken friend, down as if he were an invalid.

Zach awoke, drenched in sweat, to the cry of the muezzin calling the faithful for their morning prayers.

A rattling anxiety, the overwhelming sensation of dread, would be with him again today.

Oh Dad! Poor Dad! Why'd you do it?

Zach rolled over onto his back and feverishly searched out the crack in the ceiling.

CHAPTER ELEVEN

"Come on in, Terry. Nice to see you again. What's it been, five months?"

Terry Webster entered the small office of Paul Reilly, the Field Security Officer at Lexington Labs. "Almost six," she said. "So it's just about time for my regular visit anyhow." She immediately noticed that Reilly had already placed the records and security files she'd requested on a tidied up area of his desk. "I saw the yellow ribbons and the 'Our Thoughts Are With You' banner on my way in." An insecure smile flitted across her plain face.

"The entire company's been on edge ever since Ben's boy was ambushed. We like to think Lexington Labs is like one big family, but that this happened to Ben Pike makes the whole thing even worse."

"What do you mean?" asked Terry. Her briefcase was still in her hand and she began to blush, unsure whether to put it down or sit down herself. In just two years she had mastered the requirements of her work as a representative of the Defense Industrial Security Program, but she still struggled with the hobnobbing aspects of her position.

"Well, everybody here loves Ben—all the Pikes for that matter. Ben has not only worked here for over thirty years, he's pioneered numerous systems for us."

After an awkward moment of silence, Terry finally motioned towards a chair. "May I?"

"I'm sorry, darling," Reilly said as he slapped his forehead with the base of his hand.

Terry would have preferred a more business-like relationship with the Field Security Officer. After all, she was not here to play games or shoot the breeze. She was here to hunt.

The Industrial Security division of the Defense Investigative Service made sure U.S. industry protected all classified information in its control while carrying out government contracts or while conducting research and development. Just yesterday Terry's Boston office had received a call from DIS Headquarters in Alexandria, Virginia recommending she pay a visit to Lexington Labs. Not that they suspected anything. They merely thought it now "prudent" to update their records. Terry, on the other hand, took their call as a signal to investigate.

"Let me go straight to the point," Terry began. "Apparently, DIS has not done a background investigation of Ben Pike in over fifteen years. This despite the fact that Mr. Pike has top secret clearance and should have some kind of periodic reinvestigation check every five years." She paused, eyebrows raised. "To make matters worse, he has never been involved in a subject interview process."

Reilly exhaled loudly. He didn't care for Terry Webster's all business approach and he resented the insinuation that Lexington Labs should have somehow alerted DIS to its own lapses. He understood DIS was a casualty of governmental downsizing and had too few investigators, but he was not their keeper. His job was to assist them when they came calling, or to notify them if he suspected irregularities on the part of any of the contractor's employees.

"Until recently, Miss Webster, most of the work Ben Pike has been involved with was classified as secret. Only for the last five years has he worked on the Vulture, elements of which are considered top secret. I have Pike's security files right here for your inspection. I think you'll find that they're unremarkable. Take your time reviewing them. I have some matters to attend to, but I'll pop back here every so often to see if you have any questions."

"Thank you, Mr. Reiily."

Terry took out a pen and paper to meticuously jot down any red flag information she might come across. She began to sift through Lexington Labs' in-house security files from the early 1980's, at the point where the DIS last ran a background investigation. There were no incident reports of any data or blueprints being misplaced from restricted areas.

Credit checks were also not alarming. In fact, Ben Pike's financial fitness was excellent. He owned property outright in Brookline and the Cape, and there were sizable accounts at a bank and with three different investment firms.

Pike's travel itineraries also proved to be routine. He occasionally attended conferences and symposiums pertaining to remote piloted vehicles, but virtually all of this travel was domestic.

But then, starting in the mid 1980's, Pike began making frequent business trips to Israel. Two in 1985. Three in 86. Three in 87. Four in 1988. And on it went, at about the same rate, up until now.

" Mr. Reilly," Terry called as she saw the Field Security Officer pass by the open office door. "There's something I want to talk to you about."

Shoot. Reilly plopped into a chair while downing some antacid medication. Miss Webster was making him sick.

"What was the nature of Mr. Pike's trips to Israel?"

"Our company is involved in cooperative RPV projects with Israel. The technology transfer began a few years ago, if I'm not mistaken."

"Were all of his trips business related?"

"It seems to me there was one trip he and members of the family made several years ago which wasn't. The daughter of friends of theirs was killed in a car crash. Other than that, I don't know of any personal trips."

"Who were these friends in Israel?" asked Terry as she flipped through the files.

"I'm not certain. I believe Ben said they were friends, neighbors, who had lived for a while in the States." Reilly scratched his head while trying to remember.

"There's nothing in here mentioning Israeli friends." Terry shook the documents before her.

"Ben already had clearance. He wasn't required to inform us of any new neighbors or friends."

"That may be so but you never made any note of these friends once he told you they existed. Now, let me ask you, did you coordinate Mr. Pike's overseas work?"

"Absolutely." Reilly felt he was being cross-examined. "The U.S. has bilateral security arrangements with Memorandum of Understanding countries, of which Israel is one. Israel is required to provide proper security for classified information. This reciprocal clearance agreement we have with them is operational because their security laws and procedures are for the most part the equal of ours. But visit requests still have to be arranged with the Department of Defense Security Assistance Office in Israel, and I helped with that. The visit requests had to contain information on what subjects were to be discussed, locations to be visited, and dates of visit."

Reilly watched Terry's twitching eyes fly over the material before her. Sometimes they focused and devoured a scrap of information before they continued their prowl. She seemed like a hovering bird of prey. Suddenly her pupils dilated and she blinked rapidly.

"This is strange," she said. "On several occasions in the 80's, and virtually all of his trips in the 90's, he remained in Israel longer than the dates of his visit requests. Just two months ago he overextended his stay by one week." Her gaze fixed on Reilly, questioning and menacing at the same time.

"I remember once or twice his saying he fell ill and couldn't return. A year ago," Reilly shrugged, "he said he was staying to do some touring. Maybe some of those times he was visiting friends."

"Don't you think it a little odd that Mr. Pike still had some touring to do considering he had already been to Israel thirty or forty times before?" The question was posed more to herself than to Paul Reilly.

Terry ran through possible maneuvers. After informing Headquarters in Alexandria of her findings, they would tap into FORDTIS, their Foreign Disclosure and Technology Information System, to verify foreign facility security arrangements and international security agreements. Perhaps, given that DIS did not have overseas investigative assets, the State Department would be contacted. Perhaps even the FBI would be notified?

The ramifications were tantalizing, titillating. Terry never even heard Reilly respond as he shook his head and said doubtfully, "I suppose Ben's travel extensions are a bit peculiar at that."

Meg thought it the most beautiful place she had ever seen.

Standing on the terrace surrounding the Roman Catholic Church, it all seemed like an impressionist painting. But this was her composition, not Monet's or Manet's.

Everything looked different! The upheaval of the last few days, and now this—standing at the very spot Jesus taught from, reacquainting herself with Zvi; it all pulled at her emotions. The light of the sun diffracted at bewildering angles as blue, purple, torquoise, and green intermingled with each other. There were no borders, no clear distinctions.

The Mount of Beatitudes! The Sermon of the Mount! And tomorrow, Christmas Eve!

Her eyes took it all in: the azure sky, the Golan Heights, the tranquil Sea of Galilee, the Eden-like garden.

Zvi stood in the garden below. He leaned against a date palm tree, lost in meditation. *Blessed are the poor in spirit, for theirs is the kingdom of heaven.*

In her mind's eye Meg also saw herself, leaning over the wall of the terrace, so alone. And then suddenly the video image of Zach, tormented, vulnerable, appeared before her. *Blessed are the persecuted righteous, for theirs is the kingdom of heaven.*

She walked down to the garden and stood behind Zvi. She tried to figure out just what it was Zvi was looking at by turning and cocking her head in the same direction as his. It seemed that he was looking at nothing in particular but she knew he was seeing everything.

"It's a small country, Meggie." Zvi did not turn in her direction. "But I think it is the most special place in the entire world."

"Zvi, it's......magnificent! Inspiring!"

Nobody else called her Meggie anymore but she thought she liked it almost as much as when Zach called her *QB*.

"You're the *QB*, Zach," she had insisted soon after Zach began to call her by the nickname. "What do you mean *QB*?"

Zach burst into laughter.

"What's so funny?" she demanded.

"You are, *QB*." Zach hooked an arm around her neck. "You're so funny, *QB*. *Quality Babe!*"

From then on Meg loved the name and frequently called Zach the same thing. The acronym came to be a private, intimate password between them. Its very utterance became a way of breaking down any barriers that sometimes arose between them.

Looking now at Zvi, Meg wished she could also somehow find a way to penetrate his defenses and reach him.

"And you?" she finally asked. "What inspires you, Zvi? What do you do, where do you go when you have a problem?"

For a moment Meg thought he didn't hear her. Zvi stood motionless as a statue. Then he turned towards her with an outstretched hand and their eyes locked.

"Come. Let me show you."

Zvi's Renault spun through a series of hairpin turns and proceeded south, along the Sea by which they'd eaten St. Peter's Fish for lunch.

They spoke in punctuated intervals, about small matters, allowing the scenery to dictate the content of their conversation.

They stopped in front of the Hammat Tiberias Hot Springs and walked among tiny boiling ejections of mineral water that bubbled through deep cracks created by the fault line of the Great Syrian-African Rift. Further up the hillside they came upon a fourth-century synagogue with a remarkably preserved mosaic floor. It depicted all of the classical Jewish motifs: lions flanking an Ark, a *shofar* ram's horn, and a *menorah, the* seven-branched candelabra. But it also contained human figures characterizing the four seasons, figures wrestling in an instictive dance with the ever changing seasons.

Higher up the hill Zvi led Meg towards a domed greenish tomb. It seemed rather simple and quiet but Meg tingled with anticipation. They went in and were plunged into twilight.

"This is the tomb of Rabbi Meir Baal Ha-nes." The vault caused Zvi's words to reverberate and echo. "His name means the *Miracle Worker*. A very interesting man. He took a vow that he would not rest, he would never stop fulfilling charitable *mitzvot* commandments, until the Messiah came. Until the world became a good place, a safe place. He was therefore buried in an upright position. Over the years many miracles have been ascribed to prayer at this tomb."

"Have your prayers been answered?" Meg asked in trepidation.

"Actually, sometimes they have been. But until now I have never asked for a miracle."

Zvi abruptly turned towards her and stood powerfully close. He grabbed her arms and stared deep within her.

"I know what he's going through!" Zvi almost shouted. "I know what he's going through!" He shook Meg violently.

"Stop it, Zvi! Stop it! You're scaring me."

Zvi eased his pressure on her arms but did not let go. When he resumed talking, his voice was more controlled.

"There is a commandment called *Pidyon Shevuyim,* redemption of captives. According to our scholars there is no *mitzvah* which takes precedence over this one. A captive lives in constant danger; hungry, exposed, existing in sheer terror. Our scholars also say that when somebody saves even one life, he is actually saving the whole world. For the captive, his world is his life. And his life means everything in the world to countless other people who love him."

Zvi then released his grip and turned away. "Meggie, I'm going to go after Zach. I have to."

Meg walked in front of him and directed his look at her. It was all right there! In that instant, though she understood practically nothing, she grasped everything. She reached for him.

"I'm also going to help Zach. And I'm going to help you too," she whispered. They clung to each other, bodies pressed together, their hearts beating in unison.

That night in Ein Gev, Zvi and Meg came together in consummation of their pact.

CHAPTER TWELVE

"I'll get it!" Ben Pike yelled in the direction of the family room.

Teddy and Liz were still eating breakfast to the accompaniment of CNN reports. Sam and his wife had taken most of the grandchildren to the mall for last-minute Christmas shopping. Mary, her sister Ruth, and daughter-in-law, Jill, were in the kitchen preparing a Christmas feast.

When Ben opened the door he immediately knew that the two well-dressed young men who stood a polite distance away had come specifically to talk with him. And he knew why.

One was black, the other white. Otherwise, they were exactly alike. Both were squeaky clean, sharp, and serious. They smiled on cue in a good-natured, contrived sort of way. Ben returned a guarded smile.

"Good morning Mr. Pike. I'm special agent Mark Hriniak of the FBI."

"And I'm special agent Lionel Lane. We hope we aren't disturbing you this morning but there is something we would like to discuss with you."

"Please come in." Ben led the two men into his study and made sure to close the door behind them. He had long dreaded this moment. But now, in light of his distress for Zach, it seemed trivial and, in that way, unusually painful.

"As you know, we've been monitoring all incoming phone conversations via a direct tap ever since Zach was kidnapped. It could be that the people holding your son haven't contacted you because they seek nothing from you or your family." The man who identified himself as Lionel Lane adjusted his wire frame glasses.

"The extremists," continued Hriniak, "are politically motivated. Probably what they want to do is draw as much attention to themselves and their cause as possible. *Probably.*"

Ben was unclear whether Hriniak's last word was a question; suggestive and probing.

Despite having to catch an early six o'clock flight from Washington D.C., both men sat upright on the edge of their chairs. They had been all charged up ever since Lee Nunzio had personally instructed them last night to go to the Boston auxiliary office. Apparently a 'predicate' now existed to at least begin a counterintelligence investigation of Ben Pike. Some of his defense related exchanges with Israel appeared suspicious. Nunzio's only admonition was that they be delicate—not only because they as yet didn't really know the score—but also because of the vulnerable situation Pike's son was in.

Both Hriniak and Lane were the cream of the upcoming generation of FBI agents. They'd finished near the top of their respective classes at the Academy in Quantico. Both were the sons of police officers and had such impeccable records that they had the kind of clearance necessary for work as special counterespionage agents in Division Five. Most importantly, despite their disparate upbringings, Hriniak's in white Salt Lake City and Lane's in black Gary, Indiana, the two men possessed unusual synergism when working as a team.

"Mr. Pike," Lane said, adjusting his glasses again, "we have a tape of a phone call that was placed at the start of the week from the Galilee in Israel to your residence. A man identifying himself as Zvi spoke to Zach's girlfriend, Meg."

Hriniak took over now. "Zvi said on the tape that he would be coming to Boston the next day, and apparently he did did fly in. But then he left with Meg for Israel three days ago."

"Zvi, Meg, and my Zach all grew up together here in Brookline," Ben casually explained. "They're close friends. When Zvi heard about what happened to Zach he flew right over. I was surprised as anyone when Zvi and Meg went off to Israel together, but Meg did call when they arrived to let us know they were well. I don't know why they left so quickly. Youth is impetuous, I suppose."

"Zvi arrived with his parents," said Hriniak as he checked his notes. "Let's see, an Oded and Aviva Langer."

"Who are the Langers, Mr. Pike?" Lane asked.

"Close friends of the family. They lived in Brookline in the 80's while Oded was a student at Harvard. They returned to Israel just yesterday."

"Oded Langer is a politician of some sort over in Israel, isn't he?"

"Yes. He's now a member of the Knesset."

The questions began to be lobbed faster, in crisp cadence, in perfect measure.

How did you come to know the Langers?

Have you stayed in close contact with them over the years?

Do you have any other Israeli friends?

After a while Ben found it difficult to differentiate whether it was Lane or Hriniak that was asking a question. He found himself vaguely looking in their general direction while focusing on neither man.

All at once Hriniak and Lane exchanged a sideways glance and the questions stopped. It was as if the FBI men reached an invisible demarcation line beyond which they dared not go. At least not yet.

"I suppose," Ben leaned back and crossed his hands on the top of his head, "what you're getting at is whether this whole tragedy happened because of my family's friendship with Israelis?"

Hriniak and Lane turned to each other with half cocked heads, then resumed their watchful study of Ben.

"In one way or another, Mr. Pike, maybe that really is what this is about. Isn't it?"

Ben was not sure how to interpret that question. Were these guys simply agreeing with him over what needed to yet be determined? Or were they implying something about his secret dealings with Israel? How much, exactly, did they know?

It was enough sparring for today. He'd reached his own line beyond which he was not prepared to go.

"Well," said Ben, rising to his feet and shaking himself out, "I want to wish you both a Merry Christmas."

"Merry Christmas to you and your family, Mr. Pike," Lane said.

"We sincerely hope," Hriniak added, "the New Year finds your family reunited and well."

Hriniak and Lane did not look around as they walked out the front door and down a flagstone pathway to their car. Somewhere, Ben suspected, "G's" were in place for a picket surveillance of his house. Somewhere, perhaps even very close by, a news van was equipped with state-of-the-art eavesdropping equipment, and would from now on be listening.

Over the last few years, Meles Tekele had taught himself how to transcend the here and the now. While other political prisoners succumbed to the hardships of prison or the ghost houses, he had mastered a method of spiritual escape. It worked, some of the time. Often enough for him to still be "alive" at any rate.

He stared at the telephone before him and closed his eyes. It appeared as if he was rehearsing what he was about to say. Actually, Meles Tekele was constructing an elaborate imagery of byways over which he could move, at his discretion, between the lush Simien mountains of Ethiopia where he was born to the enchanting city of Brussels, the place he was about to call. *The place he was being forced to call.*

Tekele had fled as a refugee to Sudan in 1977. Life had become unbearable in Ethiopia. The fighting against Somalia and Eritrean rebels was never going to stop. Millions were starving and all the new military dictatorship could do was throw out Americans even as it threw thousands of dissidents into prisons in Addis Ababa.

The decision to leave Ethiopia was a wise one, at least for a few years. An official of the U.N. High Commission for Refugees in Sudan befriended Tekele at a refugee camp. Impressed by Tekele's college level education and his knowledge of English, Italian, French, and Arabic, the official recommended him to a cabinet member of Prime Minister Jaafer Numeiri's government.

In the early 1980's Tekele's Ethiopian background and firsthand knowledge of the refugee camps proved to be especially advantageous. The cabinet member, the head of the Sudanese Security Services, and Numeiri himself agreed to a covert operation with Israel. Ethiopian Jews, called Falashas, who had made a perilous migration from Ethiopia to Sudanese refugee camps, would secretly be taken to Israel. In return for their complicity, Numeiri and his aides would receive two hundered million dollars from a Reagan administration that at the time had close military and intelligence ties to Israel. Israel too deposited sixty million dollars into the personal Swiss and London bank accounts of Numeiri and his cohorts.

At first Israel managed to secretly move only small numbers of Ethiopian Jews. But with pressure by the U.S. State Department, Sudan agreed to rid herself of the Jews who were pouring across her borders. But how?

Tekele flew to Brussels as Numeiri's envoy in 1984 and there he met with a Belgian Jew, George Mittelman, and the local Mossad station chief. Mittelman owned an airline, TransEurope Air, which regularly flew Moslems from Sudan to Mecca on an annual Hajj pilgrimage.

Would Mittelman allow his planes and his pilots to fly Ethiopian Jews to Israel, by way of Brussels?

Mittelman told the Mossad chief and Tekele he would have no qualms about cooperating, as long as the Belgian government sanctioned the arrangement. As fortune would have it the Justice minister and head of the Belgian secret service, Jean Gol, was Jewish. He spoke to Wilfred Martens, the Belgian Prime Minister, and in November of 1984 TEA planes were departing from secured areas of Khartoum International for Brussels.

Operation Moses succeeded in bringing several thousand Ethiopian Jews to Israel. But early in 1985 an Israeli paper leaked details of the operation and Numeiri, under extreme pressure by other Arab League countries, immediately curtailed the flights. A thousand Ethiopian Jews remained stranded in Sudan. Vice President George Bush personally flew to Sudan to discuss the crisis with Numeiri. In March of 1985 six U.S. Hercules planes landed on an abandoned airfield near the refugee camp of Gedaref and flew the remaining Jews to Israel. Soon after, a military coup took hold. Numeiri and other "Zionist collaborators" found safe haven in Egypt.

Meles Tekele unfortunately did not.

Tekele now opened his eyes and stared once again at the telephone before him. The telephone number of the Israeli Embassy in Brussels had not changed.

"My name is Meles Tekele. I am calling from Khartoum. Does 'Red Hawk' still work there?"

The voice, suspicious and bored at the same time, told him no.

"Then let me speak with the new 'Hawk'. Tell him I am an old friend who has something very important to say."

Tekele closed his eyes while he waited for a Mossad agent. *There!* Once again he was in the Grand Place in Brussels, strolling about the Gothic square, sitting in the sun enjoying a Belgian waffle.

Had life ever really been so sweet?

A new voice came on. Tekele gripped the phone tight.

"I am calling from Khartoum. Tell Tel Aviv that Zach Pike is being held in Khartoum's Kober prison."

The voice asked how he knew.

"Associates of mine saw him go in. He has not come out."

Again the suspicious voice in his ear.

"What do I want? Why am I telling you this?" A sad, toothless smile creased Tekele's haggard face.

"It's something I have to do. Okay?" He paused to listen.

"How can I be reached? I can't…"

"No, I don't think I'll be calling again." As Tekele was about to put down the phone he thought of one other thing to say.

"Please tell 'Red Hawk' that I called. I think sometimes of our meetings together in Brussels, in the sun. It would be nice to know that he remembers me too."

Meles Tekele put the receiver down. Suddenly he was again a small boy singing with his brothers and sisters outside of their *tukul* straw hut in the Simien Mountains. His mother, draped in a cloak *shamma*, was nearby cooking sour *injera* bread on a clay board. She looked up at her children with a big smile as a cool breeze swayed a cluster of eucalyptus trees above. On a hill beyond the trees a family of curved horn walia ibex pranced in the warm sun.

Yes, life was sweet. Thank God it will forever remain so.

The long gleaming sword whirled above his head. Its sharp-edged blade sliced through the air in a blur.

Faster, in ever tighter gyrations, like a scythe sweeping across, the sword was going to mow down anything in its path.

Closer. It was closer now. In its final death spin.

The slice was so precise, so level, and so quick that Tekele's head continued to sit squarely on the base of his neck. Gradually a thin red stripe circled his neck and soon blood was running out of the slit like a waterfall.

Tekele's head lifted ever so slightly and then fell with a crack on the hard floor. His eyes remained closed, his face serene.

The executioner turned to a frail gray-bearded man wearing sunglasses. Sword still in hand, he knelt and bowed his head towards the white-gowned, white-turbaned man.

"How merciful are you, my master, my light, Sheik Amir Kasawi."

"Outrageous!"

President Earl stormed about the Blue Room alternatingly grinding a fist into the palm of his other hand and emphatically pointing his finger in no particular direction. He wore a dark tuxedo and his face was flushed.

"Don't they have any common sense! Don't they have any self-control!"

"That's the nature of tabloid television." Mark Handsman shrugged. "Anything is fair game, just so long as it's sensational."

Lou Reed had over the years and on many occassions seen Ollie Earl get his dander up. Not in school, not in the army, not in the Senate, had he ever suffered fools well. Nor could he tolerate the lax ethical standards of others. He had a steely integrity, unyielding.

"Ollie," Reed said, "relax. More than anything the piece just related background stuff on Zach Pike and his family. Yeah, it dug too much. So what? Invasion of privacy is what the media is all about. You've been in politics long enough to know that."

Earl needed some air. He rushed out of the room and went up to the second floor balcony of the south portico, the Truman Balcony. A majestic Christmas tree in the south lawn brightened the night. In the distance, beyond a snow-covered Ellipse, the Washington Monument and the Jefferson Memorial were bathed in light.

Christmas Eve! Peace on earth!

But in the far corners of the world, in the hidden recesses of many hearts, misery would not be on holiday.

The National Security Advisor followed the President out to the balcony. The air was cold but at least there was no wind. "The guests will worry about you," Reed said. "Don't you think you should go back to the festivities?"

"How could you be so naive Lou?" The President turned to his friend but did not raise his voice. "That T.V. expose didn't just encroach on the personal lives of a poor, grieving family. It preyed on them. Even worse, it raised questions and made all sorts of insinuations." He ran his hand through his hair and stared into the night sky.

"Who knows why Zach Pike was abducted? But all that Israeli stuff—pointing out that his father does some work there, that his girlfriend just went there—will only make it worse for him and harder for us. That T.V. show has just put Zach Pike in even greater danger."

Earl returned to the gathering in the East Room. He sat down beside the First Lady and took her hand while the Marine Corps Band continued their Christmas recital.

In former years, the East Room had been the setting of intense joy and bitter sorrow. Here Lynda Johnson was wed, Abraham Lincoln quartered wounded union troops, and John F. Kennedy lay in state.

And now, on the eve of what should have been a merry Christmas, as the Band played '*What Child Is This*', Mollie Earl looked over to her husband and saw something she had not seen in years.

Prayer; tearful and nourishing.

Why lies he in such
mean estate, Where ox and ass are
feeding? Good Christian fear, for
sinners here, The silent word is pleading?

Nails, spear, shall pierce him through
The cross be borne for me, for you,
Hail, hail the Word made flesh,
The Babe, the Son of Mary.

CHAPTER THIRTEEN

Creation.
Exodus.
Jerusalem.

Suspended in the reception hall of the Knesset, Israel's Paliament, Marc Chagall's three swirling tapestries were of absolutely no help at all. Instead of diverting Zvi from his myriad problems, the masterpieces seemed to heighten his anxieties. Every tapestry, every mosaic, was crammed with fanciful and bizarre images, just as his mind was crammed with chaotic thoughts.

Perched on a small hill, the Knesset afforded a commanding view of the new, modern city of Jerusalem. Zvi leaned against a large glass window and searched for his bearings through a gray mist.

To the right, beyond the Israel Museum with its white lidded dome for the Dead Sea Scrolls, would be Hebrew University's Givat Ram campus. Ordinarily he would have been there, *right now*, immersed in an archaeology book, had not his world been violently thrown off course a few scant days ago.

Off to the far left, at the end of Ruppin Boulevard, loomed the peaks of the residential Wolfson Towers and below them would be the green, familiar field of Sacher Park. Oh, how he longed to be there, *right now,* playing in a soccer game or running a post pattern in a pick up football game with American exchange students.

Somewhere in between the ball field and the Dead Sea Scrolls, nestled in a valley of olive trees, was the sketchy outline of the 7th century Monastery of the Cross. Up the hill from the Monastery lay the tranquil suburb of Rehavia and beyond that, out of sight, was the old city of Jerusalem. The holy city of Jerusalem.

Zvi had left Meggie there early that morning to do some reluctant sightseeing. By now she should have finished visiting along the Via Dolorosa and she would be winding her way among the renovated squares and alleys of the Jewish Quarter. He wanted so much to be there, with her, *right now*, as she made her way towards the Wailing Wall. There, in the shadow and shelter of the Wall, they could insert in a crevice of its massive stone blocks a handwritten note to God asking for….

"Excuse me, Mr. Langer. They will see you now." The Knesset aide, a rosy-cheeked young woman, looked at him with concern.

"Oh, I'm sorry," said Zvi. He rubbed his eyes. "Please show me the way."

They entered an elevator and descended into the lowermost floor of the Knesset. When they got out a secret service man spoke into a hand-held two-way radio. After rounding a corner, Zvi was shown into a cramped meeting room by yet another secret service man.

They were all there, but it was Prime Minister Yehuda Ben-Ziyon who stood to greet him. "Benzi", as he liked to be called, was Israel's youngest ever head of state. A relatively young country, seemingly always in danger and on the edge of catastrophe, Israel historically had looked for the experienced leadership of those who had paid long dues. Having a grizzly weather-beaten look was considered a political asset.

Appearing youthful and energetic, Benzi did not have the physical attributes of his predecessors but he did possess the requisite curriculum vitae, including a distinguished military career and a prominent and vocal background in opposition politics. Greatly influenced by the American electoral system, Benzi had pressed his party into running an

American style campaign, complete with sound bite advertisements, spin-doctoring, and even baby kissing. It worked—but then again just about everything American worked in Israel.

"Zvi, please have a seat right here next to me."

Zvi scanned the faces of the men sitting around a table laden with soda and fresh fruit not so much to find a familiar face—they were all familiar—as much as to find a friendly one, a sympathetic one. The ten bipartisan senior ministers before him were those members of the larger twenty-five man cabinet who had the most clout in determining the direction of the country.

Besides the inner cabinet those in attendance included Chief of Staff Almog, Mossad chief Itzik Ami, the Prime Minister's Advisor on Counterterrorism, Yehoshua Burg, and a grim minister without portfolio who sat at the far end of the table and did not look up to meet his eyes: Oded Langer.

Zvi's heart sank.

"You'll be happy to know that we have a solid lead in finding your friend," began Itzik Ami as if sensing Zvi's distress. "We received a call from our Brussels office reporting Zach Pike to be in Kober Prison, in Khartoum. A former agent of ours who was once involved in Operation Moses claims there were sightings of Pike being led into the prison. We are investigating that information and we have already apprised the CIA."

"Zvi, we all want to hear what you have to say," said the Prime Minister as he poured himself a glass of water. "Nu? So?"

It had only been after much insistence on his part that the cabinet had finally agreed to invite him as a consultant of sorts—not because his father was a member of Knesset, or because he was a close friend of Zach's and might have some insight as to who would harm him. It was because they were obligated to meet him.

"Obviously the extremists holding Zach Pike want to harm America," said Zvi without any hesitation, "but there is no logical explanation why this particular individual would be involved. Yes, Zach Pike is a celebrity over there, and the abduction is getting a lot of media attention. But why him? **Why him?**"

Zvi banged on the table. He searched the faces of the assembled men, and realized they were avoiding his eyes. Chief of Staff Almog did smile encouragingly, but the usual twinkle in his eyes was missing. Zvi fought against the gloom growing within him.

"I've been mulling this thing over ever since it happened," he said slowly, "and I've concluded Zach Pike was specifically targeted because of his friendship with me. Surely that has to be the most reasonable explanation."

Moti Halevy, the Foreign Affairs Minister, leaned back in his chair. "Even if that is the case, the demands made by the Sudanese Ansar Army are of America and Egypt only. This fundamentalist group wants their terrorist friends to be released from *their* jails. The ransom demand is also being made of America."

"You know as well as I do that those demands will never be met. It's a smoke screen!" Zvi took a deep breath in an effort to control his rising agitation. "Look, Israel's policy has always been to pursue and eliminate terrorists, wherever they may be, by using all of the assets at its disposal. Can I remind you of the early 70's, after our athletes were murdered in Munich and after Kozo Okamoto's Japanese Red Army massacred tens of people at Lod airport? We all know Israeli hit squads are given a free hand in deterring those responsible for terrorist acts. It's our 'secret war.'"

The ministers sat with arms folded across their chests, their chairs swiveled away from him.

It was all slipping away. They weren't listening.

He began to speak again. "Look at the recent record. You ordered the elimination of the Islamic Jihad's Hani Abed in Gaza following a spate of suicide attacks within Israel. You called on commando and Sayeret Matkal units to kill Abu Jihad in Tunis and to kill Sheik Latif in Algeria when military assistance was necessary. And by and large, your policy to pursue and eliminate has worked. But now is a time where we must pursue and rescue. We just have to. Look, everyone here knows who I am and what I've done, so why don't we stop the bullshit right now! The fact of the matter is you, and I, are responsible for freeing Zach Pike!"

"You would do well to control that temper of yours," cautioned Prime Minister Benzi. "After all, we really are on your side Zvi. We want to help your friend. All we have to decide is what form of assistance is best in this situation."

Aryeh Kutiel, the Minister of Defense, leaned forward. "If you think about it Zvi, you'll realize that militarily the Americans are probably able to do as much for Zach Pike as we can."

"This is not our battle," Itzik Ami said vehemently.

"And if we fight it, and lose it, then who do you think will get blamed for getting an American killed. 'Why'd you interfere,' they'll say." Moti Halevy shook his head. "'We would have handled it'. I can hear the Americans now."

"Zvika, I know what you're feeling." Almog's voice was soothing. "Every instinct within you wants to run to Khartoum, right now, with guns firing and free Zach. In the process you could even exact revenge on the fundamentalists holding him. But listen to your head, not your heart. It's what all of us in positions of power must always do."

They were all alligned against him. What was the point in even meeting with them if they had already made their minds up? Zvi looked towards his father but Oded Langer continued to helplessly stare at the table before him. Never had he seen his usually vibrant father quite so spent.

"If this was an innocent Jew who was incarcerated in Sudan, even if he was not Israeli, would your position be the same? That's what it all comes down to, isn't it?" Zvi's bitterness surprised even him. Where was the rage coming from?

"Shut up!" yelled Yehoshua Burg. "Who do you think you are, preaching to us? Israel has always had a moral responsibility to assist Jews whenever they are in danger. All Jews are members of the nation of Israel. All Jews are party to the same covenant. That's why all Jews have the right to instantaneously become citizens upon moving here on *aliyah*. Historically we've paid in blood to learn that most countries don't protect their Jewish citizens—will turn against them whenever the wind changes direction. I know! I came here after the war as a boy of ten, alone. Yes, we would do more for Zach Pike if he were Jewish. But he isn't. We choose to do what's best for us. We've earned that choice by blood and tears!"

"Let's all calm down." Ben-Ziyon held up his arms between Zvi and Burg.

"Zvi," he said firmly, "if it is deemed at some later point to be beneficial to the state of Israel, then we will consider military alternatives. Until then, I promise you, we will actively try to learn as much as possible about these terrorists who have seized your friend. We will share that information with Washington and cooperate as much as possible. It's the best I can do, for now. I'm sorry. I have to do what's best for the people I represent."

Damn you! Fuck you! Zvi wanted to scream. *You send me, you send my friends, to go thousands of miles to kill, but to save an innocent life you helped put in danger, that you won't do?*

It suddenly dawned upon Zvi that he had more ammunition yet at his disposal. As he was about to let loose, he looked at his father, used and despondent, and held back. Instead he thumped the table once, with all his might, and stormed out of the room.

For a moment the inner cabinet ministers sat in silence. Then, squirming in his chair, Chief of Staff Almog cleared his throat. "That's what I've always liked about him. He fights." A wry smile beamed on his face.

It had all gone so wrong! He had said things he should not have said, things he did not mean. And now that he was abandoned by others and isolated by his own folly—now what would he do?

As he walked across the cavernous reception hall, Zvi heard the echo of footsteps behind him. By the time he turned around, his father had run up beside him.

"I'm sorry. I tried everything I could to persuade them before you even got to the meeting."

"*Everything?* Everything Dad?"

Zvi's inflection was pained and accusatory at the same time. Oded looked at his son with raised eyebrows. His mouth twisted with confusion. "How long have you known?"

"Zach and I have both known about it since we were fourteen years old."

"Zvi, I put it to them directly: 'How can you not send in units to free Ben's son after everything Ben has done for Israel? You're abandoning him.' But this you've got to understand. They aren't wrapped up emotionally in this thing like you and me. They don't know Ben, or Mary, or Zach. And even if they did, Almog was still right. They have to listen to their heads."

"There's just one thing I have to know." Zvi stared into his father's eyes. "How could you compromise Ben, jeopardize a friend?"

"Ben volunteered. He was insistent. Along the way I tried to protect him as much as possible. I told him to stop but he wouldn't. He became consumed with helping Israel! Years ago he already outgrew me. Zvi, he's not just out of my control, he's *out of control!*"

They walked away from the Knesset together and into the glorious, blessed Jerusalem air. The late December haze had lifted. As they were about to part, Oded reached out to his son and hugged him. It felt awkward at first, but gradually Zvi lost himself, and then found himself, in a close huddle of family, friends, Zach, and Meggie.

We can still pull this off, he urged. *I know they're all over you out there, Zach, but don't worry. I'll find you, I'll get you the ball. Here's the play....*

"Zvi," whispered his father. "I know you. I know how you think, more than you think I do. When I was in that cabinet meeting, pleading our case, Ben and Zach were not the only people on my mind."

CHAPTER FOURTEEN

"*A*llahu Akbar!"

Tomas Bahr put down his cup of Earl Grey tea as soon as he heard Charlie Hammami's latest crow of elation. It seemed his friend always had a reason to praise Allah. Just yesterday it was as a result of his accountant's favorable earnings report. This morning's exultation came about simply because the sun had broken through a column of clouds to shine warmly upon the Hammami family as they ate breakfast in the solarium. Did Charlie always have to find the positive in everything?

"Allahu Akbar!" mouthed Tomas sarcastically as yet a second triumphal cry rang out from the room next door. He got up reluctantly from a leather recliner to see what all the commotion was about this time. As a guest he probably had a duty to feign at least some interest in his friend's perpetual good fortune.

"Just look at this, Alec!" bubbled Charlie as he pointed to his television. "No, wait a minute, let me rewind it first."

Charlie's gleeful skips to selected segments made viewing the videotape a bit distracting. But when the tape ended even Tomas was startled by the glaring innuendos the video contained.

"Ibrahim Husseini, my former employee who first sent me *Pike's Peak*, well, he happened to see this in New York on the American telly. Thank God he recorded it."

"Seems your footballer has quite the interesting family."

"More than we ever knew. At first I was thrilled just to know about his friendship with the Israeli. But now, to find out his father works on weapons systems with the Israelis, that truly is miraculous. It is indeed a double blessing."

"So now what?"

"Now my old friend, we will embark on a journey of discovery. *What projects is his father working on? What is he sharing with the Israelis?*"

"How will you do that, Charlie?"

"For one thing I can get Husseini to undertake some exploratory work. But remember Alec, even more importantly, we already possibly have a well of information yet to tap."

"Which is?"

"Why, the footballer of course!"

Suddenly, they both doubled over with laughter, Charlie amused by the serendipitous nature of it all, and Tomas sadistically delighted at the prospect of the nauseating pain that Zach Pike would surely suffer.

"There's one other thing," said Charlie while clutching his friend, still gasping with laughter, "one other point you may have noticed on the video."

"And what praise be might that be?"

"The girlfriend! She reportedly ran off with a friend—to Israel! It doesn't get any better than this, Alec. That friend is our man, our Israeli! It means God has graced us by showing us the true path. It means we were right all along. It means the Israeli will come—will come to us! Allahu Akbar!"

015-23-1186

Howard Jones punched in his social security number as he entered the compound's main building in Langley, Virginia. He looked up at a closed circuit camera and gave a rakish wink. That done he presented his I.D. card to a security officer. Then, finally, he was in.

He moved quickly, running up three flights of stairs, and then dashing through a gauntlet of halls that twisted and turned so as to better choke off internal radio transmissions. Arriving at a non-descript office door, Jones entered a special combination that unlocked it.

The office was immense and buzzing with activity. Intelligence analysts argued in one corner while Directorate for Operations officers spoke in hushed undertones in another. Elsewhere, a small group of regional experts huddled around detailed maps of Africa even as another small cluster of psychologists drew up theories several feet away. Telephones rang incessantly and runners darted between the specialized departments delivering data. At the far wall, green tinted windows electro-magnetically shielded all internal communications from the outside world. In fact, so sealed off and absorbed were the workers that no one even noticed when Howard Jones, the senior Middle East division analyst, entered the room.

Jones glanced at a large digitized clock at the center of the room: 11:58 A.M. In two minutes the task force would be convening for a joint debriefing session.

"High noon, ladies and gentlemen!" announced DCI Hurley Baker from below the clock. He clapped several times and waited for silence. It was not unusual for Baker to be in attendance when the task force assembled. The Director of Central Intelligence was very much a hands-on chief. He also would be updating the President at 1:00.

"Bill," yelled Baker. "What's the news from intelligence?"

Bill Yeoman, Deputy Director for Intelligence, noticed that Jones was standing nearby and nodded deferentially.

"I've just come from a personal meeting with Ron Yarkon, the chief Mossad representative in Washington." Jones took the floor with his usual flair. "This follows up a communique we received early this morning from Tel Aviv. Yarkon assured me that an agent of the Mossad has spoken with several people who saw Zach Pike dragged into Kober Prison, in Khartoum. Yarkon said this agent is no paper recruit. He apparently was most helpful during the rescue of Ethiopian Jews from Sudan. He has, however, been dormant for the past few years."

"What's your immediate read on this?" Baker asked.

"As a rule I put great stock in what the Mossad shares with us. However, their network of agents in that part of the world is as good, or perhaps I should say as wanting, as ours. Still, it's credible that some-body as important as Zach Pike would be kept in Kober. A ghost house wouldn't afford the kind of protection, whether from outside forces or from inside rival factions, that the fundamentalists would surely want."

"How do you suggest we verify?"

"The National Security Agency in Fort Mead now has a KH-11 recon-naissance satellite positioned over Khartoum. They'll home in on Kober to see if there's any unusual activity. They'll also naturally listen for any unusual signals communication in the Khartoum area. Assets the DO may have on the ground could also possibly confirm Pike's whereabouts."

Sharon Fisher, an intelligence analyst, nodded enthusiastically. "Five days ago the NSA decrypted a short wave radio conversation which went, and I'm paraphrasing, 'Package has safely arrived and is under lock and key.' The broadcast was made from Khartoum and went to London. The NSA could not pinpoint exact locations."

"Thanks Sharon. So Fred," Baker turned to the Clandestine Service area, "just what can your assets on the ground tell us?"

Fred Marshall, Deputy Director for Africa Operations, emerged from a knotted bunch of Directorate for Operations staff. A career CIA man, he had a reputation for leading his Africa Division forces like the marine corps drill sergeant he'd once been. Only his Office and Branch heads were considered elite enough to be called by their first names. Howard Jones knew that secretaries, military affairs experts, and counterterrorism advisors feared him. Case officers hated him for the casual disrespect he showed them. Somehow, perhaps by intimidation, possibly owing to his bottom-line effectiveness, Marshall had become powerfully entrenched in his position.

"You already know," began Marshall, a hint of disdain in his gruff voice, "that our embassy in Khartoum is closely watched. Our base chief has been rendered virtually useless by the scrutiny. Our other officers in the embassy are just as ineffective because they're followed by the Sudan Security Service. And everybody, including Sudan Security, is trailed by units of the Security of the Revolution, the National Islamic Front's own watchdogs."

Marshall paused to roll up his shirt-sleeves. Other than alternating red or blue ties, he wore plain white shirts to work every day. He just didn't care—not about office fashion nor about office etiquette. In an agency rife with *old boy* esprit de corps, Marshall did not play any of the associated games. Except for one he did find to be serviceable: He did indulge in confidences.

"We do have a NOC, a non official cover, in place. The NOC is young and inexperienced, but I do think the individual could at least find out if there has been a step-up in security around Kober, or if there has been any strange activity around the prison."

Marshall was careful to avoid revealing any particulars about the non official cover to those in the situation room. But he himself recollected the particularities of the NOC very well from the meeting he had with her before she embarked for Sudan.

At first he hadn't approved of Kelly Doyle. She was a woman, a relatively attractive one at that, but nevertheless a fragile, feeble woman. In his chauvinistic, professional world, a woman was a liability, especially one who would work overseas without diplomatic immunity in a place like Sudan. But the more he talked to Kelly Doyle, the more he grew to like her.

She'd been a marine, and from all accounts in her 201 File, a damn good one. She did what she was told, only what she was told, and she never questioned an order. The CIA's Office of Security had cleared her without reservation. Better yet, she passed every polygraph exam without raising an eyebrow. Marshall still had to pose the question directly.

"Tell me something, Miss Doyle," he'd asked her. "Say you're undercover in Khartoum and you receive a personal directive from me. Let's say it even appears a bit odd. Do you do it? Do you do it without qualification?"

"*Semper FI,*" she'd quickly responded.

"Always faithful," he repeated. "No matter what?"

"Yes, sir. Always."

He could trust her. She was a good soldier.

Hurley Baker now turned back towards his intelligence analysts. Howard Jones understood there were grave ramifications if Zach Pike truly was in Kober Prison. The President would require precise information from Baker before selecting one of the difficult options before him.

"Find out everything," Baker said, "and I mean everything, about Kober. Speak to any prisoners who may have been there. Touch base with Amnesty International. And don't forget the British, maybe they were the ones who first built it. Be very discrete."

As Baker put on his coat and prepared to take leave of the CIA situation room, he rallied his tired workers. "Keep up the good work. Our next meeting will be in four hours."

Seconds later the office was again whirling in high gear. Nobody paid attention as Baker pulled aside Marshall, Jones and Deputy Director for Military Affairs, Alan Nance. "I want a detailed DO assesment of possible covert military scenarios for that area."

They came for him in the soft hours of the night.

Voices, angry voices, were just outside. Opening his eyes, Zach saw only the continuously lit, naked light bulb of his cell. He shut his eyes quickly. Hard.

A metallic clang as they unlocked the door. It groaned as it swung open.

They were suspended over him now, boring in with their cruel eyes.

A powerful jab crunched his exposed ribs.

"Get up, get up, get up!" a high-pitched voice commanded. "Get up, get up, get up!"

Zach shuffled his chained feet as he was escorted out of the small building where he'd been since his arrival. The night air was warm, but at least it was fresh. In the moon-lit night Zach was able to distinguish the smiling face of Hassan, the man who'd whipped him several days ago.

Zach's knees buckled the moment he was brought into the long chamber. No amount of white-wash could completely cover the blood that stained its walls. Pockets of sand on the floor were saturated red. The room reeked of torn away flesh, vomit, defecation, fear.

"Bring him to the *shebba*," screamed Hassan.

His throat was wedged into the notch of a wooden fork that was fastened behind his neck with leather straps. A heavy pole that constituted the continuation of the fork was raised to shoulder height and Zach's right arm was tied to it with thongs of fresh antelope hide. It took only one excruciatingly painful instant for Zach to realize that if he lowered or raised the pole, even ever so slightly, the fork pinched his Adam's apple in a choke.

At first it took a lot of concentration to keep the pole steady, but gradually Zach dared to look around. Seated directly in front of him were two men: the Mahdi, and an elderly man wearing sunglasses. The Mahdi was spellbound with hate. He couldn't take his eyes away from Zach, yet he seemed repulsed by him at the same time. The other man gave no indication at all of what he was thinking. He sporadically pulled at his gray beard while leaning over to whisper something in the Mahdi's ear.

"You are a magnet for evil, Khawaja Pike," declared the Mahdi.

Zach did not respond. He commanded his right arm, his throwing arm, to remain still but even his fingers were now quivering under the strain of remaining motionless.

"It appears that everyone who knows you is our enemy. Perhaps you too are evil, Khawaja Pike?" Zach opened his mouth, desperately gasping for air, but he couldn't suck enough down . He glanced up, imploring for help, and saw the other man, the one with the sunglasses, signal with an open palm for the Mahdi to stop his line of questioning.

"Please permit me to give you some advice, Mr. Pike." The man spoke English with a cultured British accent. "Don't fight the pole. Relax. The more you struggle, the worse it gets. Unlike a football match, you cannot grit your teeth, hold your breath, and force yourself through the pain of one play. You are in a marathon, my friend, not a sprint. Try to relax now, if you would. You'll last much longer that way."

The elderly man's words were wise. Zach hung onto them like a drowning man clawing at a life vest. Untensing his muscles, he breathed as normally as possible. Soon the fork was only at his throat instead of compressing it. *Relax, relax, relax,* he told his trembling arm.

"Perhaps now you will be in a better frame of mind to listen and answer questions I will ask you. What is your father's occupation?"

So, he was right! This had to do with his father!

"Perhaps you did not hear my question. What does your father do?"

Zach focused on his breathing but it was turning over faster and faster. A two pound weight was added to the pole by Hassan.

"I can be merciful, Mr. Pike. But only if you do what is right. Now, your father works with weapons, does he not? Secret weapons. Weapons that could harm us?"

Another two pound weight was slung over the pole. Sweat raced down Zach's face, stinging his eyes. The questions flew at him like pellets of hail.

"Your father is an Israeli collaborator!" the old man finally yelled out of frustration.

The antelope hide now cut into his arm as it dried. *Relax, relax, relax.* Futile words. They could not help him now. Warm blood began spewing from Zach's mouth as his teeth chewed up his lips and gums. Zach screwed up his face, concentrating on the unrelenting pole.

"Zvi Langer? Tell us about your friend, Zvi Langer?"

What? What do you want of Zvi?

"Your friend is a murderer, an Israeli executioner!"

The pole began to lurch wildly. It jabbed the fork into his throat once, twice, three times. Again, and again, and again.

"Your friend is coming for you, Mr. Pike. And we are ready for him."

Zach took a long incredulous look at his mighty right arm. Where was its magic? How could it betray him so?

As hot white cinders popped before Zach's eyes, he felt a horrible sensation of falling. *Unraveling!*

"**NOOoooo!**"

CHAPTER FIFTEEN

*K*elly Doyle double bolted her apartment door. Then she pulled down her window shades until they touched the sills. It was only then, once she'd opened the typed letter from her Uncle Joe O'Brien, that her hands began trembling.

Dear Kelly,

Hope this letter finds you well. We have some great news! Jennifer has just given birth to a bouncing baby boy who cries right on cue whenever we call him by his name— Bradley Richard! But then again, he seems to cry an awful lot even when we just call him "the baby."

I think he's got some real potential as a middle line-backer. Bradley weighed in at 10 pounds, 2 ounces! Helen says he looks like Steve, but Steve says he looks like Jennifer. Darned if I can tell! Jennifer is doing well by the way. She spent only one day in the hospital.

Not a day goes by that we don't brag to somebody about the wonderful work you are doing in the name of our Saviour, Jesus Christ. From your last letter, it certainly sounds like difficult work. But if anybody can do it—you can. God would not have challenged you so if you were not strong enough to handle it.

Everybody here sends their best. Hopefully you will come and visit sometime soon. Bradley is very impatient to see you. Take care of yourself, Kelly. We love you and miss you very much.

Uncle Joe

Kelly picked up a pair of scissors from the coffee table in front of her and carefully began snipping out the last *you* in the letter. She then took it into the bathroom and submerged it in a dish of water for several seconds before placing it on a plastic lens. With the assistance of magnifying glasses, she held the lens up to the bathroom light and found the microdot instructions under the character *o*.

Subject, Zach Pike, believed held in Kober prison. Check friends and surroundings for confirmation.

Cleaning up after herself, Kelly burned the letter and the microdot instructions and flushed their ashes down the toilet. Then she made sure her daypack contained a couple of Bibles, pamphlets about *One World, One Mission*, her business visa, a visa extension issued by the Ministry of the Interior, and a valid arrival registration, compliments of the Aliens' Section of Security.

It was a short walk from her Sharia al-Qasr apartment to the bus station at U.N. Square. The route itself was almost identical to the one she'd covered an hour before when she picked up the letter at the U.S. Embassy on Sharia Ali Abdul Latif. She had gone over to the Embassy the moment they'd called to inform *One World, One Mission* of her letter.

In the five months she had been in Khartoum this was only the fourth letter to arrive for her by diplomatic pouch. Many expatriate Americans received much more correspondence via the Embassy.

It was quick and it was certain. The Sudanese postal service by contrast was slow and chancy. It often seemed that the odds of actually receiving a letter the conventional way were about as much as rolling a seven in a crap shoot.

Before purchasing her bus ticket, Kelly went into *Maxim's Burgers*, one of the very few western-style fast food eateries in the city. There, in the shadow of the Al-Kabir mosque, she made an effort to savor a hamburg drowned in ketchup, an order of fries, and a large Coke. At least it was a little bit of home in this faraway, bizarre place.

"*Sabah il-kheer, min fadlak wahid* fare to Omdurman," she said with purposeful effort.

"The bus leaves in ten minutes," answered a friendly information clerk in English. "From right here, Madam."

Kelly smiled and adjusted a straw hat to better protect her fair skin from an unimpeded sun. For the next few months, until the "rainy" season, there would not even be a cloud in the sky. But over that same period daily temperatures would soar to well over forty degrees centigrade. For now, it was a relatively comfortable thirty two degrees.

The bus, naturally, was late. And the bus was not really a bus at all. It was more a covered truck with two wooden benches in the middle. Kelly adjusted her long-sleeved, pleated, cotton dress and took a seat next to two young women who wore colorful *tobes* over their heads and shoulders. Three feet seperated them from the nearest seated man. Most of the men around her wore loose fitting jalabiyyas, although there were some wearing western clothes.

The bus unsteadily rolled forward, and then the bouncing began. Maybe it was her imagination, but Kelly could have sworn she felt eyes furtively glance her way every time her breasts jiggled to a bump in the road. She didn't blush and she didn't feel mad. It would only have been awkward to look up and chase away the curious glances. The harsh prohibitive world of *sharia* didn't change human nature, it just attempted to control it. Kelly knew that before coming to Sudan. But then again, she also thought she knew what she would be getting herself into.

As graduation day approached back when she was still Anna Amundson, all she'd known for sure was that she wanted to do something different, something meaningful and adventurous, for the next few years of her life. She was a romantic, but not in an adolescent or amorous way. She certainly daydreamed of marriage and children, but all that would just have to wait. What Anna sought was a way to express her inner values and aspirations, even if they violated society's norms.

"Oh, so you want to go a little crazy," was how a friend put it.

"I suppose I do. That's how I've always done things my entire life."

She'd grown up in the Nigerian savannas and rain forests where her father was ostensibly a teacher, her mother a nurse. In actuality, they were missionaries. Together with their four young children, they were going to save souls, and improve the world. Instilled with her parents' religious zeal and pioneering spirit, inspired by the magnificence of her surroundings, it was almost inevitable that Anna would do something unusual with her life.

After high school, she joined the Marines, reflecting her family's love of country, which coexisted with their love of God. Forced marches proved to be a minor challenge for Anna, whose years of trekking along dirt pathways in Nigeria had made her physically strong. Her religious faith had forged spiritual toughness, and her tight, disciplined family had given Anna the makings of a good soldier. But Anna wanted more.

She went to Illinois after the military in order to attend Wheaton College, a small non-denominational Christian school. Anna graduated cum laude with a major in Bible Studies and a minor in Business. And then, two weeks after commencement, she saw the ad in the Chicago Sun Times for:

THE ULTIMATE OVERSEAS CAREER

For the extraordinary individual who wants more than a job, this is a unique career—a way of life that will challenge the deepest resources of your intelligence, self-reliance, and responsibility. It demands an adventurous spirit...a forceful personality...superior intellectual ability...toughness of mind...and a high degree of integrity. You will need to deal with fast-moving, ambiguous, and unstructured situations that will test your resourcefulness to the utmost.

This is the Clandestine Service, the vital human element of intelligence collection. These people are the cutting edge of American intelligence, an elite corps gathering the vital information needed by our policymakers to make critical foreign policy decisions.

The ad went on to explain that a candidate's application would be looked on favorably if he or she had previous residency abroad, were proficient in a foreign language, and had military experience. The CIA was especially interested in candidates with backgrounds in Central Eurasian, East Asian, or Middle Eastern languages and those with degrees in international economics and business. Entrance salaries ranged from $29,721 to $45,561, depending on credentials. All applicants would have to successfully complete a medical and psychiatric exam, a polygraph interview, and an extensive background investigation.

After Anna completed her exams, she was not sent to *the farm* at Camp Peary, Virginia like other trainee officers. The CIA had decided to put her in as little contact with others as possible. In fact, they explained, they even wanted to change her name so that it did not appear on any personnel computer lists in Langley.

"There are places, Anna, where embassy case officers don't function very well. Places where they can't operate as diplomats and attend cocktail parties to listen for intelligence. In nations which sponsor or harbor terrorists, our case officers just are not effective because terrorists don't move in the same circles as diplomats, and they certainly don't go to cocktail parties. Anna, pending completion of a training program, we are offering you a position as a non official cover."

"I accept," she had said, without hesitation.

The question several weeks later as to whether or not to send "Kelly Doyle" to Sudan caused a minor schism in the uppermost levels of the Directorate of Operations. Proponents pointed to Kelly's experience in Nigeria and her knowledge of Arabic. They claimed that being a woman was actually an advantage in Khartoum because she would be viewed as somebody incapable of working clandestinely in a perilous assignment. In addition, since she would be a foreign woman in Sudan, people would go out of their way to help her, talk to her, and trust her. Most importantly, the U.S. Director of *One World, One Mission*, himself an ex-Marine, had already agreed to let a CIA operative work for his organization provided the individual truly had a solid Christian background and an unswerving commitment to evangelical Christian doctrine. Kelly satisfied all of those criteria.

An equally determined opposition argued that Kelly would stick out like a sore thumb in Sudan. Everybody who saw her would remember her. And rather than help her, they would slam doors in her face because she was so different. They would be afraid, believing that association with a western woman would be viewed as provocative.

Finally it was decided that Deputy Director for Africa Operations, Fred Marshall, make the call. After all, he would be Kelly's boss, the man who would have to accept utimate responsibility should anything happen to her. Nobody who knew Marshall gave Kelly much of a chance when she went to meet him. But Marshall surprisingly wound up approving Kelly's assignment to Khartoum. Apparently, they had reached some sort of understanding.

Kelly stepped down from the bus and into the maelstrom of Omdurman Souk. The massive market bustled with commercial activity. Craftsmen carved and peddled ebony and ivory statuettes. Goldsmiths cut jewellery while merchants in stalls hung crocodile-skin bags and shrivelled crocodile heads. Elsewhere young boys and old men who brought their camels from a nearby camel market beat the obstinant beasts with long sticks.

Kelly conspicuously bought a silk blouse from China and then set off on foot towards Kober Prison. Omdurman, unlike Khartoum, was a city that had the look of a sprawling village. There were no tall modern buildings of any kind. Goats roamed between mud homes, kicking up dust from the narrow streets.

Everywhere Kelly looked, poor children pulled heavy carts laden with goods while younger children squatted in filthy rags and in silent misery. She made a note of what she saw. After all, she was heading up the Street Children Ministry of *One World, One Mission.* As she walked along, she handed out flyers with directions to the organization's headquarters. Once there, the children could get a wholesome meal and they would be invited to stay for a Bible class.

Only those children who were deemed to be in greatest need, or who were most interested in the classes, would be invited back. The Moslem authorities kept *One World, One Mission* on a short leash. They understood what missionary work was, allowing only a limited amount of interaction with locals. In fact, the only reason they permitted the mission to function at all was for show. It was a way of saying to the world, 'See, we're an open, democratic society,' even as they tried to enforce Sharia law throughout the country, including the Christian south.

"I could sure use a tall glass of *limoon.*" Kelly rubbed a hand on her cheek, miming to the fruit juice vendor how hot she was. "I went to the souk to do some shopping and then I just started walking. Can you please tell me, where exactly am I?" Kelly threw up her hands in exasperation and half turned. Fifty yards away ten or fifteen soldiers rambled about with AK-47's slung over their shoulders. Behind them was a compound with a white fifty-foot high wall. In the corner watchtower nearest to her, Kelly spotted one soldier.

"First of all," the vendor said, laughing, "do you know you're in Omdurman?"

"That I know."

"Well, you are approximately two kilometers from the souk, in the Kober area."

"Great! That's a big help!" Kelly put her hand on her hip and looked annoyed.

The vendor laughed even harder, thoroughly enjoying her frustration. Handing her the glass of *limoon*, he pointed towards the prison.

"Maybe it's best you not know where you are because over there is one place you would not want to be."

"Is that a military base?" she asked, looking up at the watchtower.

"No, nice lady. That is a prison, for bad people and for people who are sick in the head."

"Oh, my." Kelly looked at food items behind the vendor. "Can I have some of that sesame candy and, let's see, maybe even some of those peanuts?"

A soldier began walking over to the stall. Kelly slowly took a sip of juice and tried to not look at the soldier, yet not look away from him either. He laughed with the vendor while buying a local Vimto brand soft drink. Then he left, the bottle still in his hand.

"Business is good. I hope all these soldiers stay longer."

"Aren't the soldiers always here guarding the prison?"

"Not this many. A few days ago, they came. I have even started to open my shop earlier and keep it open later because the soldiers are here all the time."

"Why, what's going on?"

"I don't know for sure. But a soldier told me there is now a very important prisoner inside."

"By the looks of things, he must be a mass murderer!"

"Oh, I don't think so. The religious courts follow *hudud* laws very closely. A murderer would probably be quickly executed."

"What in the world could he have possibly done?"

The vendor leaned on the counter, happy, it seemed, to have someone to talk to. "People who live here tell me that special security drove over here at one o'clock in the morning two nights ago. One o'clock in the morning! Can you imagine? I pity the man in there."

Two soldiers now strolled over to the stall. They purchased candy and spoke quickly in Arabic with the vendor.

"Who is the woman?" one of them asked.

"I don't know," the vendor quickly replied. "She went for a walk from the souk and got lost, poor woman."

And then, as the soldiers srarted walking away, Kelly's back suddenly stiffened. "Not as poor as the khawaja inside," she thought she overheard one of the men quietly say. Her eyes narrowed and her hands clenched into a fist. *Khawaja!* The term did not just mean mister. She too was a khawaja, a foreigner, a stranger. In a sense, in a significant and derogatory sense, she and the prisoner inside were "different."

"Well, thank you for the *limoon* and the peanuts. Could you tell me how to get back to the souk?"

The rhythm of the knocks was friendly and familiar.

"I got it." Meg went to the doorway to greet a grinning, slightly older man who wore a jeans jacket. He had a somewhat unkempt beard and almost shoulder length brown hair.

"Hi." He lowered his sunglasses. Wrinkles zigzagged around his flashing eyes in a most haphazard way. His grin never faded.

"You son of a bitch," laughed Zvi. He threw aside a book on Sudan and vaulted over a sofa. His hand slapped and then grabbed hold of the man's. "It's been what, two years or more? Couldn't you have at least contacted me?"

The man ignored Zvi's rebuke and raised his eyebrows in Meg's direction. He gave a little wink.

"This is Meg Symes, an old friend from Boston. And this is Alan, a long lost friend."

Alan lit a cigarette. He and Zvi started throwing out names of friends, each checking to see if the other knew their whereabouts.

A wife, a kid, and in L.A.

In Buenos Aires.

Bumming in Eilat.

Tel Aviv, with our community.

France, I think.

Married, working, and in Kibbutz Sde Eliyahu.

Somewhere in North Africa.

Dead. Almost a year now.

The exchange stopped, but only for an instant. Alan explained to Meg that his English was perfect because his parents made aliyah from Detroit when he was twelve years old. *Army Friends,* is how he characterized his relationship with Zvi. Then he lit another cigarette.

"How bout we go for a walk, Zvi."

Meg understood she was not invited. "Coffee will be ready by the time you get back."

"I've been in Europe for the better part of the last couple of years, primarily in Hungary and the Czech Republic." Alan sat on a dock behind Kibbutz Ein Gev, his feet dangling over the edge. This time he was smoking marijuana.

"There are all sorts of lunatics still running around over there," he continued. "Terrorists have been there for such a long time they still think of it as home, even though their communist sponsors are long gone."

Zvi leaned against a post and watched Alan stare into the rippling water. His friend's grin was thin and fragile. The grin was his last line of defense, a way to keep the enemy without, and the demons within, at bay. If ever his smile left him, if he ever lost his perspective, then he would be at their mercy. Which is to say, there would be no mercy.

"Zvi, forget Al-Omri! He may be President and Prime Minister, but Amir Kasawi is the show in Sudan. He's smart and he's ruthless. Right after Al-Omri completed the coup a few years back, Kasawi started cutting off the heads of anybody who could threaten his control of Al-Omri." Alan inhaled, held it, and blew out a thin stream of bluish smoke.

"Tell me more," Zvi said.

"Some of those rivals Kasawi did not quash fled Sudan in order to fight him another day. One I've been watching in Budapest is Farouk Mandeb, a ruthless officer who lost the power struggle to Al-Omri. When Kasawi started looking for him, Mandeb took off for Libya. Qaddafi took him in because he'd been backing Mandeb. After a short stay in Libya, Mandeb went to Budapest, which at the time was still under Soviet domination. Since then Mandeb has had Kasawi in his sights. He probably even knows about Kasawi's friends and supporters. Zvi, if you want to know more about what's going on in Sudan, then go and see Mandeb."

"Why would he help me?" Zvi asked

"You know," said Alan as he crushed his cigarette and turned his head in Zvi's direction,"you've never really been in my world. You stayed on with the Sayeret, doing some very important and difficult things. I know. But you never rolled up your sleeves to do the dirty things, the ugly little things I've been doing."

Alan lifted his shoulders, let them drop.

"Look, Mandeb won't cheerfully tell you how to help Pike. Even though he hates Kasawi on a personal level, he despises Israel and America much more. To him, we are the enemy, out to destroy not only him, but his culture and his religion. So if you want to save Pike, you'd

better start playing by the same rules as the terrorists and the fundamentalists. You can't just wait for your orders to come down from
Almog anymore, because there won't be any. You should know that
already, after your Knesset meeting of the other day."

Zvi sidearmed a flat stone into the water. It skipped along in ever
smaller leaps before dropping below the surface. "I've never worked
solo before."

"You're not really alone, Zvi." Alan looked up, his grin even wider
than usual. "I'm here with this tip on Mandeb, ain't I? You know, you
have a lot of friends, some of whom as a matter of national policy can't
openly help you. But they are with you, nevertheless."

"How old is Alan, anyway?" Meg asked while putting away dishes.
Alan had stayed for a tuna casserole lunch, then coffee and dessert.

"A year or two older than me," answered Zvi. "Why?"

"He looks ten years older than you. All that smoking, one cigarette
after another, isn't doing him any good. And I swear, when I dropped
that cup, I saw him actually get so startled he blanched. He's a wreck!"

"Well, if I'd been doing what Alan has been doing maybe I'd look the
same way. Living in constant danger has wasted him. But at least there's
not too much more they can get out of him now."

Meg looked at Zvi, her eyes perplexed, her lips parted in question.
There was so much she did not understand about Zvi, and men like Zvi.
Alan, for example.

"I could have been overseas, actively involved in the same kind of shit
Alan has been in. A lot of friends from my unit get invited. But that's not
what I wanted. I never wanted it, any of it! I stayed with military intelligence because there seemed to be some defined purpose in carrying out
their commands. Naturally, I got bloodied and scarred along the way.
But there was something still noble about it, I could still think of myself

as a soldier. But now—the exact thing I've never wanted to be, I might now have to become." Zvi put a hand over his eyes. "For Zach's sake!"

"And that thing is....?" Meg's question faded into a whisper.

"An assasin."

CHAPTER SIXTEEN

$\mathcal{T}$he black limo pulled up close to the White House. Howard Jones got out, then waited in the cold rain as Larry Duffy lumbered out the door. Duffy had never before been called to attend the President's Daily Brief, and he took the rain as a bad omen.

"I don't think he's going to like what we have to tell him."

"It's not your job to worry about that," Jones hollered over the drumming rain. He pulled the young man under a secret service agent's open umbrella. "Just answer his questions. He's supposed to be upset over things like this. He knows you're only a messenger."

The President stood by his *Resolute Desk* and nodded in the direction of Jones and Duffy as they entered the Oval Office. He wore a black cardigan sweater and looked as glum as the weather outside his windows. Lou Reed and Mark Handsman sat on one of the office's facing sofas, each engrossed in the papers before them.

"Ollie, this is Larry Duffy. He's an analyst at the National Photographic Interpretation Center." Jones pushed Duffy towards the President with a firm nudge. After a perfunctory handshake, the President showed them over to the sofas.

"Okay, this is what we know," began Jones. This was a briefing, not a meeting. There would be no introductions, small talk, or opening remarks. He sat upright on the edge of the sofa and immediately got the attention of the President's two right hand men.

"First, the Mossad informs us, through a credible agent, that Zach Pike was seen being brought into Khartoum's Kober Prison.

"Second, Fred Marshall has heard from a NOC that soldiers have been beefing up security around the prison for the past several days. Sudanese security has even been seen entering the prison in the middle of the night. Apparently there's a foreigner, probably a white caucasian, inside the prison." Jones ticked off the points with his fingers.

"Third, Duffy here has some interesting photographs to show us. These photographs confirm what the Mossad and NOC are telling us."

The speed and the informality of the briefing surprised Larry Duffy. Here he was, four years out of college, meeting with the President of the United States in the White House. He wanted to pause and savor the moment. He almost gushed about how honored he was to be in their presence. In the end the business-like tempo of the proceedings, as well as his own anxiety, influenced him to present his material right away. He removed several photographs from a polyvinyl envelope.

"These digital photos were taken from 120 miles up by an advanced KH-11 series satellite. Its telescopic camera provides high resolution, identifying objects of even a few inches. Images are grabbed, stored, and relayed to stations on the ground. This first photo—you'll notice the time of 4:09 PM in the lower right corner—shows all of Kober prison. Note these armed soldiers in front of the prison's main gate. You can also see two soldiers standing next to this particular barrack not far from the main courtyard." He flipped to the next picture.

"This blow-up of the barrack, from 5:30 PM, shows another soldier carrying a tray, probably of food, into the barrack." He went to the next photo.

"This one from 5:38 PM, shows a soldier walking with a man wearing a lab coat towards the barrack. Note the bag, possibly a medical bag, in his hand." The President, Handsman, and Reed were now all leaning forward, riveted to Duffy's documentation.

"The KH-11 moves in orbit and observes an arena for two hours. We don't currently have continuous satellite monitors over Khartoum so there is an observation gap, at least for now. This next shot was taken by a different KH-11 bird at 12:25 AM using an infrared scanner. You can see two cars parked in front of the main gate and several soldiers, as well as two men without weapons, milling about in that area. Inside the prison there are two soldiers alongside, and presumably escorting, this large man in the middle." Duffy pointed and tapped a finger at where he wanted to direct attention. For the first time in his presentation he looked up to make eye contact. "We unfortunately cannot verify this individual's identity. The pictures can't show that kind of clarity and the individual's head is bowed. However this man is certainly not wearing a jellybeeya, or any typical Sudanese style of clothing. There is this stringy-like structure down at his feet. This is probably a chain, axial resolution being better than horizontal resolution with this object. The soldiers and this individual are heading from the barrack we saw before towards this other longer barrack where two men without visible weapons are standing. Regrettably, this is the last significant photo we have for now since this KH-11 was finishing its two hour watch."

"Howard?" Earl rested his head on his hand, still gazing at the photographs.

"This is how I see it," Jones said. "Increased security around and in the prison indicates that there's somebody of value inside. This is further demonstrated by the photo showing only one tray of food being brought to the barrack. Usually barracks, and especially jails, have several prisoners inside a given cell. The prisoner inside that barrack is isolated. Further proof of the prisoner's value is the probable medical attention he is receiving. Kober undoubtedly has a small, crude infirmary. But for a doctor or nurse to be personally attending to a prisoner is highly unusual. It also, by the way, is not at all encouraging that the prisoner requires medical care." Jones let a sigh escape.

"Larry's last photo shows cars in front of Kober at 12:25 AM. A curfew exists in Khartoum from midnight to 4:00 AM. For the most part only a select group of people with passes, or security personnel, would be on the street at that hour. And activity inside Kober at that hour corroborates the NOC's account of security visits to the prison in the middle of the night. The fact that the prisoner is being led to another barrack at that time, a barrack where plain clothed individuals are situated, is very ominous. I would think the prisoner is being interrogated at a barrack better equipped for interrogation. I think you know what I mean."

"So the prisoner," the President sadly said, "is Zach Pike?"

"In my estimation, yes. What's more, it's possible that one of the men inside the prison, beside the long barrack, is Amir Kasawi, head of the National Islamic Front. But that's only a guess."

"Why do you think it might be him?" asked Handsman.

"Because of the large white turban, the *emma*, on his head. Kasawi always wears one. He also looks stooped and thin like Kasawi. But actually it really doesn't matter if it's him. The very fact that Pike is in Kober, guarded by soldiers and visited by security, implies Kasawi has to be involved in this. And if he knows about it, so do Al-Omri and the rest of the government. What we have here is proof of culpability! The smoking gun! This is a very important development in planning a response."

"And who is this other man wearing a jalabiyya, the one without a turban? The one who appears to be bald?"

"It looks to me, Mark, as if he's wearing a cap or skull-cap. I don't know who he is. Maybe he's an assistant or collaborator of Kasawi's."

"I suppose the good news is that we at least know where Pike is," Reed said.

"That's very good news. If they'd hidden him in some ghost house it would have been like trying to find a needle in a haystack." Jones shrugged and clapped his hands on his knees. "I suppose the fundamentalists decided that hiding Zach Pike was not as paramount as being ready for whoever might come for him."

"Whoever, I suppose, meaning us?" sighed Earl.

Duffy saw the President's weariness. It was a heavy burden. Americans would naturally, rightfully, once again have to do whatever was necessary to defend themselves. It was an unavoidable moral duty.

The President's secretary stepped into the office. "Lee Nunzio is here to see you. Attorney General Lopes has accompanied him."

"As you can see, Howard, it's going to be one of those days. Larry, thanks for your help." Duffy felt a little rush of pleasure. "And for Pete's sake, see if you can program more of those KH-11's to be over Khartoum, will you?"

Lee Nunzio and Victor Lopes took the sofa spots, still warm, just vacated by Jones and Duffy. *Oval Office Turnstile* is how Handsman termed the steady flow of visitors and advisors. Staying on, he resumed his previous position although Reed excused himself explaining that he had to make some urgent calls. After stretching his arms back over his head, Earl was ready for a shift of topic. But Nunzio's opening bowled him over.

"Mr. President, we have reason to believe that Zach Pike's father, Ben Pike, may be engaged in high-tech military espionage for Israel."

"What!"

"Ben Pike works for Lexington Labs on remote piloted vehicle and unmanned aerial vehicle cooperative research projects with Israel. That much you know from the T.V. segment on the Pikes. It's come to our attention that Ben Pike has been consistently extending his visit requests to Israel for several years now. Other Lexington Lab colleagues who accompany him to Israel return home when their visit requests expire, and in interviews we've conducted with them they say that immediate work assignments were completed by the time they flew back. They don't know why Ben Pike stayed on in Israel. Pike does have close friends in Israel but the records don't indicate any lengthy visits with those friends. During the time frames in question telephone bills show that Pike's wife and children placed no calls to those friends, which you'd expect if a husband or father were staying with them. And there are no calls made from the home of those friends to the Pike residence during those same unaccounted for periods."

Nunzio tapped the pile of papers in front of him. "Inconsistencies appear all over the place. At one point Ben Pike claimed he was staying on to do some sight seeing, even though he'd been to Israel on numerous occasions. There are no records of his renting a car or signing up with a tour company. In fact, we find that he stayed at the same hotel in Tel Aviv for the entire length of his extension."

"All you're telling me is that there are incongruities and suspicious behavior." Earl looked grave. "Do you have any proof that he's been spying?"

"Back in 82, slightly over a year before Israel successfully used RPV's in Lebanon, Pike and his entire family became close friends with a neighboring Israeli family. The technology used by Israel in Lebanon at the time was very similar to research Ben Pike had been working on and unsuccessfully lobbying America to use."

"That's only circumstantial," Handsman pointed out.

"We agree," said Lopes. "But considering that as yet there's no explanation why Zach Pike specifically was abducted, we think this offers a plausible reason. The kidnapping could be payback for all Ben Pike has done for Israel. It's not just a coincidence that Zach Pike is involved." Lopes stared unflinchingly at the President.

At the beginning of his term Earl had hand-picked Lopes to be Attorney General. Until then he'd been a relatively obscure San Antonio D.A. who had a reputation for being relentless and ruthless. Lopes was approximately the same age as Nunzio and shared his same outlook and approach to law enforcement. The President had hoped that the Justice Department and the FBI would, through this alliance, forge a strong base of cooperation. But the primary reason for the President's nomination of Lopes was to satisfy a Hispanic constituency who'd overwhelmingly voted for him. With his movie-star Latin looks and his frequent public appearances, Lopes had become an admired role model and a media favorite. For that Earl was grateful. But even now he didn't know what made his aggressive Attorney General tick. He was about to find out.

"When you interviewed me for the position of Federal Attorney General, you asked me if I saw the FBI as a law enforcement agency whose principal role is to catch spies or a counterintelligence agency whose main role is to learn all it can about the workings of an adversary. I clearly remember telling you that I saw the FBI as an enforcement body. Period. 'And the Justice Department should do all it can in its own capacity to find and prosecute the bastards who through their disloyalty betray the privileges of citizenship' is what I said. I meant that then, and I mean it now. Lee and I concur on this fundamental philosophy."

Perhaps it was the rapport built during his recent phone conversations with Ben Pike. Possibly it was the knowledge that this particular high profile case was too delicate and too dangerous to be simply handled with a catch-all philosophy. Maybe it was Lopes' strident, overly zealous tone. Some mix of factors made Earl suddenly fear that in his eagerness to please Nunzio and ingratiate himself with the voting public, he'd made a big mistake picking Lopes.

"Here's what we've done so far," continued Lopes. He wet his lips and leaned forward. "We've been conducting electronic surveillance, mail surveillance, and physical survellance of the Pike household in Brookline, Massachusetts for the past few days. The FBI has also parked a van that has been picking up the electromagnetic waves that cross Ben Pike's computer screen and transforming them into characters."

"In this way we can read whatever Pike writes," explained Nunzio. "The problem is that my men understandably do not want to watch a T.V. screen forever, waiting for Pike to enter something important."

"It sounds to me that what you're saying is that you have not discovered anything significant or incriminating so far." The President gripped the armrests of his chair tightly. His palms were perspiring.

"It could be the suspect is very careful. Special agents have already spoken to him so he might be alert to a misstep. It could even be that he's so careful, any trangression he committed was only verbal. In which case we simply have to try harder." Lopes shrugged. "I've approved a physical search of his home. Lee tells me that will take place sometime over the next couple of days. Maybe there's something we can uncover. One thing that can definitely be done is to plant a bug into Pike's computer. Then we can turn on his computer, call up his stored files, and send them back to us by radio modem without Pike ever knowing we entered his computer." Lopes peered at the President, tilted his head.

"Are you alright, President Earl?" he asked.

"Sorry, Victor. You know, it sounds to me like you're looking very hard to find a reason why this happened to Zach Pike. And in the process you're reaching for any conceivable evidence to support your theory. What if the extremists chose Pike just because he was as big as any hero around? He's a wholesome, red-blooded American icon. I think these extremist bastards took him because they knew exactly which button would inflict the most psychic trauma to the nation."

"We're not running a witch hunt, Mr.President. I've been in this business awhile and I'm damn good at what I do. There's something rotten here. I can smell it. We must continue with our investigation and hopefully we'll know by the time we conclude if Ben Pike is a spy or if Zach Pike was simply an American hero in the wrong place, at the wrong time."

The President took a deep breath and stared at Lopes. "Don't put words in my mouth and don't ever misconstrue what I say! Do your investigation! I want you to complete it. But you'd better be careful. Ben Pike's son is in a rat hole half way across the world. Aside from the anguish Ben Pike and his family are facing, this young man will be in greater danger if any aspect of your inquiry gets leaked."

"That's one of the reasons this investigation is done covertly, Mr. President. That's one of the reasons we have electronic surveillance and search without consent. Naturally, we don't want to inflict any needless pain or jeopardize Pike's already tenuous situation."

"There's more we need to tell you, President Earl." Nunzio looked uncomfortable with how the meeting was going. Earl sensed he had more bad news. "Ben Pike's close friend, his neighbor back in the 80's, was Oded Langer."

"Of the Knesset? Israel's Parliament?"

"That's right."

"Aw, shit!" Earl got up and ran a hand through his hair. "All the more reason to be careful. I value this nation's friendship with Israel. They're even helping us with intelligence reports in this affair. You don't know if Langer tried to get Ben Pike to convey confidential data. Hell—it's my opinion you don't even know if Ben Pike did anything wrong! But the last thing we need is for the Israelis to catch wind that we suspect, and are investigating, one of their more prominent cabinet members."

"I have to remind you, Mr. President, that the Espionage Statute, Section 794 of Title 18, does not distinguish between delivery and attempted delivery. Nor does it distinguish between hostile countries and allies." Lopes was eager to make his point. "Espionage is despicable regardless. And in my opinion, even though we don't as yet know what Mr. Pike was up to, we owe it to the people of this nation to leave no stone unturned—regardless how uncomfortable it is. Justice has to be blind."

No! Earl wanted to scream. *It has to see the whole picture! Justice doesn't live in a vacuum, just as every case can't be kept in a vacuum. If justice is only black and white, then why have a judicial system? Justice lacking in sensitivity is not justice! And a man lacking in compassion is lacking humanity.*

Mark Handsman sat slumped on the sofa. Nunzio and Lopes had left after a curt farewell. Oblivious to Mark's continued presence, the President punched his fist into the air. He then went over to a liquor cabinet along the wall and poured a glass of whiskey. The rain that beat mercilessly on the glass windows behind him only accentuated the brooding stillness that engulfed him.

The President looked so sad.

Earl tilted his head back, swallowed half of the glass's contents, and then drained the rest. It was nine o'clock in the morning.

The grandfather clock in the corner chimed, the whiskey glass came down hard on top of the cabinet, and the President strode out of the Oval Office.

Mark Handsman blinked. The moment passed. The rain kept falling.

CHAPTER SEVENTEEN

She overslept. *Again.*

Her work was simple; exhausting, yet oddly refreshing. Take the order, bring the food, take away the dishes. Later, wash the pots and pans, scrub down the tables, and mop the floor. Last night, when she had left work at kibbutz Ein Gev's fish restaurant and returned to her host family, Aviva and Odie had already gone to bed. Zvi was not about.

The full moon cast silvery beams around her room; a cool breeze gently puffed through her window. Sleep had gradually taken her over. And except for the first murky hour or so when she chased after her worries, Meg had enjoyed a relatively good rest.

Now, with the sand in her eyes and the birds chirping outside her room, she awakened to the new day in Ayelet Langer's old room. Ayelet's clothes, cosmetics,…practically everything was gone. But the morning light still touched a few cherished personal items; a doll, her books, a photograph of her with a boyfriend.

As she slipped into a pair of jeans and a T-shirt, Meg heard the morning news being broadcast in Hebrew over the radio in the kitchen. She opened her door and knew immediately that something was different. Something was wrong.

Aviva was still in her bathrobe. She was facing away, sitting by the kitchen table that overlooked her yard, and absentmindedly holding a cup of tea. Oded whispered in her ear, kissed her on top of the head, and took his briefcase as he headed out the front door. Zvi was not there. *Zvi was not there!*

"*Boker Tov,* Good Morning."

"*Boker Or,* Meggela." Aviva swiveled around and started to get up.

"No, please sit. I know my way around here well enough by now to help myself." Meg poured herself a cup of tea and took a yogurt out of the refrigerator. Then she sat down next to Aviva. "Where's Zvi?"

"He's gone."

"Gone? Gone where?"

"I don't know."

"Well, when do you think he'll be back?"

"I don't know."

Aviva sipped some tea. She gazed out her screen windows, beyond the yard and out over the glistening blue Sea of Galilee. Her eyes seemed to seek some faraway place.

"What is it? What happened?"

"When Zvi was a boy," Aviva said, putting down her cup, "of perhaps thirteen or fourteen, he bought himself a toy ship. I think it was at the Cape, no doubt when we were visiting Mary and Ben at their summer home. You can see it, actually. It's right over there in the yard, by the bushes."

A majestic clipper ship, suspended from a pole, swayed in the breeze. Large canvas sails billowed from its masts. "I remember it, Aviva," Meg said. "I was with Zach when Zvi first saw it outside a crafts shop. It was love at first sight! He was so excited! He tinkered with that thing for weeks."

Aviva nodded. "That ship has been in our back yard since we returned to Israel. At first, it seemed, the sails were always up, catching the wind. Somehow, I don't know when, Zvi took the sails down. Well, after Ayelet died, Zvi was becoming even more involved with his military unit. Oded and I never knew what he was up to, where he was. We thought we would explode with worry. We'd plead with him to tell us when he'd be on a mission, or out of the country. Zvi finally pointed out to the back yard and said, 'Look to the ship. Then you'll know.' Ever since then Meggela, whenever Zvi knew he'd be in danger, those sails howl in the wind. It's what we asked for, a sign, something, and still the sails rattle our lives. They toss us about like poor souls adrift after a shipwreck."

As Meg took hold of Aviva's hands, the kitchen table began to shake. Outside, the clipper ship began to tempestuously pitch.

"Hello. My name is Najib Pandian. I am calling from Aviation Industry, Inc. Please, I would very much like some information about your upcoming symposium in Huntsville, Alabama. The one organized by the Association for Unmanned Vehicle Systems." The caller concentrated on what the convention organizer, a woman, told him from the other end of the line. He closed his dark eyes, stroked the ends of his mustache, and inhaled the comforting aroma of hazelnut coffee as she listed the dates, hotel accomodations, and pool of participating defense contractors.

"Did you say Lexington Labs would be there?"

"Yes, sir."

"Could you please tell me who will be there from the company. I used to work for the Lab and it would be marvelous if I could meet with my old friends again."

"Let's see…Sanford Levy, Gil Gugliotti, and Barry Milstone are scheduled to take part."

"What about Benjamin Pike? Will he be there?"

The woman on the other end of the line hesitated. "He's still registered to attend. But I hardly think he'll be there, what with the tragic situation going on with his son."

"Oh, you mean Zach Pike? I never realized that was his son."

"I thought you'd worked at Lexington Labs. How could you not know Zach Pike was Ben Pike's son? It's been all over the news."

"I'm afraid I have not been paying much attention to the newspapers and television. Benjamin Pike was more of a colleague, not really a friend. He never talked to me about his family."

"Oh, I see."

The woman sounded suspicious. He should have handled it differently—said 'Oh, of course, I'd forgotten for a moment. Yes, it's terrible….' He scrambled to focus the conversation back on the symposium.

"Can you please tell me the topics that will be discussed at the meeting?"

"How about if I mail you a brochure and a program that details the whole convention?"

"Um……," said the caller reluctantly, "very well. Why not. My post office box is 1067…." *Najib Pandian? No, no! That won't do. Better not.* Ibrahim Husseini slurped down some hot coffee. "It's alright, you don't need to mail me anything. Thank you for your help."

"It's really no problem at all, Mr Pandian, I……"

"**NO!**" Ibrahim Husseini said loudly. "Maybe if Benjamin Pike does attend……Well, thank you again." Click.

Something was not right. Betty Meyers furrowed her brow. *How odd?* she wondered. As a hostess of sorts for the symposium, she knew that Ben Pike had been a dominant figure at the meetings for years, often addressing the audience over some aspect of his research. He had always been gregarious, mingling with attendees, and showering praise on all his children, especially Zach. The caller should have known Zach was Pike's son. Sparks of apprehension kept igniting, so many, so fast, that she could not possibly ignore them, let alone contain them. She picked up the phone, put down the phone, and picked it up again.

"Aviation Industry? This is the Association for Unmanned Vehicle Systems. Do you have an employee named Najib Pandian?" Betty nervously tapped a pencil on her desk. "What? What's that? You have no such employee? Well, thank you, I suppose."

She kept drumming on her telephone as she looked up another number on her Rolodex.

"You've reached Lexington Labs," a voice said.

"I would like to speak to your security division."

"You must want our Field Security Officer. Just a moment."

"This is Paul Reilly. Can I help you?"

"Yes. Yes, I think you can."

Farouk Mandeb hated the cold.

No matter which direction he turned in, regardless of the particular medieval pastel-colored *utca* he walked down in the Castle District's *Old Town*, it always seemed as if the bitter air found him out with its frigid fingers.

Budapest had its advantages to be sure; intoxicating plum *palinka*, enticing *cukraszdas* offering expresso and dobos torte, and great theater and symphony halls. Yet Mandeb dreamed of one day triumphantly returning to Khartoum, to its balm-like heat, to its maze of alleys and its souks. But Amir Kasawi, *cursed be his name*, and his puppet, Al-Omri, were still in power. They had chased him out of Sudan, into Libya, until he finally found shelter with some old military advisor friends in Hungary.

As was his custom, Mandeb continued to walk briskly. He passed Matthias Church and then stopped at Fisherman's Bastion to admire a panoramic view of Budapest. Below Fisherman's Bastion's neo-Gothic white turret platforms, the Danube River swept along regally, cutting in front of the beautiful limestone Parliament Building on the far side of the river. Before him was the Chain Bridge, one bead of the necklace of bridges linking the modern Pest to the Buda hills upon which he now stood.

At first he had been sure his exile from Sudan would last but a short time. But what should have been only months stretched into years; a veritable eternity during which he plotted, schemed, and watched Amir Kasawi from afar. Every day he asked himself what Kasawi was thinking. At every opportunity his quiet, personal time was devoted to reconstructing in his mind Kasawi's intricate network of supporters and thinking of how to break down his depraved chain of command.

But sometimes Mandeb's mind short-circuited, turning over the cards and reversing the hand against him. And now, for just a moment, his mind tricked him into thinking he was being watched, hunted.

He discreetly turned his head from side to side, seeking any shadows on the periphery. He carefully listened for any footsteps on the edge. Still not at ease, he turned around and deliberately investigated his surroundings. A grandmother knelt to bundle up her two small grandchildren. A few elderly tourists hurried back to the warm interior of their bus. Laughing at his own paranoid delusions, Mandeb continued walking. Yet he found himself quickly bypassing the Buda Castle Catacombs, whose wax figurines macabrely depicted Hungary's rather gory lore.

Approaching Gellert Hill, he craned backwards to admire Independence Monument, the gigantic stone depiction of a woman raising up a palm leaf to honor the liberation of the city by communist Russian soldiers. His arthritic shoulder and neck throbbed with the effort and he quickly decided on a change of plans. Instead of going to the thermal baths at the stately Gellert Hotel, he would visit the nearby therapeutic waters of the Rudas Baths.

He set his clothes in a locker and gingerly entered one of the Turkish Bath's secluded and steaming octagonal pools. The sulphate laden, aqua-colored water immediately began working its magic on his shoulder, his neck, his spirit. Red, yellow, and blue-colored glass in the domed cupola above transformed incoming daylight into theatrical stagelights.

It was the middle of the afternoon and he had the pool all to himself. It was so quiet, soothing. He closed his eyes and began to meditate, soon enough listing to himself all the fabulously terrible things he would do to Amir Kasawi when he caught up with him.

A metal door clanged. Opening his eyes, Mandeb saw a lithe and athletic young man approach the pool with measured steps. Despite a terry cloth towel thrown over his head, Mandeb could see that the young man's eyes were sharp and clear. As he eased himself into the far end of the pool, the young man flashed a toothy smile. Mandeb closed his eyes.

It took only a second, one infernal instant, for Mandeb to be caught in the man's fierce grip. Searing water burned his eyes, ran into his nose, and gushed out of his mouth. With all his might he vainly tried to raise his head. His arms splashed water frantically, his mind spun out of control. In panic he swallowed even more water. His every reflex fired simultaneously as his body thrashed and jerked.

All at once the strong hand tore his hair and yanked his head out of the water. He coughed and retched violently. The young man's other hand sealed his mouth. Ambushed, Mandeb realized the young man meant to kill him.

"It can get even worse, Mr. Mandeb. I want you to answer my questions." The words were hushed, but charged. "Is Amir Kasawi holding Zach Pike? If so, where?"

Mandeb's eyes teared uncontrollably as he struggled to regain his equilibrium.

"Answer!"

Mandeb shrugged. If not sent by Kasawi, then...*who?* "Why should I tell you?" he wheezed.

The young man looked at him coolly. "Because whether or not you cooperate, I'm now going to have to kill you anyway."

It was a good reason. Maybe the information he would give the young man could afford him one last chance to exact retribution. "In Knightsbridge, London. Charlie Hammami will tell you."

"Who's Hammami?"

"Kasawi's biggest sponsor."

"He'll know? He'll know about Zach Pike?"

"Yes. He'll know everything—provided you find just the right way of reminding him, coaxing him to talk," Mandeb whispered. It was a relief to tell this to someone—even to the man who was going to kill him. He would, with these his dying breaths, plant the seeds of his vengeance against Kasawi.

"Maybe," he said, "this whole business with Pike was even inspired by Hammami."

"Why do you say that?" the young man asked.

"Because Pike, anybody like him, is either taken for the vast attention it creates or to get even with somebody. Kasawi doesn't care and doesn't give in to either of those self-serving motivations. He's too practical, too smart. What he cares about is power; power to bring about a fundamentalist Islamic revolution." Mandeb strained forward to spew aqua-colored water. "Kasawi would only take Pike to win the favor of a sponsor, like Hammami, and in so doing advance his own power. And Kasawi would only hold Pike, or have him held by others to better profess his innocence, so long as it serves his needs."

"Hammami? Tell me about him."

"He's filthy rich, thanks to drug trafficing. But about his mind, I do not know. I have lived in only one mind these past few years—and that has been Kasawi's."

Mandeb rolled his eyes up and backwards. They looked into those of the assailant, *his assassin,* and then they closed acquiescingly, as if in prayer. For just an instant he was able to gratefully imagine the terror Amir Kasawi would be experiencing if it were his head in the hands of the assassin.

The young man jerked Mandeb's head up and back in one fluid motion and then swiftly twisted until he heard a distinctive snap. He hauled Mandeb out of the pool and, after checking to see that nobody was in the adjacent locker room, crammed the body into a vacant locker.

Zvi reluctantly looked at himself in a mirror. He splashed some water onto his face but still he could not wash away his revulsion. The stench of the vile deed clung to him. It started to permeate his very skin.

Outside, a dense choking fog had rolled in from the river. Zvi hurriedly left the Rudas Baths and hailed a taxi. Dazed, he did not care where he was going, just so long as it was away.

After a short ride over the Elizabeth Bridge, Zvi stumbled out of the taxi at the busy intersection with Muzeum Korut Boulevard. He opened a city map and tried to focus. As if pulled by a magnet, his eyes locked onto a site. It was nearby. So close.

Five minutes later he haltingly arrived at Budapest's Holocaust Memorial, a tree of metallic leaves bearing the names of some of the 600,000 Hungarian Jews murdered by the Nazis. Looking up, he saw the lofty stone figure of an angel throwing down a golden bolt of cloth to a martyr. Spinning around, he saw across the street a plaque indicating the birthplace of Theodor Herzl, founder of modern Zionism. Off to the side, the renovated Great Dohany Synagogue loomed, its giant moorish towers befitting the second largest synagogue in the world.

Zvi whirled around and around. It was all so confusing. Everything flowed by. Everything spattered apart. Darkness and hope juxtaposed with tragedy and faith.

The cold wind whistled past his ear as his head spun. He closed his eyes and cast himself apart from it all, to a secluded island, from where he could safely see the raging storm all around.

All at once he vomited ferociously, purging himself, healing himself. Opening his eyes to look around, he found himself adrift. *Again.*

CHAPTER EIGHTEEN

"*M*ac, you're crazy! You know that, don't you? Every time I come up here from Fort Bragg, you run me ragged. Every damn workout, every interminable run becomes a friggin' do or die challenge to my manhood. How come I have to uphold the honor of the whole U.S. army every time I see you?"

"Hey, all I'm doing is just squeezing in some time for exercise and checking to see if my fellow officers are in shape. You're the one who has to always sprint ahead and then outlift me at the weight pile, Gordy. Your problem," laughed Mac Streicher, "is that you don't like it when I fight back."

The half hour run to the Lincoln Memorial and back, across the Potomac by way of the Arlington Memorial Bridge, had been a grudging battle of wills. It passed in concentrated, intense silence. But when they got back, Admiral Mac Streicher and Brigadier General Gordy Bannister started exchanging their usual barbs and crude jokes in the Pentagon's state-of-the-art gymnasium.

Just looking at Bannister always made Mac Streicher, Chairman of the Joint Chiefs of Staff, crack up. Short and squat, Bannister had hooded fleshy eyelids and a mangled nose, the result of his middleweight boxing exploits in the service thirty-five years previous. Bannister's hair was cut in a flattop and his massive jowls always looked as if he were about to spit tobacco or dislodge great globs of epithets from his puckishly small mouth.

As an infantry officer in Vietnam, Bannister exhibited uncommon bravery on his way to earning a bunch of Silver and Bronze stars and winning the Congressional Medal of Honor. He went on to Special Forces school, ultimately serving as a lieutenant colonel with the Army Rangers. After a suffocating stint at the Pentagon as a military assistant to the Deputy Secretary of Defense, he was finally appointed to head the Joint Special Operations Command, JSOC, in Fort Bragg, North Carolina. The posting was as far as Bannister wanted his career to go, for he knew he could never again be so happy anywhere else in the military. Aside from the critical challenges of the position, Bannister, an effervescent type, loved the comraderie of the maverick officers and soldiers of the Joint Special Operations Command. The 1300 men he directed, men to whom he was unswervingly loyal, constituted the most secret units of the military. They were the elite counterterrorism and special commando teams, primarily composed of Delta Force and Seal Team-6.

"You're a lousy host, you know that don't you?" Bannister bounced alongside the taller Streicher, occasionally jabbing his finger in the air for emphasis. The two men were making their way down the Pentagon's fourth floor E-Ring to Streicher's office. "First, you suck the friggin' life juices out of me in that torture chamber you call a weight room, and then you aimlessly drag me around this monstrosity. *You're intentionally taking me the long way around!* Remember, I spent four infernal years here. I couldn't wait to get the fuck out of here then, and I'm dying to get the hell out of here now. The least you could do is offer me beer and cookies."

"Stop your bellyaching! Shape up or ship out, soldier! Pull yourself together! There's no room in this man's army for pantywaists like you, Bannister!" Streicher let loose with a rich cascade of laughter. Being around Gordy always brought back the old days, *the good old days, the fun days.* Unlike his friend, Streicher didn't disdain beaurocratic work, but he did tire at times of all the stuff shirts in Washington. Not that he would ever let on about it.

Streicher's route to the top was classic. Second in his class at Annapolis, captain of a cruiser, and later Commander-in-Chief, Pacific Command, he played by all the rules. Yet, he still found a way to respectfully voice his dissenting opinion to superiors if he felt there was a better way of doing something. If his superiors disagreed, so be it. Streicher was ideally unselfish, a consummate team player. Basically he saw the military as one big team on which everybody played a role.

He tilted back in his chair and gazed out his office window. Streicher had the utmost respect for all those countless people down there, filing in and out of the Pentagon's River Entrance. They too were part of the team, be they mid-level paper pushers, computer operators, or secretaries. He picked up the Defense Intelligence Agency's latest unified intelligence summary from his desk, the same one Paul Calloway, the Secretary of Defense, was getting one floor below.

"Handling this Pike abduction is just what my men do best, Mac," Bannister said. "It's the kind of low intensity tactical rescue operation Delta and Seal Team-6 are designed for, what we've always trained for. Surely you can see that?"

Streicher put down the summary and sighed. Of course he could see it! That was the problem! Everybody would see it—including Paul Calloway and the President!

"Mac? You do realize the Joint Special Operations Command is best prepared to handle this, don't you?"

"Regrettably, yes. But you should know that I may argue at tomorrow morning's meeting at the White House to hold off on any action, at least for now."

"What! What the hell are you talking about?"

"Gordy, I don't like surprises. Never have. It seems like practically every time special operations forces have been used in the past, something goes wrong. Catastrophically wrong! In 1980, at Desert One in Iran, a chopper hits a C-130 transport. Result—eight dead and many others burned. It was a debacle! We were lucky just to be able to beat a hasty retreat."

"That was a long time ago. A lot has been learned from that. Now there are dry runs and live ammo rehearsals. Now we make sure to always use mechanically sound equipment."

"What about Grenada? Remember Delta's discombobulation at Richmond Hill prison? Communications lines were either down or disastrously slow. It took Navy choppers two hours to come and evacuate the casualties. And the Seals fared no better! Half of their team was ambushed and wiped out while taking Radio Free Grenada. And half the force executing a low-altitude jump from C-130 transports drowned. Then another Seal contingent, God knows why, left their primary communications gear behind on a helicopter. It was a miracle they got through to a Delta squadron over another com set to finally go and get them relief."

"Look, Grenada was a poorly conceived mission from the get go, just like Iran. There were all kinds of command and control screwups. But when Congress passed that 1987 law establishing a unified Special Operations Command at MacDill mandating that both Delta and Seal Team-6 be directed from Fort Bragg—that problem was rectified. You sure as shit know that, Mac!" Bannister buzzed around the office, his jowls quivering and his face bright red.

He stopped and gestured to Streicher, making his points. "In Algiers we were all set to free the hostages on that hijacked jet, but the chicken shit Algerian government never gave us the chance. And the killers on the Achille Lauro? Delta and Seal Team-6 had them surrounded in Italy after our warplanes forced them to land the Egyptian Air plane they were on. But the Italians cut a deal with the terrorists and rather than confront Italian forces, our counterterrorist units were denied again. They're due, Mac—due for their day in the sun! It's just been bad luck, that's all!"

"That's just it, Gordy. In the unpredictable and volatile situations special ops forces are called into, there's never enough advance intelligence, back-up force, or quick-decision making ability to handle what comes up. It takes a huge amount of luck for things to work out right. Just a drop of bad luck and either it all falls down like a house of cards or there's invariably some sort of televized national humiliation."

"I don't understand you, Mac! What do you want, a huge slow build-up like the Gulf War? Well, you can't fuckin' orchestrate everything. Some situations have to be dealt with immediately, swiftly, and surreptitiously. My men are force multipliers who can more than make up the odds against them. That's why they're the best."

Streicher turned away and stared once again at the tiny people below flowing into and out of the Pentagon. He leaned against the window and lightly touched his head to the glass, once, twice.

"Mac?" Bannister said.

"You know what's always bothered me about special ops?" Streicher turned to face his friend. "It's this arrogant feeling of superiority they have. I know they have to think of themselves as better than others to pull off what they do. But then they isolate themselves from the greater military community. After a while they make themselves bigger than the real team. They think of themselves as indispensable. Gordy, I sincerely think Delta and Seals are incredible fighting men. I know they want to do what's best for the country. But they also want to do what's best for themselves—satisfy their macho cravings for adventure, fill up their own egos."

"Mac, what do you think this is, a football or basketball game? Fuck the team spirit and rah rah shit! Why should you care what's going on inside the heads of my guys? I'm tired of how the brass characterize specialized counterterrorist units. 'Troublemakers, chamelions, and thrill seekers,' they say. 'Men with puffed up egos and bulging balls.' And then we get excluded from major military exercises. You talk about Delta and Seals isolating themselves from the military mainstream, but that's a two way street. In the Gulf War we were nothing more than adjuncts on a leash." Bannister's veins throbbed at his temples.

"Mac," Bannister went on more quietly, "not far from here, in this very compound, the Pentagon's National Military Command Center has a crisis action team drawing up scenarios for a coordinated use of force in Sudan. I'm in touch with them, working with them, every single day. Do you know that every single plan of theirs involves using special operations forces? You've gotta know that, for crying out loud! There's no way around it. When diplomatic confrontation fails, we have to come in. *We're the contingency!*"

"The problem," said Streicher, stepping around his desk to put a hand on his his friend's shoulder, "is that you guys—any dangerous military intervention for that matter—should only be a contingency of last resort."

"Good morning, young Mr. Kenny Hoffman. You're up bright and early today. I trust you slept well." The dapper inn keeper at the small, family-owned Kensington Arms was amazingly just as chipper as he'd been at last night's late registration. Quite a feat, considering he'd probably hardly budged from, and could only doze in, his cushioned, wooden chair.

"Slept great, thanks. Didn't get a chance to see anything last night so I thought I'd make it a full day of sightseeing." The young tourist adjusted a day pack that was slung over his shoulder and then turned his New England Patriots cap around, pressing its bill against his neck.

The lobby of the Victorian Bed and Breakfast was decorated with dark-stained wood furniture and brass lamp fixtures. Entering the breakfast lounge, the young tourist ordered a "standard English breakfast, no bacon" from a sleepy-eyed girl. After he'd eaten a bowl of corn flakes and eggs over toast, he neatly folded a map of London into his coat pocket and left the Kensington Arms.

Zvi's old *Sayeret Matkal* army friend, Alan, had been a tremendous help. Zvi knew not to ask about his sources, but somehow Alan had provided him with the fake passport and fake driver license of a 'Kenneth Hoffman.' "But it's only temporary," he'd cautioned. "If you run into any trouble, it'll take only about seventy-two hours for local police to check, through Interpol, with authorities of the city of origin of this passport. They'll determine that the identity is groundless."

After obtaining Charlie Hammami's name from Farouk Mandeb, Zvi again had looked to Alan for help. "Call me back in three hours," Alan said. When Zvi did call back there was interesting news, disturbing news, waiting for him.

"Address: 6 Cottage Place, Knightsbridge. Fifty-six years old. Big time financial supporter of fundamentalist causes." And then there was a pause, a sigh really, that came clearly over the phone. "At one time owned a villa in Algiers. *The villa in Algiers.* The one you once visited." Zvi gasped. "Are you alright?" Alan asked. "You okay?" Zvi quickly hung up the pay phone.

Cottage Place turned out to be a quiet, dead-end street, but it did spill into the busy junction of Brompton and Cromwell roads. That was where Zvi now positioned himself. He sat at a bus stop opposite Cottage Place, a young American tourist amongst scores of British citizenry on their way to work.

A bright red double-decker pulled up and half of the rush-hour commuters at the stop climbed in. Zvi remained seated at his vantage point, looking straight down Cottage Place, occasionally glacing at a tourist book on his lap. Zvi knew that if Hammami was going to leave his mansion, one that was surely protected by an elaborate alarm system, he eventually would have to come his way either by car or on foot.

Another double-decker approached the stop, followed minutes later by a single-decker, and then a double-decker. Still there was no movement from the house. Forty-five minutes had passed. Too long to idly sit in one spot without arousing suspicion. A woman sitting nearby, a closed umbrella on her lap, was eyeing him.

"Excuse me, maa'm." Zvi scratched his head. "If I'm looking at my map and book correctly, that's the Brompton Oratory across the way, isn't it?" He pointed at a lavish 19th-century Italian-style chapel of the English Roman Catholic revival.

"That's right," the woman nodded. "I live in this neighborhood and attend Mass there. It's worth your while to visit. The Twelve Apostles in the nave are carved from the most exquisite marble. The whole interior is quite ornate." The woman leaned back to get a better look at him. "You on holiday?"

"Sure am. From Boston." The woman was getting nosy, and Zvi was not at all interested in religious adornments. "Must be some view from the top, I suppose?"

"Well, from the belfry there may be. That's where the bells are."

"I'll go over and have a look. Thank you for your help."

The chapel's vast interior was humming with activity. A service was being conducted in front and tourists solemnly walked about its gilded periphery. At the foot of a staircase, Zvi saw a sign to the *Carilon Bells*. He ran up several flights to a scaffolding holding a set of the large bells. Nobody else was about.

Zvi peered through a stone lattice outer wall and at that moment saw two teenage girls exit from the Hammami household below. They hugged their school books in front of them and got into the back seat of a black sedan that had pulled in front of the house. Zvi surmised that Hammami would not be chauffeuring his daughters, or at least he hoped he wouldn't. The car eased away from the curb.

Suddenly the mansion's front door opened. A silver-haired, well-dressed man took several steps down the walk and then turned around. He glanced down at his watch and yelled back to a middle-aged bespectacled man in the doorway. Then the man began to walk away from the house.

Zvi sprang to his feet and raced down the stairway. As he hit the bottom landing he slowed to a walk and casually continued out of the church. He picked up the trail on Brampton Rd., fifty feet behind the well-dressed man.

The man walked to Harrods and, checking his watch once again, went into the huge store. He headed straight for an Art Nouveau tiled Food Hall and read a paper, pausing occasionally to savor a scone and a cup of tea. He took no notice of the young tourist on the far side of the Hall.

Nor did the silver-haired man observe Zvi when he later strolled along the sandy track of Rotton Row, by the Serpentine lake of Hyde Park. The man appeared to be much too absorbed for that. Every so often he would stop and squint into the bright sun, clasp his hands together, and revel in the glorious path that opened up before him. Then he would go on his way again.

Just before he would have arrived at Royal Albert Hall, the man turned down Exhibition Road. On his right were the Science and Natural History museums. On his left, the Victoria and Albert museum. He went into the V & A. Zvi was very close now.

"Top of the morning, Mr. Hammami." The man in the ticket booth tipped an imaginary hat.

"Good morning, Alfred." As a patron of the museum Hammami did not purchase a ticket. Zvi dug three pounds out of his pocket, keeping one eye on the figure up ahead.

Hammami headed straight for Room 42, the Islamic Gallery on the Ground Floor. Prayer mats from around the world were carefully exhibited along one end of the room. The rest of the chamber was devoted to a gargantuan rug. Hammami clasped his hands behind his back, in apparent awe of the treasure. He abruptly turned to his right, and then looked back over to his left.

"*Allahu Akbar!* Incredible, what? It's from a Persian mosque in the year 1540, from a time when Islam was so confident of its greatness that it went untouched by the rest of the world. It's called the Ardabil Carpet, the largest in the world."

Zvi's heart skipped and then bucked. "Sure is amazing."

"Imagine the magic carpet ride this could take you on. Why, every conceivable dream one ever had could be fulfilled. Any prayer in the world would be answered from such an extraordinary carpet." Catching himself, Hammami apologetically bowed his head and made rapid outward gestures with his hand. "Oh, I'm sorry. Usually I can share my enthusiasm with a friend, a friend who should have been here by now. But unfortunately for you, you're the only person in the gallery to hear my ramblings."

He only wanted to make conversation. Share his excitement with somebody. Zvi at last drew in a breath. But his adrenalin was surging.

"Well, I'm off to the *loo*. If you see a gentleman of my age come by, please tell him I'll be but a minute."

Hammami left the gallery and went into a lavatory in the hallway. Except for an old watchman clucking to himself outside the doorway at the other end of the gallery, there was an empty silence. And an auspicious, tantalizing opportunity. Reacting impulsively, Zvi headed directly for the washroom.

As soon as the door closed behind him, Zvi sensed a lethal breath at his back. He tensed. He dropped his knees. He swiveled his head. But Hammami was all over him, precipitately riding him into a jolting crash with a sink. Flipped over backwards, Zvi grabbed hold of Hammami's forearm, but the shiny point of a switch blade knife was inexorably inching downward.

"Allahu Akbar!" Hammami muttered through tight lips. He had the awesome strength of one whose deranged mind is throttled up—way up. "I know you! I know who you are!"

There was only one thing Zvi could do. He allowed himself to slip off the sink. He slammed onto the floor in a heap, absorbing the full weight of his attacker. Hammami bit his arm, kicked him in the groin, scratched at his face. But Hammami no longer had the unfair advantage of surprise, nor was Zvi any longer caught in an a doubled back position.

Zvi kicked Hammami right back, poked him in an eye, loosened his grip on the blade by yanking his little finger backwards. Then he rolled his adversary over and took possesion of the knife.

"Who am I? *Who am I?*" screamed Zvi as he shook Hammami and slammed his head into the floor.

"The footballer's Jew friend," cursed Hammami. "The one in his book, the one from my Algiers house."

"Is he in Kober? Answer!"

"Kober, yes. He's waiting for you…"

"Who has him?"

Suddenly the lavatory door opened and a bespectacled man entered. *The one from Hammami's mansion!* The man's face blanched. He froze in his tracks.

"Help me, Alec!" yelled Hammami. "Tomas?" he implored, "please."

The man's eyes fluttered. He turned and began running for the door. *He will come—will come for us!*

"Shit!" Zvi plunged the knife into Hammami's chest and took off after the man. Like a predator chasing mismatched prey, Zvi caught the man in three easy bounds. It was only upon driving the blade into the man's back that Zvi realized the knife was still in his hand. The man's glasses fell off and, curiously, so did a salt and pepper toupee. All at once the man looked completely different. Zvi dragged him back into the washroom. Dropping the knife, he looked about, horrified at the carnage before him.

Zvi washed the blood off his hands and picked up his day pack. He hastily left the museum and when he rounded the corner onto Cromwell Road he bolted into a headlong flight, trying to outrun his rampaging mind.

The legal attache on the fourth floor of the U.S. Embassy held the telephone away from his ear and shook his head while looking at Scotland Yard's preliminary report of the crime scene. As a *legat* for the FBI, Jim Sanderson had been working with the British Police, M15 and M16, ever since the Bureau first determined that Tomas Bahr had fled to England. As the man who'd put together the team that killed Brian Sullivan, the young limo driver, and kidnapped Zach Pike, Bahr was a condemned man, a "most wanted" fugitive who now, finally, had been found.

"Jim, hold on," the Washington aide said. "I'll put you through to Lee Nunzio. He'd kill me if I didn't."

Nunzio came on the line, asking what was up.

"Well, it's good news—bad news. The Yard just found Bahr, along with a drug lord named Charlie Hammami."

"And?"

"Well, the bad news is that they're both dead. And as the British over here like to say, '*It's a bloody mess.*'"

CHAPTER NINETEEN

*M*andeb!

It was his first thought, a natural connection, on learning of Charlie Hammami's murder.

But as Amir Kasawi found out more about the strange and gruesome events taking place in Europe, a different picture began taking shape in his mind. First came the incredible news from friends in Budapest's Iranian embassy that Mandeb himself was dead, his neck broken in a bath house, *before Charlie Hammami was ever killed.*

Then tidbits of information from a paid source in British Police began to filter in. Scotland Yard was looking for a suspect, an American tourist identified by the inn-keeper of a Bed and Breakfast, and by a woman at a bus stop, as the young man later seen fleeing from the V&A museum. The man registered at the inn as *Kenneth Hoffman*, but it was becoming clear that the identity was phony. The Boston passport agency had no records of issuing a passport to any *Kenneth Hoffman* matching the particulars of the young tourist, and there wasn't any *Kenneth Hoffman* seen in England after the incident. He'd vanished, no doubt leaving the country by use of yet another passport. The only trace of personal evidence the suspect left behind was a cap, *an American football cap!*

The picture in Kasawi's mind was crystalizing. He began seeing the features of an assasin, the Israeli assasin! The one who was caught on closed circuit video killing Sheik Latif in Hammami's Algiers villa. The one whose features were those of the football-playing boy he had seen in the book Charlie Hammami had sent him.

Langer!

What was he up to?

Apparently the information about Kober prison that the Ethiopian, Meles Tekele, had been forced to provide the Mossad was not enough of a lead for the Israeli. He was now confirming the tip by interrogating sources, so to speak, in Europe. He was now learning all he could about the circumstances surrounding Zach Pike's abduction. He was now undoubtedly learning not only where his friend was held, but also *why*, and by *whom*. Zvi Langer would now not only be especially cautious, he would now be especially dangerous.

All at once Kasawi shuddered.

He was nearing a crisis situation and it didn't help any to know that one of his few remaining allies was somebody like the Mahdi. Kasawi watched him now with his straw skullcap and his bemused, crazy smile, lying face down as he recited the *Shahada,* the profession of faith. With his all-encompassing piety, the Mahdi was the perfect individual to entrust with Zach Pike. Discord with internal rivals would not arise as long as the American was in the custody of such a non-threatening holy man.

For a moment Kasawi wished that he too had the ability to so totally immerse himself, in spirituality and religion, that outside political forces and events had no special meaning. His heart ached as he realized he could not. His destiny was to restore Islam to its once glorious position by any and all means at his disposal. Like Charlie Hammami, he believed that the only way of doing that was by returning to the religion's fundamentalist roots.

But actual piety? Religious Zeal? That sadly would have to be left for others.

"My esteemed Mahdi," said Kasawi as his ally approached, "I won't trouble you with mundane details, other than to say that the news is not favorable. The Israeli has butchered a friend of mine."

"That means, however, that the Israeli swine is coming ever closer to us."

"Yes, no doubt he is. It is in our best interests to be especially vigilant in guarding our captive at this point in time."

"And what of the Americans' freeing of Sheik Omar Abdel Rahman and the rest of our brothers? Those who were involved with the World Trade Center bombing and the planned bombing of the United Nations and the tunnels? If there is no movement, should not another demand for their freedom be made by the Ansar Army?"

So, the poor Mahdi still actually thought the demand for Rahman's freedom was sincere, that it was attainable. Perhaps it would be best to keep the naive fool occupied, to continue to string him along. "Yes, by all means, go ahead and send another message by way of the television station." *What harm could it do now?*

Kasawi removed his sunglasses and cleaned the lenses with a handkerchief. Then he placed them delicately back onto the bridge of his nose. In his own mind he viewed himself as a reasonable man, a practical man. For him the whole Pike escapade never was about reprisals against Zvi Langer or about obtaining the release of Sheik Rahman. The only reason he had approved of Charlie Hammami's plan was to keep him content, to assure that Hammami's sizable remittances would keep coming in. But now, with Hammami dead, *now what?* Who would supply him with the resources he needed? Iran?

Kasawi sat straight back in his chair, unhappy with the prospect. Support from a friend was always preferable to that of a state. A friend's support was personal and based on loyalty, whereas the support from another country could change in an instant. *How to assure that the pipeline spigots from Iran stayed open? How best to utilize Zach Pike now? How best to salvage the situation?*

If only the American sportsman could have confirmed that his father did indeed provide Israel with defense-related advances—if only Zach Pike had known details of his father's secrets—then that would have been a bone to throw at Iran. But alas, Zach Pike apparently did not know. Otherwise he could never have silently endured the tortures of the whip and the *shebba*.

Kasawi stood up and walked out of Khartoum's Al-Kabir mosque. In the distant horizon to his left, an early morning sun began to rise. On his right, the fading silhouette of the moon descended into oblivion. The image was like a revelation.

The fortunes of Zach Pike would have to rise, would have to get better! Of that he was positive. It was best to rid himself of the American Football player. It was best not to get the United States upset. Perhaps he could even convince those fools in America that he initially knew nothing about Pike's kidnapping—that he'd actually interceded and won the sportsman's release?

But as for Zvi Langer, Kasawi was just as certain what his fate should be. He must kill the Israeli; *no, better yet bring him down by capturing him!* He could hand Langer over to Iran and further convince the mullahs there just how helpful an ally Sudan was, especially under his direction. Langer would be an asset to Iran—*a caged trophy!* He could even be a valuable bargaining chip for Iran should it ever have to do business with Israel.

Perhaps it would all still work out for the best? Perhaps the situation was yet salvageable? Perhaps?

"Hurley! Howard!" beckoned President Earl. "Come on over here for a moment?"

Hurley Baker and Howard Jones had been engaged in just one of many mini-confeences taking place in the Oval Office before the start of the National Security Council meeting. But they now stopped their discussion and headed over to the grandfather clock in the corner where the President and Lee Nunzio stood.

"I want to get your take on what Lee has just told me." The President nodded in Nunzio's direction.

"I was just saying that our FBI *legat* in London has learned from Scotland Yard that Tomas Bahr has been found. He was murdered along with a friend of his named Charlie Hammami. There has been no arrest yet."

"Hammami?" mumbled Jones. "That name is familiar, but I can't quite place it."

"Wasn't Kasawi's biggest rival Farouk Mandeb?" offered Baker. "Maybe he had them killed?"

"Sorry," said Nunzio, "but Mandeb's dead also. Killed in Budapest."

"What's interesting," said Earl, "is that Lee informs me that a certain book has been found in Hammami's house. It's about Zach Pike—the title is **Pike's Peak**. Apparently Hammami drew a big circle around a picture of Zach Pike as a boy, a picture where he's with family and friends on Cape Cod. Pike is circled as if he's targeted."

"What we're wondering," said Nunzio, "is whether the circle indicates that Hammami knew about the kidnapping? Did he even help direct it, and if so, why? Any ideas?"

Baker shrugged. But Jones' face suddenly brightened. "You know, I'll have to check it out, but it seems to me that three or four years ago the Israelis took out the Algiers home of somebody named Hammami and killed a visiting Egyptian Sheik."

The President momentarily pondered Jones' recollection. All at once Nunzio grabbed the President's arm and nearly whirled him around. "Do you suppose that the Israelis, knowing that Charlie Hammami was involved in abducting Pike, killed Hammami as a message? As a way of saying, 'Hey, if you took Zach Pike as a way of punishing Ben Pike for having spied for us, then think again.' As a way of saying, 'You had better release Zach Pike because we can find you and punish you.'"

"What are you talking about?" Baker asked, his eyebrows raised. "What do you mean spying for Israel?"

"I'll explain later," snapped the President, annoyed by Nunzio's lack of discretion. Unlike Nunzio, he was mindful that the CIA was still in the dark concerning the FBI-Justice Department suspicions of Ben Pike.

As Baker and Jones went for a cup of coffee, Nunzio loosened his grip on Earl's arm. "There's just one other thing that I need to tell you, Mr. President. A convention organizer for the Association for Unmanned Vehicle Systems received a bogus call from an individual who tried to find out if Ben Pike would be attending an upcoming convention. The individual let slip his post office box number but not the location. We checked out box numbers around the country and we suspect the box is in Rockefeller Plaza."

"Figures," Earl gruffly said. "That's where this whole calamity with Pike first started."

"Actually, I didn't even consider that." Nunzio, oblivious to the President's irritation, tightened his grip. "At any rate, the owner of the box is Ibrahim Husseini, an illegal immigrant with no previous record according to our National Crime Information Center. We are investigating, but we have not as yet confronted this Husseini because we thought it best to follow him for a while."

"So what you're thinking is that the Arabs are after Ben Pike because of his assistance to Israel? His *spying* for Israel, as you phrased it just a minute ago, with that brilliant theory of yours about Israel killing Hammami as retribution for harming Ben Pike's kid?" Earl was trying to control his anger but his face was by now hot red. "Listen, I don't care if every thought you have, every lead you pursue, points an accusatory finger at Ben Pike. As I warned you and Attorney General Lopes before, until you come up with *real* proof—not theories, not coincidences—you better keep them to yourself. You better be careful! Don't ever again throw your potentially harmful ideas around in earshot of other people who do not yet have a need to know!"

And then, just as members and invitees to the National Security Council meeting turned away from their small group conversations to see what all the commotion was about, the President of the United States jerked his arm away from the grip of Lee Nunzio.

"As we kick off this meeting," announced the President, still red-faced and tense, "I understand Eileen has a CNN broadcast to show us. It aired just minutes ago so as yet I have not seen it myself."

The President's secretary put a video cassette into a VCR and dimmed the lights as she left the Oval Office. All eyes were turned towards a console of monitors against the wall. It was almost an exact replay of how the last National Security Council meeting had begun.

The spokesman, dressed in traditional caftan, sat erect and spoke in a monotone. "We, the Sudanese Ansar Army, are a benevolent and patient society of freedom fighters. All we want is justice; the God-given right to throw off the West's yoke of oppression and win the release of our brothers from your jails. But our previously reasonable claims have fallen on deaf ears, numb minds, and stone hearts. There remains no recourse other than to shake the tyrants out of their stupor. To that end, we put you on alert that our patience is frayed. Due to your indifferent idleness, the life of Zach Pike now dangles from an exceedingly thin thread. Due to your cruel manipulations, soon other lives will almost certainly hang from precarious threads as well."

When the spokesman on the video finished reading his remarks, all those in attendance silently watched President Earl sit down behind his *Resolute Desk*. He took his time, deliberately tidying up a hodgepodge of items that lay scattered across the top of the desk. Folders were put away in a corner. Loose pages were straightened out and placed in a drawer. A pen was dropped into its desk set holder. The process of finding just the right place for everything was excruciatingly slow.

Braiding his fingers together on his cleared away desk, Earl looked directly at his staff. As they waited for a reassuring nod and encouraging words, they were jolted by the flashing glint in his eyes, by the crackle in his voice.

"I won't be blackmailed. We will not be threatened. We must not succumb.

"From the very start of this tragedy, our policy has been not to surrender, and God help us if we cave in now. No matter how much we value the life of every individual, concern for the well-being of the many takes precedence. We would be commiting a great disservice to the citizens of this country if we now abandoned that conviction."

He paused, then went on. "The planned focus of this meeting was to discuss a possible combat rescue mission. Especially in light of the new threats we've just heard, our agenda takes on extra urgency. But let me make it clear that whatever course we embark on today will be determined not solely by Zach Pike's best interest, but the nation's best interest." He let out a breath. "Why don't we get things rolling with a brief assesment of Sudanese military capabilities."

"Sudan has an aging and largely inoperative array of weaponry," Paul Calloway, Secretary of Defense, began. "Most of it is a jumble of old Soviet, Chinese, British, French, and yes, American merchandise. Their two main air bases, one in Khartoum International and the other in Wadi Sayyidna north of Omdurman, have squadrons flying F-5's and J-6's. They carry Soviet Atoll and American Sidewinders. Those same bases have antiaircraft guns but they're antiquated, just like their SAM's. A small base in Port Sudan flies a few Casa C-212's for limited reconnaissance over the Red Sea."

"None of this sounds very imposing. What about the quality of their personnel?" Lou Reed asked.

"Pilot proficiency is limited by constant mechanical problems and fuel shortages. As far as morale goes, it's terrible throughout the military, primarily because of the seemingly endless and exhaustive conflict with the Christian south."

"The only soldiers with any skill or spirit, the only ones treated well by the government," Mac Sreicher added, "are those of an Airborne Division at Khartoum International. They're the only ones who would put up a fight against superior American forces because they have something riding on the outcome."

"Satellite photos plus information from a non official cover in Khartoum indicates a modest build up of soldiers around Kober prison. Normally, only middle-aged civilian guards would be present there. Do you think those soldiers are from that Airborne Division?" Howard Jones asked.

"I don't know," Streicher said, "I suppose if they were it……"

"It doesn't make any difference," Gordy Bannister interrupted. "Joint Special Operations Command forces of Delta and Seal Team-6 specialize in extricating captured soldiers from impossible predicaments. According to reports from the Defense Intelligence Agency and intelligence-military affairs analysts of the CIA's Task Force, freeing Pike from Sudan is not an especially daunting assignment. Not for my men, at any rate."

"How would you go about the rescue?" Reed asked.

"The exact details of three or four possible plans are being analyzed in conjunction with the Pentagon's National Military Command Center even as we speak. But suffice it to say that all the scenarios involve stealth in inserting forces in and around the arena, surprise assault, and rapid extraction."

Alfred Brown, Secretary of State, cleared his throat. The President, Nunzio noticed, hadn't asked Brown to share his views. Lou Reed, the National Security Adviser, now had the President's ear when it came to running the foreign policy of the country. Reed was Oliver Earl's longtime friend, his appointed director of the Council, and as such the *de facto* Secretary of State. Especially no more so than in times of crisis, times like this. After years of dedicated service to the country, after a lifetime of experience, Brown was being bypassed.

"From the tenor of this discussion," Brown said, "it sounds like a forgone conclusion that military force will be used. Before we get locked into that course of action, I think we should stop and evaluate a different plan of attack. Mr. President, I know the emissary we sent to Sudan has been unsuccesful in obtaining cooperation from President Al-Omri. He denies any knowledge of the abduction and incarceration of Pike, and thus can absolve himself from providing assistance. But should we not confront him with the mounting body of evidence we have, evidence proving his and Kasawi's knowledge and sanction of this crime? In the strongest language possible we can impress on him that he had better stop assisting the terrorists and release Pike. Does it not behoove us to at least try this strategy before putting our boys in harm's way?"

Brown's concluding remarks were greeted by a chilly silence. As Brown lowered his eyes, help came from a surprising ally.

"I agree with Secretary of State Brown." Streicher conspicuously threw a sidelong look Bannister's way. "I'm no expert in diplomatic maneuverings, but I am well versed in the pitfalls of rash military ventures. Despite what the head of the Joint Special Opertions Command tells you, freeing Zach Pike will not be easy. There is always inherent risk involved in special operations, and there is always a cost. While I have the utmost confidence in the abilities of Delta and Seals, I think they should only be used when all other means have been exhausted."

"Look," Reed said, "even if we confront Sudan with our evidence, they'll only continue to deny knowing anything. Plus they'll know we're onto them. To a certain extent they'll render our intelligence over there useless. And what's worse, we'll have no element of surprise should we use special ops. If they're alerted, it wouldn't surprise me if they moved Pike just to throw us off. This would put Pike in even greater danger."

"Exactly!" Calloway looked at Bannister, his former Pentagon military assistant, and gave a supportive nod. Bannister, in turn, glared at Streicher. "Counterterrorist forces can take care of this problem now,"

Calloway said. "Why hold them back? Why allow Sudan to move Zach Pike or be more prepared for our raid? It seems to me we have a rare opportunity to use our elite forces. In so many other situations we've had to get consent from a foreign government before we could take action on their soil. In this instance we don't need Sudan's okay because it's clear there has been dupilcity on the part of their government. They've been acting in compliance with the fundamentalists anyway."

"Mr. President," said Bannister jumpimg into the fray, "in Delta and Seal Team-6 we have the most highly trained assemblage of soldiers in the world. What is the sense of having and financing them if at this, the most opportune and ideal time for their involvement, we do not call on them?"

All eyes were riveted on the President. From the firm set of his shoulders Nunzio guessed that Oliver Earl had made up his mind.

"As a proud and sovereign nation," the President said slowly, "the United States has always cherished its right to stick to principles. And what we embrace, what we love, above all else, is freedom. Since our inception, we have been willing to fight for the right to be free. *Don't tread on us!*" Earl clenched his fists as he pronounced the words. Now he turned to his advisors.

"Lou, Paul, Gordy. I agree with you about using special operations forces, and not warning Sudan first. But not for the reasons you gave.

"We have been attacked and lied to! Issuing warnings and threats is simply not a viable option under such circumstances. What we must do is respond—*take action*—on *our* own terms, at a time of *our* choosing.

"There is a line, a line of honor and decency, from which one cannot retreat. And that line must be vigilantly defended. No doubt the line is shifting, flexible,ambiguous. But it is real, nevertheless." Earl lifted his chin.

"Friends, that line has now been crossed so many times that it would not be an exaggeration to say that we have been violated. *We must defend ourselves.*"

CHAPTER TWENTY

*F*BI Special Agents Mark Hriniak and Lionel Lane walked up the now familiar flagstone pathway. An old wreath still hung from the door of the Brookline Georgian Colonial, its green holiday hue having by now faded to a silvery sage. Even the pipe organ doorbell seemed to ring solemnly and deliberately. Each long day toppled into the next like dominoes in a line.

Hriniak rang the bell again.

"Good morning Mark, Lionel," Ben Pike mechanically said. His eyes were glazed, his every movement a willful summoning of his energies. There was no fluidity anymore.

Tranquilizers? thought Hriniak.

Or was it just a question of hunkering down, coping with the ordeal by focusing on one task at a time, one thought at a time, one minute at a time? Was it just a matter of buffering himself by seeing only the detail and not the picture?

Not even Ben knew the answer. All he understood was that he had lapsed into an intimate groove, one that he had traversed, *so many years ago.*

"May we come in?"

"Oh, I'm sorry. Sure, come on in."

The house was empty. Mary was visiting at Teddy and Jill's. The grandchildren kept her occupied. Sam and Liz had returned to their homes and jobs.

A model World War II *Phantom* and *Thunderbolt* were drying on some newspapers in the den. For a change, the big screen t.v. was not only not set to CNN, it wasn't even turned on.

"When are you going to return to work, Mr. Pike?"

"I don't know. Lexington Labs doesn't seem to be in any rush. They must be getting on just fine without me."

"What about that big Unmanned Vehicle convention that's going to be taking place in Alabama? You going to that?" Lane adjusted his wireframe glasses.

"Don't know. Should I?"

"At least it would get you out of the house for a couple of days. It would probably do you some good."

"Maybe it would at that."

"Mr. Pike, we wanted to let you know that the man who organized Zach's kidnapping, Tomas Bahr…" He paused. "We found him dead…"

While Lane talked to Pike about the details, Hriniak excused himself and left the den, ostensibly heading for a bathroom. Once he was outside of the den, he altered his direction, and quietly made his way to the study.

Hriniak removed a small screwdriver from his coat pocket and pried open the back of Pike's PC. Working quickly now, he inserted a radio-activated bug that could be signaled to complete a circuit and remotely turn on the PC. The Bureau's Computer Analysis and Response Team would be able to break any code or password that might have been installed. It would have access to all of Ben's files.

Replacing the final screw, Hriniak's keen eyes scanned the study. He leafed through a personal telephone book and a report on the *Vulture* boost phase intercept Unmanned Aerial Vehicle. Tiny tripods automatically sprung out from an equally tiny 35 mm Nikon camera. Holding the camera six inches from the pages, the Nikon's macrolens captured entire pages.

Click, click, click, click, click—Done.

Hriniak wasn't through. There was something else he sought. Something about…Israel.

There!

On the bookcased wall, a volume about Israel. Next to it, a pictorial history of WWII. And between them, wedged in, a very thin, worn, brown leather booklet. He reached for it, opened to a page of closely scribbled lines.

Ben Pike's war diary!

Hriniak's eyes absorbed random pages as fast as his fingers could turn them. Without regard for consequences, without really thinking, he set the diary before the camera.

Click, click, click, click, click. And done.

Hriniak snuck out of the study and made sure to flush the toilet in the bathroom on his way back to the den.

Time elapsed? Ten minutes.

"Geez, Mark," Lane said, "lay off the fast food."

"It's the fries—they don't agree with me."

"Well, anyway Mr. Pike," Lane turned back to Ben, "just thought you should know about Bahr and where the FBI stands with its investigation."

"Thanks for keeping me up to date. It's appreciated."

Stopping at the front door, the two FBI men abruptly turned. Hriniak rested his hand on Ben's shoulder and said what he always did after one of these visits. "We want you to know that our prayers are with you. Lionel and I really are pulling for you and Zach, as hard as we can."

"Honey, come to bed already. You're exhausted!"

"In a while, dear. There's a little more work I have to do." Lee Nunzio kissed his wife Judy good-night, knowing that in a matter of seconds she would be fast asleep. Another day with their four rambunctious kids had worn her out, flying by in a non-stop rush of cooking, laundry, errands—and lots of love.

Nunzio turned down the light and began his customary rounds.

His thirteen-year-old, Brady, was in a growth spurt, his gangly feet edging over the mattress. Looking at his face, Nunzio sadly noted that a certain innocence was fading, transforming into hardness, almost before his very eyes, under the haunting watchful gaze of a football poster of Zach Pike over Brady's bed.

In the next room, secure under a pink and blue comforter pulled right up to her chin, ten-year-old Allison smiled in her sleep, a sweet angelic expression. *God Bless.*

But as for Stuart, who'd just turned eight, he tossed and moaned in his bed, despite the awesome protection of several Mighty Morphin Power Rangers. Nunzio sighed. Stuart had been having nightmares lately, of Boogey men, crazy men, bad men. A nite-lite burned at his bedside and the door to his room was kept wide open.

In the last room, curled up in her Disney characters nighty, Lisa hugged her fuzzy, white teddy bear tightly. At the morning's first light she would be running all over the house, describing her dreams with a four-year-old lisp, jumping for the sheer joy of another day.

From the kitchen a kettle whistled and Nunzio went to pour himself a cup of cocoa. From upstairs, Stuart moaned and Nunzio bolted to attention. But right in front of him, on the kitchen table, prints of Ben Pike's war diary again demanded the most attention of all.

December 15, 1944

Ten days to Christmas! All the guys seem to have a plan, if not a dream.

Jesse's going to open a diner. Billy's most definitely ready to marry Alice the moment he gets back to Philly. Hal is just plain gonna get piss drunk and get himself laid. Me? Well, I don't really know. All I really want to do is get back home to Richmond and be with family for awhile. Maybe, in time, I'll go to college, I suppose. I really don't know.

It's just like the Second Division told us it would be, right before they pulled out of this forest in Belgium. It's called the Ardennes. A picnic! they said. A ghost front! Nothing's out there! By now the Germans have retreated to Berlin, we're all sure of it.

All we did today is drill a little bit, feast on blackberries, and go sledding in the snow. All the guys here—we're the 106th Infantry Division—curse that we finished high school a few months too late. We missed out on the chance to see any real action. The older units had Normandy and a parade down the Champs—Elysee to the Place de la Concorde. All we get is a chance to get our feet wet so that we won't be quite as green as the evergreens around here.

I'm going to try to make myself comfortable in tonight's foxhole. Meanwhile, I can't help but marvel at how pretty and peaceful it all is.

December 16, 1944

They did it! I don't know how, but those fucking, Nazi bastards did it!

First came a light artillery barrage. Sarge said it was only a spoiling attack. But then it started getting worse and worse. Blue 88's and *screaming meanies* at the rate of 600 shells a minute!

The Germans are all over us like wild men! Basically, we're overwhelmed. Overrun! It's total chaos. Seasoned officers are running around panic stricken and nobody knows who's in charge.

Our company was 200 men just yesterday. I keep hearing that we're down to about 60 now. All I know is that Jesse's dead and Hal's missing.

December 18, 1944

"We have to hold them!" That's what they keep screaming at us now. At least until Patton's 4th Armored comes up from the south. At least until the 101st Airborne can get to the village of Bastogne.

The Germans are forming a bulge in our ranks. They're splitting us and pushing towards Paris. I've heard some of the brass call this the Battle of the Bulge.

We're running out of ammo, supplies, and medicine. The weather has taken a turn for the worse and they can't get us fresh supplies or any relief! Still, they keep shouting, "We have to hold them!"

But we're falling apart.

Today we left some wounded at an aid station with only a medic to watch over them. Basically, we abandoned them. "We can't get you out of here," is what we actually said. Can you imagine?

Reports and rumors fly around here just like the blowing snow. "Thousands are surrendering to the Krauts every day." "The German troops are well fed and well supplied." A little bird tells me that the rumors are all true.

The tables have turned. Just three days ago we thought we were after them. Instead, it turns out they're after us.

December 20, 1944

I left my foxhole for an instant, but Billy didn't.

I pushed his guts back in, but they slowly came back out.

I punched Billy as hard as I could, but he didn't lose conciousness.

I held his jaw, took my helmet off, and whacked him with it, but that didn't work either.

Before my eyes, Billy froze to death; bled to death.

All the while, as I held him in my arms, he cried out for his mother.

December 21, 1944

Today it really started snowing! All the planes are grounded. We're so cut off. So isolated.

The night is the worst of all. We're all so terribly afraid of it. It's then that we're left to our imaginations. We hear everything, but see nothing. All night long somebody nearby cries or screams, guys slipping into insanity, or death.

A twig snaps, the snow crunches. We convince ourselves that the enemy is sneaking up; that he's 20 yards away! We don't know, but for all we know, he really is. Maybe he's even closer, *much closer than that?*

December 23, 1944

Hallelujah! The weather's breaking. Supplies are being dropped in. We can hear the good guys pounding away with their bombs a few miles up ahead.

We're also hearing that the 101st—those "Battered, Bastards of Bastogne"—have miraculously held onto Bastogne somehow. God, they're tough. But I think when this is all said and done, we of the 106th are as well. And the same goes for the 28th, the 424th, the 99th, the 83rd, everybody.

It's turning now. I know it. Soon we're going to punish the Germans. We're gonna kill em.

December 26, 1944

For Christmas they brought in some turkey and fudge, and we all sang *Silent Night, Holy Night.*

But it wasn't.

Those damn *screaming meanies* send shivers up and down my spine. I would have thought I'd be getting used to them by now. Instead, the more often I hear them, the worse it gets.

Patton reached Bastogne today. That ass-kicker had his men on the move night and day. I guess it could have been worse—I could have been in his outfit!

December 29, 1944

I think Generals Eisenhower, Bradley, and Montgomery are shell-shocked. Instead of cutting in back of the enemy, to "bag" them like Patton wants to do, they've decided we're going to push the bulge back. *We're going to slug it out! Eyeball to eyeball, inch by inch.*

"Pick up and move, pick up and move." The problem is that it takes us a whole day to advance 500 yards! And once we cover those 500 yards we have to try and dig another foxhole into the frozen ground. Locals claim this is the worst winter ever in these parts.

December 31, 1944

Happy New Year!

January 5, 1945

We're freezing to death. Every night it's below zero. Maybe we're getting 2 hours of sleep a night, if that. Every few minutes I wake up and knock my feet together. Guys who don't do that have their feet or toes swell up and turn black. "Trench Foot", they call it.

In the daytime we prop each other up, lower our heads, and sleep while standing. That is when we're not actually sleepwalking. Then we just follow each other into some ditch like ducks all in a row.

January 9, 1945

Every day I lose a buddy, or two, or three. They rush replacements in here who have even less training than we had when the Battle began. They look at us like we're seasoned vets, which I guess by now we are.

At first the new guys are revolted by everything. But soon they too accept that dead and frozen Germans are nothing more than logs to sit on. They're beyond our pity. God, it's cold out here!

January 14, 1945

I don't know how I can go on.

They keep sending us out there like prizefighters, to bash each others brains in. We're spent! We wander around like hollow-eyed zombies, barely seeing fellow soldiers drift by.

We don't walk, we don't run. We shuffle.

We don't see the sky, just the ground. We shuffle.

The seconds of courage are like flashes, few and far between. What we do mostly is just endure all manner of hardship.

We shuffle.

January 18, 1945

If I had the strength, I would crack up.

Last night there was a new guy in my foxhole. Not a pleasant experience.

"We gotta get out of here! We gotta shoot ourselves! We gotta get out of here!"

Well, the Germans are just beyond the fog, maybe 400 yards away. Any real support is behind us about a mile away. And this poor guy is going to pieces on me, a foot away.

Wow, what a night!

January 26, 1945

It's taken us two weeks to cover the last ten miles. It's taken over a month to get back to the starting point and regain the fifty miles we originally lost in the Bulge.

There is no ceremony for us. Nothing to mark the end of the Bulge.

It just goes on. We just go on. And on. And on.

East, East, East.

The Germans are on the run now, and heaven help us if we don't finish them off once and for all.

Go, Go, Go. That's the pep talk. But actually all we can do now is stagger.

I've been reassigned to another unit—the 45th "Thunderbird" Division. I guess it makes sense; there's not very much left of my original one. Anyhow, I don't know what lies ahead. But can it possibly be any worse than the terrible barbarism just past? Not even in my worst dreams could I imagine anything quite like this again.

Upstairs Stuart was crying.

Nunzio went up and sat on his bed. Gently he began to rock him in his arms.

"Shhh. It's okay, Stuie. I'm here. Mommy and I are always here for you."

Stuart was in a deep semi-sleep. He wriggled and puffed and panted, winced and grimaced. His eyeballs thrashed wildly beneath closed eyelids.

"There's nothing to be afraid of. Nobody can harm you. Nobody would ever want to hurt you. God always watches over the little children of the world."

Slowly, as Nunzio watched, Stuart began to calm down. His body stopped fighting. His crying settled into just an occasional sigh. But his eyes kept on fluttering, as if trying to evade some horror.

He tucked Stuart in and went back downstairs to the kitchen. He flipped ahead a couple of pages and resumed reading Pike's diary.

April 29, 1945

My heart hurts, and bursts, and hurts.

My eyes have run rivers, and still I can't stop crying.

I've retched my guts out so often I worry if there's anything left of me; if I am changing from the inside out.

It is April 29, 1945; I am 18 years old and at a place called Dachau, and so much of what had until this point in my life been my life, is now gone. *It's dead.*

This morning, on our advance to Munich, we found one footbridge across a canal of Dachau that still had not been blown up. Crossing it, we came to a railroad line that serviced the concentration camp of Dachau. Our orders were to follow the line and get rid of pockets of SS resistance we encountered along the way.

We were on edge as we neared the camp. Then we came upon about forty open box cars. Suddenly some guys, even the GI's who had been with this Division in the invasion of Italy at Anzio—tough, hard guys—started crying uncontrollably. Some turned away, some stared in shock.

A moment later, I saw it too.

Everywhere, inside and outside the box cars, *all over me*, were the sickening, tangled remains of hundreds of emaciated people. Tatters of striped uniforms hung from their corpses. Yellow Stars of David fluttered over their bodies, as though watching for the vindication of their souls.

The stench knocked me off my feet. From my knees I came face to face with several bodies, heads crushed and brains oozing out from the blows of a rifle butt.

I became very angry.

I don't remember hearing any order, or anything at all for that matter, but somehow I was rushing towards the camp with other soldiers. As we ran, I started to pick up the familiar sound of sporadic enemy gunfire, then my sergeant's commands. Quickly we rounded up 200 prisoners, of whom about 30 were SS.

And then we started to look, again.

Stacked outside something called a crematorium was a very long, high row of bodies. Heads were falling backwards, falling away, in every direction. Mouths were open in a perpetual, silent scream. Eyes were sunken, mesmerizing, suffering. Nobody had died peacefully.

Chalk white stick figures, *phantoms*, began to undulate in our direction. They moved in stops and starts, crumpling every so often. Their bodies were so frail and brittle, their faces so gaunt, that every feature—bones, ears, lips, noses, eyes—were grotesque.

I became very, very angry. We all did.

Suddenly, the tension exploded into pandemonium.

Somebody cut loose with his machine gun and twelve SS prisoners fell to the ground. GI's went berserk, cursing and crying. A General from the 42nd and one of our Lieutenants squared off against each other. Officers were shouting and shoving soldiers around in an effort to keep order. "Simmer Down! Simmer Down!"

But it was too late. Revenge was the only real command that mattered.

One soldier gave a bayonet to a rail-thin survivor and watched him decapitate a guard. Some of the stronger survivors passed German guards over their heads and proceeded to tear them apart with their bare hands. Other survivors taunted their former guards and beat them into a bloody pulp with shovels.

I stood by and did nothing to stop it. Like other GI's, I just let it run its course.

I think I wanted it to happen.

April 30, 1945

This morning the remaining German guards and soldiers have begun working on burial details, carrying corpses on their backs like knapsacks. They slide the corpses into huge pits where they haphazardly fall one on top of another. An arm protrudes here, a leg sticks out there, a head......their fate is all the same. It's hard to imagine what their individual lives were like before *this*.

Their homes? Their families? Their dreams? I don't know.

We all got a chance to tour the camp. I entered one barrack and a skeleton fell to the ground and kissed my boots. Pairs of hollow eyes on a crowded bunk followed me around the room, and mouths strained themselves into wrinkled smiles.

I guess this is my parade, my Champs-Elysee.

Doctors tell us many of these people will die over the next few days of typhus and dysentary. I want to give them my K-Rations, *I want to do something for them*, but the doctors say that's counterproductive. All food is just too rich right now; too much of a shock to the system.

I was taken to a block of rooms where Nazi doctors conducted medical experiments that were supposed to be for the benefit of Luftwaffe pilots. What happens to the human body when it is deprived of oxygen at high altitudes? What happens to the human body when it is plunged into icy waters? What happens to the human body when it has to drink sea water?

Nowhere was there any concern for the human soul when it suffers.

Right now the Burgermeister of Dachau is being questioned inside an office of meticulously kept camp records, and all he keeps saying is that he and the other good citizens of Dachau didn't really know how bad the atrocities in the camp were.

"Was konnen wir tun? What could we do," he pleads.

Ever since the Bulge I've kept asking myself how I ever lived through it. And why.

I've tried to burn this whole thing into my brain: how deep the snow was, the fear in the foxholes, what Billy said to me as he was dying, the stench of decomposition, the loss of control and order, the frenzy for retribution, the shallow pleas of ignorance and weakness. And I think this diary will help.

But I suspect that I'll always remember these things anyhow, always dream them, as if they happened over the course of a long night just past.

But last night on guard duty, in the midst of all this death, a spring wind blew, and the sun rose, and for the first time in a long time I thought of the future, and my place in it. And what I've decided is that I don't want the Bulge and Dachau to be just a watershed, with the rest of my life an easy slide to some catchment. What I really want to do now, now that I've been here, is not just hold onto the memories, but to make this all matter—to let it direct me, better me, alter my thinking, and change the rest of my life.

Our "Thunderbolt" Division and the 42nd "Rainbows" are moving on today in a push towards Munich. We'll be replaced here by other units. I suppose I'll never have the opportunity to provide food, or do anything at all for the poor people of this camp. It's too late for many of them.

But someday, I'll do something.

Someday, when I ask myself, *What could I do?*—I want to answer: Something. A lot.

Lee Nunzio put away Ben Pike's war diary. He made another set of rounds of his children's rooms. He kissed his wife and went to bed.

He did not sleep.

CHAPTER TWENTY-ONE

*F*red Marshall, the CIA Deputy Director for Africa Operations, rolled up his shirtsleeves and concentrated hard on the photograph. He'd made sure his secretary would let no military affairs experts, no advisors, no phone calls—nothing—interrupt him for the next few minutes.

He recalled his conversation with Hurley Baker, who'd told him about *Pike's Peak*, the book found at Charlie Hammami's home with a circled photo of Zach Pike in it. Baker had recounted Nunzio's wild theory about the Israelis executing Hammami, a backer of Kasawi, in reprisal for Sudan's abduction of the Pike kid—a theory which was almost as crazy as Nunzio's claim that the abduction itself was payback for Ben Pike's spying on behalf of Israel. Baker had also said something about the Israelis once raiding Hammami's Algiers home.

Now, with a copy of the book before him and looking at a duplicated photo of a young Zach Pike surrounded by family and friends, Marshall called on instincts honed by years of CIA employment. The dark instincts were those of a mind trained, by a closed and secretive agency, to think surreptitiously.

Marshall's mind was so circuitous, so accustomed to hunt for vulnerabilities and exploitations, that it was able to see what ordinary minds overlooked. What Marshall saw now was that the large circle surrounded not only Zach Pike, but also a boy identified in the caption as Zvi Langer. The circle did not lasso Ben Pike.

Zvi Langer? Hadn't Zach Pike's girlfriend, Meg Symes, accompanied a Zvi Langer to Israel? Why? Why go with him? Was there something Zvi Langer could do to help Zach Pike?

Zvi Langer? According to the book, Zach and Zvi were best friends while growing up.

Vulnerability? Exploitation?

He needed Sharon Fisher, the Middle East intelligence analyst. He punched an intercom button and was instantaneously connected to the CIA's Zach Pike task force headquartered on the third floor.

"Marshall here. Get me Sharon Fisher." As soon as she picked up, he said, "Miss Fisher, I need you up here. Now. Alone."

Intentionally, as with all junior CIA personnel, he had kept his relationship with her on a last name only basis. It was just one of many ways to better delineate the seperation of rank.

Actually, he liked Sharon Fisher. She was plump and attractive, intellectually sharp, well connected to the National Security Agency, and she did what she was told to do. With a military background, she reminded him of Kelly Doyle, the Khartoum NOC. She was somebody he could trust, somebody he could control.

A moment later there was a slight ruckus coming from near his secretary's desk.

"It's all right, Miss Cooper, I sent for Miss Fisher. Please show her in."

Entering the office, Sharon walked straight into the line of Marshall's intimidating glare. He hovered above her, silent and imposing. After an eternity of seconds, he sat down on the edge of his desk.

"Please sit."

"You sent for me, Mr. Marshall?"

"I need your help. What has the task force come up with about the attack on Hammami's Algiers home?"

"The raid took place three years ago, in late March. Israel's *Sayeret Matkal* and navy commandos killed Sheik Latif, an influential Egyptian cleric Hammami was hosting at the time."

"The Arabs place a lot of emphasis on hospitality. That would have been humiliating for Hammami, yes?"

"I wouldn't know, sir. But Hammami never entertained guests there again. Shortly after the attack he sold the villa in Algiers and dismissed the villa's staff."

Marshall said nothing, but his unflinching stare made Sharon cringe, just as he'd intended. He needed more.

"You know," she said at last, "down at headquarters I was just looking at some transcripts of telephone conversations that the National Security Agency intercepted. Pretty much all the transcripts related to the Middle East go through me. Anyway, there was one in particular that was interesting. It went something like, 'Knightsbridge, London. Fundamentalist supporter. Owner of the Algiers villa. The one you once visited.'"

"And that's it?"

"Yes. It was a one-way conversation, very brief. The party that was silent made the call from Budapest."

"Where was the call going to? Who did the talking?"

"Israel."

Marshall kept his gaze on Sharon, but his mind was busy integrating what he already knew with what he had just learned.

"In the biographical research on Zach Pike, what was mentioned about Zvi Langer?"

"They were neighbors, good friends. Zvi Langer moved back to Israel with his family, to their kibbutz, when Zvi was finishing high school in Boston. Zach and Zvi maintained their friendship over the years and saw each other from time to time."

"What does Zvi Langer do?"

"After the army he enrolled at Hebrew University in Jerusalem. He's still a student, going for his first degree."

"Still a student? Only his first degree?"

"Well, his military stint must have taken some time. And his academic advancement was probably slowed by the reserve duty that Israelis are required to complete each year."

"Must be doing a lot of reserve duty, seems to me. What exactly did he do in the army?"

"I don't recall, probably because it's ambiguous."

"Miss Fisher," Marshall finally permitted himself to smile, "it's good to know that you experts down at the task force are on top of everything. As always, thank you for your help. And, as always, Shhhh." He dismissed her with a wink.

Even as she left his office, Marshall was already preparing in his mind a *For Eyes Only* message that he would send to one of his own network underlings at the CIA station in Tel Aviv.

Subject: Zvi Langer.

Identify position in army and reserves, if possible.

Ascertain recent whereabouts, i.e. Hebrew University, kibbutz, reserves.

Verify whereabouts in late March of three years ago, i.e. University, kibbutz, reserves.

Then Marshall's smile spread wide, a Cheshire cat grin. He had the goods, he was sure of it.

Zach knew he was in trouble.

He just did not know what to do about it.

Curled up in a corner, Zach leaned his head against a cool wall. A clay urinal on the far side of his cell sat only a few feet away, but it might as well have been an ocean away. Minutes passed as he deliberated whether or not to use it.

First, he would have to decide. Then he would have to will himself up. And he would have to drag his leg irons.

Every action seemed to be herculean in scope. Numbed, in a deep depression, he felt life itself as an insurmountable task.

He blinked, gazing at the naked light bulb in his cell, and peed in his pants.

His food, once again, remained untouched in a bowl by the metal door. Hunger was merely emptiness and Zach could not shake the listlessness that seemed to always be with him now. Not that he was sure he wanted to. As with everything else now, he didn't know. He just couldn't decide. In his struggle to gain some measure of control, he had somehow lapsed out of control.

His eyes swam up and around, vainly searching, but he could not really see anything.

He could endure the physical pain of torture. As in football, pain went away in time. Injuries had a way of healing all on their own. It had even been a few days since the last encounter with a whip or the *shebba*.

Yet the loneliness was unrelenting. It stung his heart and played havoc with his mind. But it was the sheer weight of mounting dread that ultimately made him crack.

How long will this continue?

What is it that they want? Dad? Zvi?

What if nobody knows where I am? What if I die here?

Worst of all was the anxiety over what his family must be experiencing. At the absolute worst times thoughts of his mother's heartache made him ill. In his most vulnerable moments, the anguish that Meg was going through made him crazy.

He realized he had been coddled and protected his whole life. Never had he gone wanting materially, emotionally. His home was full of light, food, music, and laughter. Reflecting on it, Zach knew that he had led a charmed existence. He was not only allowed, but actually encouraged, to pursue his dreams. Miraculously they had all been coming true, both on the football field and off.

It was only natural then to feel a certain amount of guilt and selfloathing. For he knew that he had been raised better, armed with enough weapons to put up a better fight.

His whole life had been around tough guys, tough people. He should have learned.

"When the going gets tough, the tough get going." "Tough times never last, tough people do." Hadn't all of his coaches taught him that, from Pop Warner all the way up to the Pros? Hadn't he seen teammates play with broken bones? Hadn't he witnessed a teammate participate in a playoff game moments after returning from the funeral of a family member?

Hadn't Meg practically raised herself out of a broken home? Hadn't Zvi always fought through whatever life dealt him? And his father; a war veteran, *a liberator*? Did he ever complain? Hadn't he always done whatever needed to be done, regardless of the difficulties or the cost?

Zach knew all this. He just did not know what to do—*about himself.*

With a start, he sensed somebody at the door's barred window.

One of his Arab guards, the one he called Ishmael.

Ishmael crouched slightly to look through the window. His narrow face, scarred according to the rituals of his nomadic Baggara tribe, was once again smiling. But his eyes were clouded in worry.

"I brought you some sweet *laban* milk." Ishmael clicked his tongue rapidly as was his tribal custom.

Zach waved his hand slightly in acknowledgement.

"You do not eat your food. Why?"

"Why should I eat it?"

"My friend, this you must understand," said Ishmael, putting the glass down on the ledge of the window. "Life is very strange. Very difficult. Over the course of a life, everybody will sometimes be in new situations, new roles. Sometimes not of one's choosing.

"Right now you are a prisoner. It is hard. It is not what you want. But, that is life.

"As a prisoner what you must do—all you must do—is survive, any way you can. There is nothing else you are called upon to do. It is difficult, but it is not complicated."

Ishmael brought a grapefruit up to the window. "This, my friend, is life. For now, it is your life. It is all that is required of you."

He began to slowly peel away the skin. The juice of the grapefruit sprayed the air with its sweet scent.

"What you must do, as a prisoner, is become a survivor. Get through this. Get by this." Ishmael held a shining yellow section of fruit up in the air. "Eat this now. Eat it." He pushed and waved the fruit furiously in Zach's direction. "Where others have survived, should you not at least try to do so?"

Zach carefully raised himself off the ground. For a moment he felt light-headed. Lifting his chains, he trudged toward the window.

The fruit exploded in his mouth, the bit of nourishment instantaneously awakening him.

Ishmael broke off another section of grapefruit.

With each piece, Zach found himself wanting more, and more.

After he finished eating even the food by his door, after Ishmael had left his window, Zach lay flat, in a prone position. With toes dug in, with hands gripping the cool floor, he pushed himself up.

One!

Two, three, four......

CHAPTER TWENTY-TWO

"Gray, cloudy, with only a slight chance—about 100%—of rain this afternoon. Just another lovely beach day here in London. And you, Lee? How's the weather there? How goes the war?"

Nunzio leaned back in his chair, peeked out his office window, and massaged his tired eyes. Jim Sanderson, the FBI's legal attache in London, always seemed to have some new and disturbing revelations for him regarding Charlie Hammami. Would this morning be any different?

"It's partly cloudy here in D.C., Jim. And as for the war," Nunzio laughed sardonically, "well, war is a messy business. Sometimes, for some people, it never really ends. It widens and finds new battlefields. It's all very confusing, Jim. But the good guys always win in the end, don't they? I mean, they should, right?"

"Ideally, I suppose. But the world's not an ideal place, not a fair place, and certainly not a simple place. You know that, Lee." Sanderson remained quiet for a few seconds, then continued. "Anyway, the Yard tells me Mr. Hammami's travel agency booked him a flight to Khartoum several weeks before Zach Pike's abduction. Eyewitnesses and airline personnel confirm that he was on board the flight to Khartoum."

"And what did he do in Khartoum? Who did he meet with?"

"That's much more difficult to determine."

"In other words, you don't know."

"The Yard does not know. For now, at any rate."

"What about other trips that Hammami took in the weeks leading up to this?"

"Well, he also flew to New York before the abduction, in fact right after returning to London from Khartoum."

"And?"

"We know which hotel he stayed in, but once again it's not clear what he did, who he saw. I'm sure the New York office can find that out."

"What about phone calls?"

"Give me two seconds." Nunzio could hear clicks and buzzes, computer noises. "Okay, I've got a list here of calls Hammami made to the States in the weeks before his murder. Most of the calls were made to investment brokers or were business-related. There were some personal calls however."

"Did he call any of those personal numbers on a regular basis?"

"Yeah, two numbers. One was Tomas Bahr's. And there's another one here. Let's see. Okay, it was placed to Brooklyn, to someone named Husseini, Ibrahim Husseini."

Jim Sanderson waited for another question from Nunzio, but all he heard was silence.

"What's the matter, Lee? You know this Ibrahim Husseini?"

"Apparently not well enough. It's only recently that we put him under observation for a stab he made at finding out about Ben Pike's convention plans for some meeting on the Unmanned Vehicle thing. It's time to get more aggressive in learning about this guy."

Right after hanging up with Sanderson, Nunzio called Victor Lopes. When he'd explained to Lopes that Hammami and Husseini had conversed on numerous occasions, the Attorney General immediately authorized an unconsented physical search of Husseini's apartment.

Husseini's calls, records, and receipts would now be investigated without his knowledge. In that way the FBI could ascertain more about Husseini, and what he was up to. That was what Nunzio wanted, what he expected.

And that was the problem.

Knowing Lopes' every move was starting to unsettle Nunzio just a little bit. He could not quite identify the apprehension he was feeling, but it seemed to involve something impending; *a clash of some kind.* Not so much with Victor Lopes the person, but with Victor Lopes' beliefs. Beliefs that were also his own, that he'd always fervently shared with Lopes. Nunzio had a strange feeling that in some way every dealing with Lopes was an unconsented search of his own beliefs; he himself was being investigated, subconsciously, and by himself. It was all very disturbing. Standing to stretch, Nunzio tried to shake off his doubts.

Ibrahim Husseini is a crackpot!

Nunzio had until just this minute been willing to bet on it. The man was lonely, obsessed with the media blitz surrounding the Zach Pike affair. Just a fantasizing misfit trying to worm his way into the picture.

But now Nunzio's professional intuition was telling him something. He flipped his Rolodex to the letter *P.*

"Lieutenant Colonel Arnie Paul, please. This is Lee Nunzio of the FBI." Waiting for Arnie to pick up, he remembered with amusement how they'd met.

At his wife's urging he'd attended one of Washington's splashier country club balls a year earlier. After a set of dances in which he'd met his dancing requirements to Judy's satisfaction, he had decided to hide out in the bar for a few minutes. There he met another dance dodger, a mildly inebriated Air Force officer. Together they had laughed, gawked at women in low cut gowns, and drunk themselves silly. They had a good time.

After half an hour they had exchanged cards and promised to get together "real soon." Of course they never had, but Nunzio hung onto Arnie Paul's card anyway. After all, this was Washington, and contacts mattered.

"Lee, what's up buddy?" Arnie Paul acted as if the ball had been just yesterday.

"Would it be possible to get together soon, Arnie? I want to tap into that highly specialized brain of yours."

"How about now?"

"Now?" Nunzio stared at the business card before him: *Lt. Col. Arnold Paul, Pentagon Ballistic Defense Organization.* "Okay. I'll be over there in half an hour."

During the drive over to the Pentagon he again ran over the latest developments. It was becoming increasingly obvious that Ibrahim Husseini was a threat, a treacherous man who might well have been involved in the sinister plan from the very beginning.

And if Husseini was a threat, then the organization he worked with was incredibly dangerous. Attuned to shifting news revelations, and flexible enough to adapt to them, this group was not only seeking revenge on Ben Pike for having assisted Israel in UAV Unmanned Aerial Vehicle know-how, it was now trying to discover the exact nature and extent of Ben Pike's current expertise.

And just what was Ben Pike's current expertise? Arnie Paul would know.

"I had kind of hoped that we'd get together again over a drink or on the links, Lee. Anywhere but in my office. Still, it's good to see you again."

"I appreciate this, Arnie. Next time we get together, soon I hope, the drinks will be on me. Anyway." He sat down, cleared his throat. "Are you familiar with UAV work Lexington Labs is contracted to do?"

"Sure. Lexington Labs is in the forefront of research being done on the Vulture."

"The what?"

"It's still being developed." Arnie locked his fingers on top of his head. "The Vulture is a high-altitude, solar-powered unmanned aerial vehicle that has boost phase intercept potential. In other words, besides carrying out reconnaisance missions, it will also be able to identify missile boost phase plumes with infrared sensors. Being high up, it can look over the horizon and take out a missile with the kinetic-kill Talon rockets that it carries."

"Tell me, Arnie, how would something like this be beneficial to the Israelis?"

"Should I ask why you're asking?"

"No."

"Fair enough. Well, I would think this would be beneficial because in the Gulf War Israel couldn't even stop a primitive SCUD. The Patriot missiles we gave them, contrary to public perception, were not at all effective. Now if Israel had formations of Vultures, platforms which could safely and vigilantly patrol for several days at a time over enemy territory, they would have a system that could intercept rockets in an endgame moments after they were fired. The Vulture would offer tremendous defensive protection for them."

"Don't we share this with Israel anyway?" Nunzio settled back in his chair, digging his palms into his knees.

"We do have Research and Development cooperation in basic versions of the Vulture. But we don't share everything, if you know what I mean. And Israel certainly won't get its hands on this technology any time soon. The money, the testing, the red-tape, they'll all slow this thing down."

"And the Arabs? How would it benefit them?"

"Aside from the same way it helps Israel, there's potentially another advantage to the Vulture. The Vulture could be designed to carry and fire weapon payloads. Israel's enemies have never been able to fly over Israel because their Air Forces are no match for Israel's. But with the Vulture they could go on the offensive."

"Couldn't Israel knock out the Vultures before they were a threat?"

"It's not so easy. The Vulture flies at over 60,000 feet and it's being developed with infrared and radio frequency defensive countermeasures. The Vulture will be hard to spot, and harder yet to destroy. Remember too that the Vulture could safely launch its rockets from within air space of far away borders."

Arnie tapped a drumbeat on his desk with a chewed-up pencil.

Nunzio leaned forward. "But why would the missiles fired from a Vulture be any more effective than missiles fired from the ground of enemy countries?"

"Because the Vulture looks down and fires up. Looking down means that as soon as it sees a target in real-time, a ground control crew can launch a missile. So the missile is not only directed according to the most recent information, but it reaches its intended target much faster than one fired from down on the ground. And since it fires up from such a high altitude, missiles that it launches could not be hit by Talon rockets of defensive Vultures which, if you remember, kill missiles shortly after being fired from the ground."

Nunzio struggled to understand the implications of what he was hearing. A moment later, Arnie spelled out his worst fears in concrete terms.

"An Arab nation, if it wanted to, would be able to seriously harm Israel. They could arm missiles on board a Vulture with chemicals, biological agents, even nuclear materials. Lee, it could be catastrophic. Potentially, it could be a mini-holocaust."

Actually, the wall was rather plain, just a marble wall with stars on it. But everytime Fred Marshall passed by it at CIA headquarters in Langley, he paused and bowed his head.

On the surface the anonymous stars seemed simple enough, but Marshall knew the story behind them. The stars represented the unknown warriors of the clandestine service. Those heroes who quietly gave of their lives, sometimes *gave* their lives, for the benefit of their country.

At times he himself felt like one of those anonymous warriors, unappreciated, misunderstood. Even among CIA colleagues, nobody knew him, the real him. To the junior staffers he was a mean ogre. Nobody grasped that his bluntness, his formality, were his way of best serving the country he loved. He watched over his heart, and hid his noble motivations, as best as he could.

Back in his office, Marshall opened the *For Eyes Only* message, the one his own Tel Aviv station crony sent him. The answers were what he'd expected.

Yes, Zvi Langer completed paratroop basic training but afterwards did not serve in a paratroop unit. The scuttlebutt was that he was in an elite intelligence unit.

No, he had not been at any of his University classes once Chanukah vacation ended. In the past few days he had not been at his kibbutz either. In fact, his whereabouts could not be tracked down anywhere in Israel.

As for late March of three years ago, well, it seems he missed an important exam that was given prior to the Passover break. Was he at Ein Gev at that time? No evidence one way or the other. But Zvi Langer hadn't run in the Tel Aviv marathon taking place at the time, one he'd registered for and had very much wanted to compete in.

The response in his hands was all Marshall needed. A vein throbbed at his temple. His face suddenly felt hot. His mind started to race.

Why? Why were commando units being considered to rescue Zach Pike? Why lose young American lives in a risky military venture? Why was the CIA once again being prevented from intervening in a crisis for which it could find a better resolution? One that wouldn't sacrifice American lives! Why should Americans have to die?

It's the Israeli that the Sudanese want; a Jew for crying out loud!

Marshall collapsed in his chair and held his head in his hands. He took a deep breath. And then another.

Something had to be done. Hurley Baker didn't even have the guts to speak up to the President and insist that the CIA, rather than the military, resolve the crisis. Why the pantload even kowtowed to Congressional oversight committees! *Clearly somebody had to do something!*

Marshall rehearsed in his mind the microdot instructions that he would personally send to Kelly Doyle in Khartoum.

Subject: The fixing of a confidential and urgent one-on-one meeting between Amir Kasawi and myself,
regarding Zach Pike.
Suggest Europe. Explain you are my Ambassador.
There is understanding that your role is now compromised.
Arrangements to follow concerning your extrication.
Be discreet. Be careful.

Semper Fi.

Something was wrong.

A gusty wind whistled through Meg's window and then huffed itself breathless. *Or did it just sigh?*

Moon rays vanished behind a passing cloud and then reappeared in a sparkling outburst of silver, magically tinseling Ayelet's doll, her books, and old photographs on top of an old dresser.

Then Meg's door slowly creaked open.

A dark stranger entered. He averted his eyes. He took a step to the right, and stopped. Unsure, even though he was back in his own home, he tottered two steps to the left, and stopped again. His arms, suspended slightly to the side, wavered as he tried to recover his balance. He cocked his head to the side, with an ear to the ground, with an ear to the sky.

The stranger moved without making any sound at all. *Was he man, was he ghost?*

To the right, to the left, winding ever closer, he felt his way along.

He was at the foot of the bed now. With hollow eyes averted, brow twisted, mouth open in question, he was a man in anguish.

He lay down beside her and rested his head on her breasts. His hands, tender and forceful, moved over her warm body. Suddenly, his hands held tight.

"Meggie," he at last said, pointing to the dresser, "that boy there in that picture, the one with the soccer ball, the one who looks so happy.

Did he ever really exist? He looks so confident, so optimistic. So ready to do something good. I just don't understand it.

"It all happened so slowly, so imperceptibly, I never saw it coming.

"Can time really be so insidious? How can it just knock us over, force us to follow its designs? Impose on us, and make us do that which we abhor?"

"Shhh, Shhh, Shhh."

"I miss the old summer days, Meggie! I miss the innocence, the friends. Meggie, I miss that boy in the picture!"

Exhausted and wrung out, the stranger, the friend—Zvi—staggered into a deep sleep. Outside, the wind began to whip itself into a tempest. And all night long, as Meg listened to the howling sails of the clipper ship in the back yard, she worried.

CHAPTER TWENTY-THREE

"*I* know it ain't much, Mac," Gordy Bannister said, waving a hand, "but welcome to the humble confines of Joint Special Operations Command at Fort Bragg, North Carolina, a.k.a. *Jay-Soc.*"

"Humble my ass! I know you've got a swimming pool, racquetball courts, and girlie bars hidden away here. And welcome? You bastard!" Streicher shook his head. "I can't believe that back at the Pentagon you had the gall to claim that I was a lousy host! Gordy, right outside this compound your unmarked patrol car goons stopped me—twice! And when they weren't stopping me, that damned electronic sensor obstacle course was a bitch to get through. The fences? The barbed wire? I bet Los Alamos doesn't have more security than this place!"

"Sorry, Mac." Bannister smiled one of his 'aw shucks' smiles. "I guess I shouldn't have told security to be extra careful for an infiltrator dressed as the Chairman of the Joint Chiefs of Staff."

Streicher roared.

The two old veterans had not met since the National Security Council meeting at the White House. Though they'd then bitterly opposed each other on the use of special operations forces, they both understood that the Commander-in-Chief had spoken. For the good of the military, for the good of the country, they would have no problems working with each other from now on. Besides, they were friends.

"So what's on the agenda? A dip in the swimming pool?"

"No, Mac. Stop number one, the House of Horrors. There's somebody there I'd like you to meet."

As soon as Bannister and Streicher seated themselves behind the glass-enclosed viewing area, a drab three-story building before them became an arcade that ignited into mayhem; a cross between an amusement park haunted house and a pin ball machine. Posters popped up, robots sprang into motion, and phantom images flew about. All the while acrobatic commandos with Heckler and Koch MP5K's fired in bursts and in single shots, a computer ping registering their deadly hits.

"This is Delta," Bannister said. "They're the best there is at room clearing. The trick is differentiating the terrorists from the hostages in just a split second. Then it's a matter of rapid aim and instinctive shooting."

"How good are they in the dark? Isn't the take down going to take place at night?"

"It is. That's why there's a set-up here to rehearse for that as well. The team dons thermal imaging sights that create a holographic picture. Night simply becomes a 3-D day."

With the barrage over, the shooting gallery now looked more like an academic discussion group. The men beyond the glass partition began to analyze every aspect of what had transpired. Soldiers spoke up, then walked through their actions, but there was one who was more animated than the others. He swiftly moved from one commando to the other, personally engaging each one with questions. He listened very seriously to their answers, his hooded charcoal eyes gleaming with excitement. His straight black hair fell forward as he exhorted some of the men, gesturing enthusiastically. Others he cuffed on the shoulder or grabbed by the arm until he was ready to move on.

The soldiers he spoke to showed no fear of him. Many actually winced in protest or frustration. But they listened attentively to everything he said, and they did not interrupt him.

"Clyde," Bannister called, once the special ops had finished their performance evaluation. "I want to introduce you to the Chairman of the Joint Chiefs."

The man with the charcoal eyes smiled in a humble sort of way. But as he approached, everything about him conveyed an aura of intensity: his eyes were alert, his steps quick, his handshake determined.

"Colonel Clyde *One Horse* Dancer," Bannister continued, "will be our point man in Khartoum."

"It's an honor, Admiral Streicher."

"Call me Mac."

Clyde Dancer looked younger than his thirty-six years, and he seemed too soft-spoken to be an elite forces officer. As far as Mac could tell he appeared too...*different*. Too different, anyway, to have achieved his position of authority without what must have been, at times, a very personal, intense struggle.

Clyde *One Horse* Dancer was a Lakota Sioux.

A long time ago Dancer had tried to explain to Bannister his motivation for joining special ops, but Bannister wasn't sure he understood.

Maybe it was in his blood? Maybe it stirred in the high winds or shallow waters of his South Dakota home? Perhaps it called to him from a wolf silhouetted before a harvest moon. But something had taken hold of him. It occupied his dreams and sang to his heart. It bequeathed upon him the tradition, and the responsibility, of ages past. Before he was ever born, Clyde *One Horse* Dancer was a warrior.

His ancestors were. They fought primarily to preserve a way of life.

His father was. He fought to defend a geographic homeland. He fought to win the kind of respect that can only go to a fighting man. So at the outbreak of World War II, he volunteered for the Army and was assigned to the 45th "Thunderbird" Division, one fifth of whose soldiers were American Indian. But as the 45th battled from North Africa, through Italy and southern France, the Ardennes forest, and ultimately to a place called Dachau, a strange thing happened.

Clyde Dancer's father, and many of the other Indians he served with, found a certain pocket of inner peace amidst all the warfare and horror around them. For once their blood was being shed side-by-side with that of the white man. Suddenly the white man's history was also their history. And in the process outward hostilities and inner strife, while not entirely forgotten, began to gradually dissolve. As a result Dancer's father, the Indians of the "Thunderbird" Division, and Indians throughout the Armed Forces, found not only a means of reconciliation, but a haven from which they could comfortably remember a way of life. And that they passed on to their children.

And so when Clyde Dancer was growing up he was both proud, and patriotic.

"Mac," Bannister said. "Clyde here is doing a great job whipping these guys into shape."

Streicher looked hard at Dancer. "What's Delta's current state of readiness?"

"We're at a C-2 level; combat ready with minor deficiencies. By the time we're ready to go, however, it will be C-1; combat ready, no deficiencies. I promise."

"And how about Seal Team—Six?"

"Who ever knows with those guys?" Dancer smiled. "They're younger, a bit more free-spirited than we are."

"Delta's gonna get Zach Pike," Bannister said. "The Navy Seals are going to neutralize Sudan's lone truly competent unit, the Airborne Division, and secure a Red Sea beachfront."

"Why am I not surprised?" Streicher shook his head. "You just can't bear seeing the Navy get the glory, can you Gordy?" Laughing, the Chairman of the Joint Chiefs turned to Dancer. "Okay, Clyde. The pressure's on you to make Gordy look good. Let's take a look around and see what it's going to take to get Delta up to C-1 status."

Leaving the House of Horrors they went to a fifty-foot climbing wall. A small group of commandos opened portable lightweight ladders even as they ran toward the wall. They positioned the ladders and shimmied up with amazing nimbleness. They then rappeled down the other side of the wall's face.

"That's how most of my men will get into Kober prison."

"That looked pretty good to me, Clyde," said Bannister.

"Well, it's never fast enough. My men will keep practicing until they shave off every possible second."

"What about the actual bust into the barrack?" Streicher asked. "Zach Pike's cell?"

"Follow me."

Range 19 Alpha proved to be a demolitions area at the far side of the compound.

"Kevin, Jacks, Little Cloud!" yelled Dancer. "Blow an *I* and an *H* for us."

"Little Cloud?" whispered Streicher to Bannister as they walked a safe distance away.

"Delta has a disproportionately large number of native Americans, Mac. They volunteer to be the best."

"Watch this," said Dancer as he rejoined the two senior officers.

The demolitions experts, wearing body armor and fire-retardant jump suits, pasted *I* and *H*-shaped charges onto a metal door and then crouched a few feet away. Five seconds later the door collapsed in smoke.

"Timing devices in the explosives insure that the top of the *I* and the *H* ignite a microsecond before the bottom. As the door goes down, the Delta commandos run right over it while lobbing flashbang concussion grenades to disorient everyone inside. It's then that they carry out the room clearing you saw at the House of Horrors."

"Impressive stuff, Mac. Don't you think?"

Streicher never heard Bannister's question. His eyes were trying to integrate the various components of what he was seeing into their correct sequence in the big picture.

"Tell me more about overall infiltration and exfiltration," he finally asked.

"JSOC also includes the Army's 160th Aviation Regiment, the 'Nightstalkers'. We train with them and their MH-60 Blackhawks. Those killer eggs are amazingly quiet, fast, and agile. Their pilots are the hottest in the business." Dancer paused, looking for a moment at the demolitions men as they examined the door and retraced their steps, analyzing the whole routine.

"Most of us will be helicoptered to the arena from ships in the Red Sea, east of Khartoum," he continued. "The choppers can refuel in flight over the desert. They'll hover over a deserted area of Omdurman, near Kober, just long enough for our men to fast-rope down. From there, under the cover of darkness, we'll go the mile to Kober's walls. The MH-60's will withdraw into the desert until they're called upon a short time later.

"As for the Seals, they're going to pin down the Sudanese Airborne Division at Khartoum International. In that way they'll also be close enough to provide support. They're arriving via their Stallion helicopters and Super Cobra gunships."

Streicher's brow remained furrowed.

'That's how most of my men will get into Kober.' 'Most of us will be helicoptered to the arena from ships in the Red Sea.' Colonel Dancer still had some explaining to do!

"What about the rest of your team? How are they getting into Kober?"

Dancer looked at Bannister, who nodded back for him to proceed.

"Some of the men, myself included, will execute a HAHO, High Altitude High Opening parachute jump from a MC-130E Combat Talon. We'll fall from 30,000 feet, sail in from 35 miles away, and land smack dab into the middle of Kober prison."

"What? You're crazy! You're both crazy!"

"Think about it, Mac." Bannister spun his friend around so they were eye to eye. "Soldiers posted in the prison's towers, unless they're all sleeping, will see Delta's approach. Even if we tried to have special ops snipers pick them off, we still wouldn't get all of them. And soldiers posted in the prison's courtyard would also be a problem. But our jumpers, camouflaged for the night with darkened chutes and black outfits and balaclavas, will eliminate soldiers in and around the prison with their silencers as soon as they've silently dropped in from the sky. Without this element of surprise, Mac, this thing just doesn't work!"

"The very best parachutists we have would be assigned to this phase of the operation," Dancer added. "We practice pinpoint drops all the time, often with the Golden Knights Parachute Team right here in Ft. Bragg. Our square chutes are like air foils, tremendously maneuvarable. We'll be wearing thermal imaging gear to help us see as if it were daylight. And since we'll jump from 35 miles away, the delivery aircraft will be out of radar range and out of earshot."

Streicher's eyes were wide in disbelief.

"Gordy, you know I fought against this entire operation. And you know why. It just seems to me that this HAHO jump will only further stack the odds against us. It's another complicating variable." He shook his head. "But since Ollie Earl decided this is what he wants, I guess this is what we'll do. I'm not here to quibble about operational details, not anymore. You and Clyde are the experts. If you say this jump is necessary, then I'm here to try and help you. God knows we all need all the help we can get."

It was a long walk back to Bannister's office, time enough to talk.

"Tell me about yourself, Clyde," Streicher said.

"I'm not sure I know what you mean, Admiral Streicher."

"You married? Kids? Home? And it's Mac, please."

"Well, I'm currently seperated from my wife." Dancer stared off at the horizon, his profile like the Indian on old nickles, strong and solemn. "Delta has put a lot of strain on our marriage. But my wife's living right next door in Fayetteville along with our two sons. I get to see them fairly often. My three sisters live in Standing Rock Lakota Reservation. My parents are gone."

"Sounds like a hard life, son. What do you like to do?"

"Fish and hunt. I've also got a Harley Davidson. And no, I don't think my life is very hard at all."

"Do you consider yourself to be a lucky sort of man, Clyde?"

"I'm not sure I know what you mean, Mac."

"Well, you've got only One Horse!"

"Yeah, but that's good—One Horse. You know, One Horse; one tribe, one unit, one country."

Streicher shook his head. And laughed.

"What's with you, Mac?" Bannister asked. "What's your point?"

Streicher laughed again, shook his head. Moments passed and only the steps of the three men could be heard on the compound's burnt out grass and asphalt paths.

"Are you lucky Clyde *One Horse* Dancer?" the Chairman of the Joint Chiefs asked again.

"The spirits have always been with me, if that's what you mean." Dancer lifted his chin, smiled confidently. "And if they're with me, then they're with us. Why would they abandon us now?"

With but an hour of daylight remaining, the sun decided to put on a show.

It distended itself into a giant, orange pumpkin and lingered magnificently just above the desert horizon. Holy men recited a blessing, observers blissfully awaited the cool night, and tourists blinked away with their cameras to forever capture the mystical and exotic moment.

But it was not the sun they had come to see.

Rather they'd gathered in front of the Hamed an-Niel mosque on this particular Friday afternoon to be amazed by the whirling dervishes of Omdurman. Following their own *tariqa* path of Islam, the ascetic dervishes would engage in a frenzied ceremonial *dhikr* to honor Sheik an-Niel, a 19th-century miracle worker and intermediary of Allah.

One of the regulars at the *dhikr* was Amir Kasawi. With eyes closed behind his aviator sunglasses, he felt the gentle breeze uplift his spirits.

But not even the wondrous, serene setting could completely calm his troubled soul. It seemed as if a miracle really was necessary for that.

Where was the Israeli? When would he present himself? How to convince the Iranians of his value?

Most of all Kasawi worried over how to gracefully and convincingly seperate himself from Zach Pike. Ever since the murder of Charlie Hammami, Kasawi had felt increasingly isolated and vulnerable. He urgently wanted more friends, and certainly did not need to rile a powerful enemy. He simply had to position himself better. But how could he curry America's bountiful graces?

The booming beat of drums shook Kasawi out of the distressing labyrinth of his thoughts. Right on cue a fluid stream of men wearing green and orange-patched jalabiyyas floated across the field by the mosque. Entering the ring of onlookers, the dervishes slowly began to chant and circle around a pole. Then, as the drums started to bang faster and faster, and the chanting discharged in a loud and flowing babble of magical incantations, the ecstatic dervishes seemed to spin themselves away from the mortal confines of earth, straight into the realm of the divine. Floating free, they flung themselves into a union with Allah.

Several spectators, mesmerized, were swept along by the convulsive circle. Nearby, delerious young boys mimicked the main festivities. Spinning in a circle, the boys whirled themselves sick, then whirled themselves right off their feet.

One young boy rolled onto the ground and came to rest at the foot of Kasawi. A flanking bodyguard momentarily stiffened out of his trance-like state, but Kasawi shooed him away with a wave. As he himself bent down to help the boy to his feet, the boy skillfully stuck something into his hand, then ran away.

With his bodyguard once again engrossed by the tumult of the circle, Kasawi glanced into the palm of his hand. He cautiously unfolded the piece of paper, a flyer describing the work of the evangelical Christian

One World, One Mission. In the right bottom corner of the flyer was a handwritten message.

Sheik Kasawi—
Do not be alarmed. I am an American with an important and personal message concerning Zach Pike.
Please look to the refreshment stand behind you.
I am wearing a straw hat and sunglasses.
Please come over and talk to me.

Turning around, Kasawi saw a conservatively dressed, western woman standing by herself to the side of a vendor's stall. He slowly stepped back so as to not arouse his security man. Then he took another step back. An instant later he was purposefully striding toward the woman.

Kelly Doyle almost choked on a swig of the soft drink in her hand. Aziz had courageously used his street urchin smarts to bring Kasawi the note. A frequent participant of her Children Ministry's meal and bible program, it was Aziz who suggested rolling on the ground. 'It will be fun,' he'd told her. But it was her own resourceful handling of Fred Marshall's ambiguous message that had brought her to this moment. And now that it was here—now that Amir Kasawi was only a few yards away—Kelly prayed she was doing the right thing.

"Who are you?" he asked bluntly.

"My name is Kelly Doyle. I work for *One World, One Mission.*"

"What is it that you want?"

"I have been instructed to tell you that a high ranking official of the CIA wants to meet you in Europe, alone, and as soon as possible. The subject to be discussed is Zach Pike."

"I know nothing of Zach Pike."

"Please excuse me, but the official has reason to believe that you do."

"Does he want to deal?"

"I don't know for sure, but I assume that he does."

"What is his name? What does he do?"

"Fred Marshall is the Deputy Director of Africa Operations."

"I do not know how I could be of any help to this Mr. Marshall. But let us assume for a moment that I am willing to meet with him. How do I know that he is an honorable man? How do I know that you are a right-eous woman? How can I know that I am not putting myself in danger?"

Kelly pondered Kasawi's question as she removed her sunglasses. "Please excuse me, but Mr. Marshall will be in the same situation as you. You will be able to observe if he too is alone. How does he know that he is not in danger?"

The giant sun, and her own image, were both caught in the reflective surface of Amir Kasawi's sunglasses. Though she could not clearly see the Sheik's eyes, Kelly sensed that they were sharp and suspicious as they bore into her. Reaching into her pack, she pulled out a bible and rested her hand upon it.

"Sheik Kasawi. I am a devout Christian. I believe in goodness. I love my God and I love God's children—all of his children. I believe Mr. Marshall is a good man, one who surely must have a fair solution; a peaceful way out. The day is short! I implore you to trust Mr. Marshall!"

The rapidly setting sun reflecting off the Sheik's glasses seemed to suddenly slow. It wavered, froze. *It almost died.* But time kept skipping along, and the sun moved down it's inexorable path.

"What does Mr. Marshall look like?"

"He's about fifty-five, large, with silver hair."

"The Alhamra palace in Granada, Spain. Monday at noon. Mr. Marshall should be alone in the Court of the Lions." Kasawi stepped away, stopped, and adjusted his sunglasses. "And Miss Doyle, you should pray that I return safely. For I will leave a directive before I go that you are not to leave Sudan until I do. Until I say so. And I won't say so until I get what I want."

When Kasawi returned unobserved to the ring of onlookers, the dervishes were still whirling and chanting. The drums were still beating. And the pumpkin sun was slipping away, sliding below the desert's barren surface.

CHAPTER TWENTY-FOUR

*L*aden with a mound of sugar, the silver-plated spoon gently sank into the cup. It swung, back and forth, with the methodical drift of a numbed hand, and a preoccupied mind. It nudged the hot coffee, then dropped into the kitchen sink.

"Thanks, Meggie." A white hand grabbed a cup, a dark brown hand scooped up a plate of cake.

From her lounge chair, Meg hugged her legs close and rested her chin on a knee. Zvi, his *Sayeret Matkal* friend Alan, and an Ethiopian Jew named Reuven, had been hunched over in discussion for three hours now. English and Hebrew flew around the Langers' Ein Gev living room as ideas were tested, discarded. Meg felt irritable, and left out.

"Look Zvi," Alan said, exasperated, "there's no getting around it. You'll have to make an overland entry into Sudan. It's just too dangerous, even with your new identity, to fly into Khartoum. The only legitimate security set-up they have is at the airport. I bet Kasawi is praying for you to fly in."

"Alan is right," said Reuven. "Sudan does not, cannot, control its borders. Refugees and smugglers always find a way of crossing."

"But Reuven, you yourself said that with the roads being as bad as they are it could take me three or four days to make my way from Ethiopia to Khartoum! That's too long! It's too long to be out of touch with what's going on!"

"Things just don't move quickly over there," Reuven said with a sympathetic smile. "You just have to get used to it."

Reuven had been among the few fortunate Ethiopian Jews brought to study in Israel in the early 1970's. He was then a bright fifteen-year-old from a prominent priestly *kes* family. The plan was that he would one day return to Ethiopia to be a religious leader. But as times worsened there for the Jews, his parents wrote him not to come back. "Not now," *not ever.*

But against his parents' wishes he eventually did; not once, but twice. Leaving his wife and children behind in Israel, Reuven volunteered to help with vital on-the-ground arrangements necessary before thousands of Jews could be flown to Israel in 1984's Operation Moses, and again in 1991's Operation Joshua. Those efforts—his whole history of harrowing experiences—enabled him to recognize the dazed look on Zvi's face.

"Zvi? Are you still with us?"

"Yes."

"Okay then. Once again, this is what I'd advise you to do. Fly from Italy or Germany, it really doesn't matter, to Addis Ababa. Take an Ethiopian Airlines flight north to my home-city Gondar. A few miles away in the Simien Mountains is the town of Debat. Look for a boyhood friend of mine, Wolde Zeleke. He is a guide who organizes hiking and horseback trips around the mountains. A few years ago, back in 1984, he led my younger brothers across the border into Sudan, almost all the way to the refugee camp at Gedaref. Wolde is an expert on the roads and trails in the region and he also knows the people of the villages."

"Do you think he has any friends among the soldiers at the border checkpoints?" Alan asked.

"I doubt it. He probably hasn't led a group towards Sudan in some time. However Wolde is a natural talker. He's relaxed, clever, and funny. Don't underestimate how much help that can be when trying to smuggle something, or somebody, across a border. And of course in that part of the world, money makes anything possible."

Zvi looked at Alan and waited. Alan had become a *mule* of sorts. He somehow had a way of obtaining everything; passports, information, airline tickets. Zvi had his suspicions, but mostly he suppressed them.

"Money?" Alan shrugged. "Yeah, I don't think that will be a problem."

"By the way, Zvi," Reuven said, "you may want to pick up some expensive liquor and some porno magazines while you're in Europe. Items that are difficult to come by are often more valuable than money. Maybe they'll help Wolde just enough to get you across the border, which is probably as far as he'll take you. From there he'll point you towards Gedaref. You know what to do once you're in Sudan, right?"

Zvi nodded.

"Oh, one other thing. Wolde won't ask for it, but leave some money for him. Do it for me. I'm sure he can use it, and after everything he's done for me, and for what he'll do for you, he deserves it."

The meeting was breaking up. Alan and Reuven turned to Meg and said good-bye, then Zvi walked them to the door. Whispering in hushed undertones, gesturing almost secretively, they stood away. *Apart.*

Motionless in her chair, Meg blankly gazed at the dirty dishes and cups strewn about. Ever since returning from Europe, Zvi had become increasingly remote. He obsessed over every facet of his plan. He focused, to the exclusion of everything else, on what he was about to do. *It wasn't fair.*

As soon as Zvi closed the door behind Alan and Reuven, she flung a cup. It shattered on the wall over Zvi's head.

"Hey!"

"Don't do this to me, Zvi! I don't deserve this!"

"What's with you, Meggie? What's the matter?"

"You're cutting me out! You bury your head in these maps, you huddle with your friends, you stare into space and carry on some sort of eerie, private conversation. Talk to me, Zvi!"

"I'm sorry, Meggie. This is how I get. I don't think I can help it."

"These friends of yours offer advice. They give you tips. They help, but only so far. Your government plays their political games, the Mossad keeps their distance, and in the end they won't let anybody really help you! No Israeli can go in with you, Zvi. But I can."

"I've been trained to work alone, if necessary, Meggie. To survive alone."

"But you're forgetting that as soon as you get Zach out of prison he will be with you. Who knows what kind of condition Zach's in? The whole country will be looking for him, looking for you. Someone has to obtain a car, set up a safe house, make travel arrangements. I can do those things! As a tourist in Sudan I can take care of these things before you ever get there!"

Like a skater in a spin, spotting a focal point with each revolution, Zvi's eyes fixed on her. He took her in his arms.

"I have to talk to Alan about this. I don't know. I just don't know." Softly he kissed her forehead, her nose, her lips. He opened his eyes, held her a little while. "Tell me Meggie, do you want to do this for me, or for Zach?"

"I suppose," she whispered, "I'm doing it for both of you. And for me." Then she rested her head on his shoulder, and blankly gazed at the clutter of the dishes.

"Welcome aboard NASA's very own George C. Marshall Space Flight Center bus tour." A honey-cheeked, saccharine blond tour guide flashed her biggest southern belle smile. "Hope ya'll enjoy your stay here in Huntsville, Alabama. You must have all come down here for the Unmmanned Vehicle Systems Conference. Where are you from, sir?"

"Boston."

"And you?"

"Umm, New York."

"And you, that's right, the couple there in back. I see you ducking. There's no reason to be bashful. Where ya'll from?"

"D.C."

"Well, today's escorted tour will take you to the Space dome, the U.S. Space and Rocket Center, and the U.S. Space Camp."

As the bus rolled forward and the tour guide droned on, Ibrahim Husseini stared at the large man, so familiar to him, who sat two rows ahead.

There had been a brief moment, not very long ago, when he'd once again felt overwhelmed by it all. Pangs of emptiness, crushing weakness, bitter isolation—it again crashed in on him when he'd learned of Charlie Hammami's murder.

But this time Ibrahim Husseini saved himself, *by himself.*

Once Hammami had instructed him to delve into Ben Pike's unmanned aerial vehicle projects, he had in effect provided Husseini with the tools to carry on after his death. Clearly information that Ben Pike possessed was of value. And surely a way could be found to tap Pike's reservoir of knowledge.

But it was not enough for Husseini to simply sift through a muddled situation. To truly rescue himself, liberate himself, he had to also find a way to shore up his painfully fragile self-esteem.

Had he not been bright enough to recognize the potential value of the picture in Zach Pike's book? Had he not taken the initiative and sent the book to Charlie Hammami? Did not Hammami have confidence in him?

It suddenly occurred to Ibrahim Husseini that he really did not need Hammami, or anyone for that matter, to guide him anymore. He could, *he would now have to*, issue himself his very own *fatwa*-like directives.

After making its first two stops, the tour bus now deposited its passengers at their final destination, the U.S. Space Camp. Husseini slipped behind Ben Pike as NASA trainees fired a rocket engine. He edged closer when they guided a spacecraft into a docking maneuver. And he was right at Pike's shoulder by the time they reached a Zero-G machine observation platform.

Husseini's breathing became disturbingly rapid; shallow and quiet. Immersed as he was in his scrutiny of Pike, Husseini did not notice the young couple from the bus carefully position a briefcase at the other end of the observation platform. In the briefcase was a parabolic microphone.

"I suppose it must be a wonderful feeling to be as weightless as these astronauts. I mean," Husseini murmured, "it must be great to rise above life's powerful control over us; to get away from its headaches and heartaches."

"I suppose it must be great at that," Ben replied as he turned his head towards the mustachioed philosopher. The swarthy man crowded him. His unblinking eyes were frighteningly opaque.

"But we can't really escape from our problems, can we, *Mr. Pike?*"

Ben turned fully towards the man, stared somberly at him. For a moment there was an uneasy silence.

"Who are you?" Ben asked quietly.

"Let me just say that I represent powerful clients, Mr. Pike. These clients are very interested in your scientific work, especially your Vulture program." His voice was low, whispering, though the rest of the tour group was by now out of earshot. "I can assure you that in return for your expertise they will compensate you with a most precious gift. One that you miss very much."

Ben felt a wave of red crash in on him.

A certain madness, reminescent of a time long ago, raced through him, lacerating his heart.

"Think about it, Mr. Pike. You're surrounded. I'm offering nothing less than a way out; for you, for your family, for your precious gift."

On the deck of the Zero-G machine an inner alarm sounded, urging Ben: *Get away! Get out!* It warned him not to get sucked in; to instead exercise the monumental self-control that is gleaned with maturity,and only by years.

With a mighty shove, Ben threw Ibrahim Husseini aside and stormed off the observation platform.

The snowy alabaster peaks of the Sierra Nevadas rose up against a heavenly blue sky. Viewed through graceful, paired windows, the vista was a canvas of stunning beauty. And yet, for most tourists, the beauty outside was surpassed by the wonder within. Tile, plaster, and marble meshed into intricately latticed art. Balconies, towers, and sunken pools flowed together in a marvelous synthesis of texture, colors, shapes.

But Fred Marshall shut out all these distractions and focused his mind. No tourist, he'd come to the fortress-palace of Alhambra to work.

After a perfunctory meeting with his Moroccan station chief in Rabat, Marshall had become unaccountable for a few hours. He'd made his way north along the P2 road to Ceuta and then boarded a hydrofoil for the short ride across the straits of Gibralter, to Spain's Andalucian town of Algericas. Bypassing the British colony of Gibralter, he drove a rented car up the coastal N-342 road until he turned inland along N-323, towards the mountainous city of Granada.

Standing now in the Court of the Lions, Marshall once again checked his watch: 12:05 P.M. Searching past slender columns and into the great halls and royal chambers on every side, he nervously scanned the awe-struck tourists who tripped out to the center of the Court. As they stood near him to gaze at the twelve whimsical lions that supported an enchanting fountain, Marshall moved left and right, forward and backward, furtively eyeing and appraising, watching and marking—*everyone*.

But still *he* was nowhere to be seen, and it was now 12:15 P.M.

Then, at the very instant he looked up, Marshall saw him!

Amir Kasawi was standing right under an elegant arch, drilling Marshall with his stare for—*who knew how long?* Without his sunglasses, a frozen eyebrow was arched skeptically over an eye that squinted in the noon day sun. The other eyebrow angled straight across a cloudy, crystalline eye. Hands clasped behind his back, feet solidly on the ground, he stood as motionless as a statue in his European-cut business suit. But when he finally moved, Kasawi was like a menacing leopard.

"Your name?" he asked.

"Fred Marshall."

"Incredible, is it not, Mr. Marshall?" Kasawi pulled on his trim, gray beard and spoke English in a softly accented voice. "To think that here on this very spot, an Islamic Moorish Kingdom of the fifteenth century was the envy of all Europe. Silk and ceramics, the arts, one could even say civilization itself, flourished in peace. While the rest of Europe was staggering out of the Middle Ages and the Black Death, Granada boasted an advanced sewage system and public baths. But do you know what happened?"

"No, I'm sorry I don't."

"After a cruel ten-year war, King Ferdinand and Queen Isabella conquered Granada. With Christian fervor they burnt Granada to the ground. After centuries of an Islamic presence in this part of Europe, the Christians began driving the Moors out. Knowing they were defeating a civilization superior to their own the Christians wept, and decided to spare this jewel, this Alhambra."

"A fascinating story," Marshall said politely. "But I like to think of the present and the future. That is why I am here."

"That is why I too am here. But it is good to remember history. I believe that what was once the past will someday be the future, again."

"You may be right. But I think we should now begin our discussion."

"Not here. Let us walk to the less crowded Generalife gardens nearby. It will be better for you there. Like most Americans, you are too tense, Mr. Marshall. It is bad for the heart. Permit me to offer you the same advice I gave to another American not very long ago: You should learn to relax. You will last longer that way."

Walking up a steep hill the two men arrived at the perpetually moving pools and fountains of the Generalife gardens. Built as a summer retreat of the Moors, alternating pavilions of marigolds and apple trees looked down upon the Alhambra.

"Listen to the birds chatter, Mr. Marshall. Do you hear the waters sing?"

"It's all very nice, but if it's all the same to you, I want to talk—now—if you don't mind!"

"Very well. Begin."

"The way I see it, you can help me obtain something I want and I can help you acquire something you want. I think we can do business!"

"I'm not sure I know what you're talking about, Mr. Marshall."

"Look, I don't care why, or even if, you took Zach Pike. But I am sure a man of your power can surely find a way of returning him to a country that desperately wants him back."

"And what is it that I want, Mr. Marshall?"

"You want America's friendship and financial support. If you help us get Zach Pike, I am sure my government will look favorably upon you. What you don't want, believe me, is to get America ticked off."

"Naturally, I value America's friendship, but I'm sorry. I hardly see how......."

"You want Zvi Langer!" Marshall blurted out.

Not totally certain of his conclusions he'd wanted to hold back and see if Kasawi would nibble on some alternate bait. But with his patience already, perhaps too easily, frayed by Kasawi's rambling history tour, Marshall impetuously played his trump card. The moment he saw Kasawi's eyes widen, Marshall knew Kasawi's gamesmanship was over.

"For all of our differences, Mr. Marshall, we really are very much alike, you and I. We understand the driving emotions that make people chase after other people. Fear, loyalty, love, revenge, self preservation; we see it all. It is a talent, I think. Now tell me, how can you help me find and catch this Israeli?"

"Certain people at my disposal can be alerted to be on the lookout for him. When we spot him, we'll tell you. It will be up to you to actually catch him."

"But he moves like a fox. Like a savage. He already has slipped into Europe to kill a dear friend of mine."

"There is somebody else we can monitor," Marshall said. "Someone who is in Israel right now. This person is not as well trained as Zvi Langer. Maybe this person will venture out in an effort to help Langer find Zach Pike. I will let you know if we locate this person, for if we do, then Langer will be close by. *Very close by.*"

Kasawi smiled. His eyes shone as he extended his hand. "I promise that as soon as I obtain the Israeli, *inchallah,* you will get your Zach Pike."

Marshall took hold of the hand, and shook it.

Exiting the Generalife gardens, heading down the Alhambra's precipitous hill, Kasawi reined Marshall back a step, leaving him with one parting piece of history.

"The year Granada fell, Mr. Marshall, was 1492. A most tumultuous year. Jews, bereft of their Moslem protectors, were at the mercy of the Spanish Inquisition. Those who did not convert to Christianity were either killed, or exiled; forced, once again, to wander in search of a mythical home.

"In that same year, Mr. Marshall, Christopher Columbus discovered America, for Spain—for Christianity.

"And as for Islam, Mr. Marshall, at this very spot, in the very same year, Islam lost its foothold in the west. Years of unstoppable expansion were over. From a chronological perspective it happened in just a blink of an eye. But with that blink a shadow started to fall over Islam, one that sadly remains to this day. In the space of that blink, when the eye was closed, a terrible, unjust misfortune befell the Islamic world. Sometimes I think it was even just a mistake?"

Kasawi sighed deeply, then gazed through the one clear eye and the one cloudy eye directly at the American agent. "But, Mr. Marshall, the world is a circle, life goes around, and maybe in tomrrow's blink there will be some new opportunities. Maybe I will blink tomorrow only to discover that the past 500 years was just a brief nightmare. A blink."

CHAPTER TWENTY-FIVE

*I*n other years, in better years, the Party had always been a joyous holiday. Even when the children had been small—long before Zach led the New York Jets to the Promised Land—the Pike Super Bowl Party was an eagerly anticipated and well-deserved day off. More than a simple break from day-to-day hardships and worries, Super Bowl Sunday was a self-ordained right to cut loose; a rare chance to jump, and scream, and laugh, and *escape*.

Ben and Mary Pike had long ago tired of the sympathetic expressions of friends. They detested being the recepients of *"I'm so sorry's."* With an iron-will they determined that family and friends would have, this, their special day.

So they swung their doors wide open. They turned on every light in the house, they decked the rooms with cheer, and they crammed every nook with food and every cranny with spirits. And then, perhaps most importantly, they made sure to hide their pain and seal their sorrow, at least as best they could.

Now, with two hours to kickoff, the guests thronged into their Brookline home. Yet with every kiss that smacked bittersweet, with every hug that lasted a second too long or clutched a bit too hard, it was becoming clear to Ben that not even a Super Bowl could deliver a needed respite. The Party was a charade, the house a prison, his mind his cell.

"Sam," Ben hollered, "I have some calls to make. I'll be back soon. In the meantime make sure everybody's having a good time. Okay?"

Ben made his break out of the increasingly congested family room. He walked sideways through a bottle neck, skirted a hub of conversation, then darted through an opening. With his drink raised high above his head he smiled, exchanged a pleasantry here and there, but never stopped moving.

IIis heart pounded, his knees buckled. By the time he locked the door of the study behind him, Ben was in a sopping sweat. He leaned against the door and closed his eyes. And then, all at once, he saw himself on a tightrope, in the very middle of a high wire. *It was a long way down.*

At one end of the wire he saw the faces of Mark Hriniak and Lionel Lane. At the other end of the wire he saw the man from the Space Center in Huntsville.

Suddenly the wire started shaking from both sides. Groping for something to hold he grasped a fistful of air. He squatted, his arms see-sawed, and for a moment his balance seemed to stabilize.

But something was wrong.

With crushing dread he began to slowly look up ahead. There, out on the wire with him, almost within reach, was Zach.

The wire was swinging wildly now. It bounced up, and tossed them up. It fell down, and dropped them...down. With each successive bounce, there was no way of knowing if their feet would once again land on the wire.

Two figures abruptly raced onto the scene! Way down below a close friend, beside himself in despair, scurried around with a net. Hopeless though it was, he vainly tried to gage which way the two men on the high wire might fall. The other figure, looking much like a younger version of the man with the net, was making his way out onto the wire. With reckless disregard for his own safety, the young man was ever so close to his friend Zach. *Excruciatingly close!*

But the wire was snapping! There was a flash! A lunge! A.......

"Dad, are you okay? The game will be starting soon."

"Teddy? Yeah, I'm fine. I just have some business to attend to. I'll be right in. Please go back and see to your mother. Please."

"I put my money on the Cowboys."

"Yeah, but you're an idiot. Four hours from now we're going to see Boston—all of New England—go bonkers over the Patriots' win. You just watch."

"The Patriots wouldn't even be in this game if the Jets had Pike. New York would have beaten them in the Conference championship."

Parked around the corner from the Pike house, the two men from the FBI's Computer Analysis and Response Team intently watched the pregame analysis, and only occasionally glanced at their computer monitor.

And why not?

For the past two weeks, ever since their FBI counterparts had planted a device in Ben Pike's computer, the Team had repeatedly turned on his computer to transfer internal files by radio modem. But there was nothing of consequence. For two weeks they had patiently waited for Pike to enter any keystroke at all into his computer. But Pike never even turned on his computer!

Weary and ambivalent, the two FBI computer experts unwrapped corn beef sandwiches. They popped open cans of coke and leaned back for the big game. But unexpectedly there was a hum, followed by a brilliant burst. One man knocked over his coke, the other wiped mustard from his mouth. In unison they swiveled their chairs to a monitor and hit a record button.

Odie—

You know what I wish?

I wish you were here. You, and Aviva, and Zvi, and *Ayelet.*

I wish that right now we'd all be safe inside this home, watching a game, in the company of friends, and laughing for a change.

But instead, I lock myself in a room, in my own house, beaten and angry. I'm angry about the terrible tragedies that have befallen you and Aviva. I'm very worried for Zvi.

And I've become sick over Zach.

I don't know how much longer I can stand the probing and poking of the media, and the FBI. Just the other day, while at a symposium, an Arab approached me and all but threatened to kill Zach if I don't cooperate on the Vulture!

It's at the point where even if I could concentrate on the Vulture, no one would let me work on it. Lexington Labs seems not to want me around anymore.

For quite a while now Mary and I have discussed retirement. But retirement is more than grandkids and golf, right? I think retirement is having the opportunity of doing what one wants to do, how one wants to do it. And what I want to do is continue working on the Vulture, in peace, at my pace, for Israel, *in Israel.*

Yes, Odie, in Israel. I really don't think I'll ever again be able to continue from the States. A little bird tells me so.

But all of that is up in the air now. God willing, let's first get our children back again. Safe and settled.

Ben—

The two FBI computer experts continued their surveillance. They practically looked over Ben's shoulder as he hit an encryption program to scramble his message. They followed along and were almost right next to him as he set his modem and telephone to transmit the coded message to......Israel. They thought they nearly heard Ben's sigh, his relief that the message was secure, when he turned off the computer.

But what the two experts really heard, was the swift high-five clap of their congratulatory hands.

It was such an extraordinary land.

He had been such a peculiar man.

It was such an exotic locale.

He had been such a peculiar man!

As the Nile Valley River Transport Corporation's passenger-ferry skimmed along the blue waters of Egypt's Lake Nasser, Meg could not quite rid herself of the bothersome notion.

The environs near the city of Aswan had been beautiful. Meg thought she could never tire of watching *felucca* sailboats glide around the palm-studded islands of the Nile. Tall bullrushes fringed Kitchener and Sehel Islands as tropical birds flew overhead. On Agilka and Elephantine Islands, ancient temples and venerable Nubians exuded an aura of mystery and romance.

Yet it was the peculiar man from the American Embassy in Cairo who kept elbowing his way into Meg's thoughts.

"When you get to Cairo," Zvi had explained, "you have to go to the American Embassy to get a new passport. Your current passport, Meggie, has an Israeli entry stamp. The Sudanese consulate won't issue you a visa if they see that stamp."

"Just remember," Alan had reminded her, "you're now Margaret S. Baines. That's what you call yourself, that's what you answer to. Meg Symes is somebody else."

It had seemed to her to be pure semantics. But to Alan, to whoever it was he reported to, what it meant was that a new and valuable identity would now not have to be found for her. And so she was on her way as soon as it was discovered that Meg Symes, the Meg Symes who was Zach Pike's girlfriend, the one mentioned in several magazine articles, actually had a real and different sounding name.

Officially she had always been Margaret S. Baines. That was the name on her birth certificate. That was the name on her passport. But at a very young age, in fact at the same moment her father, Richard Baines, had forever abandoned his family, Meg eschewed the name. Beverly

Symes may have been a drunk, and in many ways an unfit mother, but at least she was there. At least she had a name a child could latch onto for an identity.

The peculiar man at the American Embassy's Sharia Kamal ad-Din Salah address certainly seemed to take an interest in her identity. *Was it too much interest?* Meg tried not to worry about it. After all, the inquisitive man was an American, a fellow citizen. Had it been a Sudanese consular official, Meg reasoned, who was so absorbed, then there would be reason for concern.

Meg glanced at her watch. It had been a few hours since the Nile steamer departed from the High Dam of Aswan. Completed in the 1960's, the Dam regulated flood waters and provided hydroelectric power. And although it backed up the Nile's waters to create the world's largest artificial lake, the lake on which she now sailed, the Dam also forced the relocation of ancient monuments.

With a skyward gaze carrying her in imagination up and over a cliff, Meg could now almost visualize the largest of the relocation projects— Abu Simbel. Cut into blocks by a team of international archaeologists, Abu Simbel's Temple of Ramses II had been moved to higher ground and set into a cliff sculpted to match the original.

Meg imagined the four immense 65-foot statues of Ramses guarding his temple. Dwarfing smaller statues of his favorite wife, Queen Nefertari, Ramses would be wearing the double crown of Upper and Lower Egypt. Ramses would be seated, in a pose of eternal watchfulness over his desert dominion. Meg wondered what it was he needed to see; what it was that he so needed to protect?

As evening splashed a dark purple hue to the sky, Meg returned to her seat in tourist class and closed her eyes. She tried to review the steps she was supposed to take in Khartoum. But sleep soon began to overwhelm her, and instead of dreaming about grand temples and majestic monuments that she one day hoped to visit, she tossed and turned as the peculiar man in the Embassy edged his way back in.

"So, Miss Baines, you want a new passport in order to get a Sudanese visa?" The consular official in Cairo was a thin man with heavy horn-rimmed glasses. He sported a bushy mustache that shook when he laughed, rolled when he guffawed.

"Yes, Mr. Kick. Since I don't know when I'll be back in this part of the world, I figure I should do it all; Israel, Egypt, and Sudan. But friends tell me if there's evidence of having been in Israel, Sudan won't let me in."

"That's right, Miss Baines," Paul Kick said, still laughing. "I see tourists who have to play by Sudan's little games all the time. But if you'll give me just one other photo I.D., plus an additional thirty dollars, I can expedite this passport for you."

Meg had planned on obtaining an International Drivers License in Cairo, as Margaret S. Baines. But having not as yet done it, all she had with her was an old driver's license. She reluctantly handed it over to Kick.

"Meg Symes?" exclaimed the consular. His bushy mustache sniffed.

"Margaret Symes Baines is my birth name. But I've used Meg Symes for so long I guess I got my driver's license in that name."

"I'll be right back."

Meg's eyelids briefly fluttered open, saw nothing in the darkness outside the ferry's window. Still ensconced in the dream, she pulled her blanket up to her chin, never imagining what actually happened next.

Kick took the passport and driver's license and went to a back-suite of offices. He ran the names through a computer and did not see any security asterisks register next to either name. Comforted by the clearance, he then made a photocopy of the passport and the license.

"Hey Paul, don't forget to take this." Eddie Reynold's, the Station Operations Chief, picked up the photocopied license from the machine. As he was about to hand it over to Kick, he glanced at the name. His eyes suddenly bulged.

Meg Symes! Meg Symes! Wasn't that the name of the person that Fred Marshall......

"You okay, Eddie?"

"Is this Meg Symes here?"

"Yeah, Margaret S. Baines. She's right out in front. She's getting a new passport made up so she can get into Sudan."

Eddie Reynolds followed the consular official out the door. They stopped a safe distance away from Margaret S. Baines and tried to look inconspicuous.

"Listen, Paul," Reynolds said. "Do me a favor. I know you haven't done much intelligence work, but just find out, if you can, when and how she's planning on going to Sudan. Okay? I'll owe you."

Meg stirred in her sleep, her forehead tight as she recalled what next happened with the consul.

Upon returning to his desk, Kick's laugh was replaced by a nervous twitter, accentuated by the tremble of his bushy mustache.

"With luck your new passport will be available tomorrow, Miss Baines. Where can we contact you when it's ready?"

"I'm at the Luna Park Hotel. But I can contact the Embassy. It's really no......"

"When were you planning on going to Sudan, Miss Baines?"

"As soon as I get my visa."

"Are you flying into Khartoum?"

"No." She tried to catch her breath. Kick's questions pressed on her with a certain urgency. "I thought I'd see the southern part of Egypt by taking the ferry from Aswan to Wadi Halfa."

"I hear it's a great trip, Miss Baines. Quite the adventure. You'll love it." Kick's laugh cracked. He snapped his mouth shut, smoothing his mustache with a trembling hand.

A hot morning wind greeted the Nile steamer as it dragged its way into Wadi Halfa. Wiping salt, sand and sleep from her eyes with a moist towelette, Meg stood on the deck with her fellow passengers.

As billed, Wadi Halfa certainly looked like a transit port; the type of place one would want to leave as fast as possible. Everything about the town was slow and cheerless. Money changers squatted in dull silence. Corrugated tin stalls and crumbling stucco booths sat languishing and dejected. As the ferry docked at the pier, the only discernable movement was the dragging by customs officials of wooden chairs up to rotting tables.

Meg presented her visa, opened her backpack for a customs search, and then inquired about transportation to Khartoum.

"Three days till the next train."

"And the next bus?"

"Oh, that will be hot and bumpy," laughed an official, "but it will depart *bukra*, tomorrow."

Without any other option, Meg checked into the Boheira Hotel for the day. Then she walked over to the police station to obtain the necessary travel permit. *Just like any normal tourist following required procedure.*

When she returned to her ground floor hotel room, Meg lay down to rest. There had been no raised eyebrows, no alarms, no inquisitive follow-up questions.

Her eyes closed, her body relaxed. She listened to the stillness.

Suddenly a car door slammed shut. Muted voices spoke very quickly in Arabic. And then, a summons.

Knock, knock, knock!

What happened next was a slow motion blur.

She was up, she was in the middle of the room, she was by the window, she was at the door.

A cinnamon brown man, young and wearing a jalabiyya, stood in the doorway. His eyes were alive, his mouth open in a wide grin. He chuckled, giggled, snickered. With low, insinuating laughter, he relished her distress. He loved his power. He held the moment.

"And now you will come with us."

As if fog crept into her head, Meg became lost.

Queasy, numb, she blindly put items back into her pack. She hoisted the pack, left the room, climbed into a waiting car.

All at once Meg's eyes opened wide. Fear ripped through her. She wanted to scream.

There, on the back of the overhead visor, was a copy of a photograph. Distant in time and place, close to her heart and thoughts, the photo was marked with dark lines.

Three smiling kids in the summer sun of the Cape, pausing with family after a game of touch football.

A black circle drawn around Zach's head, and a check.

A black circle drawn around her head, and a check.

A black circle drawn around Zvi's head. *No check. Not yet?*

Jumpy with anticipation, the guests crowded into the family room just as the pregame show was ending. Galvanized with drink, food and each other's company, they located just the right spots from which to view the big-screen television—and simultaneously peek at the Pikes.

Having taken a seat on a sofa next to Mary, Ben realized with mounting self-consciousness that his family was part of the show. Too late, he felt the sidelong glances of the guests. *Would they be stoic? Could they laugh? Should they cry?*

Up on the screen members of the clergy somberly joined the NFL commissioner and Jets owner, Johnny Ciampana, at the fifty-yard line.

"*Psalms 70*

> *O God, hasten to deliver me; O Lord, hasten to my help!*
> *Let those be ashamed and humiliated, who seek my life;*
> *Let those be turned back and dishonored, who delight in my hurt........*"

Once again, *the probing, the poking.* Even in his own house, even at a Super Bowl party, Ben found no shelter, no escape. The words stabbed him. *The words were for him,* as well as for Zach.

> "*Let those be turned back in shame,*
> *Who say 'Aha, Aha!........*"

While the prayer continued the television cameras panned over the somber faces of a standing crowd. They zoomed in on the release of thousands of red, white, and blue balloons bearing Zach's number 16. And they hovered above Cowboy and Patriot players who knelt, together, in one huge, packed circle.

"*Psalms 121*

> *I will lift up mine eyes unto the mountains;*
> *From whence shall my help come?*
> *My help cometh from the Lord,*
> *Who made heaven and earth.*

> *He will not suffer thy foot to be moved;*
> *He that keepeth thee will not slumber.*
> *Behold, he that keepeth Israel*
> *Doth neither slumber or sleep.*

The Lord is thy keeper;
The Lord is thy shade upon thy right hand.
The sun shall not smite thee by day,
Nor the moon by night.

The Lord shall keep thee from all evil;
He shall keep thy soul.
The Lord shall guard thy going and thy coming in,
From this time forth, and for ever."

"Ladies and Gentlemen," Johnny Ciampana spoke into the microphone, "on this glorious January day in Miami's Pro Player Stadium, at this time when we ordinarily soar with unbridled enthusiasm, our hearts are wrenched.

"The past month has been grueling for us, and especially for the family of Zach Pike. But your letters of solidarity, your inspirational wishes, mean a great deal to us. They sustain us.

"I guess all I'm really here to say is what Zach's parents have requested me to say, which is—Thank You.

"And to you Zach, if you can hear me: Be strong and be strengthened. We love you. And we will find you."

As Ciampana ended his remarks the stadium began to stir and rock. It was as if a throng was moving, *mobilizing*. But the players remained, as they were, in their giant, tight huddle.

Suddenly the players all rose as one. Seeking roving sideline cameras, the players began pointing towards their chests. There, stuck over their hearts, were big, black patches with prominently emblazoned number 16's. In an instant the players were pounding their chests, thumping their black patches.

In the Pike residence friends pumped their fists and swore words of encouragement. They patted Mary's back and rained thunderous claps on Ben's shoulders. The family room throbbed with emotion.

On the screen the players were now hopping up and down. They yelled, and hollered, and roared. Like warriors, they raised and rattled their helmets as if they were sabers. They were going wild! They were going out of their ever-playin' minds!

And then they bared their teeth.

CHAPTER TWENTY-SIX

*A*nd *how many will die?*

It was going to be asked. Either of him as Chairman of the Joint Chiefs, or of Gordy Bannister as Joint Special Operations Command officer. It would be asked because—*they hated surprises.* Surprises meant *they* were not in control, and that was entirely unacceptable.

But how could he answer such a question?

No matter how well-prepared Special Forces were, Mac Streicher knew there would be mistakes, miscalculations, acts of subterfuge, and acts of God. He would want to simply shrug and say *'Shit happens,'* but that kind of response also was entirely unacceptable. They'd all gathered at the Pentagon's National Military Command Center for a last run-through of the planned scenario, and it would come down to numbers, projections—their absolute best guesses.

"The reason we wanted this meeting to take place here," the Secretary of Defense began, "inside the War Room, is so that you'd have a better understanding of our operational setup. Whether in actual fact you'll be at the White House Situation Room as the combat rescue mission is underway, or at JSOC headquarters at Fort Bragg, if you can at least picture in your minds what will be taking place here, then perhaps our lines of communication will be a bit clearer." Paul Calloway looked around the room. "And clear communication lines translates into an enhanced ability to perform our jobs, in what could be a hot situation."

There was a slight stir as bodies shifted in chairs. The tension in the room was palpable. "I will be here in the War Room with Mac monitoring and directing the overall scope of the operations," Calloway continued. "Assisting us will be the Special Technical Operations Center of the Pentagon, STOC. A staff of thirty men will be on line with the latest in high tech displays, communications, and computers. In that way we will not only be in direct contact with all of you, but also with AWACS in the area and with a Battle Group consisting most prominently of the helicopter and Harrier carriers, *U.S.S. Boxer* and *U.S.S. Essex,* in the Red Sea. Gordy, what will be happening on your end?"

"The Ops-Center of JSOC will be in touch with units in the field by way of a SATCOM satellite-transceiver. This Special Forces phone will be constantly on. In this way we will be immediately apprised, by Colonel Dancer and his men, of the situation on the ground. And just as importantly, we can direct them according to the latest data we obtain."

Howard Jones spoke up. "The CIA and the National Photographic Interpretation Center are also arranging for a KH-11 reconnaisance satellite to be over Khartoum at the time of the operation. Through the miracles of technology we can view all this unfold in real-time."

"And what about the White House?" Calloway asked.

"The Situation Room.....," Lou Reed began.

"Let me answer that," interrupted President Earl. "The National Security Adviser," he pointed to Lou, "Howard and I will be in the Situation Room. I will have the capability to instantaneously speak with any of our allies; either to explain what is going on, allay their concern, or ask for their assistance if we need it. Though Lou, Howard, and the White House Chief of Staff," he gestured toward Mark Handsman, "will advise me on breaking developments, I, as Commander-in-Chief, will ultimately decide on any operational changes. There will be no decision by committee."

A huge screen descended and lights began to dim. Gordy Bannister leaned towards Clyde Dancer and whispered, "you're on. It's your show, *One Horse*. Work it!"

Tall and striking in his Class A green uniform, the mission's Delta officer stepped out in front of the distinguished panel. In the twilight surroundings, phosphorescent visuals cast a halo around his dark features.

"The Pentagon's image perspective transformation lab has blended hundreds of still satellite photos into a digitally enhanced and animated 3-D image. Before you is the city of Khartoum-Omdurman as if we were flying over it. There you can see the airport base of Sudan's Airborne Division, a primary target of Seal Team-Six." Dancer used a laser pointer to pinpoint an area of the screen.

"We are now approaching from the east, north of Khartoum, which is the direction the MH-60 helicopters will come from after departing from the amphibious assault ships in the Red Sea. The terrain is flat, as you can see, and the helicopters will fly in low, crossing the Nile north of Khartoum. Then they will head south to Omdurman. Omdurman's buidings are scattered, and as you can appreciate there are, fortunately, huge open areas. The MH-60's will hover right here by this cemetary, half a mile from Kober prison. The helicopters are shielded from the prison's line of sight by these low buildings." He pointed again, the red beam sweeping over a row of what looked like apartment buildings.

"After fast roping down from the helicopters, part of the force will secure this lone road to Kober. The bulk of the force will move on Kober and eliminate enemy troops around the prison. Kober will be encircled and an assault team will scale its walls with portable ladders."

"Won't guards in Kober notice the commotion outside?" Reed asked. "Won't that jeopardize the mission?"

"It might. That is why there will be a surprise element in this operation. Moments before the outside assault, a team will execute a High Altitude, High Opening jump from a MC-130E Combat Talon. Unless there is a sudden *haboob* sandstorm, we can hit the drop zone inside

Kober with total precision. The jump is silent and all of our gear, including our square chutes, will be black. In all likelihood the team will eliminate the guards only after landing. But if any of the men are at very close range to guards or watchtowers as they drop, the rules of engagement call for them to open up with silenced automatic fire. We have been practicing this phase of the operation and are becoming quite proficient at it."

"And Zach Pike?" Reed asked.

"We are prepared to break into his barrack with explosives if necessary, and clear it. If Zach Pike is in good condition then we will head back towards the choppers. If he is in bad shape, or if any of my men are gravely wounded, we can call for the choppers."

"So let me be clear." Earl pointed a pen at Colonel Dancer. "You are absolutely, 100% prepared for the mission?"

"We are at C-1, Mr. President. Combat-ready, no deficiencies. The instant we get go-ahead, we will move out and board the carriers already in the Red Sea."

The President started to turn. He shifted his weight. A stern look on his face, he stared, first at Mac Streicher, then Gordy Bannister. And then, slowly, his expression softened and he asked, in an almost gentle voice,"what are the casualty estimates—Mac?"

Shit!

"If we are very unlucky—a chopper could catch fire or, say, the surprise parachute jump fail—casualties could run to upwards of thirty or forty men. But," he gazed at the ring of background light surrounding Clyde Dancer's sihouette, "I have to believe that the spirits will be with us, that they will not abandon us, and that casualties will be very light."

"Okay then," sighed President Earl. "You have go-ahead."

"There's still one item that needs to be settled on," Calloway said. "What's the code name for this? We need a code name."

Voices around the table threw out suggestions. "How about *Operation QB?*"

"Or *Special Teams?*"

"*Protective Pocket!*"

"*Deep Threat!*" Bannister drawled, lowering his voice two octaves.

Streicher shook his head, laughed. "No, no, no. One QB. One Team. One mission. *Operation One Horse!*"

"*One Horse?*" mused Earl. "Yes. Yes. *One Horse.*"

"You lose, Fred."

Hurley Baker smiled in triumph as he crossed paths with Fred Marshall in the Langley, Virginia hallway. Expecting Marshall's usual response, a gruff grumble or a snappy retort, Baker was disappointed. There was a certain pleasure in riding a curmudgeon like Marshall. So the DCI tried again.

"Cowboys really sucked, Fred. Hope you have your money wad ready."

Marshall pulled a twenty-dollar bill out of his wallet and pressed it into Baker's hand. His steel blue eyes drifted towards Baker but then slid away in distraction.

"It was only a game, Hurley. Just a lousy game." Marshall's voice trailed off as he walked off toward his office.

He had been so euphoric!

Just three days ago Eddie Reynolds, *his* Cairo Operations Chief, informed him of Meg Symes' new identity, destination, and travel plans. All Amir Kasawi would have to do was keep an eye on her. Then, when Zvi Langer met up with her, Kasawi could seize him, and most importantly, then release Zach Pike.

But Marshall's mood was now manic. The embassy in Khartoum had received a phone call from a Nile steamer passenger who befriended Margaret S. Baines. "Miss Baines did not show up for an arranged dinner in Wadi Halfa!" Concerned, the passenger had gone to Miss Baines' Boheira Hotel but still she could not be located.

Wasting no time, Marshall had instructed case officer Neal Meara, of the Khartoum base, to investigate *the alleged disappearance of an*

American citizen. Meara had dispatched a Sudanese agent, one of the very few to have actually been administered an Asset Validation System polygraph, to uncover what happened in Wadi Halfa.

Marshall now stared with apprehension at a sealed communique on his desk. Finally he tore into the envelope.

> *Asset went to subject's hotel and spoke with hotel manager.*
> *The frightened hotel manager states he saw three men pull*
> *up to subject's door. Subject immediately left room with*
> *belongings and entered vehicle. Subject appeared nervous.*
> *Subject never checked out of hotel. Subject has not been*
> *seen since the incident.*
>
> *Neal*

Suddenly Marshall lunged at the air. He ripped up the comminique, and spat.

The double crossing bastard! That son-of-a-bitch Kasawi!

Break his bones! Grind him up! Tear his cheatin' heart out!

Meg Symes wasn't supposed to be touched! Wasn't meant to be caught!

As if shot, Marshall collapsed into his chair, his mind fixed on the nightmarish scenario. *What if Kasawi doesn't even release Zach Pike or Meg Symes once he gets hold of the Israeli? What if he kills them?*

NO! There would have to be some explanation for Meg Symes' disappearance. Maybe it was all part of the Israeli's plan? Maybe she was supposed to go into deep cover?

Marshall stirred, began to think. He momentarily considered Neal Meara but then ruled him out. Unlike Eddie Reynolds, Neal wasn't really one of *his.*

He began to compose a message.

> *Subject: A meeting between Amir Kasawi and yourself.*
> *Determine if he has anything to do with the disappearance*
> *of Margaret Baines in Wadi Halfa.*

Ascertain if he has any explanation for the disappearance.
Obtain his thoughts on how to now best proceed.

Semper Fi-Kelly Doyle!

The Attorney General's dark eyes gleamed as he bursrt into Lee Nunzio's office. Lopes wet his lips, then shot a thumbs up, both hands.

"You got him?" Nunzio nervously asked.

"If you mean Ibrahim Husseini, then yeah. Legally the FBI has more than enough evidence to prosecute. The phone conversations with Charlie Hammami, proof that he mailed a copy of **Pike's Peak** to Hammami's London home, records of bank deposits that go from Hammami to Husseini, and now even sworn testimony from a couple of those already arrested in the Rockefeller incident that Tomas Bahr was seen with Husseini. And of course now there's also Huntsville and your tape of his rendezvous with Ben Pike, the threat against Zach."

Nunzio dug his elbows into his desk and rested his chin on clenched hands. He stared somberly at Lopes.

"But did you get *him?*"

"You must mean Ben Pike? That's a tough one. The Huntsville incident is of no help whatsoever—Ben Pike never even responded to Husseini. When Pike sent that computer message to Israel he came real close. But it's my legal opinion that we're not quite there." Lopes leaned towards Nunzio and continued.

"You see Lee, in an espionage case, unless agents actually witness somebody—*catch somebody*—passing classified information, there's not enough to arrest and win. We need a confession! In a way Ben Pike almost did just that when he said he wants to continue helping Israel with the Vulture. The problem is that he was contracted by the Defense Department to assist Israel with elements of the Vulture anyway!"

Lopes shook his head, shrugged. "It's crazy! I know what he meant when he said he wants to continue helping, you know what he meant, but in a court it won't stand up!"

What Nunzio did know was Victor Lopes—all too well. Instinctively, he understood what the Attorney General wanted. *He wanted the kill!*

"You want to squeeze him."

"The Behavioral Science Unit can do it, Lee. They say Ben Pike is falling apart! Expert coaxing, just the right nudge, and he'll break! The Unit will commiserate with what he's been through. 'We understand,' they'll say. They'll appeal to his patriotism. They'll assure him the Vulture project with Israel will continue. They'll promise him that if he confesses, the Justice Department will be told he cooperated; that his family won't be interviewed or investigated; that he"ll get off light; that the media......."

"You can't do anything to him! Not in the predicament his kid's in! Nothing, *nothing* can be done now! If the Islamic extremists holding Zach Pike catch wind that we're investigating—let alone prosecuting—his old man for having helped Israel, then Zach Pike's dead!"

"Calm down, Lee. I know that. But this Zach Pike thing won't last forever. One way or the other it will be resolved. God forbid, if the kid is killed I know this will never see the light of day. But if things work out okay, when it blows over, *we* can do it. *We* can show President Earl all the evidence. *We* can convince him that all *we* need is a confession. *We* can......."

The graying man with the neatly trimmed beard once again vainly looked beneath the ferris wheel of Mogran Amusement Park. He slammed on his blue cap and meandered over to a stand to buy an orange popsicle. It instantly started to melt in Khartoum's sultry evening air.

The Park's colorful lights and carnival music brought glee to the faces of its patrons. Beaming children tugged the long jalabiyyas of their fathers, pointing towards rides that went up, down, and sideways. For Zvi, the man with the blue cap, everything suddenly began to spin. And every swirling, twinkling light, every gleeful laugh that rose up around him, jarred his memory and chillingly reminded him that—*somebody was missing.*

"I'm looking for Wolde Zeleke."

"I am Wolde Zeleke," the man had said. He looked over the propped up hood of a Land Rover and smiled. In the background a cassette was playing Bob Marley's, *No Woman, No Cry.*

"You have regards from a friend—Robel Tekle."

"Oh," laughed the man. His eyes sparkled. "You mean Reuven. How is he? How are his parents, and his brothers, and his sisters? I miss them very much. Why don't they write more? How are Reuven's children? How is their life in Izrael? It must be very lovely there, I would think. Look at what Reuven sent me from Izrael. Look!"

Wolde held up a gold Star of David from a chain around his neck. Then he lifted up another charm, a silver lion.

"I am not a Jew, but I am proud to wear the Star, and of course my Ethiopian Lion of Judah. Together they bring me much luck and happiness. They protect me."

Wolde ran over and effusively shook Zvi's hand. He seated Zvi on top of a wooden crate and poured him a tall glass of mint tea. After cutting several slices of *injera* bread, he talked. And talked.

And talked!

He spoke of his life in the Simien Mountain town of Debat; of his wife and seven children; his tour guide business; his dreams and his hopes.

He wanted to know everything about Reuven. Was he happy? Was he healthy? Would he ever come and visit?

Wolde's smile never disappeared, the glint in his eye never clouded over. Three hours of conversation raced by in a blink.

"And now my friend," Wolde abruptly inquired, "what can I do for you?"

"I have to go to the Sudanese city of Gedaref."

"Oooh, no problem, no problem."

Wolde knew all the back roads. He skillfully steered his Land Rover around pot holes, sink holes, and flooded holes. He chased away goats, ibex, and baboons. He refueled the Land Rover from Jerry cans. He negotiated with a former Eritrean guerilla on a fair price for an AK-47. And he cooked up a delicious stew of *Kuk Wat* peas and vegetables the one evening they camped out in the bush.

"Wolde," Zvi said as they sat by a warm glowing fire, "you have not seen Reuven for a long time. Why do you do this?"

"I think it is like this: Good friendship grows and deepens. Actually, it becomes even more important if the friend is not near you. A good, old friend pulls at your heart from afar. When the friend is not near you, not with you, every memory touches your heart and waters your eyes. It is very sad. So you feel the touch and the tears and you wish, so so hard, that you could have the friend once again. And if you are so fortunate as to be able to help the friend, in any way, you do so. Then you have the friend near to you again. For after all, what is a friend if not somebody that you help? But you understand that, don't you?"

Zvi was silent, under the fire's spell. He threw in some twigs and then got up. "Thank you, for Reuven, for myself. Good night, Wolde."

The next day Wolde parked the Land Rover around the corner from an Ethiopian border checkpoint. He grabbed some liquor and several erotic magazines.

"Stay put! Do not get out. Leave this to me." Then he vanished, leaving Zvi to swelter.

After an hour Wolde appeared at the door and got in. His face was taut, his grin was gone; his shirt clung with perspiration.

"Is everything okay? What happened?"

"Just stay down low!"

Zvi crouched in front of the back seat and felt for the AK-47. Wolde drove slowly and evenly. A minute passed by, then another.

"Welcome to Sudan," Wolde chirped, his big grin returning.

"What?" Zvi said from the back. "We're across?"

"Welcome to Africa," Wolde laughed. "A Sudanese soldier was at the Ethiopian checkpoint borrowing coffee. I also gave him some of the money you gave me, and some of the liquor. So he waved to his friend at the Sudanese checkpoint to let the Land Rover through."

Zvi put the AK-47 into his pack and took out a blue cap. On it was the United Nations High Commissioner for Refugees logo, the one depicting hands sheltering a refugee. Then he put a UNHCR name tag onto a chain and fastened it around his neck. He shoved a United Nations *Laissez Passer* passport into his pocket.

"I am a Jew, Wolde. And right now I wish I could wear the same Star of David you have. But I can't. So for now I have to hope that this chain will protect me."

Wolde let the 'UNHCR representative' off at the town of Showak. He pointed the way to Gedaref, and beyond that the way towards Khartoum itself. Then the two men shook hands, held a long final look, and simultaneously said, "Thank you."

Alone, way up high, in a rocking ferris wheel seat that overlooked an alien city, the man with the blue cap blinked, then flinched. He had no firm recollection of the past few minutes, no solid impression as to the course of events that brought him—*to this!* It was a long, dizzying way down.

All at once the man was a boy once again, hiding in a tree limb on the Cape, having just overheard a disturbing revelation.

The ferris wheel seat began to dangerously teeter. Petrified, the man looked to the side, but this time there was no friend to grab him, steady him, guide him down.

ZACH! ZVI! Where are you? A voice from below, a girl's voice.

I'm up here! the man screamed. *Meggie? Where are you? Why aren't you here?*

The man leaned forward, cocked his head to the side, and waited for a response.

There was none.

CHAPTER TWENTY-SEVEN

*K*elly Doyle ran.

Her arms pumped, her strong legs chugged, her unwieldy *One World, One Mission* pack bounced at her back. Her face reddened from a healthy pink to deep crimson. Like a missile she flew. Like an angel she took wing.

Closer—Faster.

She was running headlong towards something, but she did not really understand what. All she knew was that the microdot message, the one she'd received via diplomatic pouch at the American embassy, sounded urgent. An American woman named Margaret S. Baines was missing! And perhaps Amir Kasawi would know what happened to her. It was her job, her responsibility, to find out.

Kelly raced past U.N. Square and the Al-Kabir mosque. Stunned worshippers gawked; merchants gasped.

Faster!—Closer!

This time she couldn't wait until Friday, couldn't wait for the Whirling Dervishes of Omdurman. She had to speak to Kasawi. *Right now!*

Kelly could see the waters of the Blue Nile before her now. She turned right on Sharia el-Nil and headed towards the *Qasr ash-Shab*, the People's Palace.

There, approaching a limousine, was Sheik Amir Kasawi. He was turning to say something to Prime Minister Al-Omri, turning to……

"Stop!"

To the soldier with the M-16, Kelly was quite a sight. Sweaty and red, with curly hair tousled and her back pack off kilter—*she was crazy!*

"I must talk to Sheik Kasawi," she panted. "Please! It's very important."

"No! I can't allow it. Stop. Stop!"

"But he knows me! If he would just look my way, he'd speak to me!"

"Stop!" barked the soldier, pointing his gun. "Go back!"

"He'll recognize me," pleaded Kelly, reaching into her pack. "If you could just show him…."

The shot crackled Khartoum's listless air. The bullet tore up Kelly's chest. Her hand convulsed and a book sailed upwards.

She staggered and the book landed just as she toppled to the ground. She gazed up, and except for her quivering lips, she was very still.

> *The Lord is my shepherd; I shall not want.*
> *He maketh me to lie down in green pastures.*
> *He leadeth me beside the still waters.*
> *He restoreth my soul.*
> *He guideth me in straight paths for his Name's sake;*
> *Yea, though I walk through the valley of the Shadow of Death,*
> *I will fear no evil,…….*

A sudden wind, a kind wind, blew through. It caressed her purplish lips, combed her matted hair, kissed her pale face, and hovered over Anna Amundson's soul.

Then the wind leaped.

It swirled over to the book, hovered, then frantically leafed through its pages.

> *Surely goodness and mercy shall follow me all the days of my life;*
> *And I shall dwell in the house of the Lord, forever.*

Warden Hassan paraded out of Kober prison's main gate, a lofty smile radiating from his brownish face.

"*Masa-il-Kheer*, Good evening. *Tisbah ala-Kheer*, Good night!" he chimed while saluting the soldiers outside the prison's walls. "You should have a pleasant watch."

For such a young man, warden Hassan had a long reputation. An expert practitioner of the *curbash* whip, a skilled manipulator of the forked *shebba* torture, warden Hassan was notoriously cruel. But what seperated him from other thugs, what made warden Hassan truly evil, was the delight he took in his atrocities. For him, brutality was the ultimate in power, the pinnacle of domination. And more than merely appreciating the usefulness of brutality, the warden *liked it*.

Driving along Sharia al-Murradah, along the banks of the White Nile, Hassan now contemplated his business at Omdurman's camel market. Owing to his name he would naturally have no problems buying the best camels and obtaining the best guides. Those were the most critical aspects of the travel arrangements which He wanted, what He.......

With a glance in his rear view mirror, Hassan was momentarily startled to see the same white Renault that he'd first noticed near the prison. But it was about fifty meters behind him, and it was not gaining any ground.

Comforted, he sped by Tuti Island, his eyes following a sign pointing towards the Tomb of the great nineteenth-century Mahdi.

Now there was a man who understood the applications of power! True, the current Mahdi had not as yet humbled the West, but he was a man who appreciated the relevance of fear in the modern world. He understood that only a return, no matter what the cost, to strict *Sharia* law would.......

The Renault was twenty meters behind now, *and closing!*

Hassan floored his accelerator and precipitously veered left onto Sharia Shambat. But the Renault was still right there, *still right behind!*

Closer, closer...., Hassan allowed the Renault to close the gap. Then he cut his wheel sharply to his right.

In open desert now, kicking up a cloud of sand, Hassan frantically looked over his left shoulder only to see a white man with a blue cap throw his hand brake up and execute a 180 degree turn. The man's tires screeched as they accelerated in pursuit, hummed as they hit the sand.

Deeper and deeper into the desert. The Renault had an answer for every juke, every swerve. So many that after two minutes Hassan was swooning. *Nothing was working.* The driver of the Renault was a fiend, well versed in spin, a master of sway.

Dizzy and lost, Hassan was succumbing. The Renault devoured the last few meters that seperated them, and then it rammed Hassan's car on the side.

Again, and again, and harder. The Renault was relentless!

Suddenly Hassan's car rode up on its two right wheels, and flipped.

By the time the Hassan opened his eyes, before he could even fumble for his revolver, an AK-47 was aimed between his eyes. Blood gushed from a gash in his forehead, practically blinding him. His white jalabiyya was red.

"*Ana batkallim arabi*, I speak Arabic," said the man.

"So you have finally come."

"I want some answers. A friend I was supposed to meet in Khartoum is missing. Where is she?"

Hassan smiled. His eyes crinkled. After a kick to the stomach he laughed outright.

"Where is Zach Pike?" screamed the man, kicking once more.

Hassan's smile was insane. It was sadistic, masochistic.

Reaching up to his window visor, Hassan plucked down a copy of a photograph. As the man examined the relic of his youth, of his memories, of what once was, he went berserk.

For an instant the desert erupted into tumult: a shrill, a howl, the sharp crack of a club. And then silence, *silence,...silence.*

Tenderly Zvi picked up the photograph. Staring into his past, he spotted the handwriiten *fatwa* decree on the back side.

One, two, three.
The world will reel when it sees the might of true faith.
It will quake as it hears the march of resurrected power.
You are the Ansars!—the followers, the helpers, the soldiers.
I am your.......

Suddenly the putt-putt of an engine could be heard as it made its way closer to investigate the accident. Leaping into the rented car, the man pulled himself away from the photo, from the past. His white Renault jolted him, *forward.*

CHAPTER TWENTY-EIGHT

What the hell's going on here? Neal Meara wanted to know. He was the goddam CIA case officer, so how come he was the last one to be in the know?

It was bad enough the Sudanese were apparently holding Zach Pike.

But now he'd learned an American identified as Margaret S. Baines had vanished in Wadi Halfa. Then, hours later, an American missionary worker named Kelly Doyle was shot in front of the People's Palace at point blank range by a Sudanese soldier!

So Meara raised his voice. He slammed his fist on the nearest table and physically imposed himself at the People's Palace.

"Listen to me," he told a desk clerk. "I don't care if it is the middle of the night. If I don't get an immediate audience with Sheik Amir Kasawi, there'll be hell to pay. Do you read me? And I will personally single you out as obstructing all of my efforts."

"Wait here," moaned the clerk. "I'll see what I can do."

Minutes later Meara stormed into Kasawi's office. Waiting for him, standing but five feet away, was the Sheik. He was ready to defuse the American, and to make good his own escape. Kasawi bowed in respect, then rushed towards Meara, grasping both his hands.

"I am so sorry, so sorry. On behalf of my country, I extend my heartfelt condolences. That such a thing would happen in Sudan is indeed a tragedy."

Kasawi led Meara to a grand chair made of Lebanese cedars and Genoan velvet. Then he sat down on a folding chair right in front of him.

"Why did your guards shoot that girl?" Meara asked.

"It was a mistake. The guard panicked when he saw her running towards Prime Minister Al-Omri. The woman ignored the guard's command to stop. But let me assure you that the incident is being investigated and that the guard is currently under arrest."

"What possible reason would this girl have to charge towards Al-Omri?"

"There is something I must tell you," Kasawi sighed. He pulled his chair closer and removed his sunglasses. His deformed eye, opaque, fixed, was at once both hideous and spellbinding. "I believe Kelly Doyle wanted to see me. Did you know she worked for your CIA?"

"What? I don't understand. How could I not have known this?"

"Our intellgence sevices, our *mukhabarat*, have known for some time that Kelly Doyle was working under cover. In fact, so far under cover that you would not have been told of it."

"You mean a non official cover?"

"If that's what you call it, then yes. Anyway, Mr. Meara, when I found out that Zach Pike was indeed being held in Sudan, I was in a very precarious position. Naturally I wanted to help resolve the matter and inform your government of what I had learned. But I had to be very careful and secretive because, Mr. Meara, *I have enemies in this country.* They render me less powerful than I may appear. So I decided not to go by way of a conventional route, that is to say not to inform you or directly contact your government. It would have been too dangerous for me. So I approached Kelly Doyle and she arranged a meeting for me to share what I had learned."

"A meeting with whom?"

"I met in Spain with somebody by the name of Fred Marshall."

"Marshall! Why wouldn't he tell the agency what he learned from you?"

"Because, Mr. Meara, Fred Marshall is a bad man. A rogue. I noticed that as soon as I met him. He would have nothing to do with passing on my offer of help to others. He was, how do you say it, *cutting his own deal.*"

"What deal? What are you talking about?"

"Marshall somehow found out that my enemies, the ones actually holding Zach Pike, were using him as bait; a lure to catch a close friend of Pike's named Zvi Langer. Apparently this Langer is an Israeli assasin, somebody who has killed Islamic fundamentalist leaders. At any rate, Marshall made an arrangement with my rivals to help them catch Zvi Langer in exchange for the release of Zach Pike."

"What on earth was Marshall's rationale?"

"He knew America was not capable of making such a deal. He took it on himself to do it, figuring it was a way of insuring the safe release of Zach Pike without risking further American lives." The Sheik was calm and forceful in his explanations, very convincing.

"And just how was Marshall going to help your adversaries catch this Israeli?"

"Ah, that's where the missing American in Wadi Halfa fits in. You see, Mr. Meara, in all likelihood Margaret Baines is actually Meg Symes, the girlfriend of Zach Pike and the good friend of Zvi Langer. Fred Marshall must have given her name to my rivals knowing that she might come to Sudan and help lead them to the Israeli."

"But why was Meg Symes abducted? Why not leave her alone and let the Israeli come to her?" Kasawi was smooth, but his story still didn't quite hold water.

"I believe that the same group who kidnapped Pike and made the deal with Marshall must have assumed that if they grabbed Meg Symes, then there would be even more incentive for the Israeli to show up. That it would even improve the chances of capturing him."

"And Kelly Doyle? Why was she in such a rush to see you?"

"I theorize that when Marshall discovered he had been cheated in the deal he made with my enemies, he realized he had made a terrible mistake by not letting me help. So he sent this poor woman who was at his beck and call to try and see me. It was he, Fred Marshall, who sent this woman to her horrible death."

Meara did not want to leap to conclusions. For all he knew Kasawi himself could have double-crossed Marshall. He was more than capable.

But like many in the CIA, Meara had always considered Fred Marshall a Directorate *cowboy*. And what Kasawi was saying sounded just like Marshall: arrogant, hot-tempered, secretive. A snake.

"Sheik Kasawi, do you have any idea where Meg Symes might be?"

"I'm sorry, I don't."

"Well, where is Zach Pike? Maybe she's with him?"

"He is at Kober prison, Mr. Meara."

"And these enemies of yours, *of ours,* those who kidnapped Zach Pike and may have Meg Symes—who are they?"

Amir Kasawi drew Neal Meara closer with a wave of his finger. Looking nervously around his office he cupped his hands around the case officer's ear, smiled, and whispered.

The calls were placed and the messengers were sent at exactly 7:30 P.M.

One was found at his home. Another was contacted at a restaurant by way of his portable phone. A beeper signaled yet a different man. Still others were hunted down among byways and alleyways all over Capitol Hill.

In each instance the confidential summons basically reiterated: *Emergency, Emergency. Drop what you're doing. Get your ass over to the White House, **now**, And shut your mouth.*

Limos, cars, even an occasional taxi, began arriving at the White House almost immediately. Before any of the Congressional members could exchange any hearsay, they were quickly ushered by an expanded White House staff down to a lead-encased conference area near the Situation Room.

Over in the Press Room of the West Wing, beat writers who may have noticed the commotion were told in no uncertain terms to '*sit on it!*'

Other members of the press headquartered across the street in the Old
Executive Office Building were kept away.

At 8:15 P.M. the doors of the Situation Room conference area were
locked. Any late arriving Congressional leaders were sequestered
upstairs in the Roosevelt Room.

At 8:16 P.M. President Earl hurried into the conference area.
Following close behind him were the Vice President, the Attorney
General, and the White House Chief of Staff. The President opened his
mouth as if about to speak, but then suddenly stopped. He personally
knew each and every man before him: the Speaker of the House; the
President Pro Tem of the Senate; majority and minority leaders; the
Chairman and ranking members of both the Armed Services
Committee and the Foreign Affairs committee. Now they all sat
upright, hanging for his every word. Looking over the assembled faces,
Oliver Earl tried to instill confidence in each mind, hope in each heart.

"At 7:00 P.M. our time, that's 1:00 A.M. in Sudan, an array of MH-60
Blackhawk, Super Stallion, and Super Cobra helicopters took off from
the *U.S.S. Boxer* and *U.S.S. Essex* in the Red Sea. Thus begins the mission code-named *Operation One Horse,* to rescue Zach Pike.

"The operation is a concerted and coordinated effort that involves
elements of our very best units and special forces. The operation calls
for surprise infiltration and quick exfiltration. We expect it to be over
within a matter of hours. But we are prepared for complications should
they arise.

"The circumstances necessitating the introduction of U.S. armed
forces are well known to all of you. Terrorists, with the knowledge and
cooperation of a foreign government, killed one U.S. citizen in
Manhattan and have kidnapped another from this country. They have
spirited him away to their shores and they dangle his young life and
make all manner of threats in order to alter American foreign policy. It
is tantamount to an attack on this country. In their most recent video,
the Sudanese Ansars threaten other American lives. We have reason to

believe they are even trying to obtain information that directly affects national security. The actions of the Ansars, and the culpability of the government of Sudan, is outrageous! Our response is appropriate, measured. But strong."

For an instant the President and Victor Lopes looked at each other and nodded in unison, their past differences momentarily suspended. Then the Attorney General stepped forward and went to bat.

"It is my judgement, and it is the opinion of Justice Department lawyers, that the President as Commander-in-Chief has authority to conduct this military venture. Article II, Section II, of the Constitution states that it is the President's right to employ forces as he sees fit.

"Of course Congress too has a role. You and your counterparts provide for and augment the forces and you determine what guidelines would best serve them. But that is for normal military situations. What we have before us is a crisis.

"So in conjunction with the War Powers Resolution, the President is not only notifying you within the required 48-hour period of his deployment of forces, but also is consulting you as he is required to do before engagement of forces. Your legitimization of this military action strengthens the effective conduct of the mission. The President turns to you for support."

It was an ambush! At least some Congressional members felt so. As in so many other instances, the President had acted unilaterally to usurp their voice and circumvent their power. He had consulted them only after already deciding to deploy and begin a military campaign. He had consulted them only when the commencement of operations was imminent.

One Congressman squirmed. Another coughed. Some shot disgruntled glances at each other. But the repercussions and rebukes would have to wait for another day. For now their front would be united. It had to be. *And they understood it had to be.*

Nobody protested. No advice was given. There was no debate. Their silence was their blessing.

A moment later several of the President's more ardent backers raced up to shake his hand. And as the President and his entourage rapidly departed they called to him, "Godspeed!"

Entering the Situation Room, the President loosened his tie and sat down between Lou Reed and Howard Jones. Before them was a video satellite feed of Kober prison. All around them a dozen technicians manned their computer and monitor stations.

"As you can see Ollie, it's still quiet. But that'll change soon enough."

"How soon, Lou?"

"In another twenty minutes Clyde Dancer and his Geronimo squad will jettison from the MC-130. It'll take them awhile to touch down since it's a high opening jump, from 35,000 feet. But two or three minutes after their touch down the rest of the Deltas should be on top of those walls."

"Okay. Get me the Pentagon and Fort Bragg."

"Mr. President, you can do it for yourself if you want," a technician explained. "Just hit that switch."

The President clicked up a green toggle and leaned forward. "Paul? Paul Calloway? Mac? You read me?"

"Yes sir, Ollie. This is Paul. Everything's fine in the War Room."

"Are the Sudanese on to any of this?"

"No. The AWAC's J-Star Joint Surveillance Target Radar System hasn't picked up anything out of the ordinary. And the ALQ-8 electronic countermeasures are sending out signals to the Sudanese that there's no aircraft at all in the sky. It also helps that the choppers are flying low over vast desert areas."

"What about the Seals?"

"They're well on their way. In twenty minutes they should be on the ground. Then they'll take up positions around the Airport and pin down the Airborne Division."

"And how about the status in the Red Sea?"

"I'll answer that. This is Mac, Mr. President. The *Essex* and *Boxer,* as well as the carrier Teddy Roosevelt, are on alert. Four Harriers are skyborne and ready if called upon."

"Gordy?"

"JSOC headquarters reporting, Mr. President. *One Horse* just told me his guys are skyhigh, if you'll pardon the pun." Bannister chuckled, though nobody else did. "Hey, Mac buddy!" he said after a pause.

"What, Gordy?"

"Relax, will ya! It'll be okay."

The President turned down the green toggle and leaned back. He looked again at the shadowy video feed of a serene Kober prison. His hands started to tremble.

"I'm lucky to have an old friend like you here," he said, turning to Lou Reed. He breathed in, held it. "Okay Lou," he said, finally, kneading his hands together. "This is it."

Chapter Twenty-nine

*L*aden with gear, snug under the layerings of their military armor, the ten men who sprawled in the guts of the fuselage prepared themselves for war. To the steady drone of the engines, in the persistent, soft illumination of an orange light, the ten men drifted in and out of a jumpy slumber. Every time anticipation and fear awakened them, they would tell themselves that it was best to rest, best to distance their minds.

But now, enevitably, finally, *it really was time.*

So they roused themselves, shook themselves. Looking at themselves, looking at each other, they checked and rechecked, *everything.*

The eleventh man never did drift off to sleep the whole time. Ever vigilant, he now paced to the cockpit of the MC-130E Combat Talon one last time. Then, equipped with the latest flight pattern coordinates and weather reports, Clyde Dancer lined his squad up for inspection. He wanted to know that they truly were ready.

After adjusting the combat vest of one of his men, he pounded and pounded the soldier's shoulders. Then he reassuringly tapped the soldier's chin. He examined another's parachute, slapped the chute, then massaged the nape of the soldier's neck. Approaching the final man, Dancer smeared black war paint over a small, smudged-away area in the corner of the man's eye.

The man, Lieutenant Colonel Jim Lonestreet, grimaced, shuddering slightly. Dancer had seen it before; the loss of focus, an instant of panic.

Somehow the second-in-command hadn't awakened just right. Somewhere, along some fine line, Jim Lonestreet had stumbled.

Reacting quickly, Dancer reached for Lonestreet, held him in his strong hands. Fixing him with a warrior's eye, Dancer found him, and saved him. The crisis passed.

"There is only one thing more noble than freeing a captive," Dancer said to his men. "And that is returning his soul back to the place it yearns for, the safety and love of his home. We have been blessed with just such an opportunity, and such a responsibility.

"Know this—Zach Pike is one of us. *He's just like us.* And like us, he can't fight forever, can't fight alone. It is imperative that we free him. We have to take him home!"

Suddenly the fuselage's luminous orange light turned emerald green. All eyes quickly sought out the jumpmaster. Wearing headphones, he grimly waited for his cue. He nodded his head, raised his thumb.

Eyes darted, seeking contact, but only for an instant. There wasn't time, *because the time was now!*

Dancer positioned his night-vision goggles over his eyes and ran to an open ramp. He looked back over his shoulder to the ten men behind him.

Crouching in a line, each man with an arm outstretched to touch the man right before, the squadron readied to pounce. The cold air whipped in torrents. The black night was everywhere.

Clyde *One Horse* Dancer leaped, hurling himself into the dark.

"Ollie." Paul Calloway said. "They're out! They've jumped!"

"How long till touch down?"

"About another twenty minutes."

"How are the choppers doing, Gordy?"

"Delta's MH-60's are two minutes behind where we thought they'd be. Winds from a small localized *haboob* storm forced them to swing a bit further west. But it should be okay. They'll fast rope down near Kober in another five minutes and make up for the lag."

Mac Streicher sensed it. *Something was wrong?* He recognized the concern in Bannister's voice. *Something was missing?* Years of experience told him so. With a furrowed brow he glanced at a monitor in the War Room. A blue dot depicting the location of the Stallions was still blinking.

"Shouldn't the Seals be landing now? And setting up perimeter positions around Khartoum International?"

"We've got a slight problem here, Mac. The helicopters' forward-looking infrared systems picked up a small convoy of military trucks on a road near the airport. The Seals are in a holding pattern till the convoy pulls farther away."

In the ensuing silence President Earl narrowed his eyes and abruptly turned towards Lou Reed and Howard Jones. He hunched his shoulders, raised his hands in question. They in turn weakly shrugged.

In the War Room, Mac Streicher doubled over, a long groan escaping along with his breath. He knew he had to quell the concern in the White House, answer the questions the President seemed hesitant to ask, *to say something—damn it*. But all he could do for now was lunge forward, toward the monitor before him.

Clyde Dancer pulled his rip cord seconds after the jump. As if attached to a giant rubber band, his billowing chute jerked him upwards with whip-lash force.

Other than an initial and faint "yee-hah," Dancer heard nothing and saw even less. The darkened C-130 stole away, his men, camouflaged, disappeared into the night sky, and the ground was still over five miles below. Even the drop zone was some twenty-five miles away.

With his arms by his side, not over his head where they would have frozen, Dancer reached for the control system on his chest. He checked his altimeter and then looked at his GPS Global Positioning System. An overhead satellite provided position coordinates and locked in the drop zone with a shiny yellow *x*. His own position flashed red.

As a backup he and his men carried a CADS Controlled Aerial Delivery System. In case of GPS failure, or if anybody were to become totally disoriented, they could simply latch onto a homing device that had been successfully dropped within two miles of the prison earlier that night. However, so far the weather was fine, the wind blew in a steady southerly direction, and Dancer hoped that his men were nearby and would not need to employ the CADS system. But as yet there was just no way of knowing.

Referring to his GPS, Dancer steered by pulling right or left on his toggles. As he parasailed he went ever lower and closer to the drop zone. He could now see the lights of Khartoum, and across the Nile the sparse lights of Omdurman.

Suddenly, as his eyes squinted through dark night, he discerned the dim but definitive rectangular lights of Kober prison. From here on he would rely on sight coordinates to guide him in. The ground, and whatever lay in wait, would careen towards him at full tilt.

With one thousand feet showing on his altimeter, Dancer began his final approach. As he turned into the wind to reduce his speed, he looked above and behind him.

His heart skipped!

There, faintly visible in the lights of the city, was a beautiful circular formation. Quickly he counted square canopies.

One…two…three, four, five, six, seven, eight, nine,……and ten!

The canopies were softly flapping as the team S-turned. Clutching his short barrel Heckler and Koch MP5K, Dancer could not yet clearly see into the prison's towers. Though no guards were visible in the courtyard, a group of soldiers sat in front of Kober's main gate.

200 feet, 150……

Sailing right over a tower, Dancer's finger stroked the sensitive trigger. He was about to pull, the tower guard having lit a cigarrette,……. *NO! NO! It was too fast!* Flaring into a brake, he pulled both his steering toggles down hard.

All at once he heard the loud shatter of glass. Snapping his head around, he saw the guard with the cigarette topple out of the tower. But an errant shot from one of his men, silenced as it was, had also exploded a prison light.

Crash!

Diverted by the ruckus, Dancer smashed into the ground. Rolling onto his knees he unsnapped his harness and then bolted for the cover of a barrack. With the shattered glass already alerting other guards, successive members of the team fired furiously towards the remaining towers as they descended.

With one immense sweep, the main gate of the prison swung open and a column of soldiers poured through into the courtyard. Dancer emptied magazine after magazine in their direction as he gave cover to his exposed team. Four Sudanese soldiers fell immediately. Two others were cut down as they fled. But many others got away! They slammed the main gate shut.

And then it got crazy.

Prisoners began banging on their doors. Some clanged on window bars and wailed insanely. Bullets from the towers whizzed into the courtyard and smacked into the ground as dull thuds. And an ancient siren moaned hideously, incessantly.

Scrambling from the glaring spotlight focused on the courtyard, Dancer's men sprinted for protective shadows. But one team member hopped on one leg even as his other leg dangled oddly at the knee. Another man was scooped up onto the shoulders of a friend. His arms and his legs kicked in the air as the man carrying him raced for cover.

"Clyde!" hollered Jim Lonestreet from a nearby barrack wall. "Tony's a stomach, Hobbie's a leg!"

"I want those two to watch the gate. Now listen! Shots are coming from there, that barrack window. It looks like the barrack Pike's supposed to be in. You, Kevin, and Jacks are going to come with me and circle around it.

I want the others to get that tower over there, and that other tower. Grenade launchers, sniping, anything. Just get 'em!"

Dancer pulled his SATCOM transceiver from a vest pocket and unfolded the webbed antenna. He keyed the microphone and a moment later he reached the JSOC Ops Center of Fort Bragg.

"Surprise is compromised! Surprise is compromised! Two wounded. Moderate resistance, but we're going after Pike. We'll need exfil! Repeat, need exfil!"

Dancer's eyes scanned the top of the prison walls. Delta squadrons should have long ago roped down from the Blackhawks. Even if a small group of Sudanese soldiers outside put up a fight, Delta should have covered the few hundred yards to Kober. They should have controled the main gate. They should have planted their portable ladders up against the walls. They should have been just about on top of those walls, over the.........

"Gordy? Where's Delta? *Where the fuck is the rest of Delta?*"

The real-time satellite video feed was a cruel mistake. No Commander-in-Chief should ever have to view something like this.

President Earl stared at the monitor before him and could not breathe. Even from a distant overhead angle he saw them splatter onto the courtyard, rise in confusion, and writhe in pain.

"We've got casualties," Gordy announced in a strained voice. "They're proceeding towards Zach Pike."

"We've got a problem," Mac blurted. "The Seals couldn't land in time to secure the airport. It seems units of Sudan's Airborne Division have been notified and are now on the move towards Kober."

"And what about Delta?" the President asked, tensely.

"Delta never made up for that lag time. They're out of their choppers, but now besides storming Kober, they've got to get ready for the Airborne."

"How bad is this, Mac?"

"The Super Cobras and Blackhawks will provide effective air support. But there's no getting around it, there's going to be a little war out there. There will be some casualties. And there won't be as much help inside Kober for Dancer's team. It's going to take a little longer."

The President buried his face in his hands. "And Zach Pike?"

There was a pause from the Pentagon's National Military Command Center. "We'll reach him, but now...." Another pause. "Whoever's guarding him has for some time now been alerted. It's not good, Mr. President. Not good."

From shadow to shadow. From cover to cover. Along whitewashed walls, by a circuitous path, Clyde Dancer, Jim Lonestreet, Kevin Mcvie, and Ira Jackson closed in. In sprints, and dives, and rolls they continuously outdistanced a trail of bullets.

Just as they reached the backside of their intended barrack, one tower was silenced. Then, seconds later, the other tower vanished in a fireball.

Working quickly, Kevin and Jacks affixed *I* and *H* shaped charges onto a heavy back door. They lit a fuse, ducked, and counted out their prayers with numbers.

One, two, three, four, five........

The door buckled and fell. Lobbing flash-bangs through the blown-away door, Dancer and Lonestreet screamed like banchees over the thunderclap of the magnesium-based grenades. Then they charged.

With tinted goggles they cut through the flash, ready to kill the instant they made an identification. Lonestreet immediately found a Sudanese soldier frozen in place. The soldier looked his way but saw nothing, other than an oncoming headlight. A moment later he was practically severed at the waist.

A very tall, very thin soldier ran out of a cell. His hands were up in the air, his face was decorated with tribal scars. Unexpectedly he opened his mouth as if to speak. But Dancer's nerves were fraying, his ingrained instincts ran deep, and he shot the Sudanese soldier dead between the eyes.

"Zach! Zach!" yelled Dancer. "Where are you? We've come to take you home!"

Suddenly a lone whistle pierced the confusion of the barrack. It whined horribly, echoed. And Clyde Dancer descended to his knees, to his stomach, face down on the flagstone floor.

A Sudanese soldier by the barrack window crouched low, trying to hide his guilt. But Jim Lonestreet found him in the midst of the clangor and flash, and sprayed his blood all over an ivory white wall.

Running over to Dancer, Kevin McVie plugged a gauze bandage into a gaping hole that had been his uppermost chest. But the bandage spurted out with the ryhthmic squeeze of his pulsing aorta.

In a frenzy, Lonestreet and Ira Jackson ran to every corner of the barrack. Then they and other members of Clyde Dancer's team ran to every corner of the prison.

"He's not here! He's not here!"

Jim Lonestreet's agitated SATCOM cry shook the Ops Center, the War Room, the Situation Room.

"Jim," Gordy Bannister asked tersely," where's *One Horse*?"

"He's dying!"

"And Pike? Are you telling us Zach Pike's not there?"

"He's not here! He's not here!"

President Earl's ashen face matched the ghostly gray of the video monitor. Far away, standing in the middle of a lonely courtyard, a soldier seemed to be looking up to the satellite; seemed to be looking up to the heavens.

"Ollie?" Howard Jones cleared his throat and gently tried again. "Ollie?"

"Yeah, Howard."

"Darndest thing? Langley just put a call through to me from Khartoum. Neal Meara, our case officer, insisted on talking to me. He says he just came back from Amir Kasawi's office. Seems Kasawi told him the strangest story. Kasawi claims he's innocent, that he's actually been trying to reach us ever since he found out Zach Pike was in his country. To that end Kasawi had a clandestine meeting with the CIA's Director for Africa Operations, Fred Marshall. But Marshall, according to Kasawi, didn't relay anything to us because he'd made an arrangement with the real kidnappers of Zach Pike."

"Look here, Howard. I've got a crisis on my hands right now. We've got boys dying out there and we suddenly have no idea where the hell Zach Pike is. Now unless what you have to tell me is somehow pertinent to what's going on, it'll just have to wait."

"Kasawi told Neal Mcara that Pike was in Kober but......."

"But he's not in Kober, Howard! You can see he's not!"

"But that's just it! Kasawi wasn't lying when he said Zach Pike was in Kober. We ourselves have known for a long time that he was there. Well, if Kasawi wasn't lying about that, then maybe the rest of his story is credible. Or at least elements of it."

Jones ran through Kasawi's story—how Pike was a lure for an Israeli friend who'd killed fundamentalist leaders, how Marshall was working on a trade of this Israeli for Pike.

"Ollie, if any of this is true, then maybe Israel has some idea where Pike is."

"This all sounds crazy to me, Howard. We know Kasawi is a criminal and a liar. Can you give me a solid reason to believe him?"

"Well, Zach Pike's girlfriend went to Israel after the abduction to be with this mutual friend. And we know for a fact that she is now missing—*in Sudan!*"

The President sighed and threw up his hands, exasperated. One more piece of bad news. "Okay," he said finally. "What's the name of this friend, this killer, that I'll ask Israel about?"

"Zvi Langer."

Langer? Langer! Wasn't that the same last name the FBI had mentioned? A friend of Ben Pike's, a Knesset member named Oded Langer, whom they claimed Ben Pike supplied information to.

The President opened his eyes. He suspected that it was all regrettably true—as real as the dying man on his video monitor, who was being rushed to the middle of a prison courtyard.

"Okay, Howard, get me the Israeli Ambassador and Prime Minister Ben-Ziyon. And Howard, just who did Kasawi claim was holding Zach Pike?"

Circling.

They were circling now.

The infinite sky above had no end. It knew no limits.

And why now, *just now,* at thirty-six years of age, was everything opening up?

In the distance, like drums the cannons fired, like cries the bullets shrieked.

But there was also song. Beautiful Sun Dance songs that cradled his heart and massaged his dreams. And sprinkles from a Lakota Medicine Man's pipe fell onto him like the peaceful falling of snow.

But for him, it wasn't going to be *that easy.* For what made him a warrior also held him tight. With his final struggle he tensed, he shook, he opened his eyes, he gasped.

And then his sisters at Standing Rock and his sons in Fayeteville took hold of an immense white cloth. In one sudden violent pull, they ripped the cloth and released his spirit.

And *One Horse* lived on.

CHAPTER THIRTY

*O*ne could get lost in a desert.

But one could also lose oneself in a desert.

Trekking across crescent-shaped sand dunes, traversing endless red and black mineral-laden dry *wadi* riverbeds, the caravan of fifty camels and nomadic tribespeople was picture perfect. In the pre-dawn moonlight, preparing to leave behind the shadowy date palm trees and scrubby shrubs of the Shabb oasis, the caravan appeared to be a romantic Saharan fantasy, an adventure daydream. But in reality, it was a nightmare.

"*Sabah il-kheer,* Good Morning," said an expert desert guide, a *khabir.* From the Kababish tribe of Nubia, the bedouin *khabir* stood by an immense boabab tree, sizing up the coming day just as he savored a cup of muddy Turkish coffee. A guide by trade, Rashid made his real livelihhood as a smuggler. And he not only knew every shrub and every boulder in the region for the landmarks they were, he could also read the winds and the stars, using them for a compass.

"*Alhamdulillah,* Praise be to God," a man with a skull cap of palm straw answered Rashid's greeting. "With the miracle of this new day, we will reach our destination, yes?" The man's smile was sudden, revealing a *falsa* aperture between his front teeth.

"*Inshallah.* Now that our swift dromedaries have eluded the Camel Corps and have slipped across the border, even the way bows before you, my *Mahdi.*"

Like the prophet Mohammed, and just like the great nineteenth century Mahdi before him, Mahdi Ahmed Mohammed ibn Sayid decided
he too was required to execute a *hegira*, a flight. For he too had a mission.

Amir Kasawi had thought him naive. Amir Kasawi had considered
him to be a little crazy. Amir Kasawi had played him for a fool.

But in the end it was Kasawi who was the fool! *He was so weak!* A
pandering politician who hid behind the spiritual cloak of a holy man.
A sheik who in times of trouble was not strong enough to believe that if
he only put his entire faith in Allah, all would be well.

*Did Kasawi really believe that a Deliverer such as himself would be sat-
isfied to merely take custody of such Prizes? Couldn't Kasawi see that the
Prizes were actually Gifts? Could Kasawi not realize that the Gifts were
sacrificial pawns in a great struggle?*

"Mahdi? Mahdi?"

"Yes Rashid."

"The sun will be up in but two hours. The air is cool, the distance
short, and as you can see, my men have almost finished loading the
camels. Do we have your consent to push on?"

Beyond the boabob tree, showered with a thousand desert stars,
bathed in a a full desert moon, a Gift was bound inside an empty water
skin and then hoisted up over the pack saddle of a disagreeable one-
humped dromedary. Close by, a second stuffed water skin was raised
onto another camel.

And then, if only for a moment, the skins crawled to life, from within.

"*Yalla,*" the Mahdi announced. "Let us go forward."

"What the hell is a Mahdi?" President Earl erupted. "Who is this
guy, Howard?"

"A Mahdi is a messenger of God, an emissary of Mohammed. He is
divinely sent to lead his people. The best known Mahdi was the one
who fought the British at the end of the last century. As for this current
Mahdi, all I have heard is that he is gaining a following. Reports have

him pegged as a charismatic religious leader who preaches strict adherence to Sharia law. A fanatic believed to be beyond and above political interests and issues. Now it seems perhaps those reports were wrong. Then again, perhaps the Mahdi is changing."

"If what Kasawi told Neal Meara is correct and the Mahdi really has them, what's your analysis of this, Howard?"

Howard Jones, the preacher's son, rose to his feet and slowly swayed from side to side. "A terrorist, as you know, is driven by hate, jealousy, and revenge. Eventually these emotions become the object of practically all of his actions. But even with that, a terrorist can appreciate how his actions fit into the larger scheme of things. There is some brake on his actions because he retains in his mind both macrocosmic and microcosmic perspectives. He still sees the consequence of his actions in the larger global environment, and his world of human one-on-one relationships, his universe in miniature, is still intact.

"But Ollie," Jones said quietly, "there is one thing more dangerous than a terrorist. And that's a terrorist who is a religious fanatic. For that individual is not accountable to any country or person, only to God. If this Mahdi has Zach Pike and his girlfriend in his possession, then God help them, because only God knows where they are."

The black and white monitor in front of Earl seemed as grim as Jones's words. In a few minutes the KH-11's orbit would move the satellite away from Khartoum. And then, even the semblance of control the video feed provided would be lost, as far out of reach as the whims of a Mahdi.

"President Earl!" Bannister's voice came through static from Fort Bragg's JSOC Headquarters. "I think we caught a break."

"Why's that Gordy?"

"*One Horse's* men have already taken control of the prison, which means Delta forces outside are able to concentrate solely on the Airborne. They're peppering them right now with crossfire. And the

TOW's and Hellfires of the Super Cobras are smashing the Airborne's armored personnel carriers on the road from the airport to Kober."

"Casualties?"

"Light. A round of 25 mm. cannon fire from one armored carrier wounded three Deltas. And that's it, other than the two wounded in Kober." Bannister paused. "And of course, *One Horse.*"

"Mac?" the President said.

"I read you, Mr. President."

"What happens now?"

"A Stallion is going to medivac the wounded back to the USS Boxer. And the other choppers can exfil everybody within a half hour, by which time the fight should be stopped."

"No, no. *What happens now?*" the President repeated.

"I'm not sure I follow."

"The mission's not accomplished! *One Horse* hasn't attained it's objective!"

"Unless we know where *they* are, what more can we do?"

"Mr. President," said a communications technician, "Israeli Ambassador Yonah Yardeni is on line five."

"Major General Yardeni, this is President Earl. The armed forces of the United States are in the midst of a rescue operation in Omdurman, Sudan. We have just received some intelligence briefs which lead us to believe that an Israeli friend of Zach Pike, an individual named Zvi Langer, may be in Sudan attempting to rescue Pike and possibly a missing friend named Meg Symes. We need......."

"Mr. President," interrupted the technician, "We have Prime Minister Ben Ziyon on line one."

"Benzi, Ollie here. I'm going to have my technicians set up a secure three way line between your embassy and the two of us."

"Ollie, make it a four way line. I'm in touch right now with Chief of Staff Almog and the head of our *AMAN* military intelligence, Rafi Cohen."

"Okay Benzi, will do. I was just telling the Ambassador that we are in the middle of a rescue......"

"We know about it Ollie. We have a RC-135 spy plane in the area. It's tracking your choppers, Harriers, and MC-130's."

"I can only assume then that you have a significant interest in what's going on in Sudan?"

"Yes."

"You know then why I'm calling?"

"Yes, I believe I do. Zach Pike is not in Kober, is he?"

"No, he's not. *What's going on Benzi? Who is Zvi Langer?*"

"He is one of our top soldiers. And more important, he's best friends with Zach Pike. Ever since the abduction, Zvi Langer has believed that his past military exploits are responsible for what happened to Zach Pike. We never verefied if that was true. We thought there may have been......*another reason*......for what happened to Zach Pike. We never really knew for sure. In any case, Zvi took it upon himself to help his friend. What he is doing is not sanctioned by the State of Israel. He does not have our blessing! But for all that Zvi has done on behalf of Israel, and as a son of one of our Knesset members, he has our respect and affection. We've given him some privileged consideration—as we would a rebellious son—meaning that we've helped him where we could, and we never, ever, let him just go. We always wanted to know where he was, and how he was."

Another voice came over the wire. "Mr. President, I'm Rafi Cohen, military intelligence. At our insistence, Langer let us track his movements in Sudan. He is carrying a small LSI circuit homing device in his bag. It works as a personnel locator system radio. When on, the device's frequency hops at preset times, so his signal can't be picked up by enemy forces."

"You know where Zvi Langer is?" asked the President.

"The radio works like a transponder, supplying ranging and identification information. To preserve the lithium battery, Langer only turned on the device at times of his choosing. Four days ago a listening post of ours in Ethiopia was sporadically picking up his signal. But two days ago they lost it and a communications facility in our Negev desert faintly began hearing the signal. And just now, the RC-135 spy plane has identified definitive bearings for him because his device has been steadily on. Apparently he has left it on!"

"Well, where is he?"

"Langer has now crossed into Egypt."

"*EGYPT!*"

"Mr. President." Yet another voice cut in. "Chief of Staff Moti Almog here. I have come to know Zvika Langer very well over the years. He is the consummate soldier; daring, calculating, and committed. If he has moved into Egypt, if he has chosen to leave his device on, there must be a very good reason."

"Do you think he may have already rescued Zach Pike and Meg Symes, and crossed into Egypt with them? Is that what you're saying?"

"No. If the two Americans were okay, if they were already in Egypt, then we would know about it. What I am saying is that Zvika Langer crossed into Egypt because the two Americans have been moved there. They are not yet free, and he has left his device on because he is in danger. They are all in danger."

"Moti!" Mac Streicher interrupted his Israeli counterpart, his tone brusque. "What are Zvi Langer's current coordinates?"

"There was a time," explained Rashid, "when it was easier for a desert guide like me. A time when the skeletons of thousands and thousands of camels would mark the way. Just west of here, Mahdi, along the great *Darb al-Arbain* Forty Days Road, camels laden with slaves and all manner of ivory and copper, hippo teeth and ostrich feathers, parakeets and monkeys, would sail across the sands like mighty galleons. For centuries the Road north went from western Sudan on to the very heart of Egypt. But then the British built military posts all along this area. And in their zeal to crush the Mahdiyya and eradicate the Road's trade, the Road ended."

"It will begin again some day soon Rashid," the Mahdi said patiently. "But for now, do not speak to me of Forty Day Roads. These two days on a camel are enough for me." He grimaced as he rode beside the guide, swaying slightly as the camel dipped and rose. "Please do not misunderstand. We are grateful to have you. After warden Hassan was murdered, it looked as though we would not be able to find camels and a guide to meet us at Wadi Halfa, so close to the border. We are fortunate too in that before he was murdered, warden Hassan had already been directed by Amir Kasawi to follow the American woman as she crossed the border into Sudan. Were it not for that, we never would have caught her and broken through the sordid and mysterious web she, the Israeli, and Zach Pike had spun."

Cresting a steep sand dune, the Mahdi suddenly directed Rashid to stop the caravan. Shimmering in the sun's very first rays, like a vast and distant mirage, lay the stunning deep blue waters of Lake Nasser. And hovering by the side of the waters, hewn into blood red cliffs, the unblinking four Colossi of Ramses II watched over the magnificent Sun Temple of Abu Simbel like regal sentries.

Looking over the waters and the desert, *arrogantly looking down on them*, the Temple and its Titanic statues were the very embodiment of all that the Mahdi detested. The Temple honored false Gods. Its builders were infidels and heathens. Their blasphemous idols symbolized the subjugation of the people, the exploitation of others. *And they would have to be obliterated.*

Only the destruction of the statues, and the associated deaths of a modern-day American idol and his girlfriend, would be a mighty enough display to send tremors up and down the spine of the oppressive west. Only such a demonstration would rattle Egypt, the puppet of the west, and warn other Moslems not to allign themselves with the infidel.

If only,…if only, Zach Pike and the American woman had lured the Israeli, *then the scenario would have been perfect!*

"Ollie," Lou Reed wondered aloud. "Isn't it a little peculiar that Israel didn't let us know from the get-go that they thought Zach Pike might have been kidnapped as a means of getting back at one of their own? I mean, assuming it's true, Israel certainly knows it would not be held responsible if years later someone wanted to punish us for a past security or military escapade of theirs? Clearly it's our responsibility to rescue Pike, not theirs. It doesn't really make sense. What do you suppose Prime Minister Ben Ziyon meant when he said there may have been *'another reason'* for what happened to Zach Pike? What is it that they would want to hide?" He scratched his forehead. "Ollie?"

The President was silent, with a faraway look in his eyes. Reed reached out, touched his arm.

President Earl blinked, reared back. Then, as if to rid himself of whatever apparition he'd been seeing, he shook himself.

"Mr. President," Streicher's voice came over the line, "the Israelis have given me Zvi Langer's bearings. He's forty kilometers over the border, definitely in Egypt."

"Is he on the move, Mac?"

"Negative. His bearings place him at a spot called Abu Simbel."

"Anybody know anything about this place?" asked Earl.

"Abu Simbel is the greatest archaeological site in southern Egypt," Jones said authoritatively. "Immense seated statues of Ramses II make up the facade of a magnificent temple. About thirty years ago the entire edifice was moved up a cliff when Egypt built the High Dam that flooded Nubia and created Lake Nasser."

"Sounds pretty isolated. If the Israelis are right about Pike and the girl being moved, how would the Mahdi take them to a place like Abu Simbel?"

"I'm not real sure, Ollie. The border road between Sudan and Egypt is very tough to get through. Basically, only frequent business travelers or international human rights workers with proper papers can cross into Egypt. It's also possible to sail from Sudan's Wadi Halfa, though Egyptian security vessels usually stop and search small craft. But once in Egypt, one could drive, take a hydrofoil—you can get to Abu Simbel in myriad ways. If the Mahdi is determined to take his captives from Sudan to Abu Simbel, he probably could find a way."

"Wait a minute, wait a minute," Reed said. "We're getting ahead of ourselves here in even assuming Pike and Meg Symes are in Egypt. Don't you think it best that we call President Abdallahi? He'll be able to find out what's going on at Abu Simbel."

"But once we call the Egyptian President," Jones said, "he will never allow us to operate inside his country. He will want to handle everything. Is that what we want, Ollie?"

"Naturally it's best to do this by ourselves," said President Earl. "You both make valid points, though. I can't fly reconnaissance without alerting Egypt. And before I can decide to deploy special forces into Egypt, I have to know whether Zach Pike and Meg Symes really are there. I can't in good faith commit our forces just because this Israeli Zvi Langer may be in trouble there."

A hush descended over the Situation Room, the War Room, and JSOC Headquarters. Pressed as they were by time, they needed to come up with a creative plan, and quick.

"I think I have an idea," Jones spoke up. "Mac, how far is it from Omdurman to Abu Simbel?"

"A little over seven hundred kilometers."

"Ollie, I'm sure the National Security Agency can divert the next scheduled KH-11 satellite to go from Khartoum to southern Egypt. That way we can see if there's anything unusual going on at Abu Simbel. What I suggest for now is redeploying the MH-60's, Super Cobras,and Stallions north towards Egypt. By the time we would have to commit them to cross over into Egyptian air space, we would already know whether or not the situation in Abu Simbel warrants their use. And we would not have to notify Egypt and deal with their protestations until the fly over was imminent."

"Mac, what's your opinion?" the President asked.

"Mr. President, you're the one who has to deal with Egyptian national security violations and diplomatic fallout. The only thing I can tell you is that from a military standpoint Howard's idea is risky. We don't know what this Mahdi guy is bringing to the table. In addition, Delta and the Seals have not specifically trained for combat at Abu Simbel. And don't forget, Egypt may not like this. They may fight us. This could escalate, dangerously!"

"And Gordy, what do you think?" asked President Earl.

"I think Howard's a fuckin' genius," Bannister said enthusiastically. "I know my men and they're ready to take on whatever's out there at Abu Simbel. They're totally focused on retrieving Pike. Remember, these guys are the best. And they won't just be supported by the choppers. I don't think it will be necessary, but we do have Harriers in the area and we can scramble F-14 Tomcats from the USS Teddy Roosevelt."

"Isn't it a hell of a long way to Abu Simbel, Gordy?"

"The choppers can refuel in flight with the fuel drogues of the MC-130 Talons. But because it is a long way, there's no time to lose. If we're going to send them, we better do it now!"

"Lou!" the President said sharply. "I want your opinion."

"Assuming we now start to transfer forces north, we're obviously going to have to notify Egypt as the helicopters get close to the border. So you'll have to be very forceful with President Abdallahi. Remind him in no uncertain terms about the billions America provides to his country each year. But if you can't convince him this is a top priority *American* issue, if he is adamant and refuses to let us in, then scrap it! Regardless of how prepared Gordy says we are, this ain't worth going to war with an ally."

There was a brief silence, then Reed went on. "But if there isn't going to be a war, then I say, *do it!* Otherwise Ollie, you're going to be hearing: *MIS-SION—UNACCOMPLISHED!* in your dreams, from now to forever."

"Okay." President Earl slowly brought his clenched fist down on the table. "Pending what the KH-11 shows us, looks like I'll just have to tell Egypt to butt out! Mac, Gordy—go get 'em!"

CHAPTER THIRTY-ONE

*H*overing expectantly, the great vultures spread their outstretched wings. Motionless, silent, they lurked high above, scanning the ground below using specially adapted areas in the center of their eyes to magnify and pinpoint even the smallest details. With a keen sense of smell, an uncanny sense of premonition, they patiently waited for their opportunities.

Standing beneath the Sun Temple's Hypostyle Hall ceiling of decorated vulture motifs, a camel man in a long coarse *araagi* shirt and baggy *sirwel* trousers peered at the Hall's northern wall from under his layered headcloth. In an expanse running from the ceiling to the floor, the relief of the Great Kadesh Battle Scene depicted over one thousand figures.

In one corner of the relief spies supplied secret information to Ramses. In a middle panel Ramses marched his infantry and chariots on to the city of Kadesh. Elsewhere, Ramses' army fought the Hittite enemy in fierce hand-to-hand combat until the arrival of reinforcements. And everywhere, rows upon rows of tragic prisoners were led by their captor, like animals deprived of freedom, like commodities without intrinsic human worth.

At any other time the camel man would have been thrilled to study the relief, for it held great academic fascination. But right now, after everything, all that the camel man saw was carnage and chaos. And like

a vulture the one thing he could sense, or dare to expect, was his
opportunity; his opportunity to pluck free that which his eyes watched
for—that which his heart longed for.

> *You are the Ansars! The followers, the soldiers.*
> *I am your.........Mahdi!*

Warden Hassan, dying in the desert by his overturned car, was the
one who unintentionally pointed him in the right direction. From the
moment Hassan derisively presented him with the photocopied picture,
from the instant he read the Mahdi's handwritten *fatwa* on the back
side, Zvi began shadowing the Mahdi.

He watched him and his band of disciples as they fled from Kober
prison. He stalked them as they drove north to Wadi Halfa. He searched
them out as they abandoned their vehicles to join up with a caravan of
camels. And then, when the caravan was alone and removed from him
in the vastness of the desert, Zvi hunted them in his mind and physically paralleled their movements north—*to Egypt!*

Once again donning his United Nations High Commissioner for
Refugees blue cap, and displaying the chained UNHCR identification
around his neck, Zvi had driven his rented white Renault to the
Egyptian border. And as any relief worker would, he had presented the
authoritative Laissez Passer passport of a humanitarian aid officer. The
border guard, intimidated by the official documents of a foreigner,
mindful that the United Nations Secretary General was himself an
Egyptian, waved Zvi through. It was then a sprint to the first and only
Egyptian locale of any distinction—*Abu Simbel.*

The high ground of Abu Simbel's cliff offered Zvi an opportunity to
hide his car behind a rocky hill. And after changing into the camel
herder clothes he'd purchased at Wadi Halfa, Zvi entered a mountain-
side museum dedicated to the amazing archaeological rescue of Abu
Simbel from the rising waters of Lake Nasser. Exhibits in the museum
explained how fragile red sandstone had been fortified with injections

of synthetic resin. Dramatic film footage depicted mighty cranes lifting twenty ton blocks for reassembly two hundred meters further back and sixty meters further up from the original site. Vivid footage even documented how compressed air drills levelled the top of the mountain so as to ensure that the Temple and four statues of Ramses would sit on a site that had the exact same dimensions, angles, coloring and landscaping of the original cliff.

And that's when it had hit home—*the mountainous cliff was artificial. A reinforced concrete dome. A fake! A fake buried with landfill!*

Now knowing what to look for, Zvi exited the Hypostyle Hall with its remarkable reliefs and adorned vulture ceiling. And he went deeper into the Temple. He entered a second and smaller hall and went still deeper. He entered a vestibule and went ever deeper. On through three doors that opened off the rear of the vestibule and into.......

The Sanctuary—a place so holy that it had been alligned by its architects to be kissed by the sun's rays only on Ramses' February 21st birthday and on his October 21st coronation date. A place so hallowed that its ageless paintings were meant never to be altered by time; its divine statues never to be mutilated by man.

In the low ceiling of a gray corner, in a spot that never was warmed by the sun, was the sign of human tampering: a neglected open hatch that had been installed to serve as an emergency exit for the miners who had worked on relocating the Temple.

Suddenly Zvi sprang from the ground, his hand barely grabbing onto a steel rung. An almost audible groan escaped as he began to pull himself straight up.

As Zvi scaled the rungs of the ladder, a horrible darkness soon enveloped him. The narrow walls of the vertical tunnel he was in seemed to close and press. On occasion he would pause, amid ensnaring cobwebs and phantom scorpions, and look up, hoping to see the light, the sky...a way out...the smiling faces of friends. But all he saw was a black emptiness, like death, like oblivion.

NO! He went higher.

NO! He climbed faster.

The tunnel drew him on like a vortex. The spiraling abyss carried him up. All at once his hand smacked into a door, an old wooden door weighed down by shifting sands. Pushing as hard as he could, he budged the door ever so slightly as the winds of the desert rushed through a newfound crack. Pushing again, the warm rays of the sun touched recesses that had not seen light for years. And then, pushing a third time, Zvi pressed himself against the tunnel wall as desert sand cascaded through the open hatch.

The door was situated on the leeward side of a dune. Zvi carefully emerged from the tunnel and when he crawled at an angle up to the crest of the dune, he gasped.

The cliff face was one hundred yards away to the east, and beyond and below it glittered the aqua waters of Lake Nasser. Around the downward shoulder of a hill to the north, a quarter of a mile away, stood a ticket kiosk. Off to the west lay the Western Desert of the Sahara, its rainbow of multi-colored sand and rock stretching away, forever. But it was the view to the south that was most breathtaking of all.

For a moment Zvi thought it must be an illusion, a mirage that undulated elusively in the distance. But as he watched the caravan's march, Zvi saw that it had the distinctive beat and compelling outline of reality. Easing onto his back, Zvi allowed himself to gently slide down the dune. But the slide became a roll, faster and wilder. And as he jarred to a halt, as he lay motionless on the desert floor, his squinting eyes spun crazily towards the sun.

Leaping to his feet he kicked sand this way, that way, until he was satisfied. Then he slipped back into the tunnel, keeping his head above the door, and waited.

Not again, not once more, but for one last time.

"Mac, where are they?" the President asked.

"The Blackhawks and Super Cobras are currently over the Nubian Desert, just east of the Nile's Third Cataract."

"Estimated Time of Arrival?"

"The lead choppers have been refueled and are 250 kilometers away—*and they ain't cruising*, Mr. President. They can be there in about an hour. One Hour! That is if you actually send them over into Egypt."

The President glanced at a wall clock and swiveled his chair. "Damn it, Howard, it's 9:05 A.M. in Egypt. What's going on?"

"Ollie, Larry Duffy of the National Photographic Interpretation Center is on line nine. Go ahead, Larry."

"Mr. President. We now have a KH-11 over the target area. In just a moment we're going to hook you up to its feed."

The video monitor before President Earl flickered back to life. "Okay, got it."

"As a matter of orientation," said Duffy, "what we see is Lake Nasser on the right of the screen. Next to it is the cliff of Abu Simbel. And towards the top of the screen you'll see a couple of parked tour buses."

"What's this down at the bottom?"

"A bedouin caravan. They're common in the area."

"Do you see anything that's at all peculiar?"

"No, nothing so far."

"Larry, Howard here. What are those markings in the sand? There by the cliff?"

"Probably tracks of some tourist who ventured up there recently."

"Can you magnify that, Larry?"

"Hold on."

Zooming too close too fast, the video picture blurred out of focus. Overcompensating with a reel back, the picture again became unreadable. Backwards and forwards the camera focused with smaller and more subtle adjustments, until finally it was right there.

"What is it?" the President asked.

"Just a line. A line in the sand."

"And that? That next to it?"

"Another line, a perpindicular line."

"That ain't no line," the President said, peering closely. "That's an exclamation point!"

"I don't know," Lou Reed said with a shake of his head. "I don't see it."

"Look at it for crying out loud! See that dug out area below the line. *That's the point!*"

"Now wait a minute, Ollie. Let's not get overly excited about this. Even if something's there, so what? What does it mean? We can't send our guys in with guns-a-blazin' based on that. Who are they gonna shoot at? Where's Zach Pike and the girl? The choppers are already dangerously close to venturing into Egypt. Once they've done that, Ollie, you've as good as commited them! So what's it gonna be?"

"Lou," the President said, "until we can be reassured that nothing's going on over there, we simply cannot risk abandoning Americans who may be in peril. MAC!"

"Yes, Mr. President."

"Keep the choppers going for now. We're going to push this for as long and as far as we possibly can."

"Do I have your consent?" asked the desert guide. "My Mahdi, may I command the charges into action?"

"Yes, Rashid. Time cannot be stopped, fate cannot be altered."

Standing majestically on the saddle of his camel, Rashid silently orchestrated an intricate series of maneuvers. As he thrust his arms downward, his men whipped their camels into a trot as they fanned out into perimeter positions. With a wave of his hand, the Mahdi's brigade began running in the direction of the ticket kiosk and parking lot. And upon squeezing an imaginary trigger with a finger of his outstretched arm, specialized detonation experts started up pneumatic drills. Others prepared fuses and a trailing line that would be placed by the drilled holes and wired to a detonator and plunger. Still others carefully blended a highly explosive gel mix of nitrate RDX, TNT, and aluminum that would be poured into the holes.

Now, aided by Rashid, the Mahdi climbed up to the top of the saddle and gazed at two waterskins that hung on the sides of a nearby camel. Then he nodded.

Two men immediately drew their sharply curved knives and began hacking away at the leathery skins. Though their movements appeared crude, their flashing chops were actually skilled sweeps. Suddenly, almost magically, as the perforations became larger, the skins gave birth to two living beings. Dragged out of their wombs, the two bodies huddled together on the ground. One of the creatures wore chains around his bleeding ankles.

A man arose. One defending angel. Not flying down dramatically from the sky, but quietly rising up from the sand.

Unobserved, from right in the midst of the chaotic activity, seemingly from nowhere, the camel man began to amble.

CHAPTER THIRTY-TWO

"Forty kilometers to the border of Egypt!" Mac Streicher practically screamed from the Pentagon's War Room. "Just eighty to Abu Simbel!"

"Mr. President, this is Larry Duffy. Something very strange is going on."

As the President looked at his monitor, it jolted to life. Suddenly animated and active, the characters on the desert stage threw off show roles and ran forward for their curtain call. So professional were they in demeanor, so forthright and purposeful, that there was now no doubt they were up to something—*and it was no good.*

"The bastards!" The President slammed his hand onto a table.

"I don't believe it," Howard Jones muttered.

"We've already got President Abdallahi on line two," Reed said.

"President Abdallahi," said the President. He breathed in, blew it out. "We've got an emergency situation transpiring in the southern part of your country, at Abu Simbel. We have excellent reason to believe that extremists are threatening the lives of Americans, including that of Zach Pike. The deployment of American helicopter units from Sudan is imminent. I repeat, imminent. I am asking you not to interfere with any actions they may undertake in the resolution of this crisis."

"President Earl. We are a sovereign nation. If criminal elements are executing an attack on our soil, then it is our problem. With all due respect, it is our obligation to handle this matter, not yours."

"We are already in position to handle this. President Abdallahi, every second could be paramount. Your troops would arrive too late. Please understand that our goal is a simple one—to save our people. We have no desire to usurp Egypt's sovereignty. We understand your concerns and appreciate that Egypt bears responsibility for apprehending the criminal elements who brought this crisis to its shores. We must work together in a way that will best preserve both of our national interests. The United States must rescue its people, and Egypt will, I hope, apprehend the extremists."

"I have to consult with my advisors. I must get their assesment of your impending actions as it relates to our national security. I cannot for now guarantee, President Earl, that your proposal will be accepted."

"It is not a proposal. And I suggest you deliberate quickly. We prefer that you join us in resolving this matter, but let me be blunt: The United States is determined and ready to go. And if you fight us, there will be grave consequences."

They never truly saw him coming.

Squinting into a morning sun, Rashid's knife-wielding henchmen could only sense the specter of a man approaching from due east. The powerful sun at the man's back masked his features, his intentions. And when the camel man was upon them he pointed persuasively in the direction of the Mahdi and then pointed innocently towards himself.

As he knelt to take custody of the two human bundles their hollowed eyes widened, their poor souls swooning in shock.

"*Shhhh,*" whistled the wind. "*Shhhh,*" hissed the apparition, the old friend.

Meg was trembling—and she looked awful. But at least she was not bound and could assist in saving herself. Zach, on the other hand, looked almost helpless. Shackled, with the wounds and bruises of torture, he'd been diminished to a wasted caricature of himself.

Zvi tenderly lifted Meg to her feet, then gently pulled Zach onto his. For a moment Zach swayed in the desert wind, his skeletal frame staggering. But then he gritted his teeth. He winked a hard and gleaming eye. And the trio stirred to life.

Zvi's intention was to head, as inconspicuously as possible, for the white Renault that he'd parked behind a hill. But as soon as Zvi looked up he saw a formidable obstacle blocking their path of escape. Amidst all the caravan's chaotic activity was a stiff figure dressed all in white—the Mahdi!

Zvi looked into his face and saw the fiery countenance of the zealot. The Mahdi was almost beyond his comprehension; unfathomable and dark.

"Come on," urged Zvi as he turned Zach and Meg in the opposite direction. "Walk faster!" he said, unable to shake himself free of the Mahdi's stare, his hypnotic mastery.

Zvi could sense the Mahdi's incredulity, what he was thinking. *They're getting away? NO!*

"Stop them!" the Mahdi finally shouted. "Stop them!"

Bending down Zvi quickly lifted Zach onto his shoulders. He grabbed Meg's hand. And then they ran for their lives.

The downward slope of the ground pushed them headlong almost to the point of falling. The pounding of their hearts propelled them to run as fast as they possibly could. And soon all they could see were the glistening waters of Lake Nasser, teasing them, pulling them, closer and closer and closer. To the very brink.........of the cliff of Abu Simbel!

"Go, Go, Go!" Gordy Bannister yelled to Jim Lonestreet. "You're in charge of *One Horse*," he exhorted.

Jim Lonestreet leaned over the shoulder of his pilot's lead Blackhawk and tried to peer beyond a wall of blue water. Barely thirty feet above Lake Nasser, the rotors of the chopper whipped up rippling swells.

"Gordy, there's two Egyptian F-16's way up on our right," Lonestreet said. "No communication initiated. So far no threatening advances."

"The AWAC's monitoring the situation. And we've got Harriers backing you up. Now listen up, Jim. The caravan is scattered all over the top of the cliff. There are also tourists and civilians milling around the entrance of the Temple that's by the foot of the statues. You and the forces at your command will not fire unless fired upon. Even when you identify Pike and the girl, do not fire unless they are in immediate danger. Just get in, get them, and get out!"

The pink sandstone slab was headwall steep at its top. But at least its seventy degree angle would be as daunting to their pursuers as it was to them.

Zvi held onto Meg's hand and lowered her two feet to a position where she could cling to a crack. Her left foot found a scoop, her right foot swung freely. Then Zvi had Zach piggyback himself onto him.

"Wrap your arms around me. Keep yourself as close to me as you can."

Zvi knew from rappelling in the Judean Desert that free climbing had more to do with balance and friction than it did with brute strength. But Zach still weighed more than he did, even in his emaciated condition. As soon as he lowered himself with a pinch grip, Zach's weight on his back carried him farther away from the cliff face than he wanted to be. Dangling in air, Zvi craned his neck to look up and then desperately looked downward, past his flailing legs, to get his bearings. His grip was slipping.

Zvi thought he saw the waters of Lake Nasser behind him, the Temple floor far below him. The blue sky over his head was both dizzyingly close but unreachable. And for an instant he could not help thinking that the sky was about to zoom away, forever.

"Zvi!" shrieked Meg. "You've got a ledge right below your right foot. You can edge onto it!"

Zvi toed his foot over, tried a resting stance. He caught a foothold and faced into the rock, gulping down mouthfuls of thin air.

"Where are we Meggie?" Zvi kept asking during the first ten feet of their descent. "How far are we?"

And Meg came through. Having to look up to Zvi and Zach, she seemed able to ignore what should have been her own paralyzing fears by concentrating on their next best move. From grip to grip, from foothold to foothold, Meg coaxed them along. Every movement was measured in groping increments, achieved with reckless faith.

And then, at about the same time as the cliff face jutted out into a somewhat more obtuse and manageable angle, Zvi heard the distant whiring of wings at their backs.

It was a most amazing sight.

Tiny specks of humanity crawling on the sheer wall above the colossal statues of Ramses, clinging to life by their very nails.

"We see them," cried Lonestreet. "They're on the cliff face fifteen feet below the rim, about twenty feet above the heads of the statues. Pike's hanging on to somebody dressed like a nomad. It could be the Israeli. The woman is very close by. There's a group of Bedouins standing by the top and it looks like a couple of them are starting to climb down after them."

"How close can you get?" Bannister asked.

"Not close enough. The cliff angle.... But if they......"

"Jim? Jim?"

"Aw, shit! Aw, shit! Pull back!"

"Jim!"

"They got Stingers, Gordy! My pilot spotted a white plume in the nick of time and infrared jammed the missile's acquisition."

"Where'd you see the initial signature come from?"

"The top of the cliff. My gunner's M-60 is returning fire but the Stinger's shooter and spotter just ducked behind a boulder."

"Okay, we'll get the Super Cobras to circle around, nap of the earth hug the terrain, and destroy them with their 20 mm cannons and rockets."

"But who knows how many Stingers are out there, Gordy? We can't really do anything till those damn Stingers are taken out!"

The shrieks of panicked tourists reverberated from the depths of the Temple where they had run for cover. Their cries echoed in the recesses of rock until they grew faint, but the rock still carried the remnants of their muffled pleas as vibrations that permeated to the fingertips of the climbers.

In labored and gasping breaths the climbers inched towards a carved ledge, one with a baboon motif, along the summit of Abu Simbel's facade. Their sharp groans called up reserves of courage, called out their desire to live.

Zvi was talking to himself: "One more......one more step, Zvi." Reaching for the ledge, he glanced up only to see the leg of a pursuer kick out against the blue sky. The pursuer was closing the gap, *very quickly*.

"It's ten feet to the top of the statue's crown," Zvi said urgently. "We have to jump."

The surface area of the crown was not very large. Any miscalculation or slip, and they'd plummet seventy feet to the base of the statue.

"I'll go first. Then you go Meggie. Then you Zach. I'll catch you, I promise."

Zvi concentrated on the very center of the crown. Leaning his toes over the ledge, he pushed away and landed on his hands as well as his feet. The four pointed landing prevented him from awkwardly rolling or stumbling away.

"Your turn, Meggie," he encouraged, looking up.

Without any hesitation Meg leaped forward. But her spring carried her away, and she landed only a foot from the crown's edge. Zvi scooped her back safely into his arms.

Despite his weakened and pained condition, Zach's aim was quarterback perfect. He nailed his leap. And as he flattened Zvi, a great boom sounded from atop the cliff.

"Holy cow!" Jim Lonestreet whistled as cannon fire from a Super Cobra exploded into a bucket of RDX gel mix.

Lapping a fiery tongue in pursuit of a Stinger missile team, brilliant flashes of yellow and white also leaped into the air like pyrotechnics. Burning torches of human flesh raced in panic all about the desert ground, screaming horribly.

Lonestreet blocked out the mayhem and made his report. "That makes three Stingers knocked out. It's bedlam on the top of the cliff."

"What's with Pike and the girl?" Bannister asked. "Where are they now?"

"They're on the top of one of the statues, about thirty feet below the edge of the cliff."

"Are the Egyptians still behaving?"

"Their F-16's are circling, Gordy. They must be salivating by now. I don't think they'll stay out of the fray much longer."

"Radar shows that they also have a helicopter unit closing from the north."

"Gordy?"

"What? Jim, what is it? Where are you?"

"I've just had a word with my pilot. We have an idea."

The KH-11 satellite had a blind spot.

Though the inferno on the cliff summit was playing live on the monitor, the cliff face was invisible.

"What the hell is going on?" President Earl demanded above the din in the Situation Room. The cramped quarters could barely contain the wild emotions of its inhabitants. "Gordy? Gordy!"

"Oh, my God," crackled the JSOC officer's voice. A moment of silence, and then his sharp command could be heard in the confines of the Situation Room as they also rang out to units halfway around the world. "Cover them! Cover them!"

With a sudden dip and a plummeting dive, Jim Lonestreet's Blackhawk swept in on its target, a beeline straight and true. And then, all at once, it pulled into a sheer stall, its massive rotors angling backwards so as to narrowly miss hitting the red rock of the cliff.

Crouching away from the hazardous winds of the helicopter, the three friends held onto each other tightly. All about them bits of loose rock flew like lethal projectiles.

With a gunner clinging white-fisted to his vest, Lonestreet dived onto his belly and wriggled his upper torso out of the Blackhawk's door.

"Grab the line!" he screamed. "Get into the harness!" The furious noise of the helicopter muted his cry, his mouth contorted in vain. Squirming even further out of the Blackhawk, Lonestreet raised a STABO rescue harness above his head and unleashed it. But the harness snapped away from Zvi's outstretched fingers.

As he was about to reel the harness back for a second attempt, Lonestreet began to swing the rope instead. Back and forth—*closer, closer*—the harness drew tantalizingly close when at last Zvi snatched it!

He pulled the harness' snaplink straps over Meg's legs and tightened. He helped Zach climb into a set of canvas loops, fastening them.

And then came a surprise.

The harness had yet another pair of belts. It could accomodate three people. *There was room, room enough, room for him as well!*

As he was about to latch himself into the harness, a body, diving from above, slammed him. Zvi saw the sky…a knife. He fell back, he pushed forward. *He let go of the harness.*

"NO!" Meg cried out.

"ZVI!" Zach lunged. But the helicopter was already veering back, surging away.

The tip of the knife touched Zvi's heart. A hand compressed his neck. Desperate, Zvi clawed at the killer's face. He tore his nose, bit his hand. He kicked and punched. Then, slowly, he lifted the man up—and threw him over the edge of the statue's crown.

But there were more.

Looking up, Zvi saw other pursuers—four, maybe five—on the cliff face. They were closing in, readying themselves to pounce. To kill.

Zvi leaped through the air. He plunged thirty feet, spraining his ankle as he landed on Ramses' lap.

"ZVI!"

Lifting himself up he jumped down another thirty feet, breaking his other ankle on the stoned feet of Ramses.

"ZVI!"

Picking himself up, he began to stagger. He was hobbling, and falling, and trying to get away, and live.

"Run him down!" raged the Mahdi. "Hunt him down, Rashid. Track him from the sides of the cilff!"

"For God's sake," President Earl screamed, "help him." Then, strongly, he ordered it: "Help him!"

The azure waters of Lake Nasser became one with the blue sky. The heavenly blue was right before him, almost within his grasp. Zvi stumbled towards it, the pain in his ankles ripping him to pieces.

Zach and Meg witnessed his every buckling step. Dangling helplessly from the end of a rope that pulled them behind Jim Lonestreet's racing Blackhawk, they saw Zvi carry himself towards the water. In horror they realized, just moments before Zvi himself saw it—*there was nowhere left to go!*

Zvi turned round and round. The winds off Lake Nasser whipped in from below. Waves of attackers were streaming down from above. And a mysterious giant shadow was swooping in from behind.

Diving from the sky, risking the fire of remaining Stinger teams, an MC-130 Combat Talon was heading straight for him. As it screamed by it jettisoned a kit that was joined to a helium balloon by a flexible rope.

Zvi knew of the Fulton Surface to Air Recovery System. But just in case he didn't, the brief instructions on the outside of the kit were chillingly explicit.

Attach the enclosed harness.
Raise the balloon.
Pray.

The Combat Talon circled sharply back over the water. Then it slowly straightened its wings, flashed its lights, lowered its nose, and thundered in on its second pass.

Zvi forgot to breathe, dared not blink; life perched on a precipice, in a still vacuum.

Guided by locator beacons, the Combat Talon zeroed in on the rope that now hung vertically below the helium balloon. *Closer, closer, closer,* a yoke on the front of the Talon plowed into the rope, catching it, engaging it.

The violent pull jerked Zvi off the ground. His head flew back, his arms and his legs all but tore out of their sockets. Zvi bounced wildly in the air, sideways, upside down, right side up.

The rope tossed him like a rag doll. But gradually the vibrations of the rope lessened and Zvi was soon flying horizontally. All at once his hand shot up, he signaled to the Talon's crew, he pumped a fist for all to see, "*Here I am. Here I am!*"

But a hot *sirocco* wind suddenly sprang up. Blowing in from the Saharan desert, it whistled and whipped itself over the hazy waters of Lake Nasser. It kept going, and going, aiming itself against the sails of some distant clipper ship, as if appointed to rip the ship from its safe moorings.

The AK-47's bullet knocked Zvi into a tight, terrifying spin. He felt himself looking through a kaleidoscope; each slight twist altered every shape, changed every color. Zvi closed his eyes.

"*Shema Yisroel,* Hear O Israel: the Lord is our God, the Lord is One."

His body slumped in his harness.

"ZVI!"

His face caught the warmth of the sun.

"NO!"

A winch at the rear ramp of the Combat Talon slowly began pulling him aboard, pulling him ashore.

CHAPTER THIRTY-THREE

"*I* want the ball," President Earl said. "Hut one, Hut two, Hike!"

A young military aide lobbed a snap in the President's direction. Then he stood and watched, flabbergasted at the President's giddy demeanor.

Rushing forward to the first light of a new day, the President tucked away a small brown satchel as if it were a real football. Playfully cradling the portable case designed to electronically link him with the Situation Room, Earl tore through the South Lawn of the White House. A squad of Secret Service agents ran interference as they cheerfully followed him in the direction of the West Wing.

The President hadn't slept a wink, but he was ecstatic. *It's over*, he thought. *The worst is over.*

Mark Handsman greeted him by the entranceway of the Wing. "Hurley Baker, Victor Lopes, and Lee Nunzio are already here to see you."

"Just as well," the President sighed. He walked with his Chief of Staff back to the Oval Office and reluctantly settled himself behind the Resolute Desk. "It's best to make sure we're all on the same team before the morning press conference begins. Show them in."

"You've still got some nifty moves, Ollie," Baker laughed, entering the Office. "We were watching you from the Rose Garden."

"Good news is a potent elixir. It can make even me an old fart like me feel young again. I trust you guys have even more good news for me."

"I'm not sure I do," Baker said more soberly. "I confronted Fred Marshall the very moment Howard Jones told me of Neal Meara's phone call to him last night."

"Well?" the President stared into his CIA Director's gray eyes.

"It's true. What Amir Kasawi told Meara is basically true. Marshall all but admitted as much."

"And you knew nothing of this?"

"No. Marshall was secretly cutting a deal with the fundamentalists believing it to be the safest way to win the release of Zach Pike."

"But damn it, Hurley, how could you not know anything about it?"

"You have to understand that Fred Marshall has been with the CIA for over thirty years. That's a long time, Ollie. Somewhere along the way we stopped watching him, stopped looking for warning signals in his behavior. We allowed him too much power to run his Division and his personnel as he saw fit." Baker's face was bright, embarrassed no doubt.

"You know," the President said, "the Egyptians captured the Mahdi at Abu Simbel as soon as our forces departed. Maybe the Mahdi will shed some light on how Marshall contacted him to set up the deal."

"That, by the way, is where Marshall's account of events differs from Kasawi's. Marshall told me it was Kasawi who took Zach Pike and it was with him that he made a deal. Marshall said he didn't even know about the existence of any Mahdi."

The President shook his head. "Frankly Hurley, at this point I trust Marshall about the same as I trust Kasawi; that's to say—*not at all*. Regardless, Kasawi's going to be in power for some time to come. We'll watch him like a hawk from now on but we can't really do anything about him. The question is, what do we do about Marshall?"

"Mr. President," Victor Lopes broke in, "you know where I stand on this. The FBI, with the full cooperation of the Justice Department, should investigate. And if necessary, prosecute."

"I don't think that's a good idea," Baker said. "Once the House Select Committee on Intelligence gets wind of a Justice Department-FBI probe, they'll be hauling Fred Marshall's ass down to the Rayburn Building lickety-split."

"So what?" Lopes shrugged, his face unpleasantly challenging. "At least your CIA goons won't be able to bury their mistakes like they've done so many times before. At least maybe a scoundrel like Fred Marshall will actually get his comeuppance and there'll finally be some justice meted out to individuals in the intelligence community!"

"I don't think you understand, Victor." Baker tried to remain composed. "Fred Marshall knows too much. As Director for Africa Operations, he's the authority on every officer, non official cover, and agent over there. Hell, he runs them! If this goes public our entire network in Africa could collapse. Even more, our personnel there could be jeopardized. That's tantamount to a shakedown!"

"So for the sake of protecting secrets, ethics lose out?" Lopes glared at Baker.

"No, Victor." Baker's voice was straining to stay under control. "For the sake of protecting lives, guarding our national interests, and preserving the few fledgling democracies in that part of the world, secrets must be kept. Ollie, you know what's going on with those Congressional intelligence committees! For years now they've been ordering us to slash our budgets and shrink our staffs. I made almost fifty appearances on the Hill this past year in order to defend the budget. How many times can I explain that though the cold war is over, the world is still a very dangerous place? If Congress gets to use Marshall as fodder, the CIA will be working with one hand tied behind it's back!"

"Victor," said President Earl, "I'm sorry. But I think that you'd agree, even if Fred Marshall ever made it anywhere near the courts, there would be strong cause for invoking the Classified Information Procedures Act. Marshall will never be prosecuted. Prosecution of this case would be too damaging to our nation's best interests."

The President clapped a hand on Baker's shoulder. "Hurley, go ahead and run your internal investigation. Be discreet, but be effective. If the

Directorate doesn't learn from this mess, if your only action is to hand Marshall an early retirement with a full pension and full benefits, you'll have about as much influence with me as an Amir Kasawi or a Fred Marshall. Got that?"

"Ollie," Baker said, his voice suddenly vibrating with emotion, "a young non official cover named Anna Amundson was recently killed by Sudanese Security Forces. Kasawi indicated to Meara that Marshall ran this girl ragged, had her jump through hoops for him. I can guarantee you that if we find Marshall had anything to do with sending this girl to her death, he'll rue the day he was born."

"And what's that supposed to mean?"

"There are people in the Clandestine service who don't take kindly to this type of thing. These people are different from you and me—they operate by a different code of behavior. In a best case scenario Marshall will be shunned and it'll be as if his CIA career never existed. If he's not so lucky, people will snoop and pounce the instant he screws up. And if he's really unlucky, well,…he's just unlucky."

Is it over? The President was beginning to relax, hoping it was.

Victor Lopes corrected him. "There's another matter."

In an instant the euphoria of the early morning romp around the South Lawn drained away. His heart sank, his muscles froze—and the strangest thing was, the President himself did not quite understand why.

"Ben Pike," Lopes said.

He didn't even have to hear it, really, but Lopes' words hit him hard.

"Now that his boy is safe," Lopes continued, "I think it's time we decide what to do with Ben Pike. As I told Lee, if transfer of classified material has not actually been witnessed, then it's very hard to prove verbal transfer of material in court. Under such circumstances the only way to obtain an arrest is if the Internal Security section of the Justice Department gives its approval. In other words, if I consent. But I won't consent unless there's enough evidence to prosecute, and I won't prosecute unless there's enough evidence to convict. We almost came up with the evidence we needed when we tapped Pike's computer and got that bit addressed to Oded Langer, indicating that he helped Israel with the Vulture program. The problem is that Ben Pike was sponsored by the Defense Department to assist Israel with elements of the Vulture program anyway."

"So you can't come up with the evidence you need?" the President tentatively asked.

"As I've told Lee, what we need is a confession."

"What makes you think Ben Pike will confess?"

"Pike's a rational man. We'll confront him with the evidence we already have. We'll promise him the joint Vulture program with Israel won't be affected if he cooperates. We'll promise him his family won't be dragged into this and that he'll get off relatively easy."

"I don't know about this, Victor. Is this what we want to do?"

Lopes pressed his case, gesturing as he laid out the whole Justice Department strategy. "The Behavior Unit has already designed a plan of attack. A Special Agent will call. 'Mr. Pike,' he'll say. 'I need to talk with you about a very important matter.' When Ben Pike meets him, the casually dressed Agent will say, 'Mr. Pike. We want to tell you a story about a hypothetical person. This person grew up in Virginia and went overseas to honorably serve his country in World War II. He was impressionable, and what he saw in the war left a terrible mark. Nevertheless, this person went on to a prestigious Boston college, and then got a job with a Boston-based defense contractor. He raised a wonderful family, and he was proud and happy with his life. But then a visiting Israeli befriended him. This friend dredged up old feelings, opened old wounds. And before long this friend persuaded him to start assisting Israel with the supply of secret defense information.' Well, I think you get my drift, Mr. President. In this non-confrontational encounter, Pike will recognize the person as himself. The FBI will even seem sympathetic because of the way the story was told."

"You want to trip him up!" the President exclaimed. "You want to squeeze him, manipulate him! I say forget it! He's been through enough with the abduction of his kid. Just forget it, Victor!"

Lopes was ready. He took a deep breath and exhaled. "Ibrahim Husseini. We have to try him in a court of law. And when we do, out pops Ben Pike."

"Wait a second," Lee Nunzio finally spoke up. "Ben Pike never did respond to Husseini when he was confronted by him at the Space Center in Huntsville. He ignored Husseini's threats. He didn't cooperate."

"True," said Lopes. "But we have to try Husseini for attempting to elicit classified information from the United States, and Ben Pike's name is going to be dragged all over the place. How long do you think it'll be before the press digs up things we already know about Pike? When they do, how are we going to explain our negligence in not going after Pike? The press will have a field day! Don't you see? It's like with Fred Marshall. One way or another, in the end, justice catches up with a criminal. It has to!"

For a moment it seemed to President Earl as if the walls were swaying. Ibrahim Husseini would have to be tried. There was no getting around it.

"Victor." Lee Nunzio carefully broke the momentary silence. "Didn't you say that we already have the goods on Ibrahim Husseini? You told me we have records of his phone conversations with Charlie Hammami. We have evidence of his mailing *Pike's Peak* to Charlie Hammami. We have money transfers going from Hammami to Husseini. And even those we have already arrested in connection with the Rockefeller Center incident will testify they saw Husseini meet with Tomas Bahr."

"And?"

"So you're right about justice, one way or another, catching up to a criminal. We don't need to prosecute Husseini on espionage-related activities because we have enough to prosecute and convict him for the murder of Brian Sullivan and the abduction of Zach Pike!"

"In that way," the President said, the revelation now dawning, "Ben Pike doesn't need to be brought up at all. There won't be any charges filed nor questions raised of Husseini that would concern him."

"You can't do that!" Lopes practically yelled. "You can't decide in smoky back rooms what manner of justice applies. To whom it applies. Look, Mr. President, I recognize you're my boss. You're the chief executive charged with the execution of law. And when you wanted me to do my job and go to bat for you in convincing Congressional members of the propriety of the War Powers Resolution, I did it. But now, blocking the conscientious performance of my duty as Attorney General is unprecedented. It's beyond the pale! You need a reason for deciding this, one for the record. If I don't get one then I'm resigning. And if I do, this whole Ben Pike thing is going to come out!"

"Okay then, Victor, here's a reason: The Vulture is still a classified Defense project and secrets that are vital to the interests of the United States could be lost. Here's another official reason: Oded Langer is a member of the Knesset, and your pursuit of this matter could harm relations with Israel. That too would be detrimental to the interests of the United States."

"Mr. President, why are you doing this?" Lopes asked. His head drooped, his body slumped in resignation. "Really, why are you doing this?"

"You said to me not very long ago, in this very office, that justice has to be blind. But you're wrong. Every person and every case must be judged individually, in their entirety. Justice has to see......*everything*! And it's got to be sensitive. Justice leavened with mercy and kindness."

"And you, Lee? What do you have to say?"

"All I can tell you," Nunzio softly said, "is that even before his son was kidnapped, Pike had looked into the jaws of Hell. Trust me. Have a little compassion here, Victor. Let it rest. Don't resign—just let it go."

It was a spectacular morning. The sun was just starting to warm up the crisp, late January day as they walked out to the South Portico's Truman Balcony. Off in the distance the city was coming to life. Governmental beaurocrats and military employees on their way to work were just now learning the good news. They honked their horns as their radios informed them of what had happened. Tourists at the Washington Monument and the Jefferson Memorial rejoiced as they heard of the miracle at Abu Simbel. The whole city, the entire country, celebrated as people watched the media interview Ben and Mary Pike in front of their Brookline home.

"Lee, come on over here," the President said, smiling. "Lou and I were just about to light cigars. Will you join us? Please."

"I don't smoke, but okay. Actually, maybe it'll do me some good."

Despite the euphoria all around him, Lee Nunzio was tired. And torn. His whole life was dedicated to an ongoing battle against evil, in any form it came in. Some battles were won, some lost—it never ended. Along the way there were costs, casualties: Dancer, the NOC Anna Amundson. Yet one had to at least strive or else....... But never before had he been forced to choose between justice, and what might be a higher justice.

"You know, Lee, I don't know a damn thing about Ben Pike. Sure, I spoke to him a few times. I learned a little about his background, what he did here, what he did there. Maybe because he was at the Bulge, maybe I just felt sorry for him because of his kid, I don't know—but I like him. The thing is......*I don't know him.* But what you said a few minutes ago, the way you said it—I have this feeling that you really do know him. So tell me, why didn't you side with Victor back there?"

"Well," Nunzio slowly said, "the Ben Pike I see is eighteen years old. Just a little older than my own children. The Ben Pike I know is an eighteen-year-old kid who has the terrible misfortune of stumbling on a world gone insane. But despite the cataclsym all around him, he somehow pulls himself together and pulls through. He's full of hopes and ideas and he vows to make the world better. In part he does this, can do it, because he is eighteen years old. He's naive—but I mean that in a good sense. He's so naive that he sees things as they should be. He's so innocent that he's good. And being innocent, he's vulnerable." He raised his eyebrows, tilted his head. "The Ben Pike I don't know, an older version, has faults, to be sure. But I still believe him to be eighteen years old in the sense of that innocence."

Nunzio squinted into the sun and continued. "Did you see the Super Bowl?"

"Sure. I saw it."

"Remember there was this guy from the clergy who recited psalms?"

"Yeah." President Earl shrugged, and waited.

"Well, I simply could not bear to see people point at Ben Pike, mock him, and say, *'Aha, Aha!'*" Nunzio turned fully towards the President. "The Ben Pike I know—his intentions and motives—are just."

More than anything, it was a deliriously buoyant ride, down a narrow path composed of staff well-wishers who spontaneously yelled their congratulations. All along the way to the press room, the President acknowledged his supporters but never broke stride. He couldn't stop; not yet, not now.

He could see the press room's raised platform, the blue curtain with the White House logo, the White House spokesman. He saw the expectant press corps jumped to their feet. He was very close. It was almost over. He had to ride it to its end, see it to its end. He had to hear himself say, *it's over.*

"It's over! It's over!"

But, of course, that was not quite so.

CHAPTER THIRTY-FOUR

$\mathcal{M}$ay.

The larks and the laughing gulls were coming home for the season. The bayberry and beach plum thickets were alive with light and color. The airy winds were sweet.

Way down below tiny boats in the Cape Cod Canal bobbed up and down like toys. Way up high the steel cables of the Bourne Bridge stretched heavenward to support a great silvery arch. The long, narrow, magical bridge spanned forward, *and it spanned back*.

Old memories, new feelings—the SUV's radio sang to them songs of what was and what could be. For they were free, they were young, and they could *dance, dance, dance*.

They were going to open up the summer house in Falmouth, the house that was in their dreams, and in their hearts.

Zach glanced away from the wheel. He'd gained back weight, energy. He was strong. "The Jets have a three day minicamp coming up soon. Can you believe it Meg? That it's practically the time of year again for training camps to open?"

"No, I can't," Meg said. She leaned toward him and tickled. "The two-a-day workouts in the hot summer sun, the sweating bodies, I tell you Zach, the beach is really going to exhaust me this summer. How ever do I do it?"

"Aw, poor Meg. It's hard, I know. But be brave. You'll manage somehow. You always do."

Glancing right, Zach looked at Meg again, the spring sun had put a blush on her cheeks. Then he looked past her, toward the back seat. Meg smiled, straightened, looked back too.

Zvi was grinning wildly. His eyes shone bright, contrasting his pale skin.

"Do you realize," he said, "just how many years it's been since the three of us have been together like this?"

"Well it wouldn't have taken quite so long," Meg teased, "if you hadn't been in the hospital for so long."

"Yeah, Zvi. I screamed at you to duck that last bullet, but oh no, you had to be a hero. It's your fault!"

"*Geez*, what was I thinking? Bouncing around in the air there, how could I not have missed it? Zach, Meggie, will you ever forgive me?"

"Well, make sure it never happens again."

Heading down Route 28A, the SUV slowly rolled past sandy beaches, quaint little harbors, and salt marshes. The side roads and dirt paths all looked familiar now. Some of the roads and paths beckoned, an invitation to travellers to share in the beauty at the road's end. But some did not. They led off to isolated places—private places.

They knew that.

Zvi rubbed his tired eyes, his hand swiped at his creased brow. He was drifting a bit, again; looking into the eyes of the Mahdi. Unlike Zach or Meg, in many ways still on the cliff.

"I still can't believe," said Meg, with a sudden turn toward Zach, "that your parents moved to Israel. It seemed so out of the blue."

"I'm not really surprised."

"You're not?"

"No." Zach kept his eyes on the road ahead.

"And you, Zvi? I'm sure your parents are thrilled to have Mary and Ben so close by, but don't you think it's kind of strange?"

"No." Zvi kept his eyes on the dunes and brush at the side of the road.

"Well, I'm going to miss them."

"They're coming back for a visit in July," Zach said. "They're not about to sell the Cape house. You'll be able to see them then, with me, right here." Zach smiled apprehensively, his eyes expectant.

"And remember," Zvi quickly added, "you could always see them in Israel, whenever you visit me."

Meg gazed out the window, wistful, silent.

They were very close now. And conversation ended.

The SUV turned onto Church Street, banked right onto the shore road, and then crawled up a small hill. The SUV stopped as a Garth Brooks song played on the radio. Zach took Meg's hand. Meg took Zvi's.

> *And now,*
> *I'm glad I didn't know,*
> *the way it all would end,*
> *the way it all would go,o-o-o-o,*

From their vantage point the house below them was as pristine as it had been years ago. They did not see that its shingles were slightly weathered, that its gingerbread gables were a bit crumbled. They didn't notice that the green grass was fringed with brown, that the lilac-laced picket fence needed paint, that the big oak tree in the front yard was now a little bent.

Below their cottage, out on the point, the Nobska Lighthouse stood like a beacon to the ships that sailed around the Elizabeth Islands and across Vineyard Sound.

> *Our lives,*
> *are better left to chance,*
> *I could have missed the pain,*
> *but I'd have had to miss, the, dance.*

Suddenly a boy with a football ran to a spot on the grass. His father fell in behind him and placed his hands on his son's youthful shoulders. Family members closed in all around. A girl in a tank top cuddled up next to the boy. And then a friend nestled in beside the girl.

They were smiling and laughing. They were very happy.

Click.

"We're here!"

ABOUT THE AUTHOR

*A*fter serving a portion of his service in an elite unit of the Israel Defense Forces, Gabe Galambos travelled extensively in England, Spain, and Hungary, locales that appear in the novel. Sent to Sudan in 1983 by the American Association for Ethiopian Jewry to assist in the clandestine rescue and relocation of Jews to Israel, he was captured. While under house arrest he and a fellow prisoner escaped through the brush to Zaire, but were later returned to Sudanese custody. After spending time in a prison and a Khartoum jail, the two were finally released when several Congressional members interceded on their behalf.

He is a diagnostic cardiac sonographer and a resident of Brookline, Massachusetts.

REFERENCES

"Stealing Pike's Peak is in the best tradition of political suspense stories. It never lets up".

Bill Phillips—Screenwriter; "Seduction In A Small Town", "Rising Son", "The Beans of Egypt, Maine"

The Polyol Paradigm and
Complications of Diabetes

Margo Panush Cohen

The Polyol Paradigm and Complications of Diabetes

With a Foreword by Harold Rifkin

With 25 Figures

Springer-Verlag
New York Berlin Heidelberg
London Paris Tokyo

Margo Panush Cohen, M.D.,Ph.D.
Professor of Medicine and Director
Division of Endocrinology and Metabolism
University of Medicine and Dentistry of New Jersey
Newark, New Jersey 07103
USA

The quotation on pp. 2–3 is reprinted by permission of *The Wall Street Journal*, © Dow Jones and Company, Inc. 1986. All rights reserved.

Library of Congress Cataloging in Publication Data
Cohen, Margo P.
  The polyol paradigm and complications of diabetes.
  Bibliography: p.
  Includes index.
  1. Diabetes—Complications and sequelae.
2. Polyols—Physiological effect. 3. Aldose
reductase. I. Title. [DNLM: 1. Diabetes Mellitus—
complications. 2. Diabetes Mellitus—enzymology.
3. Sugar Alcohol Dehydrogenases—metabolism.
WK 895 C678p]
RC660.C474 1987   616.4'62   86-26022

Typeset by Publishers Service, Bozeman, Montana.
Printed and bound by Quinn-Woodbine, Woodbine, New Jersey.
Printed in the United States of America.

9 8 7 6 5 4 3 2 1

ISBN 0-387-96418-5 Springer-Verlag New York Berlin Heidelberg
ISBN 3-540-96418-5 Springer-Verlag Berlin Heidelberg New York

To Louis and Tillie Panush

and to Perry, Michael, Daniel,
and Jonathan Cohen

Foreword

In the last decade, it has become increasingly evident that the clinical and morphologic changes underlying many of the complications of diabetes, including cataract formation, retinopathy, nephropathy, neuropathy, and macrovascular disease, are preceded by a variety of disturbances of biochemical and physiologic origin. Dr. Cohen has recently written a superb monograph, entitled *Diabetes and Protein Glycosylation: Measurement and Biologic Relevance*, in which she thoroughly explores how enhanced nonenzymatic glycosylation in uncontrolled diabetes underscores the pressing need for maintenance of long-term euglycemia. In the present volume, *The Polyol Paradigm and Complications of Diabetes*, she reviews, in a most succinct and thorough manner, how another biochemical mechanism, involving the polyol pathway, is involved in the pathogenesis of such diabetes complications as retinopathy, neuropathy, nephropathy, and cataract formation.

Dr. Cohen gives us a clearly written and comprehensive monograph, reviewing the chemistry of the polyol pathway and of the aldose reductase inhibitors, and the pathophysiologic significance of increased polyol pathway activity in a variety of tissues affected by diabetes mellitus. She insightfully describes the relationship of increased polyol pathway activity to altered metabolism of inositol-containing phospholipids and to changes in various tissue concentrations of *myo*-inositol. Finally, she provides us with a careful review of the existing experimental and clinical studies with a variety of different aldose reductase inhibitors that have been and are being performed in the hope of preventing or reversing long-term complications of diabetes.

This monograph is a most welcome addition to the literature on diabetes and its chronic complications, particularly since its author is a world-renowned endocrinologist and diabetes specialist who, throughout the years, has focused the major portion of her research activities on the biochemical and metabolic aberrations underlying the long-term complications of diabetes. It should appeal to the basic and clinical investigator, as well as to the clinician, and should be present in every medical school and hospital library where it is easily accessible and available to all who are concerned and involved with the management of diabetic patients.

HAROLD RIFKIN, M.D.

Clinical Professor of Medicine
Albert Einstein College of Medicine

Professor of Clinical Medicine
New York University School of Medicine

Principal Consultant
Diabetes Research and Training Center
Albert Einstein College of Medicine
Montefiore Medical Center
New York, New York

Preface

The polyol paradigm is one of two major theories that have been advanced to explain the pathogenesis of the complications of diabetes. The other, which implicates excess nonenzymatic glycosylation, has been described in the companion volume *Diabetes and Protein Glycosylation*, also published by Springer-Verlag.

The polyol pathway originally was described in the ocular lens, where it was implicated in the development of sugar cataracts. It now is clear that the polyol pathway is present in diverse tissues, where it may participate in the pathogenesis of diabetic neuropathy, retinopathy, and microvascular disease.

The pathway involves two enzymes, aldose reductase and sorbitol dehydrogenase, the first of which converts sugars into their respective alcohols (polyols). It is believed that activation of the polyol pathway has deleterious metabolic effects in several organs. Blocking the pathway by inhibiting aldose reductase, the responsible enzyme, thus may interrupt or forestall development of tissue damage in diabetes.

The Polyol Paradigm and Complications of Diabetes comprehensively reviews the biochemistry and pathophysiologic consequences of enhanced polyol pathway activity, with discussions oriented around the organ systems affected. Insights gained from experimental studies and clinical trials with aldose reductase inhibitors are critically analyzed.

M.P. COHEN

Contents

CHAPTER 1

Introduction

The polyol paradigm is one of two major theories that have been advanced to explain complications of diabetes. The other theory concerns the nonenzymatic glycosylation of proteins,[1] a process that is increased in the presence of hyperglycemia. Like excess nonenzymatic glycosylation, activation of the polyol pathway occurs in tissues that do not require insulin for glucose transport and can dispose of glucose via insulin-independent pathways. It is of more than passing interest that such tissues are the sites of several characteristic complications of diabetes, a fact that increases the attractiveness of the concept that enhanced flux of glucose through certain biochemical pathways in cells that are freely permeable to glucose is a mechanism underlying the development of chronic complications of diabetes.

The polyol pathway involves two enzymes, aldose reductase and sorbitol dehydrogenase, the first of which converts sugars into their respective alcohols (polyols). Initially reported to be operative in the development of sugar cataracts in the ocular lens, the polyol pathway, it is now clear, is present in diverse tissues, where it may participate in the pathogenesis of diabetic neuropathy, retinopathy, and microvascular disease.

The concept that tissue accumulation of polyol pathway products, or some consequence thereof, has deleterious effects in involved organs has gained credence in recent years, as has the notion that blocking the pathway by inhibiting the responsible enzyme could interrupt or forestall the evolution of tissue damage in patients with diabetes. Indeed, these ideas have attracted the attention not only of physicians and scientists concerned with the treatment, prevention, and biochemical basis of diabetic complications, but also of patients, the pharmaceutical industry, drug analysts, and investment houses. Excerpts from a feature article that appeared in the *Wall Street Journal*[2] attest to the interest that has been generated in the pharmaceutical and financial communities and among the lay public regarding the polyol pathway and aldose reductase inhibitors:

> In 1966, Mr. Dvornik, then chief biochemist at Ayerst Laboratories, listened as two Harvard University scientists described the previously unknown chain of biochemical events through which diabetes ravages the body. Disrupt that chain with a synthetic chemical, the two scientists reasoned, and Ayerst would have the first drug for treating the complications that can cripple, and sometimes kill, diabetics.
>
> Today, Ayerst, a unit of New York-based American Home Products Corp., is one of six companies racing to the market with drugs based on the two scientists' idea. Although the anti-diabetes drugs may still be years away from pharmacy shelves, expectations for them are high. The drugs, called aldose reductase inhibitors (ARI), "may revolutionize the treatment of diabetes". . . .
>
> The ARI drugs are among the first fruits of the so-called rational approach to drug research that has been the source of much optimism in the industry. . . .
>
> The development of the drug, however, . . . has been slowed by difficult and expensive testing and by competition with other drug companies to come up with the most effective product. Almost every pharmaceutical company is pursuing ARI research because it's based on such a clearly defined scientific approach. And with five million diabetics in America, the potential for profit is high.
>
> Diabetes is caused by a shutdown in production of insulin. Without insulin, muscle and fat cells can't process the glucose, or sugar, that they use as fuel. High levels of unused sugar back up in the bloodstream, then nerve, eye and kidney cells, which don't need insulin to process the glucose, gorge themselves on the excess sugar.
>
> Scientists now believe that years of such overconsumption eventually damages the eye's cells, causing cataracts and even blindness; disrupts nerve

cell activity, causing severe pain or loss of feeling; and upsets kidney cells, sometimes so severely that the organ stops functioning.

But scientists were powerless to stop the process until they found a chemical switch to close the pathway involved in the cells' sugar feast. As with many of the diseases that have been approached rationally, the key to the diabetes pathway was an enzyme. And it wasn't until 1969 that chemists figured out how to interrupt the activities of enzymes, which are enormously powerful proteins that act as catalysts and speed up biochemical reactions.

The enzyme that unlocked the mystery of the diabetes pathway was noticed in 1963 by Jin Kinoshita.... "We figured we'd locked into the common pathway through which diabetes affected all organs," says Dr. Kinoshita... "The next moves seemed relatively simple: Inhibit the enzyme, block the pathway, and disrupt the disease"....

Ayerst, which had believed itself to be alone in the ARI field, received a shock: Pfizer, Inc., which had been doing its own ARI research, had developed a drug called Sorbinil that was as effective as Ayerst's but was 25 times more potent....

But proving the drug's effectiveness has been a slow process. Recent studies published in medical journals show that the drug's ability to reduce nerve damage in longtime diabetes is limited. Doctors who have worked with ARIs believe that "once the damage has been done to the cells, nothing can truly reverse it".... Meanwhile, Dr. Gabbay is worried that as a preventative, the drugs will be used to block the action of the aldose reductase enzyme for many years. "Since we still don't know what the enzyme's job in healthy tissue is, blocking the enzyme over the course of a lifetime may be very dangerous."

This book is written in the belief that cognizance of the potential pathophysiologic consequences of activation of the polyol pathway by hyperglycemia will reinforce the conviction that every effort should be made to achieve and maintain normalization of blood glucose levels in diabetic patients. Like its recently published companion volume, *Diabetes and Protein Glycosylation*,[1] *The Polyol Paradigm* adds another dimension to the concept that the guilt of glucose in the pathogenesis of complications of diabetes can no longer be denied. The chapters that follow review the chemistry of the polyol pathway and of aldose reductase inhibitors, discuss the metabolic and pathophysiologic significance of enhanced polyol pathway activity, and analyze the insights gained from experimental and clinical studies with aldose reductase inhibitors. Although the ultimate role of the polyol pathway in the sequence of events leading to several of the complications of diabetes, and of aldose reductase inhibitors in the treatment or prevention of these complications, remains to be determined, it is believed that comprehensive discussion of this topic is of timely importance to all concerned with the management of diabetic patients and interested in the mechanisms responsible for the complications characteristically associated with diabetes.

References

1. Cohen MP: *Diabetes and Protein Glycosylation: Measurement and Biologic Relevance*. New York, Springer-Verlag, 1986.
2. Waldholz M: Researchers use logic to uncover, then break, the chain of diabetes. *The Wall Street Journal*, February 5, 1986, p 31.

Chemistry

Aldose Reductase and Sorbitol Dehydrogenase

Aldose reductase is a member of the aldo-keto reductase enzyme family that is present in mammalian tissues. It is a monomeric NADPH-binding protein that catalyzes the reduction of aldoses to their corresponding sugar alcohols. Using NADPH as coenzyme, aldose reductase catalyzes the initial reaction of the sorbitol pathway, also called the polyol pathway.[1-3] Oxidation of sorbitol to fructose, catalyzed by the enzyme sorbitol dehydrogenase, which uses the cofactor NAD as the electron acceptor, constitutes the second reaction in this pathway, according to the scheme depicted in Figure 2-1.

Both aldose reductase and sorbitol dehydrogenase have broad substrate specificities, including glucose and galactose for the former enzyme, and xylitol (to form D-xylulose) and ribitol (to form D-ribulose) for the latter. Notably, however, sorbitol dehydrogenase has limited ability to further metabolize galactitol, the sugar alcohol formed from galactose. This feature has been exploited experi-

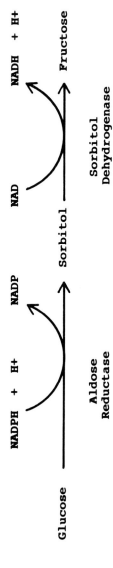

FIGURE 2-1 The sorbitol pathway: Aldose reductase (alditol-NADP+ oxidoreductase, EC 1.1.1.21) and Sorbitol dehydrogenase (L-iditol dehydrogenase) (EC 1.1.1.14).

mentally with the use of galactose-fed models to probe the consequences of polyol accumulation in various tissues.[4]

Because of their low affinity for glucose, the aldose reductases are normally operative at low catalytic rates when glucose concentration is in the physiologic range. In the presence of hyperglycemia or galactosemia, however, their activity increases substantially, causing increased formation of the correspondent sugar alcohols sorbitol and galactitol.[5,6] This fact, coupled with the recognition that sugar alcohols penetrate cell membranes poorly, and hence, once formed, are trapped intracellularly, led to the proposal that osmotic effects consequent to polyol accumulation are instrumental in the development of certain chronic complications of diabetes.[7-9] This theory is discussed more fully in later sections. Appreciation of the potential role of the polyol pathway in the pathogenesis of diabetic complications also generated considerable interest in the identification and characterization of aldose reductases in various tissues, and led to the search for effective inhibitors of aldose reductase that might prove clinically useful for the treatment or prevention of diabetic sequelae.

Biochemical studies have confirmed the presence of aldose reductase activity in diverse tissues, including seminal vesicles, placenta, lens, brain, erythrocyte, muscle, renal papillae, and aorta.[1,2,10-42] In early reports, the distinction between aldose reductase and other enzymes, such as aldehyde reductases or hexonate dehydrogenase, that have closely related substrate specificities was sometimes imperfect; however, immunologic studies have clearly established the separate identity of aldose reductase.[36,37,42,43] Immunohistochemistry also has demonstrated widespread distribution of aldose reductase in mammalian tissues[44-46] (Tables 2-1, 2-2). The enzyme is present in lower organisms such as yeast, which has provided a stable and convenient source of aldose reductase with high specific activity that has proved useful for studies of the reaction mechanism.[47,48] It is also found in the muscle of the parasitic nematode *Ascaris suum*.[49]

Aldose reductase is a member of a class of several pyridine nucleotide-linked enzymes which share common structural and functional characteristics and which catalyze the oxidation and reduction of aldehydes. Although it has broad substrate specificities which overlap those of aldehyde reductases, the enzyme has some

TABLE 2-1 Tissue Distribution of Aldose Reductase Detected by Immuno-histochemistry

Tissue	Localization
Adrenal cortex	Glomerulosa, fasciculata, reticularis
Cerebral cortex	Pyramidal cells, choroid plexus (epithelium)
Blood vessels	Intima (endothelium), media
Eye	Lens, retina, cornea, ciliary processes, optic nerve
Intestine	Lamina propria of jejunal villi
Kidney	Interstitial cells, collecting tubules, Henle's loop, papillae (epithelium)
Ovary	Medulla, oocyte, granulosa cord cells
Peripheral nerve	Schwann cells
Salivary glands	Ductal epithelium
Spinal cord	Anterior horn cell bodies, white matter neuroglia cells
Testis	*Leydig cells, Sertoli cells, epididymis

Data from Kern and Engerman.[44]
*According to Ludvigson et al.,[45] aldose reductase is specifically located in the Sertoli cell and is not detected immunocytochemically in any other testicular cell type.

affinity for D-glucose and other aldo-sugars, resulting in retention of its separate name and classification as an aldose reductase. However, the aldehyde form of D-glucose may be the true substrate in the reduction of D-glucose by the enzyme. Aldose reductase is an A-type enzyme, meaning that the reaction it catalyzes occurs with the direct and stereospecific addition and removal of hydrogen from the para position of the nicotinamide ring of the nucleotide.[15,21,50-52] Sorbitol dehydrogenase is also an A-type enzyme. Aldose reductase in the lens, the tissue that has been most intensively studied, of several species is a monomeric acidic enzyme having a molecular weight in the range of 35,000 to 40,000 and an isoelectric point of 4.75 to 4.85.[25,26,29,30] Human brain aldose reductase is a monomer of molecular weight 38,000 with an isoelectric point of 5.9.[21]

Human placental aldose reductase has an apparent molecular weight of 37,000 on SDS-gel electrophoresis.[14] On immunodiffusion or immunoelectrophoresis, antibodies raised against this preparation give a single line of identity with either human placental or human lens aldose reductase, but not with rat lens aldose reductase.

TABLE 2-2 Tissues in Which Immunohistochemical Evidence of Aldose Reductase Is Lacking

Adipose tissue
Adrenal medulla
Kidney cortex
Lung
Microvasculature
Oviduct
Parathyroid
Prostate
Salivary gland acini
Epidermis and dermis
Spleen
Thyroid
Umbilical cord
Uterus

Data from Kern and Engerman.[44]

Thus, lens aldose reductases from different species are not immunologically identical. On the other hand, antibodies against purified rat lens aldose reductase, which appears as a closely spaced doublet with a molecular weight of approximately 38,000 on SDS-gel electrophoresis, show cross-reactivity with human placental aldose reductase. Both enzymes are activated by sulfate ions and inhibited by chloride ions, and have similar substrate specificities with higher affinities for aromatic and aliphatic aldehydes than for hexose sugars, greater activity with aromatic than with aliphatic aldehydes, and greater preference for short-chain than for long-chain aliphatic aldehydes. In purified form, neither shows any activity when L-gulonate (gulonic acid) is used as substrate, thus differentiating them from L-hexonate dehydrogenase.

When isolated from brain, lens, and other tissues, aldose reductase is closely associated with an enzyme of the glucuronic acid-xylulose shunt, NADP-L-hexonate dehydrogenase (NADP+ 1-oxidoreductase; EC 1.1.1.19). In muscle, the properties of one of two major aldehyde reductases, which had been designated ARI and ARII (AR 1 and AR 2), appear to be similar to those of lens aldose reductase. This "low-K_m" aldehyde reductase in muscle has immunologic identity with similar low-K_m aldehyde reductases of brain and kidney and with lens aldose reductase.[37,38] These muscle and kidney low-K_m aldehyde reductases, and probably the high-K_m aldehyde reductases as well, are inhibited by the commercial aldose reductase inhibitors alrestatin and Sorbinil. Thus, it has been argued that a separate designation for aldose reductase is not necessary. However, with the impetus provided by the pharmaceutical industry and the emergence of aldose reductase inhibitors in the clinical arena, this designation is now too firmly entrenched to be easily supplanted by a revised nomenclature.

In some studies, bovine, rat, and human lens aldose reductase have exhibited unusual kinetic characteristics, with a deviation from classic Michaelis-Menten kinetics that consisted of a concave downward curvature in Lineweaver-Burk double reciprocal plots at higher substrate concentrations. This behavior may reflect the presence of two enzymes. Although aldose reductase was originally described as a single species, recent studies with rabbit lens have identified two bands of aldose reductase activity by anionic polyacrylamide gel electrophoresis.[38] Purified rat lens aldose reductase also migrates as a closely spaced doublet, but one of the bands may represent a product of proteolysis. In the rabbit lens, these closely migrating bands represented monomeric enzymes, and had electrophoretic mobilities identical to those of two aldose reductases (aldose reductase 1 and aldose reductase 2) purified from skeletal muscle of male rabbits. Double immunodiffusion studies showed that antiserum to the muscle aldose reductase 1 cross-reacted with complete identity with muscle aldose reductase 2 and 1, and that antiserum to muscle aldose reductase 2, which almost completely blocks the activity of this enzyme, cross-reacted with complete identity with the lens aldose reductases. The molecular weights of the lens and muscle aldose reductase 1 and the muscle aldose reductase 2 were respectively estimated at 40,200 and 41,500, based on a curve derived from the relative mobilities of standard proteins plotted against their molecular weights. However, on gel filtration the molecular weights of the two muscle aldose reductases were indistinguishable at about 34,000. Like the lens aldose reductases, the enzymes from rabbit skeletal muscle are inhibited by the commercial aldose reductase inhibitors alrestatin and Sorbinil and by the flavinoid quercetin. According to one report, pig lens aldose reductase, in contrast to enzyme in the lens of the above-mentioned species, does not show homotrophic cooperative effects and does not appear to contain isoenzymes.[27] On the other hand, Markus and co-workers found that aldose reductase was present as two or more isoenzymes in all mammalian lenses they studied (human, cat, dog, guinea pig, monkey, pig, rabbit, rat, and sheep) except those of mouse.[53]

Although the presence of aldose reductase in red cells has been argued, it appears that human erythrocytes contain an aldose reductase that has kinetic, immunologic, and structural properties similar to the lens enzyme.[36,42] Despite some early confusion with the hexonate dehydrogenase present in these cells, it appears that erythrocyte aldose reductase is a separate enzyme since antiserum raised against the former enzyme does not cross-react with the latter. Aldose reductase from human erythrocytes has been purified to homogeneity.[36] The molecular weight of this enzyme, based on Sephadex gel filtration and polyacrylamide gel electrophoresis, is 32,500. It has an isoelectric pH of 5.47, a pH optimum of 6.2, and a requirement for lithium sulfate (0.4 M) for full expression of its activity. The enzyme is inhibited by various aldose reductase inhibitors and, in general, has properties similar to those exhibited by aldose reductases from bovine lens and brain and from human brain.

Under physiologic conditions, red cell aldose reductase exists in activated and unactivated forms, and exhibits biphasic kinetics.[54,55] The activated form reduces glucose to sorbitol with about seven times greater efficiency than does the unactivated form. Activation can be accomplished by preincubation of the enzyme with glucose-6-phosphate, NADPH, and glucose, 10 μM each. Aldose reductase in other tissues may also exist in activated and unactivated forms (Figure 2-2),[56] which could account for the previously observed anomalous kinetics and would help explain the increased aldose reductase activity and consequent polyol accumulation associated with hyperglycemia. Interestingly, the activated enzyme is less susceptible to inhibition by aldose reductase inhibitors such as Sorbinil, alrestatin, and quercitrin (Figure 2-3). This may explain the need in vivo for higher plasma levels of inhibitor to accomplish lowering of the sorbitol concentration in the erythrocytes of diabetic subjects than are required in vitro under standard assay conditions. Similarly, aldose reductase prepared from normal human lens exhibits properties similar to native enzyme from other tissues,

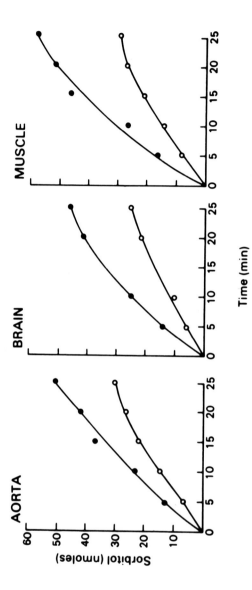

FIGURE 2-2 Formation of sorbitol by aldose reductase from various tissues. ○——○, unactivated enzyme; ●——●, enzyme activated by incubation with glucose-6-phosphate, NADPH, and glucose. Reproduced with permission from the American Diabetes Association, Inc. From Das B, Srivastava SK: Activation of aldose reductase from tissues. *Diabetes* 1985; 34:1145–1151.

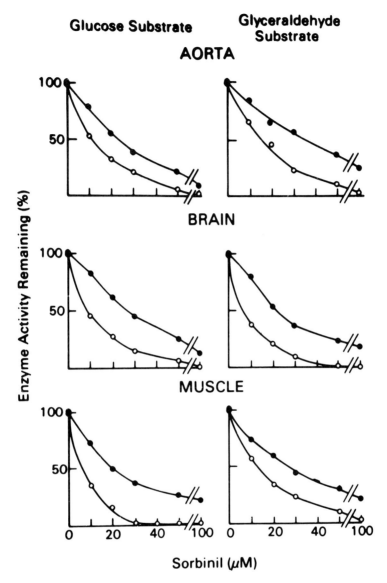

FIGURE 2-3   Inhibition by Sorbinil of activated (●——●) and unactivated (○——○) forms of aldose reductase from various tissues. Reproduced with permission from the American Diabetes Association, Inc. From Das B, Srivastava SK: Activation of aldose reductase from tissues. *Diabetes* 1985; 34:1145–1151.

whereas aldose reductase prepared from lens of hyperglycemic diabetic subjects exhibits properties similar to those of enzyme activated in vitro.

Aldose Reductase Inhibitors

The identification of aldose reductase in a variety of tissues in which
complications of diabetes occur has led not only to a mechanistic
theory, discussed in detail in the following chapters, proposing that
hyperglycemia can alter the metabolism and function of cells in
these tissues via sorbitol accumulation, but also to the search for
inhibitors of aldose reductase that are nontoxic and effective in vivo
with an appropriate duration of action. The hope is that such compounds will prove useful therapeutically for those complications of
diabetes in which activation of the polyol pathway is believed to play
a role.

A variety of structurally unrelated compounds possess aldose
reductase-inhibiting properties. Early studies showing that long-
chain fatty acids and α-keto fatty acids could inhibit aldose reductase when galactose, glucose, or xylose was used as substrate led to
the development and in vitro testing of tetramethylene glutaric
acid.[2,6,57-61] However, this compound did not prove useful in vivo
because of its inability to penetrate plasma membranes.[62,63] Later, a
number of heterocyclic compounds were found to be capable of
inhibiting the enzyme. These include quinolones, spirohydantoins
and structurally similar isoxazolidines, xanthones, flavinoids and

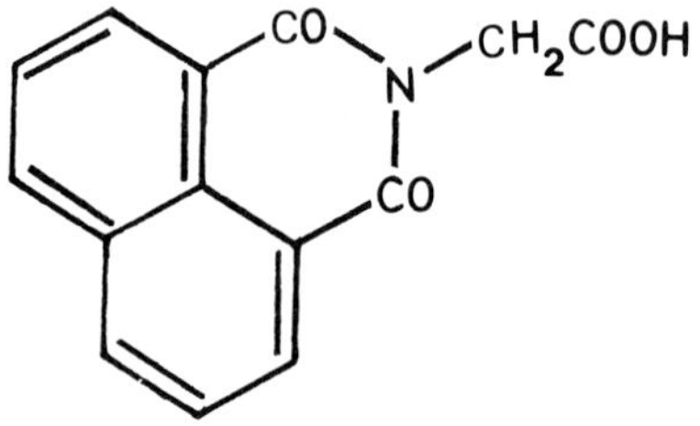

FIGURE 2-4 Structure of alrestatin (1,3-dioxo-1H-benz[de]isoquinolone-
2(3H)acetic acid).

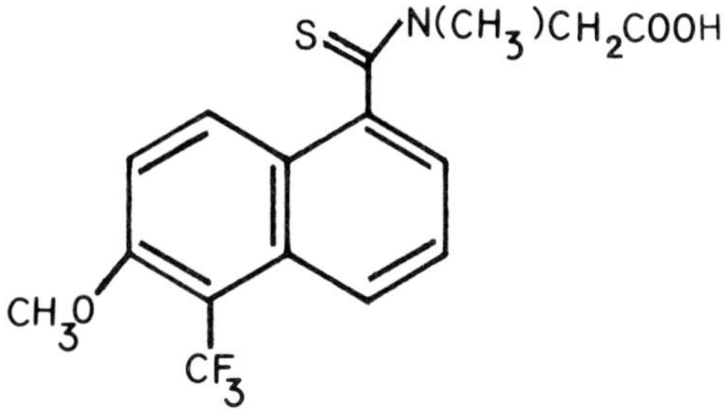

FIGURE 2-5   Structure of tolrestat (Alredase®; *N*-[5-trifluoromethyl)-6-methoxy-1-naphthalenyl]thioxomethyl]-*N*-methylglycine).

structurally related quercitrins, and numerous other compounds that contain a chromone ring system.[64-87] Several of these various compounds, such as alrestatin (Figure 2-4), tolrestat (Figure 2-5), Sorbinil (Figure 2-6), Clinoril® (Figure 2-7), Syntex (Figure 2-8), quercitrin (Figure 2-9), and antirheumatic drugs such as salicylates, indomethacin, and oxyphenbutazone, are now well known. Others such as Statil (ICI 10,5552; 1-[3,4-dichlorobenzyl]-3-methyl-1,2-dihydro-oxiquinol-4-ylacetic acid) and ONO 2235 ((E-3-carboxy-methyl-5)[(2E)-methyl-3-phenylpropenylidene]rhodanine)   have begun to appear in the literature more recently.

Kinetic studies show that most of these inhibitors act by noncompetitive or uncompetitive inhibition, indicating that they do not compete with either the substrate or the nucleotide cofactor site (Refs. 67,70,77,78,85,88–90). In fact, competition studies suggest

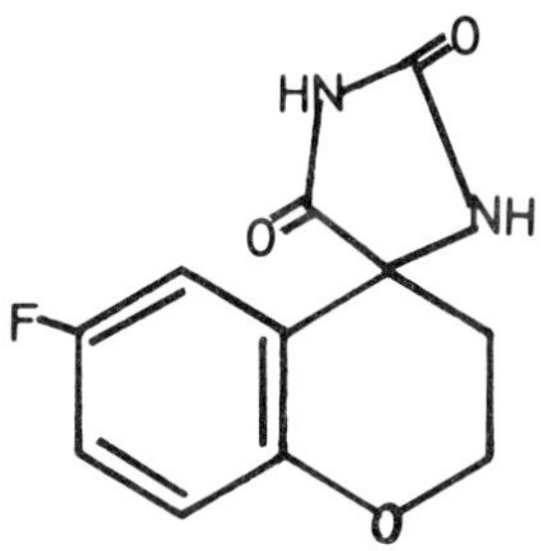

FIGURE 2-6   Structure of Sorbinil (d-6-fluoro-spiro(chroman-4-4'-imidazolidine)-2',5'-dione).

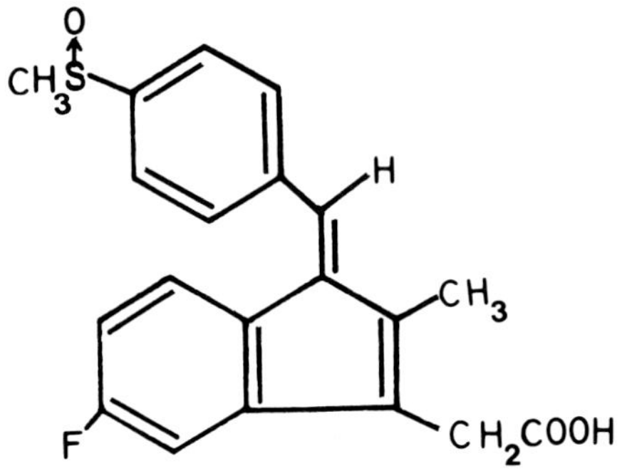

FIGURE 2-7   Structure of sulindac (Clinoril®; 2-(5-fluoro-2-methyl-1-[*p*-methyl-sulfinyl)benzylidine]indene-3-acetic acid).

that compounds with aldose reductase-inhibiting properties can interact reversibly at a common site, called the inhibitor site, on the aldose reductase enzyme. Inhibitors may act to convert the active enzyme to inactive forms, whereas maintenance of activity appears to require protection by thiols.[57,91] Moreover, it appears that aldose reductase inhibitors can also act as antioxidants, and in this manner may decrease tissue levels of toxic dicarbonyl compounds and free radicals produced spontaneously from auto-oxidation of monosaccharides.[83,92,93] In view of the superoxide theory of cataractogenesis, discussed in the chapter on aldose reductase and complications of the eye, this property must be taken into account in any interpretation of the beneficial effects of aldose reductase inhibitors on the development of sugar cataracts.

The inhibitor site of aldose reductase enzymes appears to be structurally distinct from those sites that bind either the substrate or the

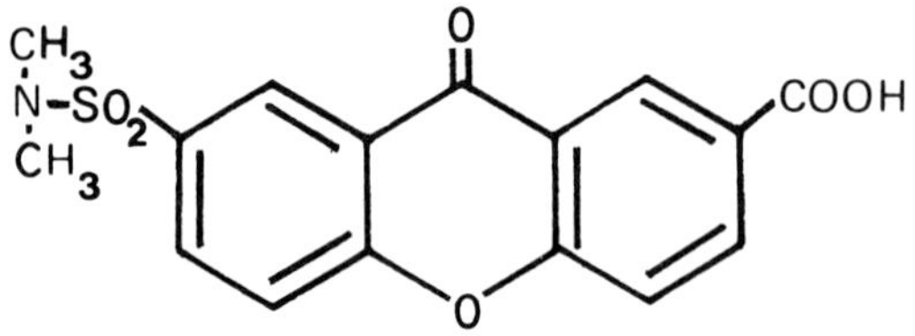

FIGURE 2-8   Structure of Syntex (7-dimethyl sulfamoyl-xanthone-2-carboxylic acid).

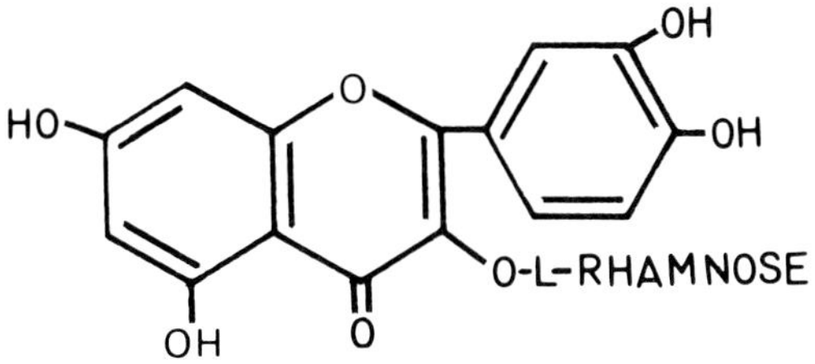

FIGURE 2-9 Structure of quercitrin (2-(3,4-dihydroxyphenyl)-3-O-rhamnosyl-5,7-dihydroxy-4-oxo-4H-chromen).

nucleotide cofactor. It can distinguish between various inhibitors stereochemically, recognizing stereospecific differences in inhibitor molecules.[88] The inhibitory property of various agents depends on the presence of components that are subject to nucleophilic attack. For compounds containing the benzopyran ring system, inhibitory activity has been correlated with the ability to undergo a charge-transfer interaction at a reactive carbonyl group by accepting a pair of electrons from the enzyme.[78] According to Kador and Sharpless, the inhibition of aldose reductase by diverse compounds could result from several mechanisms.[90] For example, binding of the inhibitor could alter the three-dimensional configuration of the enzyme, which could in turn lead to a hindrance of the catalytic site, either by conformational distortion or by steric interference produced by overlapping of the bound inhibitor. These possibilities could arise directly from nucleophilic attack of the reactive carbonyl to form a reversible tetrahedral intermediate, or from a charge-transfer bridge formed between the nucleophilic residue on the inhibitor site and an acidic moiety on another region of the protein. In the latter situation, the reactive carbonyl would be acting to allow nonproximate amino acid residues in the aldose reductase protein to interact. Tyrosine and arginine have been proposed as the respective acidic and basic residues involved in such an interaction. This would fit with the proposal that arginine, possibly together with lysine and histidine, is part of a basic center necessary for activity of the enzyme.[33,91]

These investigators have further postulated that enzyme inhibitor interactions involve a three-point site, and have offered a model for the inhibitor site based on information gained from computer molecular modeling, molecular orbital calculations, structure-activity relationships, and protein modifications. This model includes hydrophobic binding with two lipophilic regions on the enzyme and a charge-transfer interaction between the nucleophilic residue and the reactive carbonyl group of the inhibitor.

The foregoing studies were undertaken to define minimum requirements for aldose reductase inhibitory activity, and thereby provide a framework for the design of new agents with greater potency and specificity. This approach promises replacement of random screening techniques by development of rationally and specifically designed compounds. Such compounds could include agents that do not inhibit hexonate dehydrogenases, as many of the present aldose reductase inhibitors do.[67,94] For example, a recent study found that Sorbinil, alrestatin, and quercitrin are potent inhibitors of liver aldehyde reductase I and brain, liver, and erythrocyte aldehyde reductase II, as well as of purified lens and brain aldose reductase.[95] It could also allow development of inhibitors targeted for the aldose reductase of particular tissues, thus overcoming the differences in susceptibility to inhibition of the enzyme from different tissue sources that have been identified.[96-98] For example, the order of relative potency of four compounds against human placental aldose reductase was chromone derivatives > alrestatin > quercitrin > tetramethyleneglutaric acid, whereas the order of potency of these compounds against rat lens aldose reductase was quercitrin > alrestatin > chromone derivatives = tetramethylene glutaric acid.[96] These findings further suggested that evaluation of aldose reductase inhibitors for potential clinical use may require testing against human aldose reductase. Finally, the results of at least one study suggest that, in some tissues, aldose reductase might be associated in vivo with a factor that renders it insensitive to inhibitors.[99] This could have pharmacologic significance in the development and design of agents targeted for specific tissues.

References

1. Hers HG: Le mécanisme de la transformation de glucose en fructose par les vesicules séminales. *Biochim Biophys Acta* 1956; 22:202–203.
2. Hayman S, Kinoshita JH: Isolation and properties of lens aldose reductase. *J Biol Chem* 1965; 240:877–882.

3. Gabbay KH: The sorbitol pathway and complications of diabetes. *N Engl J Med* 1973; 288:831–836.

4. Cogan DG, Kinoshita JH, Kador PF, et al: Aldose reductase and complications of diabetes. *Ann Intern Med* 1984; 101:82–91.

5. Kinoshita JH, Futterman S, Satoh K, et al: Factors affecting the formation of sugar alcohols in ocular lens. *Biochim Biophys Acta* 1963; 74:340–350.

6. Chylack LT, Kinoshita JH: A biochemical evaluation of a cataract induced in a high glucose medium. *Invest Ophthalmol* 1969; 8:401–412.

7. LeFevre PG, Davies RI: Active transport into the human erythrocyte: Evidence from comparative kinetics and competition among monosaccharides. *J Gen Physiol* 1951; 34:515–524.

8. Wick AN, Drury DR: Action of insulin on the permeability of cells to sorbitol. *Am J Physiol* 1951; 166:421–423.

9. Kinoshita JH: Cataracts in galactosemia. *Invest Ophthalmol* 1965; 4:786–799.

10. Hers HG: Le mécanisme de la formation du fructose séminal et du fructose foetal. *Biochim Biophys Acta* 1960; 37:127–138.

11. Hastein T, Velle W: Placental aldose reductase activity and foetal blood fructose during bovine pregnancy. *J Reprod Fertil* 1968; 15:47–52.

12. Hastein T, Velle W: Purification and properties of aldose reductase from the placental and seminal vesicle of the sheep. *Biochim Biophys Acta* 1969; 178:1–10.

13. Clements R, Winegrad AI: Purification of alditol NADP oxidoreductase from human placenta. *Biochem Biophys Res Commun* 1972; 47:1473–1480.

14. Kador PF, Carper D, Kinoshita JH: Rapid purification of human placental aldose reductase. *Anal Biochem* 1981; 114:53–58.

15. Hoffman PL, Wermuth B, von Wartburg J-P: Human brain aldehyde reductases: Relationship to succinic seminaldehyde reductase and aldose reductase. *J Neurochem* 1980; 35:354–366.

16. Dons RF, Doughty CC: Isolation and characterization of aldose reductase from calf brain. *Biochim Biophys Acta* 1976; 452:1–12.

17. Boghosian RA, McGuiness ET: Affinity purification and properties of porcine brain aldose reductase. *Biochim Biophys Acta* 1979; 567:278–286.

18. Moonsammy GI, Stewart MA: Purification and properties of brain aldose reductase and L-hexonate dehydrogenase. *J Neurochem* 1967; 14:1187–1193.

19. O'Brien MM, Schofield PJ: Polyol pathway enzymes of human brain. *Biochem J* 1980; 187:21–30.

20. Boghosian RA, McGuiness ET: Pig brain aldose reductase: A kinetic study using centrifugal fast analyzer. *Int J Biochem* 1981; 13:909–914.

21. Wermuth B, Burgesser H, Bohren K, et al: Purification and characterization of human-brain aldose reductase. *Eur J Biochem* 1982; 127:279–284.

22. Ris MM, von Wartburg J: Heterogeneity of NADPH-dependent aldehyde reductase from human and rat brain. *Eur J Biochem* 1973; 37:69–77.

23. Turner AJ, Tipton KF: The characterization of two reduced nicotinamide-adenine dinucleotide phosphate-linked aldehyde reductases from pig brain. *Biochem J* 1972; 130:765–772.

24. Jedziniak JA, Chylack LT, Cheng H-M, et al: The sorbitol pathway in human lens: Aldose reductase and polyol dehydrogenase. *Invest Ophthalmol Vis Sci* 1981; 20:314–326.

25. Sheaf CM, Doughty CC: Physical and kinetic properties of homogeneous bovine lens. *J Biol Chem* 1976; 251:2696–2702.

26. Hayman S, Lou MF, Merola LO, et al: Aldose reductase activity in the lens and other tissues. *Biochim Biophys Acta* 1966; 128:474–482.

27. Branlant G: Properties of an aldose reductase from pig lens. *Eur J Biochem* 1982; 129:99–104.

28. Crabbe MJC, Halder AB: Affinity chromatography of bovine lens aldose reductase, and a comparison of some kinetic properties of the enzyme from lens and human erythrocyte. *Biochem Soc Trans* 1980; 8:194–195.

29. Conrad SM, Doughty CC: Comparative studies on aldose reductase from bovine, rat and human lens. *Biochim Biophys Acta* 1982; 708:348–357.

30. Hermann RK, Kador PF, Kinoshita JH: Rat lens aldose reductase: Rapid purification and comparison with human placental aldose reductase. *Exp Eye Res* 1983; 37:467–474.

31. Inagaki K, Miwa I, Okuda J: Affinity purification and glucose specificity of aldose reductase in bovine lens. *Arch Biochem Biophys* 1979; 216:337–344.

32. Tanimoto T, Fukuda H, Kawamura J: Purification and some properties of aldose reductase from rabbit lens. *Chem Pharm Bull (Tokyo)* 1983; 31:2395–2403.

33. Doughty CC, Lee S-M, Conrad S, et al: Kinetic mechanism and structural properties of lens aldose reductase, in Weiner H, Wermuth B (eds): *Enzymology of Carbonyl Metabolism: Aldehyde Dehydrogenase and Aldo/Keto Reductase*, pp 223–242. New York, Alan R. Liss, 1982.

34. Attwood MA, Doughty CC: Purification and properties of calf liver aldose reductase. *Biochim Biophys Acta* 1974; 370:358–368.

35. Halder AB, Wolff S, Ting H-H, et al: An aldose reductase from human erythrocyte. *Biochem Soc Trans* 1980; 8:644–645.

36. Das B, Srivastava SK: Purification and properties of aldose reductase and aldehyde reductase II from human erythrocyte. *Arch Biochem Biophys* 1985; 238:670–679.

37. Cromlish JA, Flynn TG: Pig muscle aldehyde reductase. Identity of pig muscle aldehyde reductase with pig lens aldose reductase and with low Km aldehyde reductase of pig brain and pig kidney. *J Biol Chem* 1983; 258:3583–3586.

38. Cromlish JA, Flynn TG: Purification and characterization of two aldose reductase isoenzymes from rabbit muscle. *J Biol Chem* 1983; 256:3416–3424.

39. Gabbay KH, O'Sullivan JB: The sorbitol pathway in diabetes and galactosemia: Enzyme localization and changes in kidney. 1968; *Diabetes* 17:300.

40. Gabbay KH, Cathcart ES: Purification and immunologic identification of aldose reductases. *Diabetes* 1974; 23:460–468.

41. Morrison AD, Clements RS Jr, Winegrad AI: Effects of elevated glucose concentrations on the metabolism of the aortic wall. *J Clin Invest* 1972; 51:3114–3123.

42. Srivastava SK, Ansari NH, Hair GA, et al: Aldose and aldehyde reductase in human tissues. *Biochim Biophys Acta* 1984; 800:220–227.

43. Wirth H-P, Wermuth B: Immunochemical characterization of aldo-keto reductases from human tissues. *FEBS Lett* 1985; 187:280–282.

44. Kern TS, Engerman RL: Immunohistochemical distribution of aldose reductase. *Histochem J* 1982; 14:507–515.

45. Ludvigson MA, Sorenson RL: Immunohistochemical localization of aldose reductase. I. Enzyme purification and antibody preparation—localization in peripheral nerve, artery and testis. *Diabetes* 1980; 29:438–449.

46. Ludvigson MA, Sorenson RL: Immunohistochemical localization of aldose reductase. II. Rat eye and kidney. *Diabetes* 1980; 29:450–459.

47. Sheys GH, Arnold WJ, Watson JA, et al: Aldose reductase from *Rhodotorula*. *J Biol Chem* 1971; 246:3824–3827.

48. Sheys GH, Doughty CC: The reaction mechanism of aldose reductase from *Rhodotorula*. *Biochim Biophys Acta* 1971; 242:523–531.

49. Goil MM, Harpur RP: Aldose reductase and sorbitol dehydrogenase in the muscle of *Ascaris suum* (Nematoda). *Parasitology* 1978; 77:97–102.

50. Halder AB, Crabbe MJC: Bovine lens aldehyde reductase (aldose reductase). Purification, kinetics and mechanism. *Biochem J* 1984; 219:33–39.

51. Feldman HB, Szczepanik PA, Harne P: Stereospecificity of the hydrogen transfer catalyzed by human placental aldose reductase. *Biochim Biophys Acta* 1977; 480:14–20.

52. Crabbe MJC, Halder AB: Kinetic behavior under defined assay conditions for bovine lens aldose reductase. *Clin Biochem* 1979; 12:281–283.

53. Markus HB, Raducha M, Harris H: Tissue distribution of mammalian aldose reductase and related enzymes. *Biochem Med* 1983; 29:31–45.

54. Srivastava SK, Hair GA, Das B: Activated and unactivated forms of human erythrocyte aldose reductase. *Proc Natl Acad Sci USA* 1985; 82:7222–7226.

55. Das B, Hair GA, Srivastava SK: Activated and unactivated forms of aldose reductase and its role in diabetic complications. *Fed Proc* 1985; 44:1391(A).

56. Das B, Srivastava SK: Activation of aldose reductase from tissues. *Diabetes* 1985; 34:1145–1151.

57. Jedziniak JA, Kinoshita JH: Activators and inhibitors of lens aldose reductase. *Invest Ophthalmol* 1971; 10:357–366.

58. Kinoshita JH, Dvornik D, Kraml M, et al: The effect of an aldose reductase inhibitor on the galactose-exposed rabbit lens. *Biochim Biophys Acta* 1968; 158:472–475.

59. Kinoshita JH, Fukushi S, Kador P, et al: Aldose reductase in diabetic complications of the eye. *Metabolism* 1979; 28(suppl I):462–469.

60. Hutton JC, Williams JF, Schofield PJ, et al: Polyol metabolism in monkey-kidney epithelial-cell cultures. *Eur J Biochem* 1974; 49:347–353.

61. Obazawa H, Merola LO, Kinoshita JH: The effects of xylose on the isolated lens. *Invest Ophthalmol Vis Sci* 1974; 13:204–209.

62. Hutton JC, Schofield PJ, Williams JF, et al: The failure of aldose reductase inhibitor 3,3′-tetramethylene glutaric acid to inhibit in vivo sorbitol accumulation in lens and retina in diabetes. *Biochem Pharmacol* 1974; 23:2991–2998.

63. Gabbay KH, Kinoshita JH: Growth hormone sorbitol, and diabetic capillary disease. *Lancet* 1971; 1:913.

64. Chylack LT Jr, Henriques HF, Cheng H-M, et al: Efficacy of alrestatin, an aldose reductase inhibitor, in human diabetic and nondiabetic lenses. *Ophthalmology* 1979; 86:1579.

65. Varma SD, Mukuni I, Kinoshita JH: Flavinoids as inhibitors of lens aldose reductase. *Science* 1975; 188:1215–1216.

66. Dvornik D, Simard-Duquesne N, Kraml M, et al: Polyol accumulation in galactosemic and diabetic rats: Control by an aldose reductase inhibitor. *Science* 1973; 182:1146–1148.

67. Okuda J, Miwa I, Inagaki K, et al: Inhibition of aldose reductases from rat and bovine lenses by flavinoids. *Biochem Pharmacol* 1982; 31:3807–3822.

68. Segelman AB, Segelman FP, Varma SD, et al: *Cannabis sativa L.* (Marijuana) IX: Lens aldose reductase inhibitory activity of marijuana flavone C-glycosides. *J Pharm Sci* 1977; 66:1358–1359.

69. Beyer-Mears A, Farnsworth PN: Diminished diabetic catactogenesis by quercitin. *Exp Eye Res* 1979; 28:709–716.

70. Peterson MJ, Sarges R, Aldinger CE, et al: CP-45,634: A novel aldose reductase inhibitor that inhibits polyol pathway activity in diabetic and galactosemic rats. *Metabolism* 1979; 28(suppl 1):456–461.

71. Fukushi H, Merola L, Kinoshita J: Altering the course of cataracts in diabetic rats. *Invest Opthalmol Vis Sci* 1980; 19:313–315.

72. Poulson R, Boot-Hanford RP, Heath H: Some effects of aldose reductase inhibition upon the eyes of long-term streptozotocin-diabetic rats. *Curr Eye Res* 1982; 2:351–355.

73. Jacobson MJ, Sharma RJ, Cotlier E, et al: Diabetic complications in lens and nerve and their prevention by sulindac or Sorbinil: Two novel aldose reductase inhibitors. *Invest Ophthalmol Vis Sci* 1983; 24:1426–1429.

74. Richon AB, Maragoudakis ME, Wasvary JS: Isoxazolidine-3,5-diones as lens aldose reductase inhibitors. *J Med Chem* 1982; 25:745–747.

75. Sohda T, Mizuno K, Imamiya E, et al: Studies on antidiabetic agents. 5-Arylthiazolidine-2,4-diones as potent aldose reductase inhibitors. *Chem Pharm Bull* 1982; 30:3601–3616.

76. Schnur RC, Sarges R, Peterson MJ: Spiro oxazolidinedione aldose reductase inhibitors. *J Med Chem* 1982; 25:1451–1454.

77. Pfister JR, Wymann WE, Mahoney JM, et al: Synthesis and aldose reductase inhibitor activity of 7-sulfamoylxanthone-2-carboxylic acids. *J Med Chem* 1980; 23:1264–1267.

78. Kador PF, Sharpless NE: Structure-activity studies of aldose reductase inhibitors containing the 4-oxo-4H-chromen ring system. *Biophys Chem* 1978; 8:81–85.

79. Simard-Duquesne N, Greslin E, Dubuc J, et al: The effects of a new aldose reductase inhibitor (tolrestat) in galactosemic and diabetic rats. *Metabolism* 1985; 34:885–892.

80. Sestanj K, Bellini F, Fung S, et al: N([5-(trifluoromethyl)-6-methoxy-1-naphthalenyl]thioxomethyl)-N-methylglycine (tolrestat), a potent orally active aldose reductase inhibitor. *J Med Chem* 1984; 27:255–256.

81. Inagaki K, Miwa I, Yashiro T, et al: Inhibition of aldose reductases from rat and bovine lenses by hydantoin derivatives. *Chem Pharmacol Bull* 1984; 30:3244–3254.

82. Chaudhry PS, Cabrera J, Juliani HR, et al: Inhibition of human lens aldose reductase by flavinoids, sulindac and indomethacin. *Biochem Pharmacol* 1983; 32:1995–1998.

83. Crabbe MJC, Freeman G, Halder AB, et al: The inhibition of bovine lens aldose reductase by Clinoril, its absorption into the human red cell and its effect on human red cell aldose reductase activity. *Ophthalmic Res* 1985; 17:85–89.

84. Kikkawa R, Hatanaka I, Yasuda H, et al: Effect of a new aldose reductase inhibitor, (E)-3-carboxymethyl-5[(2E)-methyl-3-phenylpropenylidene] rhodanine (ONO-2235), on peripheral nerve disorders in streptozotocin-diabetic rats. *Diabetologia* 1984; 24:290–292.

85. Sharma YR, Cotlier E: Inhibition of lens and cataract aldose reductase by protein bound anti-rheumatic drugs: Salicylate, indomethacin, oxyphenbutazone, sulindac. *Exp Eye Res* 1982; 35:21–27.

86. Kador PF, Sharpless NE, Goosey JD: Aldose reductase inhibition by anti-allergy compounds, in Weiner H, Wermuth B (eds): *Enzymology of Carbonyl Metabolism: Aldehyde Dehydrogenase and Aldo/Keto Reductase*, pp 243–259. New York, Alan R. Liss, 1982.

87. Ono H, Hayano S: 2,2′,4′4′-Tetrahydroxybenzophenone as a new aldose reductase inhibitor. *Nippon Ganka Gakkai Zasshi* 1982; 86:353–357.

88. Kador PF, Goosey JD, Sharpless NE, et al: Stereospecific inhibition of aldose reductase. *Eur J Med Chem* 1981; 16:293–298.

89. Varma SD, Kinoshita JH: Inhibition of lens aldose reductase by flavinoids. *Biochem Pharmacol* 1976; 25:2505–2513.

90. Kador PF, Sharpless NE: Pharmacophor requirements of the aldose reductase inhibitor site. *Mol Pharmacol* 1983; 24:521–531.

91. Halder AB, Crabbe MJCC: Inhibition of aldose reductase by phenylglyoxal, diethylpyrocarbonate and thiol modifiers. *Biochem Soc Trans* 1982; 10: 401–403.

92. Wolff SP, Crabbe MJC, Thornally PJ: Autoxidation of glyceraldehyde and other simple monosaccharides. *Experientia* 1984; 40:244–246.

93. Thornally PJ, Wolff SP, Crabbe MJC, et al: Autoxidation of glyceraldehyde and other monosaccharides catalyzed by buffer ions. *Biochim Biophys Acta* 1984; 797:276–287.

94. O'Brien MM, Schofield PJ, Edwards MR: Inhibition of human brain aldose reductase and hexonate dehydrogenase by alrestatin and Sorbinil. *J Neurochem* 1982; 39:810–814.

95. Srivastava SK, Petrash JM, Sadana IJ, et al: Susceptibility of aldehyde and aldose reductase of human tissues to aldose reductase inhibitors. *Curr Eye Res* 1982; 2:407–410.

96. Kador PL, Merola LO, Kinoshita JH: Differences in the susceptibility of aldose reductase to inhibition. *Doc Ophthalmol Proc Ser* 1979; 18:117–124.

97. Kador PF, Kinoshita JH, Tung WH, et al: Differences in the susceptibility of aldose reductase to inhibition. *Invest Ophthalmol Vis Sci* 1980; 19:980–982.

98. Yoshida H: The characteristics of aldose reductase in human lens, placenta, and rat organs. *Nippon Ganka Gakkai Zasshi* 1981; 85:865–869.

99. Maragoudakis ME, Wasvary J, Gaigiulo P, et al: Human placental aldose reductase: Sensitive and insensitive forms to inhibition by alrestatin. *Fed Proc* 1979; 30:255(A).

Aldose Reductase and Complications of the Eye

Cataracts

The paradigm for the participation of the polyol pathway in the pathogenesis of a complication of diabetes is the ocular lens, the first tissue in which an association between excess sorbitol formation and a pathologic change was described. The discovery by Von Heyningen that the lenses of rats in which cataracts had been induced by diabetes, or by galactose or xylose feeding, contained increased amounts of the respective sugar alcohols sorbitol, galactitol, and xylitol provided an explanation for certain histopathologic features that had been observed in developing cataracts.[1,2] These features consisted of the early appearance of hydropic lens fibers, followed by rupture of the swollen fibers, liquefaction, and replacement by vacuoles or interfibrillar clefts.

Although the identified sugar alcohols are not themselves toxic to the cell, they are osmotically active substances which can cause transcellular movement of water. It was quickly appreciated that accumulation of sugar alcohols in lens fiber cells could lead to hypertonicity with entry of excess water and cellular overhydration, exaggerated by the fact that these substances penetrate cell membranes poorly and hence, once formed, remain trapped within the cell.[3,4] Indeed, Kinoshita and colleagues demonstrated in a number of studies that polyol accumulation in the lens is accompanied by a parallel increase in water content and lens hydration,[5-12] thus suggesting a mechanism for the initiation of cataract formation that had definite histopathologic correlates, as noted above. The disruption of fiber structure that follows osmotic swelling ultimately leads to loss of transparency.[13] This sequence of polyol accumulation and lenticular swelling also helped explain the long-recognized occurrence of semiacute changes in the refractive index in diabetic patients, with myopia due to lens swelling during hyperglycemic phases and hypermetropia when the blood glucose is lowered.[14-16]

Polyol-induced hypertonicity of the lens promotes entry of sodium ions along with water. As osmotic swelling proceeds, membrane permeability is altered, resulting in loss of potassium ions and amino acid concentrating ability, and efflux of *myo*-inositol.[10,12,17-25] Other changes include decreased ATP levels, loss of reduced glutathione, and leakage of peptides (Figure 3-1). The synthesis of lens crystallins is depressed during development of galactose-induced cataracts, but synthesis of noncrystallin proteins is unaffected; leakage of crystallin proteins from cataractous lenses also occurs.[26] The onset of cataracts in galactosemic and diabetic rats is accompanied by a reduction in NADPH and an increase in NADP$^+$ levels,[27] and progression of lens opacity in galactosemic rats is accompanied by decreased Na/K-ATPase activity.[28] Interestingly, treatment with the aldose reductase inhibitor sorbinil prevents the drop in Na/K-ATPase activity, as has been found in other tissues (see Chapters 4 to 6). In diabetic rats, the lens content of glucose-6-phosphate and glycerol-3-phosphate as well as of sorbitol and fructose is increased.[29-31] Glycerol-3-phosphate, but not glucose-6-phosphate, is normalized by treatment with Sorbinil. The ability of Sorbinil to restore glycerol-3-phosphate prompted the suggestion that aldose reductase inhibition affects a wide network of glycolytic reactions in the lens, possibly by influencing altered redox states of NAD$^+$/NADH and NADP$^+$/NADPH that are generated by shifts in the activity of the pentose shunt pathway in the diabetic state.[31]

The decrease in reduced glutathione that is observed during sugar-induced cataract development has been interpreted as evidence

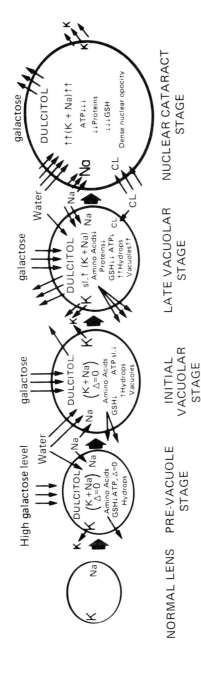

FIGURE 3-1 Sequence of changes involved in the development of sugar cataracts, as proposed by Kinoshita. Reprinted with permission from Kinoshita JH: Cataracts in galactosemia. *Invest Ophthalmol* 1965; 4:786–799.

supporting an alternative or concomitant theory of cataractogenesis, namely, oxygen-dependent oxidative stress on the lens. This theory notes that superoxide and its derivatives can cause lens injury, possibly by polymerization/depolymerization or denaturation reactions involving various macromolecules and by generation of toxic waste products, and that the amount of oxidized proteins is higher in cataractous than in noncataractous lenses.[32-38] The observation that the development of opacities in lens incubated with high glucose concentration is arrested when reduced glutathione or vitamin E, which inhibit superoxide-dependent oxidative reactions, is added to the incubation media seems to support the hypothesis that the decrease in reduced glutathione that follows lens polyol accumulation and swelling is a major factor in cataractogenesis.[39] Similarly, treatment of diabetic rats with daily injections of vitamin E prevented the appearance and evolution of lens changes that were observed in untreated diabetic rats, namely, irregular structure of equatorial fiber cells at 4 days, followed by twisting of and protrusions from these cells at 1 to 2 weeks, disorganization at 3 weeks, and extensive subcapsular globular degeneration of cortical fiber cells at 6 weeks.[40] Notably, the levels of fructose and glucose in the vitamin-treated diabetic animals were increased to the same extent as in untreated diabetic rats, and lens sorbitol levels remained elevated in the rats that received vitamin E, indicating that the protective effect of vitamin E did not derive from a direct influence on the activity of the polyol pathway. However, a more recent study found that the addition of vitamin E or reduced glutathione failed to protect against the development of cataracts that were induced by incubation of rat or gerbil lenses with medium containing a high (55.5 mM) glucose concentration.[41] Aldose reductase inhibitors do not appear to consistently influence peroxidation reactions in diabetic rat lenses,[42] but can restore normal levels of glutathione.[31]

Three additional lines of reasoning, bolstered by experimental evidence, support the hypothesis that polyol accumulation participates in the pathogenesis of sugar cataracts, at least in animal models. First, the development of cataractous changes and the rate of cataract formation, either in vivo in animals with spontaneous or experimental diabetes, or in vitro when lenses are incubated in media containing high glucose concentrations, is greater in lenses in which there is a high level of aldose reductase activity. For example, a mouse model with congenital diabetes and low levels of aldose reductase activity in the lens accumulates little polyol and does not develop cataracts despite persistent hyperglycemia, whereas a rodent model with high levels of aldose reductase activity in the lens develops cataracts within a few weeks after the onset of mild hyperglycemia.[12,43-46] Additionally, lenses from gerbils cultured in medium containing 55.5 mM glucose develop cortical opacities after 24 hours, whereas rat lenses incubated under the same conditions do not develop opacities until 96 hours; aldose reductase activity in gerbil lens is about twice that in rat lens.[41] Gerbils given a high (50%) galactose diet develop cataracts about twice as fast as do galactose-fed rats, and dulcitol accumulation in the lenses of these animals is more pronounced than it is in the lenses of galactosemic rats.[47] Second, cataract formation is accelerated when sugars that have a K_m for aldose reductase that is lower than glucose are used, since they are better substrates, or if the inducing agent is a sugar that forms an alcohol but is not further metabolized to a keto sugar via sorbitol dehydrogenase. Thus, xylose and galactose promote the formation of lenticular opacities or cataracts more efficiently than does glucose.[11,41,43,44,48] Third, prevention of polyol accumulation by inhibition of aldose reductase delays or prevents the onset of cataracts. This has been demonstrated repeatedly in galactose-fed and diabetic animals, and with a variety of compounds, from the earliest available to the most recently developed aldose reductase inhibitors including tetramethyleneglutaric acid[19,49]; Ayerst's alrestatin and tolrestat[50-53]; Pfizer's Sorbinil[54-58]; compounds developed by ICI, Eisai, and ONO[59,60]; flavinoids such as quercitrin[46,61-63]; and the structurally similar xanthones.[64] Although the ability of a variety of other, structurally unrelated compounds such as sulindac (Clinoril®), salicylates, and indomethacin that can act as inhibitors of aldose reductase to forestall the development of sugar cataracts in animal models has not been established, there is interesting clinical information to suggest that they could do so.[65-69]

Treatment with an aldose reductase inhibitor has also been reported to reverse the cataractogenic process after it has been initiated in galactose-fed or streptozotocin-diabetic rats.[70,71] After 5 days of galactose, fiber disintegration and vacuole formation in the pre-equatorial and equatorial cortex were noted; treatment with

Sorbinil despite continued high-galactose feeding during the subsequent 5 days reversed these changes. The lenses of untreated diabetic rats showed increased fiber thickness, edematous granulation of the cell surface, and absence of fiber interdigitation by 16 days after induction of diabetes; subsequent treatment for 5 days with Sorbinil resulted in recovery of fiber contour and interdigitation and appearance of new fibers.

Whole-body irradiation in young rats prolongs the latency period for development of galactose-induced cataracts.[72,73] It is therefore of interest to note the report that whole-body irradiation inhibits the normal age-associated increase in lens aldose reductase activity, either by an effect on enzyme synthesis or by causing production of faulty protein.[74]

A few studies directly support the relevance of findings in experimental sugar cataracts to cataract formation in human diabetes. For example, analysis of cataracts removed from human diabetic subjects has shown that the contents of sorbitol and fructose are increased in specimens removed from patients with elevated fasting blood glucose concentrations[63,75] (Figure 3-2). In one series of patients with diabetes and cataracts, the content of fructose and sorbitol in their cataracts correlated with their fasting blood glucose concentrations and glycosylated hemoglobin levels.[76] Another study, however, found no differences in the lens aldose reductase activity of normal, nondiabetic cataract, and diabetic cataract specimens.[77] Human lenses, obtained from donated eyes kept in an eye bank, synthesize substantial amounts of sorbitol and fructose when incubated in the presence of 30 mM glucose.[51] The tacit assumption that the lens is exposed in vivo to increased concentrations of glucose in human diabetic patients appears to be correct, since the mean glucose concentration in the aqueous humor of cataract patients with diabetes is higher than that in the aqueous humor of nondiabetic subjects.[78] Additionally, increased aqueous humor glucose concentration is reported to elevate the sodium concentration in human lens. However, despite the presence of polyol pathway enzymes in the ciliary body, sorbitol does not accumulate in this tissue in diabetes, at least in rabbits, and enhanced polyol activity thus does not appear to contribute to other diabetes-associated changes in the aqueous humor, such as the reduction in amino acid levels.[79-81]

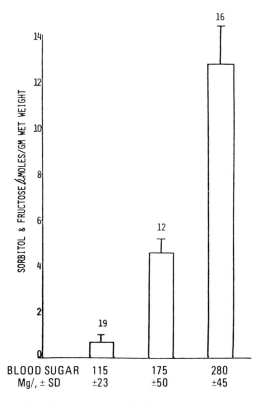

FIGURE 3-2 Relationship between sorbitol plus fructose contents and fasting blood glucose concentrations in cataracts from diabetic subjects. Reprinted with permission from Varma SD et al: Implications of aldose reductase in cataracts in human diabetics. *Invest Ophthalmol Vis Sci* 1979; 18:237–241.

Despite the above considerations, the exact contribution of the polyol pathway to the development of cataracts, either diabetic or senile, in human patients is not entirely clear, and this information must be interpreted in the context of other theories regarding cataractogenesis in diabetic or nondiabetic populations. One of the most prominent among these is that linking the nonenzymatic glycosylation of proteins to cataract formation.[82] That treatment with an aldose reductase inhibitor reportedly prevented cataracts in galactosemic rats without altering the level of nonenzymatic glycosylation of lens proteins could be taken as evidence favoring the primacy of the polyol pathway as a pathogenetic influence.[83] Similarly, Sorbinil has no effect on the level of glucose-6-phosphate, an efficient reactant for nonenzymatic glycosylation, in the lens of diabetic rats.[31] However, these results do not address the issue of animal versus human cataracts, or of the suitability of extrapolating effects induced by galactose, which is not further metabolized to fructose, to those of glucose, which is. These considerations assume particular importance in view of the findings that, on a per lens basis, the level of aldose reductase in human lenses is roughly one order of magnitude lower than that found in many animals, that the specific activity of human lens aldose reductase is less than that of rat or rabbit, and that the ratio of activity of aldose reductase to sorbitol dehydrogenase in human lens is the reverse of that in all other animal lenses that have been studied.[77] Relative to animal lenses, the human lens contains high levels of sorbitol dehydrogenase and limited levels of aldose reductase. Thus, sorbitol is the predominant polyol product in animal lens, but fructose is the main metabolite in human lens. However, fructose could exert a significant osmotic effect, assuming that it is not freely diffusable from the cell and that it is not further metabolized to a great extent. Reports that the prevalence of cataracts in patients receiving aspirin is significantly lower than that in matched populations not receiving aspirin could be taken as evidence that inhibition of nonenzymatic glycosylation (via acetylation of free ϵ-amino groups of lysine residues in lens proteins) prevents cataract formation, but these observations could relate to the aldose reductase-inhibiting properties of salicylates.[68,69,84]

The relationship between sugar-induced cataracts according to the osmotic theory, and cataract formation according to the depletion of reduced glutathione/oxidative dependent oxidative stress theory is not entirely clear, as discussed earlier in this chapter. Further, the potential involvement in cataract formation of abnormalities in the glycolytic pathway or in the metabolic regulation of glycolysis, and how these relate to enhanced polyol pathway activity, have not been fully defined.[85-89] One unifying hypothesis that takes into account the diverse factors that have cataractogenic potential is that which postulates that a combination of two or more such factors may actually be required for development of cataracts. Each factor may be subcataractogenic if operative alone, and may act in concert with or potentiate another, possibly in stepwise fashion.[40,89,90] The contributing factors may not be identical in individual patients. Thus, the decreased lenticular glycolysis, phosphofructokinase, and hexokinase activity, and the excess nonenzymatic glycosylation of lens crystallins that occur with aging may, in combination, contribute to the formation of senile cataracts.[77,85-87] These factors, perhaps coupled with the added stress of sorbitol and fructose accumulation, may explain the increased risk for senile cataracts conferred by the diabetic state.[91] Similarly, it is likely that other and various combinations of stress factors for cataractogenesis pertain in diabetic populations. If this hypothesis is correct, the potential benefit of eliminating at least one subcataractogenic influence, such as polyol accumulation via inhibition of aldose reductase, can be readily appreciated. In fact, a recent study presenting evidence that the addition of 0.1 mM H_2O_2 to lenses incubated in the presence of 36 mM glucose reduces sorbitol production and accumulation suggests that inhibition of aldose reductase renders the lens better able to cope with oxidative stress.[92] The theory underlying this postulate recognizes that aldose reductase and glutathione reductase both require NADPH as a cofactor and that both oxidation and sorbitol production will activate the hexose monophosphate shunt, the principal source of NADPH in the lens. Thus, activation of the polyol pathway may result in a competition for available NADPH that impairs the tissue's ability to scavenge oxidants.

Retinopathy

The capillaries of the retina contain two types of cells: the endothelial cells and the intramural pericytes.[93-95] Endothelial cells line the capillary lumen and form a permeability (blood-retinal) barrier, derived to a large extent from the tight junctions by which these cells are joined.[96] They produce and are surrounded by a basement membrane, which is continuous with that which envelops the pericyte. Intramural pericytes, also known as mural cells, are selectively lost early in the course of diabetic retinopathy,[97-99] leaving a ghost-like pouch of surrounding basement membrane.

This specific mural cell loss is believed to be a primary event contributory to the retinopathic process, even though it might be obscured by capillary closure later in the course of retinopathy.[100] Breakdown of the blood-retinal barrier is another early feature.[101-103] Dilatation and endothelial cell proliferation occur in the capillaries in which there is a loss of mural cells, while adjacent capillaries have diminished perfusion and eventually become acellular tubes consisting solely of basement membrane.[104] Dilated capillaries develop microaneurysmal outpouchings, leak intravascular fluid, and may eventually give rise to growth and proliferation of new capillaries (neovascularization).

A link between the polyol pathway and the mural cell dropout characteristic of early diabetic retinopathy was first suggested with the demonstration that aldose reductase is present in the retinal microvasculature,[105] and specifically in the mural cells. Immunohistochemical studies using antibody raised in goats or rabbits against human placental aldose reductase have localized the enzyme in the perinuclear cytoplasm of mural cells of human retinal vessels.[106] In these studies, the successful demonstration of immunoreactivity was ascribed to the use of short-term trypsin digestion to prepare well-preserved human retinal vessels with intact basement membranes, since two previous studies of frozen retinal cross sections had failed to find or had shown only scattered histochemical evidence of the enzyme in rat and dog retinal vessels.[107,108] Another, more recent study also failed to find aldose reductase immunohistochemically in frozen sections of the retinal vessels, but it was impossible to identify specific mural cell bodies in these sections of retinal capillaries.[109] Aldose reductase activity has also been demonstrated by radioimmunoassay in rhesus monkey mural cells that have been maintained in tissue culture.[110] The radioimmunoassay utilized rabbit antibody that was prepared against purified human placental aldose reductase, and cross-reacted with the enzyme in rhesus lens. It was able to detect aldose reductase in whole retinas as well as in cultured mural cells, but not in freshly isolated retinal capillaries, perhaps because of the paucity of pericytes in such preparations and the consequent low relative concentration of aldose reductase (Table 3-1).

When mural cells from rhesus monkey are maintained in tissue culture medium that contains a high (40 mM) glucose concentration, sorbitol accumulation occurs. Retinal mural cells also contain higher levels of fructose when grown in 40 mM glucose than they do

TABLE 3-1   Aldose Reductase in Retinal Tissue From
Rhesus Monkeys

Sample	Aldose Reductase (ng/mg protein)
Retinal capillaries	Negligible
Whole retina	69
Cultured mural cells	441

Data from Buzney et al.[110]

when the culture medium contains 10 mM glucose, indicating that
these cells contain sorbitol dehydrogenase activity. The sorbitol
accumulation is evident after 3 days of culture in 40 mM glucose,
rises dramatically between the third and the seventh day of exposure
to high glucose, and thereafter plateaus (Figure 3-3). Retinal

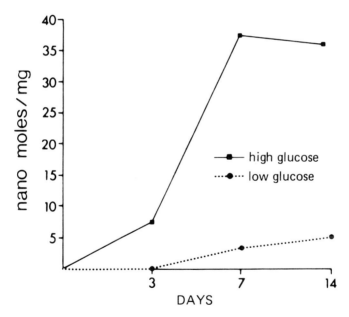

FIGURE 3-3   Sorbitol accumulation in cultured retinal mural cells. High glucose,
40 mM concentration; low glucose, 10 mM concentration. Reprinted with permission from Buzney SM et al: Aldose reductase in retinal mural cells. *Invest
Ophthalmol Vis Sci* 1977; 16:392–396.

TABLE 3-2   Galactitol Production by Retinal Microvessels

Condition	Galactitol μmol/g protein)
30 mM galactose	24.5 ± 4.1
30 mM galactose plus 2.5 × 10⁻⁵ Sorbinil	11.0 ± 1.3

Data from Kern and Engerman.[111]

microvessels isolated from dogs and incubated with a high (30 mM) galactose concentration produce dulcitol (galactitol), the hexitol resulting from aldose reductase activity on galactose substrate.[111] This galactitol production is prevented when an aldose reductase inhibitor is included in the incubation medium (Table 3-2).

Aldose reductase activity has been demonstrated by enzymatic assay and by immunologic techniques in a retinoblastoma cell line maintained in tissue culture.[112] Unfortunately, the exact retinal cell of origin of this cell line is not known, making the findings difficult to interpret from the perspective of pericyte dropout and diabetic retinopathy. The retinoblastoma cells accumulate dulcitol when placed in media containing 30 mM galactose, and this accumulation is prevented by inclusion of the aldose reductase inhibitor Sorbinil in the tissue culture media.

The foregoing observations have helped formulate the postulate that polyol accumulation occurs in, and is injurious to, the retinal microvascular mural cell in diabetes. It appears that retinal peri-cytes, like peripheral nerves and other tissues affected by complications of diabetes, do not require insulin for glucose transport. Cultured bovine retinal capillary pericytes have been found to possess a saturable, stereospecific, carrier-facilitated transport mechanism for D-glucose and its analog, 3-O-methyl-D-glucose.[113] These recent findings help support the fundamental hypothesis that the hyperglycemia of diabetes, via shunting of glucose from insulin-dependent to insulin-independent metabolic processes such as the polyol pathway, damages the mural cell. Indeed, polyol content is increased in the retinas of animals with experimental diabetes[114,115] (Figure 3-4). Further, mural cells maintained in tissue culture with medium containing a high glucose concentration have been noted to undergo degenerative changes,[110] consisting of clumping and multilayering of the cells amid extracellular debris, whereas cells grown in 10 mM glucose remained in monolayer and the cultures contained minimal cellular debris (Figure 3-5). The cell multiplication rate and the mitotic rate are reduced when bovine retinal microvessel pericytes are grown in 20 mM compared to 5 mM glucose, but high glucose concentration stimulates protein and collagen synthesis by these cells.[116]

Three additional findings in retinal tissue help support the hypothesis that polyol accumulation contributes to the retinopathic process. First, dogs maintained on a high-galactose diet sufficient to produce galactosemia develop retinal microaneurysms reminiscent of those found in typical diabetic retinopathy[117] (Figure 3-6). Second, the basement membrane in retinal capillaries of rats fed a high-galactose diet for 28 to 44 weeks is thickened, and this thickening is prevented by including an aldose reductase inhibitor in the diet[118] (Figure 3-7). However, these latter findings have to be reconciled with the report that the increased rate of collagen synthesis induced by culture of bovine retinal capillary pericytes in high glucose concentration is not corrected by inclusion in the incubation media of the aldose reductase inhibitor Sorbinil[119] (Figure 3-8). Third, fructose-fed diabetic rats develop retinal microvascular changes that include pericyte loss, microaneurysms, endothelial proliferation, and capillary basement membrane thickening, and treatment with the aldose reductase inhibitor ONO-2235 reduces the severity of these changes.[120]

It is not clear whether polyol accumulation per se, or associated metabolic changes, is (are) deleterious to the retinal microvasculature, and if so, how. According to one group of investigators, the absolute level of sorbitol that accumulates in the retinas of diabetic rats (1.5 μmol/g protein) is insufficient to be of osmotic significance.[114] However, another group noted that, since aldose reductase activity is sequestered in specific cellular locations, accumulated sorbitol might not be evenly distributed throughout the retina and could be a significant osmotic force in individual cells.[107] Further, retinal sorbitol concentrations may have been underestimated in some studies, since levels are considerably higher (68.5 and 243 μmol/100 g tissue; normal and diabetic sucrose-fed rats, respectively) in specimens dissected in situ and placed in perchloric acid within 5 seconds.[121] On the other hand, it has been argued that

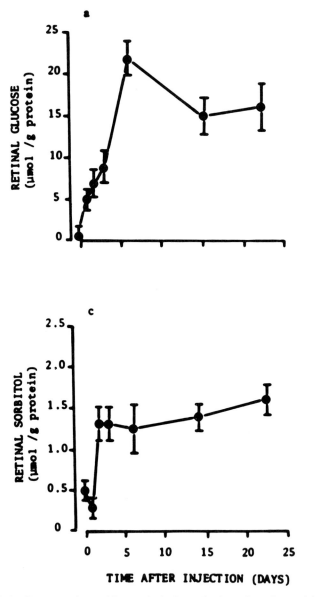

FIGURE 3-4   Concentrations of free carbohydrates in the retina of rats with streptozotocin diabetes. Reprinted with permission from Hutton JC et al: Sorbitol
metabolism in the retina: Accumulation of pathway intermediates in streptozotocin
induced diabetes in the rat. *Aust J Exp Biol Med Sci* 1974; 52:361–373.

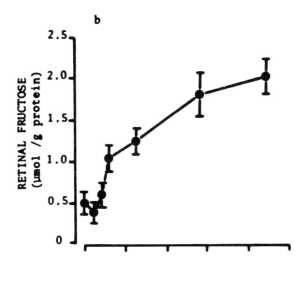

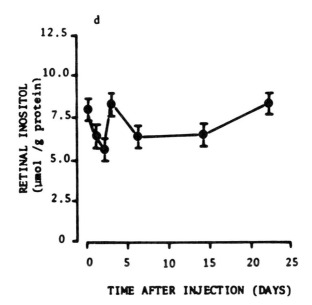

TIME AFTER INJECTION (DAYS)

FIGURE 3-4 *Continued.*

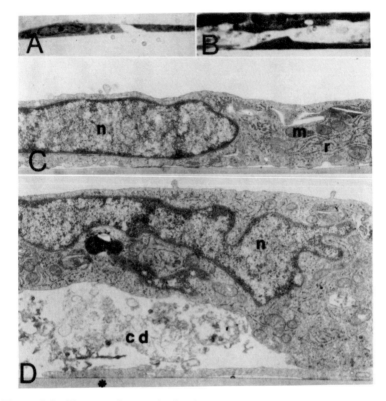

FIGURE 3-5   Electron micrograph of retinal mural cells maintained in 10 mM (C) and 40 mM (D) glucose concentration; n, nucleus; m, mitochondria; r, rough endoplasmic reticulum; cd, cellular debris. Reprinted with permission from Buzney SM et al: Aldose reductase in retinal mural cells. *Invest Ophthalmol Vis Sci* 1977; 16:392–396.

the quantitatively similar levels of aldose reductase activity in retinal and cerebral microvessels militate against a major role of this enzyme in the pathogenesis of diabetic retinopathy, since the retinal but not the cerebral microvasculature is typically damaged in diabetes.[122]

The possibility that other changes in cell nutrients or enzymatic activities accompanying polyol accumulation in the diabetic retina contribute to the pathogenesis of retinopathy is intriguing. One group of investigators found that increased retinal sorbitol in alloxan-

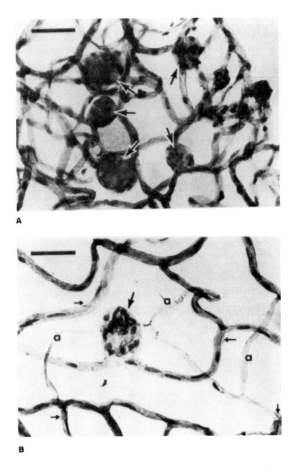

FIGURE 3-6   Retinal vascular changes in experimental galactosemia. A, Capillary aneurysms (large arrows); B, acellular capillaries (a) and ghosts of intramural pericytes (small arrows). Reproduced with permission from the American Diabetes Association, Inc. From Engerman RL, Kern TS: Experimental galactosemia produces diabetic-like retinopathy. *Diabetes* 1984; 33:97–100.

diabetic rabbits is associated with *myo*-inositol depletion and reduced Na/K-ATPase activity,[115] as has been observed in other tissues, notably peripheral nerve and renal glomeruli. Another group, however, noted that rat retinal *myo*-inositol concentrations were unaffected by streptozotocin diabetes.[114] Interestingly, the polyol accumulation induced in cultured retinal mural cells by exposing

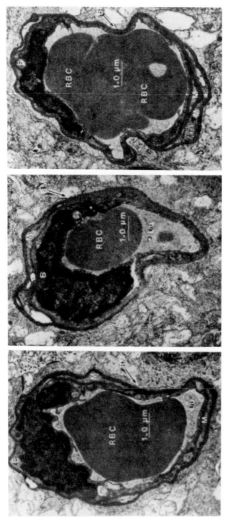

FIGURE 3-7 Electron micrographs of retinal capillaries from control (left), galactose-fed (middle), and Sorbinil-treated, galactose-fed (right) rats. BM, Basement membrane; E, endothelial cell; Lu, lumen; M, mural cell; RBC, red blood cell. Copyright 1983 by the AAAS. From Robison WG et al: Retinal capillaries: Basement membrane thickening by galactosemia prevented with aldose reductase inhibitor. *Science* 1983; 221:1177–1179.

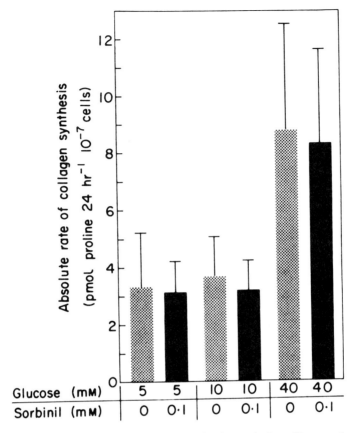

FIGURE 3-8 Collagen synthesis in cultured bovine retinal capillary pericytes. Shaded bars, without Sorbinil; Solid bars, with Sorbinil. Reprinted with permission from Li W et al: The effects of glucose and an aldose reductase inhibitor on the sorbitol content and collagen synthesis of bovine retinal capillary pericytes in culture. *Exp Eye Res* 1985; 40:439–444.

them to high glucose concentration is not accompanied by reduced inositol levels.[110] Nevertheless, the reported changes in retinal *myo*-inositol and Na/K-ATPase activity in diabetes were prevented with inhibition of aldose reductase, suggesting that they are in some way consequent to the enhanced polyol pathway activity. Further, they are associated with a functional alteration, manifest as a reduction in the electroretinogram C wave, that also corrects with aldose reductase inhibition or with *myo*-inositol supplementation.[123,124]

Although the reduced oscillatory potential of the electroretinogram observed after 12 to 16 weeks of diabetes in the rat was not corrected by an aldose reductase inhibitor, the drug significantly improved the change in peak latency shortening of the electroretinogram observed after 8 weeks of diabetes.[125] The relationships between mural cell dropout and/or endothelial cell proliferation and the abnormalities in *myo*-inositol content, Na/K-ATPase activity, and deterioration of the electroretinogram need to be delineated. Studies examining these questions will undoubtedly proceed in conjunction with experiments seeking to unravel analogous relationships that exist in other tissues subject to diabetic complications. The recent description of a sodium-dependent, glucose- inhibited transport system for *myo*-inositol in retinal capillary pericytes[126] suggests that mechanisms underlying metabolic, and perhaps functional, defects in the retinal microvasculature and in the peripheral nerve in diabetes are similar.

There is disagreement whether one abnormal retinal function consistently found in diabetic patients[102,127] and experimental animals[103] is linked to enhanced polyol pathway activity, namely, the breakdown of the blood-ocular barrier to the passage of organic anions such as fluorescein. This abnormality can be quantitated by the technique of vitreous fluorophotometry, which measures the vitreous concentration of fluorescein after its intravenous administration. The increased ocular accumulation of fluorescein observed in rats with streptozotocin diabetes was not duplicated by rendering rats galactosemic with a diet containing 50% galactose, and treatment of diabetic rats with either of two different aldose reductase inhibitors failed to correct the abnormal vitreous fluorophotometric measurements associated with untreated experimental diabetes of 3 weeks duration.[128] On the other hand, treatment for 6 months with sulindac (Clinoril) or Sorbinil, two inhibitors of aldose reductase, was reported to significantly lower leakage on vitreous fluorophotometry in patients with insulin-dependent and non-insulin-dependent diabetes.[129,130] However, the relationship between breakdown of the blood-retinal barrier, as assessed by vitreous fluorophotometry, and the traditional microaneurysmal and neovascular lesions of diabetic retinopathy is not clear. In fact, the former may reflect a structural defect in the retinal pigment epithelium and/or a decreased transport of fluorescein out of the eye, and may not be part of the same putative process that promotes capillary leakage in the retinal microvasculature or in other sites of microangiopathic complications. Nevertheless, the report that Sorbinil diminished the rate of progression over a 6-month period of the penetration of fluorescein across the blood-retinal barrier in 32 patients with non-insulin-dependent diabetes has encouraged the suggestion that aldose reductase inhibition may alter the course of early diabetic retinopathy.[131]

The retina contains sorbitol dehydrogenase as well as aldose reductase, and hence generates increased amounts of fructose when the polyol pathway is activated.[110] It has been proposed that one way in which enhanced retinal polyol metabolism might contribute to the retinopathic process is by rapid and uncontrolled channeling of excess fructose, after phosphorylation, into the glycolytic pathway. This would raise the concentration of retinal lactate, believed by some to be of significance in the development of diabetic retinopathy.[132,133] In this context, it is interesting to note that one aldose reductase inhibitor can reduce lactate output in cultured kidney epithelial cells incubated for several hours in a high (55 mM) glucose concentration,[134] and that another, given in vivo, can normalize the concentration of lactate in the retinas of streptozotocin- diabetic rats.[135] However, this compound, ICI 10552, had no significant effect on the elevated retinal concentrations of sorbitol and fructose in diabetes.

Keratopathy

Although a variety of corneal lesions are known to occur spontaneously in diabetes,[136,137] interest in diabetic keratopathy, as these abnormalities are collectively called, was spurred with the advent of vitrectomy for the treatment of certain retinal complications of diabetes. Since the cornea in diabetic subjects heals slowly even with minor trauma,[138,139] and since the corneal epithelium often is intentionally removed during vitrectomy, the problem soon became apparent. Several reports have described the propensity for the development of corneal abnomalities in diabetic patients after vitreous surgery.[140-144] These are ascribed to a delay in the re-epithelial-ization of the cornea after surgical manipulation, resulting in a persistent corneal epithelial defect and, occasionally, stromal edema.

The possibility that increased polyol pathway activity might contribute to diabetic keratopathy was dramatically highlighted in a recent case report that describes the response of severe keratopathy in a young woman with insulin-dependent diabetes to treatment with an aldose reductase inhibitor.[145] The woman had bilateral persistent corneal epithelial defects complicated by reduced corneal sensation and keratitis sicca. Response to conventional therapy for more than a year was inadequate, with recurrence of the corneal defects and intraocular inflammation. After the patient had received Sorbinil in one eye and placebo in the other for 2 months, only the Sorbinil-treated eye showed diminution in the size of the epithelial defects and in the signs of inflammation. Subsequently, both eyes received Sorbinil, resulting in marked clinical improvement.

Aldose reductase has been localized immunohistochemically, using specific antibodies raised in rabbit and goat against purified human placental aldose reductase, in the human corneal endothelium and epithelium.[146] The presence of the sorbitol pathway and its activation in vitro by high glucose concentration have been demonstrated in the rabbit corneal epithelium.[147] In this tissue, glucose uptake and glycogen formation are the same without or with insulin added in vitro, indicating that corneal epithelial cells are insulin-insensitive and thereby suggesting that they would accumulate sorbitol if exposed to a hyperglycemic milieu. Bovine corneal epithelium incubated in xylose-containing medium accumulates xylitol, and inclusion of an aldose reductase inhibitor in the

TABLE 3-3 Sugar Contents in Human Corneal Epithelium

| | uM/g dry wt | |
Sugar	Normal	Diabetic
Fructose	—	2.2
Glucose	1.8	12.2
Sorbitol	—	0.62

Data from Foulkes et al.[142]

FIGURE 3-9 Re-epithelialization of cornea after denudation in normal (A), galactosemic (B), and Sorbinil-treated galactosemic (C) rats. Reprinted with permission from Datiles MD et al: Corneal re-epithelialization in galactosemic rats. *Invest Ophthalmol Vis Sci* 1983; 24:563–569.

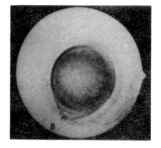

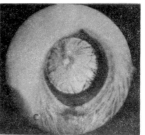

incubation prevents the synthesis of xylitol.[12] Corneal epithelium from diabetic patients reportedly contains elevated levels of glucose, sorbitol, and fructose, as well as two other unidentified sugars that are not present in the epithelium of nondiabetic patients[136,142] (Table 3-3). Thus, aldose reductase functions in the corneal epithelium and can be activated by increased intracellular concentrations of sugar. It has been proposed that sorbitol accumulation in corneal epithelial cells results in osmotic changes that make the diabetic tissue more vulnerable than usual to intraoperative damage,[138] although it is arguable whether the sorbitol level is sufficient to produce an osmotic effect.[147]

Support for the hypothesis that aldose reductase is involved in the development of keratopathic lesions is derived from studies with experimental animal models of diabetes and galactosemia. Diabetic and galactosemic rats both exhibit delayed healing after scraping of the corneal epithelium; treatment with an aldose reductase inhibitor restored the rate of healing of the denuded corneal epithelium to that observed in normal animals.[12,145,148,149] The ability of aldose reductase inhibition to hasten regeneration of the epithelium in diabetic rats was not specific to a particular compound since several different inhibitors had similar beneficial effects. Inhibition of aldose reductase also promoted healing, characterized by a clear and transparent cornea, in contrast to the cloudiness and edema found in the re-epithelialized cornea of untreated diabetic or galactosemic rats[148,149] (Figure 3-9).

The manner in which the polyol pathway participates in the development of diabetic keratopathy or the persistence of corneal defects in diabetes is unknown. Nevertheless, the single description of a dramatic clinical response and the report of a significant experimental response to inhibition of aldose reductase activity in the cornea suggest that the accumulation of polyol products or consequences thereof are involved. These findings offer promise that aldose reductase inhibitors might beneficially influence corneal abnormalities in diabetes, and should encourage further work to assess the therapeutic potential of these agents for diabetic keratopathy.

References

1. Van Heyningen R: Formation of polyols by the lens of the rat with sugar cataracts. *Nature (Lond)* 1959; 184:194–195.

2. Van Heyningen R: Metabolism of xylose by the lens. Rat lens in vivo and in vitro. *Biochem J* 1959; 73:197–207.

3. LeFevre PG, Davis R: Active transport into the human erythrocyte: Evidence from comparative kinetics and composition among monosaccharides. *J Gen Physiol* 1951; 34:515–524.

4. Wick AN, Drury DR: Insulin and permeability of cells to sorbitol. *Am J Physiol* 1951; 166:421–423.

5. Kinoshita JH, Merola LO, Satoh K, et al: Osmotic changes caused by the accumulation of dulcitol in the lenses of rats fed with galactose. *Nature (Lond)* 1962; 194:1085–1087.

6. Kinoshita JH, Merola LO, Dikmak E: Osmotic changes in experimental galactose cataracts. *Exp Eye Res* 1962; 1:405–410.

7. Kinoshita JH, Merola LO, Dikmak E: The accumulation of dulcitol and water in rabbit lens incubated with galactose. *Biochim Biophys Acta* 1962; 62:176–178.

8. Kinoshita JH, Merola LO: Hydration of the lens during the development of galactose cataract. *Invest Ophthalmol* 1964; 3:577–584.

9. Kinoshita JH, Futterman S, Satoh K, et al: Factors affecting the formation of sugar alcohols in ocular lens. *Biochim Biophys Acta* 1963; 74:340–350.

10. Kinoshita JH: Cataracts in galactosemia. *Invest Ophthalmol* 1965; 4:786–799.

11. Kinoshita JH: Mechanisms initating cataract formation. *Invest Ophthalmol* 1974; 13:713–724.

12. Kinoshita JH, Fukushi S, Kador P, et al: Aldose reductase in diabetic complications of the eye. *Metabolism* 1979; 28:462–469.

13. Kuwabara T, Kinoshita JH, Cogan DC: Electron microscopic study of galactose-induced cataract. *Invest Ophthalmol* 1969; 8:133–149.

14. Duke-Elder WS: Changes in refraction in diabetes mellitus. *Br J Ophthalmol* 1925; 9:167–187.

15. Vere DW, Verrel D: Relation between blood sugar level and the optical properties of the lens of the human eye. *Clin Sci* 1955; 14:183–196.

16. Varma SD, El-Aguizy HK, Richards RD: Refractive changes in alloxan diabetic rabbits. Control by flavinoids. *Acta Ophthalmol* 1980; 58:748–759.

17. Kinoshita JH, Merola LO, Hayman S: Osmotic effects on the amino acid-concentrating mechanism in the rabbit lens. *J Biol Chem* 1965; 240:313–315.

18. Kinoshita JH, Merola O, Tung B: Changes in cation permeability in the galactose-exposed rabbit lens. *Exp Eye Res* 1968; 7:80–90.

19. Chylack LT Jr, Kinoshita JH: A biochemical evaluation of a cataract induced in a high glucose medium. *Invest Ophthalmol* 1969: 8:401–412.

20. Varma SD, Kinoshita JH: Sorbitol pathway in diabetic galactosemic rat lens. *Biochim Biophys Acta* 1974; 338:632–640.

21. Cotlier E: *Myo*-inositol: Active transport by the crystalline lens. *Invest Ophthalmol* 1970; 9:681–691.

22. Broekhuyse RM: Changes in *myo*-inositol permeability in the lens due to cataractous conditions. *Biochim Biophys Acta* 1968; 163:269–272.

23. Sippel TO: Changes in the water, protein and glutathione contents of the lens in the course of galactose cataract development in rats. *Invest Ophthalmol* 1960; 5:568–575.

24. Kinoshita JH, Barber GW, Merola LD, et al: Changes in the levels of free amino acids and *myo*-inositol in the galactose-exposed lens. *Invest Ophthalmol* 1969; 8:625–632.

25. Reddy VN, Schauss D, Chakrapani B, et al: Biochemical changes associated with the development and reversal of galactose cataracts. *Exp Eye Res* 1976; 23:483–493.

26. Kador PF, Zigler S, Kinoshita JH: Alterations of lens protein synthesis in galactosemic rats. *Invest Ophthalmol Vis Sci* 1979; 18:696–702.

27. Lee SM, Schade SZ, Doughty CC: Aldose reductase, NADPH and NADP$^+$ in normal, galactose-fed and diabetic rat lens. *Biochim Biophys Acta* 1985; 841:247–253.

28. Unakar NJ, Tsui JY: Inhibition of galactose-induced alterations in ocular lens with Sorbinil. *Exp Eye Res* 1983; 36:685–694.

29. Gonzalez AM, Sochor M, McLean P: Effect of experimental diabetes on glycolytic intermediates and regulation of phosphofructokinase in rat lens. *Biochem Biophys Res Commun* 1980; 95:1173–1179.

30. Gonzalez AM, Sochor M, Rowles PM, et al: Sequential biochemical and structural changes occurring in rat lens during cataract formation in experimental diabetes. *Diabetologia* 1981; 21:5.

31. Gonzalez AM, Sochor M, McLean P: The effect of an aldose reductase inhibitor (Sorbinil) on the level of metabolites in lenses of diabetic rats. *Diabetes* 1983; 32:482–485.

32. Bhuyan KC, Bhuyan DK, Katzin DM: Amizol-induced cataract and inhibition of lens catalase in rabbit. *Ophthalmic Res* 1973; 5:236–247.

33. Reddy VN: Metabolism of glutathione in the lens. *Exp Eye Res* 1971; 11:310–328.

34. Varma SD, Kumar S, Richards RD: Protection by ascorbate against superoxide injury to the lens. *Invest Ophthalmol Vis Sci* 1979; 18(suppl):98.

35. Varma SD: Superoxide and lens of the eye. A new theory of cataractogenesis. *Int J Quantum Chem* 1981; 20:479–484.

36. Goosey JD, Zigler JS Jr, Kinoshita JH: Cross-linking of lens crystallins in a photodynamic system. A singlet oxygen mediated process. *Science* 1980; 208:1278–1279.

37. Dische Z, Zil H: Studies on the oxidation of cysteine to cystine in lens protein during cataract formation. *Am J Ophthalmol* 1951; 34:104–113.

38. Garner MH, Spector A: Selective oxidation of cysteine and methionine in normal and cataractous lens. *Proc Natl Acad Sci USA* 1980; 77:1274–1277.

39. Creighton MO, Trevithick JR: Cortical cataract formation prevented by vitamin E and glutathione. *Exp Eye Res* 1979; 29:689–693.

40. Ross WM, Creighton MO, Stewart-DeHaan PJ, et al: Modelling cortical cataractogenesis: 3. In vivo effects of vitamin E on cataractogenesis in diabetic rats. *Can J Ophthalmol* 1982; 17:61–66.

41. Chand D, El-Aguizy K, Richards RD, et al: Sugar cataracts in vitro: Implications of oxidative stress and aldose reductase I. *Exp Eye Res* 1982; 35:491–497.

42. Kadoya K, Hashi H, Yui MNH, et al: Influences of aldose reductase inhibitor on peroxidation reaction in the lens of streptozotocin diabetic rats. *Nippon Ganka Kiyo* 1983; 34:2172–2176.

43. Cogan DG, Kinoshita KH, Kador PF, et al: Aldose reductase and complications of diabetes. *Ann Intern Med* 1984; 101:82–91.

44. Gabbay KH: The sorbitol pathway and complications of diabetes. *N Engl J Med* 1973; 288:831–836.

45. Varma SD, Kinoshita JH: The absence of cataracts in mice with congenital hyperglycemia. *Exp Eye Res* 1974; 19:577–582.

46. Varma SD, Mikuni I, Kinoshita JH: Flavinoids as inhibitors of lens aldose reductase. *Science* 1975; 188:1215–1216.

47. El-Aguizy HK, Richards RD, Varma SD: Sugar cataracts in mongolian gerbil (*Meriones unguiculatus*). *Exp Eye Res* 1983; 36:839–844.

48. Obazawa H, Merola LO, Kinoshita JH: The effects of xylose on the isolated lens. *Invest Ophthalmol* 1974; 13:204–209.

49. Kinoshita JH, Dvornik D, Kraml M, et al: The effect of an aldose reductase inhibitor on the galactose-exposed rabbit lens. *Biochim Biophys Acta* 1968; 158:472–475.

50. Dvornik D, Simard-Duquesne N, Kraml M, et al: Polyol accumulation in galactosemic and diabetic rats: Control by an aldose reductase inhibitor. *Science* 1973; 182:1146–1148.

51. Chylack LT Jr, Henriques HF, Cheng H-M, et al: Efficacy of alrestatin, an aldose reductase inhibitor, in human diabetic and nondiabetic lenses. *Ophthalmology* 1979; 86:1579–1585.

52. Simard-Duquesne N, Greslin E, Gonzalez R, et al: Prevention of cataract development in severely galactosemic rats by the aldose reductase inhibitor, tolrestat. *Proc Soc Exp Biol Med* 1985; 178:599–605.

53. Simard-Duquesne N, Greslin E, Dubuc J, et al: The effect of a new aldose reductase inhibitor (tolrestat) in galactosemic and diabetic rats. *Metabolism* 1985; 34:885–892.

54. Peterson MJ, Sarges R, Aldinger CE, et al: CP-45,634: A novel aldose reductase inhibitor that inhibits polyol pathway activity in diabetic and galactosemic rats. *Metabolism* 1979; 28(suppl 1):456–461.

55. Beyer-Mears A, Cruz E, Nicolas-Alexandre J, et al: Sorbinil protection of lens protein components and cell hydration during diabetic cataract formation. *Pharmacology* 1982; 24:193–200.

56. Datiles M, Fukui H, Kuwabara T, et al: Galactose cataract prevention with Sorbinil, an aldose reductase inhibitor: A light microscopic study. *Invest Ophthalmol Vis Sci* 1982; 22:174–179.

57. Peterson MJ, Sarges R, Aldinger CE, et al: Inhibition of polyol pathway activity in diabetic and galactosemic rats by the aldose reductase inhibitor CP-45,634. *Adv Exp Med Biol* 1979; 119:347–356.

58. Fukushi H, Merola L, Kinoshita JH: Altering the course of cataracts in diabetic rats. *Invest Ophthalmol Vis Sci* 1980; 19:313–315.

59. Poulsom R, Boot-Hanford RP, Heath H: Some effects of aldose reductase inhibition upon the eyes of long-term streptozotocin-diabetic rats. *Curr Eye Res* 1982; 2:351–355.

60. Ono H, Nozawa Y, Hayano S: Effects of M-79,175, an aldose reductase inhibitor, on experimental sugar cataracts. *Nippon Ganka Gakkai Zasshi* 1982; 86:1343–1350.

61. Beyer-Mears A, Farnsworth PN: Diminished diabetic cataractogenesis by quercetin. *Exp Eye Res* 1979; 28:709–716.

62. Varma SD, Mizuno A, Kinoshita JH: Diabetic cataracts and flavinoids. *Science* 1977; 195:205–206.

63. Varma SD, Shockert SS, Richards RD: Implications of aldose reductase in cataracts in human diabetics. *Invest Ophthalmol Vis Sci* 1979; 18:237–241.

64. Beyer-Mears A, Cruz E, Nicolas-Alexandre J, et al: Xanthone-2-carboxylic acid effect on lens growth, hydration and proteins during diabetic cataract development. *Arch Int Pharmacodyn Ther* 1982; 259:166–176.

65. Sharma YR, Cotlier E: Inhibition of lens and cataract aldose reductase by protein-bound anti-rheumatic drugs: Salicylate, indomethacin, oxyphenbutazone, sulindac. *Exp Eye Res* 1982; 35:21–27.

66. Jacobson M, Sharma YR, Cotlier E, et al: Diabetic complications in lens and nerve and their prevention by sulindac or Sorbinil: Two novel aldose reductase inhibitors. *Invest Ophthalmol Vis Sci* 1983; 24:1426–1429.

67. Crabbe MJC, Freeman G, Halder G, et al: The inhibition of bovine lens aldose reductase by Clinoril, its absorption into human red cell and its effect on human red cell aldose reductase activity. *Ophthalmic Res* 1985; 17:85–89.

68. Cotlier E, Fagadau W, Cicchetti DV: Methods for evaluation of medical therapy of senile and diabetic cataracts. *Trans Ophthalmol Soc UK* 1982; 102:416–422.

69. Cotlier E, Sharma YR, Niven T, et al: Distribution of salicylate in lens and intraocular fluids and its effect on cataract formation. *Am J Med* 1983; 75(6A):83–90.

70. Hu T-S, Datiles M, Kinoshita JH: Reversal of galactose cataract with sorbinil in rats. *Invest Ophthalmol Vis Sci* 1983; 24:640–644.

71. Beyer-Mears A, Cruz E: Reversal of diabetic cataract by sorbinil, an aldose reductase inhibitor. *Diabetes* 1985; 34:15–21.

72. Hockwin O, Bergeder HD, Kaiser L: Über die Galaktosekatarakt junger Ratten nach Ganzkorperröntgenbestrahlung. *Ber Dtsch Ophthalmol Ges* 1967; 68:135–139.

73. Hockwin O, Bergeder HD, Ninnemann U, et al: Untersuchungen zur Latenzzeit der Galaktosekatarakt von Ratten. Einfluss von Röntgenbestrahlung und Diätbeginn bei verschieden alten Tieren. *Graefes Arch Klin Opthalmol* 1974; 189:171–178.

74. Keller H-W, Stinnesbeck TH, Hockwin O, et al: Investigations on the influence of whole body X-irradiation on the activity of rat lens aldose reductase (E.C.1.1.1.21). *Graefes Arch Klin Opthalmol* 1981; 215:181–186.

75. Chylack LT Jr, Henriques H, Tung W: Inhibition of sorbitol production in human lenses by an aldose reductase inhibitor. *Invest Ophthalmol Vis Sci* 1978; 17(ARVO suppl):300.

76. Lerner BC, Varma SD, Richards RD: Polyol pathway metabolites in human cataracts. *Arch Ophthalmol* 1984; 102:917–920.

77. Jedziniak JA, Chylack LT, Chen H–M, et al: The sorbitol pathway in the human lens: Aldose reductase and polyol dehydrogenase. *Invest Ophthalmol Vis Sci* 1981; 20:314–326.

78. Davies PD, Duncan G, Pynsent PB, et al: Aqueous humor glucose concentration in cataract patients and its effect on the lens. *Exp Eye Res* 1984; 39:605–609.

79. Reddy DVN, Kinsey VE: Transport of amino acids into intraocular fluids and lens in diabetic rabbits. *Invest Ophthalmol* 1963; 2:237–242.

80. Reddy DVN: Amino acid transport in the lens in relation to sugar cataracts. *Invest Ophthalmol* 1965; 4:700–706.

81. Reddy VN, Chakrapani B, Steen D: Sorbitol pathway in the ciliary body in relation to accumulation of amino acids in the aqueous humor of alloxan diabetic rabbits. *Invest Ophthalmol* 1971; 100:870–875.

82. Cohen MP: *Diabetes and Protein Glycosylation: Measurement and Biologic Relevance.* New York, Springer-Verlag, 1986.

83. Chiou SH, Chylack LT, Bunn HF, et al: Role of nonenzymatic glycosylation in experimental cataract formation. *Biochem Biophys Res Commun* 1980; 95:894–901.

84. Cotlier E: Aspirin effect on cataract formation in patients with rheumatoid arthritis alone or combined with diabetes. *Int Ophthalmol* 1981; 3:173–179.

85. Bous F, Hockwin O, Ohrloff C, et al: Investigation on phosphofructokinase (EC 2.7.1.11) in bovine lens in dependence on age, topographic distribution and water soluble protein fractions. *Exp Eye Res* 1977; 24:383–389.

86. Chen HM, Chylack LT Jr: Factors affecting the rate of lactate production in rat lens. *Ophthalmic Res* 1977; 9:381–387.

87. Ohrloff C, Zierz S, Hockwin O: Investigations of the enzymes involved in the fructose breakdown in the cattle lens. *Ophthalmic Res* 1982; 14:221–229.

88. Siddiqui MA, Rahman MA: Effect of hyperglycemia on the enzyme activities of lenticular tissue of rats. *Exp Eye Res* 1980; 31:463–469.

89. Chylack LT, Cheng H-M: Sugar metabolism in the crystalline lens. *Surv Ophthalmol* 1978; 23:26–34.

90. Hollows JC, Schofield PJ, Williams JF, et al: The effect of an unsaturated fat-diet on cataract formation in streptozotocin-induced diabetic rats. *Br J Nutr* 1976; 36:161–177.

91. Kahn HA, Liebowitz HM, Ganley JP, et al: The Framingham eye study. II. Association of ophthalmic pathology with single variables previously measured in the Framingham study. *Am J Epidemiol* 1977; 106:33–41.

92. Barnett PA, Gonzalez RG, Chylack LT, et al: The effect of oxidation on sorbitol pathway kinetics. *Diabetes* 1986; 35:426-432.

93. Kuwabara T, Cogan DG: Retinal vascular patterns. VI. Mural cells of the retinal capillaries. *Arch Ophthalmol* 1963; 69:492-502.

94. Hogan MJ, Feeney L: The ultrastructure of the retinal vessels. II. The small vessels. *J Ultrastruct Res* 1963; 9:29-46.

95. Ishikawa T: Fine structure of retinal vessels in man and the macaque monkey. *Invest Ophthalmol* 1963; 2:1-15.

96. Shakib M, Cunha-Vaz JG: Studies on the permeability of the blood retinal barrier. IV. Junctional complexes of the retinal vessels and their role in the permeability of the blood retinal barrier. *Exp Eye Res* 1966; 5:229-234.

97. Speiser P, Gittelsohn AM, Patz A: Studies on diabetic retinopathy. III. Influence of diabetes on intramural pericytes. *Arch Ophthalmol* 1968; 80:332-337.

98. Yanoff M: Diabetic retinopathy. *N Engl J Med* 1966; 274:1344-1349.

99. Addison DJ, Garner A, Ashton N: Degeneration of intramural pericytes in diabetic retinopathy. *Br Med J* 1970; 1:264-266.

100. Cogan DG, Toussaint D, Kuwabara T: Retinal vascular patterns. IV. Diabetic retinopathy. *Arch Ophthalmol* 1976; 66:366-372.

101. Ashton N: The blood-retinal barrier and vaso-glial relationships in retinal disease. *Trans Ophthalmol Soc UK* 1965; 85:199-230.

102. Cunha-Vaz J, DeAbreau JRF, Campos AJ, et al: Early breakdown of the blood-retinal barrier in diabetes. *Br J Ophthalmol* 1975; 59:649-656.

103. Waltman S, Krupin T, Hanish S, et al: Alteration of the blood retinal barrier in experimental diabetes mellitus. *Arch Ophthalmol* 1978; 96:878-879.

104. Wise GN, Dollery GT, Henkind P: *The Retinal Circulation*, pp 290-324, 350-420. New York, Harper & Row, 1971.

105. Gabbay KH: Purification and immunological identification of bovine retinal aldose reductase. *Isr J Med Sci* 1972; 8:1626-1628.

106. Akagi Y, Kador PF, Kuwabara T, et al: Aldose reductase localization in human retinal mural cells. *Invest Ophthalmol Vis Sci* 1983; 24:1516-1519.

107. Ludvigson MA, Sorenson RL: Immunohistochemical localization of aldose reductase. II. Rat eye and kidney. *Diabetes* 1980; 29:450-459.

108. Kern TS, Engerman RL: Distribution of aldose reductase in ocular tissues. *Exp Eye Res* 1981; 33:175-182.

109. Akagi Y, Yajima Y, Kador PF, et al: Localization of aldose reductase in the human eye. *Diabetes* 1984; 33:562-566.

110. Buzney SM, Frank RN, Varma SD, et al: Aldose reductase in retinal mural cells. *Invest Ophthalmol Vis Sci* 1977; 16:392-396.

111. Kern TS, Engerman RL: Hexitol production by canine retinal microvessels. *Invest Ophthalmol Vis Sci* 1985; 26:382-384.

112. Russell P, Merola LO, Yajima Y, et al: Aldose reductase activity in a cultured human retinal cell line. *Exp Eye Res* 1982; 35:331-336.

113. Li W, Chan LS, Khatami M, et al: Characterization of glucose transport by bovine retinal capillary pericytes in culture. *Exp Eye Res* 1985; 41:191–199.

114. Hutton JC, Schofield PJ, Williams JF, et al: Sorbitol metabolism in the retina: Accumulation of pathway intermediates in streptozotocin induced diabetes in the rat. *Aust J Exp Biol Med Sci* 1974; 52:361–373.

115. MacGregor LC, Rosecan LR, Laties AM, et al: Microanalysis of total lipid, glucose, sorbitol, and *myo*-inositol in individual retinal layers of normal and alloxan diabetic rabbits. *Diabetes* 1984; 33:89A.

116. Li W, Shen S, Khatami M, et al: Stimulation of retinal capillary pericyte protein and collagen synthesis in culture by high-glucose concentration. *Diabetes* 1984; 33:785–789.

117. Engerman RL, Kern TS: Experimental galactosemia produces diabetic-like retinopathy. *Diabetes* 1984; 33:97–100.

118. Robison WG, Kador PF, Kinoshita JH: Retinal capillaries: Basement membrane thickening by galactosemia prevented with aldose reductase inhibitor. *Science* 1983; 221:1177–1179.

119. Li W, Khatami M, Rockey JH: The effects of glucose and an aldose reductase inhibitor on the sorbitol content and collagen synthesis of bovine retinal capillary pericytes in culture. *Exp Eye Res* 1985; 40:439–444.

120. Hotta N, Kakuta H, Fukasawa H, et al: Aldose reductase inhibitor and fructose-rich diet: Its effect on the development of diabetic retinopathy. *Diabetes* 1984; 33(suppl 1):199A.

121. Heath H, Hamlett YC: The sorbitol pathway: Effect of streptozotocin induced diabetes and the feeding of a sucrose-rich diet on glucose, sorbitol and fructose in the retina, blood and liver of rats. *Diabetologia* 1976; 12:43–46.

122. Kennedy A, Frank RN, Varma SD: Aldose reductase activity in retinal and cerebral microvessels and cultured vascular cells. *Invest Ophthalmol Vis Sci* 1983; 24:1250–1258.

123. MacGregor LC, Matschinsky FM: Treatment with aldose reductase inhibitor or with *myo*-inositol arrests deterioration of the electroretinogram of diabetic rats. *J Clin Invest* 1985; 76:887–889.

124. MacGregor LC, Matschinsky FM: Correlation of biochemical and electrophysiological abnormalities in retinas of experimentally diabetic animals. *Diabetes* 1985; 34(suppl 1):13A.

125. Yamani T: Effect of aldose reductase inhibitor on the oscillatory potential in ERG of streptozotocin diabetic rats. *Folia Ophthalmol Jpn* 1983; 34:2237–2244.

126. Li W, Chan S, Khatami M, et al: Inhibition of *myo*-inositol uptake in cultured bovine retinal capillary pericytes by D-glucose: Reversal by Sorbinil. *Invest Ophthalmol Vis Sci* 1985; 26(Suppl):335.

127. Krupin T, Waltman SR, Oestrich C, et al: Vitreous fluorophotometry in juvenile-onset diabetes mellitus. *Arch Ophthalmol* 1978; 96:812–814.

128. Krupin T, Waltman SR, Szewczyk P, et al: Fluorometric studies on the blood retinal barrier in experimental animals. *Arch Ophthalmol* 1982; 100:631-634.

129. Cunha-Vaz J, Mota C, Leite E, et al: Effect of aldose reductase inhibitors on the blood-retinal barrier in early diabetic retinopathy. *Diabetes* 1985; 34(suppl 1):109A.

130. Cunha-Vaz JG, Mota CC, Leite EC, et al: Effect of sulindac on the permeability of the blood retinal barrier in early diabetic retinopathy. *Arch Ophthalmol* 1985; 103:1307-1311.

131. Cunha-Vaz JG, Mota CC, Leite EC, et al: Effect of Sorbinil on blood-retinal barrier in early diabetic retinopathy. *Diabetes* 1986; 35:574-578.

132. Heath H, Kang SS, Philippou D: Glucose, glucose-6-phosphate, lactate and pyruvate content of the retina, blood and liver of streptozotocin-diabetic rats fed sucrose- or starch-rich diets. *Diabetologia* 1975; 11:57-62.

133. Hamlett YC, Heath H: The accumulation of fructose-1-phosphate in the diabetic rat retina. *IRCS Med Sci* 1977; 5:510.

134. Boot-Hanford R, Heath H: The effects of aldose reductase inhibitors on the metabolism of cultured monkey kidney epithelial cells. *Biochem Pharmacol* 1981; 30:3065-3069.

135. Poulsom R, Mirrlees DJ, Earl DCN, et al: The effects of an aldose reductase inhibitor upon the sorbitol pathway, fructose-1-phosphate and lactate in the retina and nerve of streptozotocin-diabetic rats. *Exp Eye Res* 1983; 36:751-760.

136. Schultz RO, VanHorn DL, Peters MA, et al: Diabetic keratopathy. *Trans Am Ophthalmol Soc* 1981; 79:180-199.

137. Hyndiuk RA, Kazarian EL, Schultz RO, et al: Neurotrophic corneal ulcers in diabetes mellitus. *Arch Ophthalmol* 1977; 95:2193-2196.

138. Pfister RR, Schepens CL, Lemp MA, et al: Photocoagulation keratopathy: Report of a case. *Arch Ophthalmol* 1971; 86:94-96.

139. Kanski JJ: Anterior segment complications of retinal photocoagulation. *Am J Ophthalmol* 1975; 79:424-427.

140. Perry HD, Foulks GN, Thoft RA, et al: Corneal complications after closed vitrectomy through the pars plana. *Arch Ophthalmol* 1978; 96:1401-1403.

141. Brightbill FS, Myers FL, Bresnick GN: Postvitrectomy keratopathy. *Am J Ophthalmol* 1978; 85:651-655.

142. Foulks GN, Thoft RA, Perry HD, et al: Factors related to corneal epithelial complications after closed vitrectomy in diabetes. *Arch Ophthalmol* 1979; 97:1076-1078.

143. Blankenship GW, Machemer R: Pars plana vitrectomy for the management of severe diabetic retinopathy: An analysis of results five years following surgery. *Ophthalmology (Rochester)* 1978; 85:553-559.

144. Faulborn J, Conway BP, Machemer R: Surgical complications of pars plana vitreous surgery. *Ophthalmology (Rochester)* 1978; 85:116-125.

145. Cogan DG, Kinoshita JH, Kador PF, et al: Aldose reductase and complications of diabetes. *Ann Intern Med* 1984; 101:82–91.

146. Akagi Y, Yajima Y, Kador PF, et al: Localization of aldose reductase in the human eye. *Diabetes* 1984; 33:562–566.

147. Friend J, Snip RC, Kiorpes TC, et al: Insulin insensitivity and sorbitol production of the normal rabbit corneal epithelium in vitro. *Invest Ophthalmol Vis Sci* 1980; 19:913–919.

148. Fukushi A, Merola LO, Tanaka M, et al: Re-epithelialization of denuded corneas in diabetic rats. *Exp Eye Res* 1980; 31:611–621.

149. Datiles MD, Kador PF, Fukui HN, et al: Corneal re-epithelialization in galactosemic rats. *Invest Ophthalmol Vis Sci* 1983; 24:563–569.

CHAPTER 4

Diabetic Neuropathy

Among the several mechanisms that have been proposed to explain the pathogenesis of diabetic neuropathy, the scheme invoking the polyol pathway as contributory to the nerve dysfunction in diabetes is one that has perhaps gained the most credence in recent years. In part this relates to a better understanding of the morphologic, functional, and metabolic abnormalities that underlie the neuropathic syndromes, and in part to the impetus provided by the pharmaceutical industry with premarketing publicity for the clinical use of aldose reductase inhibitors in the treatment of diabetic neuropathy.

Although the clinical manifestations of diabetic neuropathy may vary, the electrophysiologic and morphologic features reflecting neural involvement are fairly constant. Slowing of the motor nerve conduction velocity is the most traditionally recognized parameter of peripheral neuropathy, but sensory disturbances and autonomic nerve dysfunction can also be quantitated by techniques such as measurement of the sensory threshold, sensory nerve conduction velocities, and microneurography.[1-5] Histologically, there is segmental demyelination, loss of Schwann cells, and axonal shrinkage and degeneration.[6-9] Similar electrophysiologic and morphologic changes have been repeatedly observed in peripheral nerves of animals with experimental diabetes.[10-18]

The capillaries of the endoneurium of peripheral nerves in diabetic subjects display abnormalities reminiscent of those characteristically found in other tissues subject to diabetic complications, notably the retinal and glomerular microvasculature. These include thickening and reduplication of the capillary basement membrane, endothelial hyperplasia, and fibrin or platelet plugging.[19-22] Such abnormalities are believed to be associated with distal polyneuropathic syndromes, and should not be construed as tantamount to occlusive atherosclerotic lesions, nor confused with the ischemic vascular insults now recognized to be causally associated with mononeuropathic disease[23-25] (Table 4-1). However, the questions of how or if they contribute to, or if they result from, the primary pathogenetic process responsible for diabetic polyneuropathy remain enigmatic. Thickening of the perineurial cell basement membrane of the sural nerve and the dorsal root ganglion is also found in human diabetes.[26,27] These changes may arise from increased vascular permeability, perhaps related to the foregoing capillary changes, although some doubt has been cast on this hypothesis.[27,28]

The notion that increased activity of the polyol pathway might be involved in the pathogenesis of diabetic neuropathy was bolstered by the finding that sorbitol and fructose are present in high concentration in normal peripheral nerve,[29-32] and the observation that these substances further accumulate in the nerves of animals with experimental diabetes.[33-37] Sorbitol and fructose concentrations are also increased in peripheral nerves obtained from patients with diabetes,[8,38] and the level of sorbitol in cerebrospinal fluid of diabetic

TABLE 4-1   Etiologic Classification of Diabetic Neuropathies

Etiology	Syndrome
Ischemia	Mononeuropathy (e.g., cranial, radiculopathy)
Metabolic abnormalities	Distal symmetrical polyneuropathy
Ischemia plus metabolic abnormalities	Diabetic amyotrophy Diabetic neuropathic cachexia

subjects is higher than that in nondiabetic individuals.[39,40] Nerve is one of the tissues that do not require insulin for glucose transport,[41,42] and hence the glucose concentration in Schwann cells and within axons mirrors that of the extracellular compartment. The rise in intracellular glucose accompanying hyperglycemia in the diabetic state would be expected to activate the polyol pathway, increasing the formation of sorbitol and fructose in the nerve. When hyperglycemia is controlled with insulin therapy, the elevated levels of sorbitol and fructose in the nerve fall significantly, confirming that hyperglycemia resulting from insulin deficiency is primary to their increase.[33,34,36]

Biochemical and immunohistochemical studies have consistently demonstrated the presence of aldose reductase in the Schwann cell.[29,43-47] The enzyme is localized to the cytoplasm of the cell body and is not present in the axon, the perineurial structures, or the endoneurial space. This is compatible with earlier studies that had suggested that aldose reductase was confined to the cell cytoplasm, since activity persisted in Wallerian degenerated nerves, a model in which axons are resorbed but Schwann cells persist and proliferate.[43,44]

The traditional explanation implicating the polyol pathway in the pathogenesis of diabetic neuropathy has invoked damage resulting from the osmotic effects of accumulated sorbitol. In this construct, the sorbitol-induced edema of the Schwann cell would cause cell lysis and, eventually, demyelination due to loss of the myelin-sustaining role of these cells. However, electron microscopic studies have not shown that Schwann cell edema exists in animals with experimental diabetes[12,18,48-50]; in fact, one often-cited study found that the cytoplasmic volume of the Schwann cell was decreased, not increased, in diabetic rats.[14] Although cellular edema in peripheral nerve biopsies from patients with recent-onset diabetes has been described,[19] the inability to consistently document Schwann cell edema in experimental diabetes has dislodged this hypothesis from its position of primacy. Nevertheless, the concept that osmotic influences resulting from sorbitol accumulation compromise nerve function remains viable from another perspective. This relates to changes observed in the endoneurial compartment of peripheral nerves obtained from diabetic and galactose-fed animals. In the latter model, edema in the endoneurial interstitium and increased endoneurial pressure have been noted.[51-54] Decreased nerve conduction velocity, along with galactitol accumulation, accompanies these changes.[55,56] Endoneurial swelling has also been noted in nerves from hyperglycemic animals, although not invariably.[14,57,58]

Although it has been suggested that dehydration due to severe hyperglycemia might obscure tissue edema,[59] such dehydration consequent to a hyperosmolar stimulus might itself be injurious. One pathogenetic scheme that has been advanced invokes dehydration of the axon, resulting from hyperosmolarity of the endoneurial fluid, to explain the axonal shrinkage that is a morphologic hallmark of diabetic neuropathy.[9,50,58] In contrast, another hypothesis implicates endoneurial swelling, with dilution of the normal hypertonicity of the endoneurial fluid, in the compromise of axonal function.[14,59] Although seemingly dichotomous, both postulates subscribe to the view that axonal damage rather than demyelination is the primary nerve fiber lesion in diabetic neuropathy. If this is so, changes in the Schwann cell, albeit the neural reservoir of aldose reductase activity, would ensue secondary to axonal damage. Since inhibition of aldose reductase decreases swelling of the sciatic nerve in galactose-fed rats[60] and reduces the sorbitol concentration and improves motor nerve conduction velocity in the sciatic nerve of streptozotocin-diabetic rats,[61] it is believed that there is a causal link between enhanced polyol pathway activity, depressed nerve function, and neural edema, even if edema does not occur in the Schwann cell itself.

Another manner in which enhanced polyol pathway activity may alter axonal metabolism pertains to its influences on nerve *myo*-inositol. This cyclic hexitol is a ubiquitous constituent of cells and a component of tissue phosphoinositides, which are believed to have an important role in neural function. It has been known for a number of years that diabetic patients have greatly exaggerated excretion of *myo*-inositol.[39,62-66] Although the kidney appears to play a major role in the regulation of plasma *myo*-inositol levels in normal subjects,[67] *myo*-inositol metabolism may be altered in diabetic individuals who do not have a significant compromise in renal function. Diabetic patients also exhibit intolerance to oral inositol, due perhaps in part to impaired utilization.[62,68] One site where uptake is diminished is the peripheral nerve, which can normally maintain its free *myo*-inositol content against a large concentration gradient.

TABLE 4-2   Restoration of Sciatic Nerve Conduction Velocity and *myo*-Inositol Content in Streptozotocin-Diabetic Rats with *myo*-Inositol Feeding

Experimental Group	Plasma Glucose (mg/dL)	Plasma *myo*-Inositol (μM)	Sciatic *myo*-Inositol (mmol/kg)	Conduction Velocity (m/s)
Control	< 200	26–30	2.76 ± 0.06	61.9 ± 0.6
Diabetic	600	24–38	2.27 ± 0.17*	51.0 ± 1.0*
Diabetic, 1% MI in diet	600	207–285	4.63 ± 0.14**	60.5 ± 0.6**

*Significantly different from control.
**Significantly different from untreated diabetic.
MI, *myo*-inositol.
Data from Greene et al.[74]

Myo-inositol content is significantly decreased in the peripheral nerves of rats with experimental diabetes[33,69,70]; decreased *myo*-inositol in peripheral nerves obtained from human patients with diabetes has been found by some[37] but not all[8,35] investigators, and the *myo*-inositol content of cerebrospinal fluid in patients with neuropathy is less than that in patients without neuropathy.[71,72] The reduced peripheral nerve *myo*-inositol in experimental diabetes is associated with slowing of the conduction velocity.[25,63] Treatment with *myo*-inositol prevents both nerve *myo*-inositol depletion and the reduction in nerve conduction velocity[33,73-75] (Table 4-2). The corrective effect of oral *myo*-inositol supplementation occurs despite persistent severe hyperglycemia, whereas insulin therapy that does not adequately control hyperglycemia fails to restore either nerve *myo*-inositol levels or the depressed conduction velocity (Table 4-3). These findings firmly implicate hyperglycemia and/or insulin deficiency in the genesis of nerve *myo*-inositol depletion, and the reduction in nerve *myo*-inositol content in the genesis of the slowed nerve conduction velocity in diabetes.

A link between these findings and the polyol pathway was provided by the demonstration that inhibition of aldose reductase prevents not only the increase in nerve sorbitol but also the fall in nerve *myo*-inositol and the reduction in nerve conduction velocity.[75-78] Although the mechanism by which inhibition of one of the enzymes of the polyol pathway mediates this effect is not clear, the fact that an aldose reductase inhibitor can do so opens new windows

TABLE 4-3   Effect of Insulin Treatment on Sciatic Nerve Conduction Velocity and
myo-Inositol Content

Experimental Group	Conduction Velocity (m/s)	*myo*-Inositol Content (mmol/kg)
Control	64.6 ± 0.9	3.17 ± 0.25
Diabetic, untreated	50.1 ± 0.9*	2.19 ± 0.11*
Diabetic, insulin treated, inadequate control	51.4 ± 1.1	2.52 ± 0.13
Diabetic, insulin treated, meticulous control	62.9 ± 0.9**	2.98 ± 0.22**

*Significantly different from control.
**Significantly different from untreated diabetic.
Data from Greene et al.[33]

concerning the undoubtedly complex relationship among activation of the polyol pathway, altered *myo*-inositol metabolism, and the pathogenesis of diabetic neuropathy. It also renders imperfect, if not obsolete, an earlier explanation that had been put forward to explain the association of hyperglycemia with nerve *myo*-inositol depletion. This postulate developed from the observation that glucose competitively inhibits in vitro *myo*-inositol uptake in endoneurial preparations derived from rabbit sciatic nerve[79] (Table 4-4). In this preparation, more than 90% of the *myo*-inositol uptake occurs by a transport system that is sodium dependent and saturable, and the proposed hypothesis suggested that the hyperglycemia of diabetes inhibits the sodium-dependent *myo*-inositol uptake and is thereby responsible for the reduction in nerve *myo*-inositol content. Since inhibition of aldose reductase corrects *myo*-inositol depletion without altering the glucose concentration, it is clear that this construct is incomplete. One possibility is that glucose-induced polyol accumulation increases *myo*-inositol efflux from the cell. Support for this hypothesis derives from studies with lenses, in which increased *myo*-inositol efflux has been demonstrated when incubations are performed in media containing high glucose concentrations.[80-82]

The next link in the scheme relating altered polyol and *myo*-inositol metabolism to compromised nerve function in diabetes pertains to the recently described interrelationships of these substances

TABLE 4-4 Glucose Inhibition of Sodium-Dependent Uptake of [³H]-Labeled *myo*-Inositol by Rabbit Sciatic Nerve Endoneurial Preparations

Incubation Conditions	Uptake (nmol/kg/min)
5 μM *myo*-inositol	
5 mM glucose	78 ± 4
20 mM glucose	57 ± 3*
50 μM *myo*-inositol	
5 mM glucose	415 ± 43
20 mM glucose	310 ± 15*

*Significantly different from 5 mM glucose.
Data from Greene and Lattimer.[79]

with the activity of sodium/potassium adenosine triphosphatase (Na/K-ATPase), an enzyme critically involved with maintenance of sodium concentrations in the axon. Na/K-ATPase activity is reduced in the sciatic nerve of rats with experimental diabetes, and this abnormality is believed to cause an increase in the intra-axonal sodium concentration, resulting in impaired sodium influx during depolarization and a consequent compromise in the propagation of nerve impulses.[83,84] Decreased neural Na/K-ATPase activity is corrected by either dietary *myo*-inositol supplementation or treatment with the aldose reductase inhibitor sorbinil[85,86] (Table 4-5). These observations not only implicate *myo*-inositol depletion in the genesis of impaired Na/K-ATPase activity, but also indicate that enhanced polyol pathway activity, perhaps via reduction in cell *myo*-inositol levels, contributes to the defect in neural Na/K-ATPase activity in diabetes. Nerve conduction velocity, *myo*-inositol content, and Na/K-ATPase activity also are decreased in Bio-Breeding diabetic (BB/D) rats. Vigorous treatment with insulin normalizes these parameters and also prevents the progression of associated structural changes.[87] One such structural change consists of a decrease in the number of intramembranous particles in replicas of freeze fracture surfaces of the internodal myelin membranes of large sciatic nerve fibers.[88] This change, which may represent the structural correlate of the reported decrease in electrical resistance of internodal myelin in diabetes, is prevented by treatment with insulin or by dietary *myo*-inositol supplementation.

TABLE 4-5 Effect of Diabetes and Sorbinil Treatment on
Rat Sciatic Nerve ATPase Activity

Experimental Group	Na/K-ATPase (μmol/g/hr)
Control	104.3 ± 4.4
Untreated diabetic	56.8 ± 2.9*
Sorbinil-treated diabetic	95.7 ± 5.0**

*Significantly different from control.
**Significantly different from untreated diabetic.
Data from Greene and Lattimer.[86]

Na/K-ATPase is a membrane-bound enzyme complex intimately associated with phospholipid-related cell cycles and components, particularly phosphatidylinositol. This inositol-containing phospholipid is both a precursor to synthesis and a breakdown product of the polyphosphoinositides, which are present in high concentration in the peripheral nerve, where they are associated with myelin. Phosphoinositide turnover is markedly increased during neural stimulation, impulse generation, and synaptic transmission, and may be involved with the generation of ionic fluxes that accompany these processes.[89-94] Thus, diminished *myo*-inositol content may compromise phosphoinositide synthesis or metabolism, in turn impairing neuronal Na/K-ATPase activity and contributing to faulty neuronal transmission. This could create a self-perpetuating cycle of negative influences on nerve function, as Green[83,86,95] has proposed (Figure 4-1).

One of the problems with this construct is that corresponding quantitative changes in the phosphatidylinositol or polyphosphoinositide content of peripheral nerve in diabetes have not been definitively established.[70,73,96,97] However, several studies have shown that the activities of enzymes concerned with phosphatidylinositol and polyphosphoinositide synthesis are decreased in preparations of nerves obtained from diabetic animals.[69,97-99] Additionally, the in vitro incorporation of [^{32}P]orthophosphate into sciatic nerve polyphosphoinositides, particularly phosphatidylinositol-4,5-bisphosphate (PIP$_2$), is increased in preparations from diabetic rats, and these increases are prevented by treatment with insulin.[100,101] The finding that the glucose-induced inhibition of *myo*-

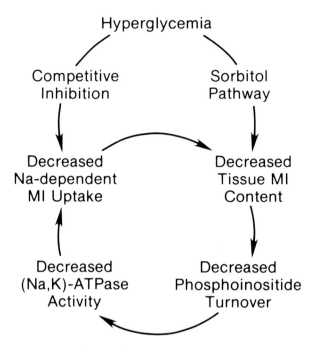

Hyperglycemia

Competitive
Inhibition

Sorbitol
Pathway

Decreased
Na-dependent
MI Uptake

Decreased
Tissue MI
Content

Decreased
(Na,K)-ATPase
Activity

Decreased
Phosphoinositide
Turnover

FIGURE 4-1 Proposed interaction of hyperglycemia, sodium-dependent *myo*-inositol (MI) uptake, inositol phospholipid metabolism, and sodium-potassium ATPase [(Na,K)-ATPase] activity in the pathogenesis of diabetic neuropathy. Reproduced with permission from the American Diabetes Association, Inc. From Greene DA, Lattimer SA: Protein kinase C agonists acutely normalize decreased ouabain-inhibitable respiration in diabetic rat nerve. *Diabetes* 1986; 35:242–245.

inositol uptake in adipocytes is associated with decreased phosphatidylinositol formation also offers support for this hypothesis.[102] Finally, Greene and Lattimer recently reported that agonists of protein kinase C, a putative messenger regulated by phosphoinositide turnover, normalize the reduced oxygen consumption that reflects diminished Na/K-ATPase activity in endoneurial preparations from alloxan-diabetic rabbits.[95] This suggests that nerve *myo*-inositol depletion impairs Na/K-ATPase activity by a mechanism involving protein kinase C, and that altered phosphoinositide metabolism, presumably related to *myo*-inositol deficiency, underlies the defect in protein kinase C. Other evidence linking phosphoinositide turnover, Na/K-ATPase activity, and *myo*-inositol metabolism has been found in aortic tissue (see Chapter 6), and an analogous sequence of metabolic abnormalities has been identified in peripheral nerve. In rabbit tibial nerve endoneurial preparations, deprivation of *myo*-inositol results in associated decreases in resting energy utilization, Na/K-ATPase activity, and phosphatidylinositol metabolism in a compartment of rapid basal turnover. [103,104]

Recently, defects in axonal transport, known for several years to occur in peripheral nerve of animals with experimental diabetes, have been linked to the accumulation of polyol pathway products. [77,105-113] Axonal transport is assessed by measuring the accumulation of endogenous components of the axoplasm after constriction of the nerve trunk; accumulation in nerve segments proximal to the constriction reflects orthograde transport, whereas accumulation distal to the ligature is an index of retrograde transport. The orthograde axonal transport of choline acetyltransferase and acetylcholinesterase is diminished in sciatic nerves of streptozotocin-diabetic rats. The implication of this abnormality is that there is restricted availability of neuronal proteins and nutrients to distal portions of the axoplasm, and that this restriction contributes to the axonopathy of diabetic neuropathy. Decreased conduction velocity accompanies impaired axonal transport, and insulin treatment normalizes both parameters. More importantly, from the perspective of the interrelationships between changes in this axonal function and alterations in polyol and/or *myo*-inositol metabolism, treatment with the aldose reductase inhibitor Sorbinil or with dietary *myo*-inositol supplementation restores axonal transport in streptozotocin-diabetic rats. Since either of these treatments also restores nerve *myo*-inositol levels, *myo*-inositol depletion is believed to underlie this defect in axonal transport. However, nerve *myo*-inositol levels were not decreased in diabetic BB/D rats that were treated with insulin but remained hyperglycemic, and choline acetyltransferase did not accumulate after constriction of the sciatic nerve in these animals. Although differences in the nature of the diabetes (experimental versus spontaneous) in the animals used for these two studies may account for the seemingly dichotomous results, the findings in the latter study are compatible with the interpretation that *myo*-inositol depletion is prerequisite to this impairment in axonal transport. On the other hand, neither aldose reductase inhibition nor *myo*-inositol supplementation prevents the deficit in the slow anterograde transport of labeled protein in motoneurons of rats with diabetes of 4 weeks' duration.[114,115]

The aldose reductase inhibitor Statil, developed by Imperial Chemical Industries (ICI 128436), prevented sorbitol accumulation, *myo*-inositol depletion, and the defective accumulation of choline acetyltransferase activity occurring after ligature in the vagus nerve of streptozotocin-diabetic rats.[116] Choline acetyltransferase activity in cholinergically innervated organs such as the terminal ileum and iris is reduced in streptozotocin diabetes, and treatment with Statil prevents these reductions.[117] *Myo*-inositol levels and Na/K-ATPase activity are reduced in the superior cervical ganglia of diabetic rats, and these changes are prevented by treatment with Sorbinil.[118] The implication of these findings is that the mechanisms underlying autonomic neuropathy are similar to those responsible for peripheral neuropathy, at least in the experimentally diabetic rat.

At least three interrelated and fundamental concerns have limited the translation of the intriguing results from these studies with tissue from diabetic animals to the problem of diabetic neuropathy in humans and its possible treatment with aldose reductase inhibitors. First, there is no assurance that the biochemical abnormalities associated with defects in nerve function in animal models of diabetes are the same as those responsible for the development of diabetic neuropathy in people. Second, many of the studies have employed measurement of motor nerve conduction velocity to detect the appearance of functional deficits or restoration of functional integrity by various manipulations, yet nerve conduction reflects function only in that small fraction of total nerve fibers that are the largest and most rapidly conducting. Further, decreased nerve conduction velocity can occur in the absence of structural changes such as segmental demyelination and axonal loss. Third, in view of the fact that functional defects in diabetic neuropathy are associated with structural as well as metabolic abnormalities, there is no guarantee that agents having a favorable impact on dysfunction related to metabolic disturbances will also alleviate abnormalities arising from structural changes. Indeed, available evidence suggests dissociation of the underlying structural and metabolic factors in chronic diabetes. After 12 weeks of untreated diabetes followed by 6 weeks of vigorous treatment with insulin, sural nerve conduction velocity in BB rats was only partially restored despite normalization of nerve *myo*-inositol and Na/K-ATPase activity.[119] The residual defect in nerve conduction was associated with a persistent morphologic change consisting of a disappearance of paranodal axoglial junctional complexes. This abnormality has also been identified in the sural nerve of human patients with distal symmetrical diabetic polyneuropathy.[120] It is not yet known whether some of the structural changes found in experimental diabetes of lesser duration are reversible. Such changes would include the expanded size and number of filaments in the proximal axons and the shrinkage in cross-sectional area of distal axons of the sciatic nerve system in rats with streptozotocin diabetes of 4 to 6 weeks' duration.[121] Paranodal nerve fiber swelling, believed to be an ultrastructural precursor of axoglial dysjunction, is prevented by treatment with insulin or oral *myo*-inositol.[122]

References

1. Chochinov RH, Ullyot LE, Moorhouse JA: Sensory perception thresholds in patients with juvenile diabetes and their close relatives. *N Engl J Med* 1972; 286:1233–1237.

2. Graf RJ, Halter JB, Halar E, et al: Nerve conduction abnormalities in untreated maturity-onset diabetes: Relation to levels of fasting plasma glucose and glycosylated hemoglobin. *Ann Intern Med* 1979; 90:298–303.

3. Pfeifer MA, Weinberg CR, Cook DL, et al: Correlations among autonomic, sensory and motor neural function tests in untreated non-insulin-dependent diabetic individuals. *Diabetes Care* 1985; 8:576–584.

4. Valbo AB, Hagbarth K-E, Torebjork HE, et al: Somatosensory, proprioceptive and sympathetic activity in human peripheral nerves. *Physiol Rev* 1979; 59:919–957.

5. Fagius J: Microneurographic findings in diabetic polyneuropathy with special reference to sympathetic nerve activity. *Diabetologia* 1982; 23:415–420.

6. Thomas PK, Lascelles RG: The pathology of diabetic neuropathy. *Q J Med* 1966; 24:489–509.

7. Behse F, Buchthal F, Carlson FI: Nerve biopsy and conduction studies in diabetic neuropathy. *J Neurol Neurosurg Psychiatry* 1977; 40:1072–1082.

8. Dyck PJ, Sherman WR, Hallcher LM, et al: Human diabetic endoneurial sorbitol, fructose and *myo*-inositol related to sural nerve morphometry. *Ann Neurol* 1980; 8:590–596.

9. Clements RS, Bell DHS: Diagnostic, pathogenetic and therapeutic aspects of diabetic neuropathy. *Spec Top Endocrinol Metab* 1982; 3:1–43.

10. Powell H, Know D, Lee S, et al: Alloxan diabetic neuropathy: Electron microscopic studies. *Neurology* 1977; 27:60–66.

11. Schlaepfer WW, Gerritsen GC, Dulin WE: Segmental demyelination in the distal peripheral nerves of chronically diabetic chinese hamsters. *Diabetologia* 1974; 10:541–548.

12. Yagihashi S, Kudo K, Nishihira M: Peripheral nerve structures of experimental diabetes in rats and the effect of insulin treatment. *Tohoku J Exp Med* 1979; 127:35–44.

13. Jakobsen J: Axon dwindling in early experimental diabetes. I. A study of cross-sectioned nerves. *Diabetologia* 1976; 12:539–546.

14. Jakobsen J: Peripheral nerves in early experimental diabetes. Expansion of the endoneurial space as a cause of increased water content. *Diabetologia* 1978; 14:113–119.

15. Jakobsen J: Early and preventable changes of peripheral nerve structure and function in insulin-deficient diabetic rat. *J Neurol Neurosurg Psychiatry* 1979; 42:509–518.

16. Monckton G, Pehoevich E: Autonomic neuropathy in the streptozotocin diabetic rat. *Can J Neurol Sci* 1980; 7:135–142.

17. Moore SA, Peterson RG, Felten DL, et al: Reduced sensory and motor conduction velocity in 25-week-old diabetic [C57BL/Ks (db/db)] mice. *Exp Neurol* 1980; 70:548–555.

18. Sima AA: Peripheral neuropathy in the spontaneously diabetic BB-Wistar rat. *Acta Neuropathol* 1980; 51:223–227.

19. Bischoff A: Morphology of diabetic neuropathy. *Horm Metab Res* 1980; 9(suppl):18–28.

20. Timperley WR: Vascular and coagulation abnormalities in diabetic neuropathy and encephalopathy. *Horm Metab Res* 1980; 9(suppl):43–49.

21. Timperley WR, Ward JD, Preston FE, et al: Clinical and histological studies in diabetic neuropathy: A reassessment of vascular factors in relation to vascular coagulation. *Diabetologia* 1976; 12:237–243.

22. Williams E, Timperley WR, Ward JD, et al: Electron microscopic studies of vessels in diabetic peripheral neuropathy. *J Clin Pathol* 1980; 33:462–470.

23. Raff MC, Asbury AK: Ischemic mononeuropathy and mononeuropathy multiplex in diabetes mellitus. *N Engl J Med* 1968; 279:17–22.

24. Asbury AK, Aldridge H, Hershberg R, et al: Oculomotor palsy in diabetes mellitus: A clinico-pathologic study. *Brain* 1970; 93:555–566.

25. Dreyfus PM, Hakim S, Adams RD: Diabetic ophthalmoplegia: Report of a case with postmortem study and comments on vascular supply of human oculomotor nerve. *Arch Neurol Psychiatry* 1957; 77:337–349.

26. Johnson PC, Brendel K, Meezan E: Human diabetic perineurial cell basement membrane thickening. *Lab Invest* 1981; 44:165–170.

27. Johnson PC: Thickening of the human dorsal root ganglion perineurial cell basement membrane in diabetes mellitus. *Muscle Nerve* 1983; 6:561–565.

28. Seneviratne KN: Permeability of blood nerve barriers in the diabetic rat. *J Neurol Neurosurg Psychiatry* 1972; 35:156–162.

29. Gabbay KH, Merola LO, Field RA: Sorbitol pathway: Presence in nerve and cord with substrate accumulation in diabetes. *Science* 1966; 151:209–210.

30. Sherman WR, Stewart MA: Identification of sorbitol in mammalian nerve. *Biochem Biophys Res Commun* 1966; 22:492–497.

31. Stewart MA, Passoneau JV: Identification of fructose in mammalian nerve. *Biochem Biophys Res Commun* 1964; 17:536–541.

32. Stewart MA, Sherman WR, Anthony S: Free sugars in alloxan diabetic rat nerve. *Biochem Biophys Res Commun* 1966; 22:488–491.

33. Greene DA, DeJesus PV, Winegrad AI: Effects of insulin and dietary *myo*-inositol on impaired peripheral motor nerve conduction velocities in acute streptozotocin diabetes. *J Clin Invest* 1975; 55:1326–1336.

34. Stewart MA, Sherman WR, Kurien MM, et al: Polyol accumulation in nervous tissue of rats with experimental diabetes and galactosemia. *J Neurochem* 1977; 14:1057–1066.

35. Ward JD: The polyol pathway in the neuropathy of early diabetes, in Camerini-Davalos RA, Cole HS (eds): *Vascular and Neurologic Changes in Early Diabetes*, pp 525–532. New York, Academic Press, 1973.

36. Ward JD, Baker RWP, Davis BH: Effect of blood sugar control on the accumulation of sorbitol and fructose in nervous tissues. *Diabetes* 1972; 21:1173–1178.

37. Poulsom R, Heath H: Inhibition of aldose reductase in five tissues of the streptozotocin diabetic rat. *Biochem Pharmacol* 1983; 32:1495–1499.

38. Mayhew JA, Gillon KRW, Hawthorne JN: Free and lipid inositol and sugars in sciatic nerve obtained postmortem from diabetic patients and control subjects. *Diabetologia* 1983; 24:13–15.

39. Pitkänen E, Servo C: Cerebrospinal fluid polyols in patients with diabetes. *Clin Chim Acta* 1973; 44:437–442.

40. Servo C, Pitkänen E: Variation in polyol levels in cerebrospinal fluid and serum in diabetic patients. *Diabetologia* 1975; 11:575–580.

41. Greene DA, Winegrad AI: In vitro studies of the substrates for energy production and the effects of insulin on glucose utilization in the neural components of peripheral nerve. *Diabetes* 1979; 28:878–887.

42. Greene DA, Winegrad AI: Effects of acute experimental diabetes on composite energy metabolism in peripheral nerve axons and Schwann cells. *Diabetes* 1979; 30:967–974.

43. Gabbay KH, O'Sullivan JB: The sorbitol pathway in diabetes and galactosemia: Enzyme and substrate localization. *Diabetes* 1968; 17:239–243.

44. Gabbay KH: The sorbitol pathway and complications of diabetes. *N Engl J Med* 1973; 288:831–836.

45. Gabbay KH: Hyperglycemia, polyol metabolism and complications of diabetes. *Annu Rev Med* 1975; 26:521–536.

46. Ludvigson MA, Sorenson RL: Immunohistochemical localization of aldose reductase. I. Enzyme purification and antibody preparation-localization in peripheral nerve, artery, and testes. *Diabetes* 1980; 29:438–449.

47. Kern TS, Engerman RL: Immunohistochemical distribution of aldose reductase. *Histochem J* 1982; 14:507–515.

48. Brown MJ, Sumner AJ, Greene DA, et al: Distal neuropathy in experimental diabetes. *Ann Neurol* 1980; 8:168–178.

49. Hanker JS, Ambrose WW, Yates PE, et al: Peripheral neuropathy in mouse hereditary diabetes mellitus. I. Comparison of neurologic, histologic and morphometric parameters with dystonic mice. *Acta Neuropathol (Berl)* 1980; 51:145–153.

50. Sugimura K, Windebank AJ, Natarajan V, et al: Interstitial hyperosmolarity may cause axis cylinder shrinkage in streptozotocin diabetic nerve. *J Neuropathol Exp Neurol* 1980; 39:710–721.

51. Low PA, Dyck PJ, Schmelzer JD: Mammalian peripheral nerve sheath has unique responses to chronic elevations of endoneurial fluid pressure. *Exp Neurol* 1980; 70:300–306.

52. Low PA, Dyck PJ, Schmelzer JD: Chronic elevation of endoneurial fluid pressure is associated with low-grade fiber pathology. *Muscle Nerve* 1982; 5:162–165.

53. Myers RR, Costello ML, Powell HC: Increased endoneurial fluid pressure in galactose neuropathy. *Muscle Nerve* 1979; 2:299–303.

54. Powell HC, Myers RR: Schwann cell changes and demyelination in chronic galactose neuropathy. *Muscle Nerve* 1983; 6:218–227.

55. Sharma AK, Baker RWR, Thomas PK: Peripheral nerve abnormalities related to galactose administration in rats. *J Neurol Neuropathol Psychiatry* 1976; 39:794–802.

56. Gabbay KH, Snider JJ: Nerve conduction defect in galactose-fed rats. *Diabetes* 1972; 21:295–300.

57. Powell HC, Costello ML, Myers RR: Endoneurial fluid pressure in experimental models of diabetic neuropathy. *J Neuropathol Exp Neurol* 1981; 40:613–634.

58. Dyck PJ, Lamberg EH, Windebank AJ, et al: Acute hyperosmolar hyperglycemia causes axonal shrinkage and reduced nerve conduction velocity. *Exp Neurol* 1981; 71:507–514.

59. Powell HC: Pathology of diabetic neuropathy: New observations, new hypotheses. *Lab Invest* 1983; 49:515–518.

60. Cogan DG, Kinoshita JH, Kador PF, et al: Aldose reductase and complications of diabetes. *Ann Intern Med* 1984; 101:82–91.

61. Yue DK, Hanwell MA, Satchell PM, et al: The effect of aldose reductase inhibition on motor nerve conduction velocity in diabetic rats. *Diabetes* 1982; 31:789–794.

62. Clements RS, Reynertson RH, Starnes WS: *Myo*-inositol metabolism in diabetes mellitus. *Diabetes* 1974; 23:348A.

63. Daughaday WH, Larner J: The renal excretion of inositol in normal and diabetic human beings. *J Clin Invest* 1954; 33:326–332.

64. Clements RS: Diabetic neuropathy—Newer concepts in etiology. *Diabetes* 1979; 28:604–611.

65. Clements RS, Reynertson R: *Myo*-inositol metabolism in diabetes mellitus. Effect of insulin treatment. *Diabetes* 1977; 26:215–221.

66. Pitkanen E: The serum polyol pattern and the urinary polyol excretion in diabetic and uremic patients. *Clin Chim Acta* 1972; 38:221–230.

67. Clements RS, Diethelm AG: The metabolism of *myo*-inositol by the human kidney. *J Lab Clin Med* 1979; 93:210–219.

68. Barbosa J: Plasma *myo*-inositol in diabetics including patients with renal allografts. *Acta Diabetol Lat* 1978; 15:95–101.

69. Clements RS, Stockard CR: Abnormal sciatic nerve *myo*-inositol metabolism in the streptozotocin-diabetic rat. Effects of insulin treatment. *Diabetes* 1980; 29:227–235.

70. Palamano KP, Whiting PH, Hawthorne JH: Free and lipid *myo*-inositol in tissues from rats with acute and less severe streptozotocin-induced diabetes. *Biochem J* 1977; 167:229–235.

71. Servo C: Sorbitol and *myo*-inositol in the cerebrospinal fluid of diabetic patients. *Acta Endocrinol* 1980; 94(suppl 238):133–138.

72. Servo C, Bergstrom L, Fogelholm R: Cerebrospinal fluid sorbitol and *myo*-inositol in diabetic polyneuropathy. *Acta Med Scand* 1977; 202:301–304.

73. Winegrad AI, Greene DA: Diabetic polyneuropathy: The importance of insulin deficiency, hyperglycemia and alterations in *myo*-inositol metabolism in its pathogenesis. *N Engl J Med* 1976; 295:1416–1421.

74. Greene DA, Lewis RA, Lattimer SA, et al: Selective effects of *myo*-inositol administration on sciatic and tibial motor nerve conduction parameters in the streptozotocin-diabetic rat. *Diabetes* 1982; 31:573–578.

75. Gillon KRW, Hawthorne JN, Tomlinson DR: *Myo*-inositol and sorbitol metabolism in relation to peripheral nerve function in experimental diabetes in the rat: The effect of aldose reductase inhibition. *Diabetologia* 1983; 25:365–371.

76. Gillon KRW, Hawthorne JN: Sorbitol, inositol and nerve conduction in diabetes. *Life Sci* 1983; 32:1943–1947.

77. Mayer JH, Tomlinson DR: Prevention of defects of axonal transport and nerve conduction velocity by oral administration of *myo*-inositol or an aldose reductase inhibitor in streptozotocin-diabetic rats. *Diabetologia* 1983; 25:433–438.

78. Finegold D, Lattimer SA, Nolle S, et al: Polyol pathway activity and *myo*-inositol metabolism: A suggested relationship in the pathogenesis of diabetic neuropathy. *Diabetes* 1983; 32:988–992.

79. Greene D, Lattimer SA: Sodium and energy-dependent uptake of *myo*-inositol by rabbit peripheral nerve. *J Clin Invest* 1982; 70:1009–10018.

80. Cotlier E: *Myo*-inositol active transport by the crystalline lens. *Invest Ophthalmol* 1970; 9:681–691.

81. Chylack LT, Kinoshita JH: A biochemical evaluation of a cataract induced in a high-glucose medium. *Invest Ophthalmol* 1969; 8:401–412.

82. Broekhuyse RM: Changes in *myo*-inositol permeability in the lens due to cataractous conditions. *Biochim Biophys Acta* 1968; 163:269–272.

83. Greene DA, Lattimer SA: Impaired energy utilization and sodium-potassium ATPase in diabetic peripheral nerve. *Am J Physiol* 1984; 246:E311–E318.

84. Brismar T, Sima AAF: Changes in nodal function in nerve fibres of the spontaneously diabetic BB-Wistar rat: Potential clamp analysis. *Acta Physiol Scand* 1981; 113:499–506.

85. Greene DA, Lattimer SA: Impaired rat sciatic nerve sodium-potassium ATPase in acute streptozotocin diabetes and its correction by dietary *myo*-inositol supplementation. *J Clin Invest* 1983; 72:1058–1063.

86. Greene DA, Lattimer SA: Action of sorbinil in diabetic peripheral nerve. Relationships of polyol (sorbitol) pathway inhibition to a *myo*-inositol mediated defect in sodium-potassium ATPase activity. *Diabetes* 1984; 33:712–716.

87. Sima AAF, Lattimer SA, Yaghihashi S, et al: Biochemical, functional, and structural correction of diabetic neuropathy in the BB-rat after insulin treatment. *Fed Proc* 1984; 43:375A.

88. Fukuma M, Carpentier J-L, Orci L, et al: An alteration in internodal myelin membrane structure in large sciatic nerve fibres in rats with acute streptozotocin diabetes and impaired nerve conduction velocity. *Diabetologia* 1978; 15:65–72.

89. White GL, Larabee MG: Phosphoinositides and other phospholipids in sympathetic ganglia and nerve trunks of rats. *J Neurochem* 1973; 20:783–798.

90. White GL, Schellhase HU, Hawthorne JN: Phosphoinositide metabolism in rat superior cervical ganglion, vagus and phrenic nerve: Effects of electrical stimulation and various blocking agents. *J Neurochem* 1974; 28:149–158.

91. Hawthorne JN, Pickard MP, Griffin HD: Phosphatidylinositol, triphosphoinositide and synaptic transmission, in Wells WW, Eisenberg F (eds): *Cyclitols and Polyphosphoinositides*, pp 145–151. New York, Academic Press, 1978.

92. Henrickson HS, Reinertsen JL: Phosphoinositide interconversion: A model for control of Na^+ and K^+ permeability in the nerve axon. *Biochem Biophys Res Commun* 1971; 44:1258–1264.

93. Michell RH: Inositol phospholipids and cell surface receptor function. *Biochim Biophys Acta* 1980; 415:81–147.

94. Tetjak AG, Limarenko IM, Lossova GV, et al: Interrelation of phosphoinositide metabolism and ion transport in crab nerve fiber. *J Neurochem* 1977; 28:199–205.

95. Greene DA, Lattimer SA: Protein kinase C agonists acutely normalize decreased ouabain-inhibitable respiration in diabetic rat nerve. *Diabetes* 1986; 35:242–245.

96. Jeffreys JGR, Palmano KP, Sharma AK, et al: Influence of dietary *myo*-inositol on nerve conduction and inositol phospholipids in normal and diabetic rats. *J Neurol Neurosurg Psychiatry* 1978; 41:333–339.

97. Natarajan V, Dyck PJ, Schmid HO: Alterations in inositol lipid metabolism of rat sciatic nerve in streptozotocin-induced diabetes. *J Neurochem* 1981; 36:413–419.

98. Hothersall JS, McLean P: Effect of diabetes and insulin on phosphatidylinositol synthesis in rat sciatic nerve. *Biochem Biophys Res Commun* 1979; 88:477–484.

99. Whiting PH, Palmano KP, Hawthorne JN: Enzymes of *myo*-inositol and inositol lipid metabolism in rats with streptozotocin-induced diabetes. *Biochem J* 1979; 179:549–553.

100. Bell ME, Peterson RG, Eichberg J: Metabolism of phospholipids in peripheral nerve from rats with chronic streptozotocin-induced diabetes: Increased turnover of phosphatidyl-4,5-bisphosphate. *J Neurochem* 1982; 39:192–200.

101. Berti-Mattera L, Peterson R, Bell M, et al: Effect of hyperglycemia and its prevention by insulin treatment on the incorporation of [^{32}P] into polyphosphoinositides and other phospholipids in peripheral nerve of the streptozotocin diabetic rat. *J Neurochem* 1985; 45:1692–1698.

102. Kaplan SA, Lee W-NP, Scott ML: Glucose inhibits *myo*-inositol transport and phosphatidylinositol formation in adipocytes. *Diabetes* 1985; 34(suppl 1):183A.

103. Simmons DA, Winegrad AI, Martin DB: Significance of tissue *myo*-inositol concentrations in metabolic regulation in nerve. *Science* 1982; 217:848–851.

104. Winegrad AI, Simmons DA, Martin DB: Has one diabetic complication been explained? *N Engl J Med* 1983; 308:152–154.

105. Schmidt RE, Matschinsky FM, Godfrey DA, et al: Fast and slow axoplasmic flow in sciatic nerve of diabetic rats. *Diabetes* 1975; 24:1081–1085.

106. Giachetti A: Axoplasmol transport of noradenaline in the sciatic nerves of spontaneously diabetic mice. *Diabetologia* 1979; 16:191–199.

107. Jakobsen J, Sidenius P: Decreased axonal transport of structural proteins in streptozotocin-diabetic rats. *J Clin Invest* 1980; 66:292–297.

108. Tomlinson DR, Moriarty RJ, Mayer JH: Prevention and reversal of defective axonal transport and motor nerve conduction velocity in rats with experimental diabetes by treatment with the aldose reductase inhibitor Sorbinil. *Diabetes* 1984; 33:470–476.

109. Sidenius P: The axonapathy of diabetic neuropathy. *Diabetes* 1982; 31:356–363.

110. Tomlinson DR, Holmes PR, Mayer JH: Reversal, by treatment with an aldose reductase inhibitor, of impaired axonal transport and motor nerve conduction velocity in experimental diabetes. *Neurosci Lett* 1982; 31:189–193.

111. Mayer JH, Tomlinson DR: Axonal transport of cholinergic transmitter enzymes in vagus and sciatic nerves of rats with acute experimental diabetes mellitus; correlation with motor nerve conduction velocity and effects of insulin. *Neuroscience* 1983; 9:951–957.

112. Mayer JH, Herberg L, Tomlinson DR: Axonal transport and nerve conduction and their relation to nerve polyol and *myo*-inositol levels in spontaneously diabetic BB/D rats. *Neurochem Pathol* 1984; 2:285–293.

113. Tomlinson DR, Mayer H: Defects of axonal transport in diabetes mellitus—a possible contribution to the aetiology of diabetic neuropathy. *J Auton Pharmacol* 1984; 4:59–72.

114. Mayer JH, Tomlinson DR, McLean WG: Slow orthograde axonal transport of radiolabelled protein in sciatic motoneurones of rats with short-term experimental diabetes: Effects of treatment with an aldose reductase inhibitor of *myo*-inositol. *J Neurochem* 1984; 43:1265–1270.

115. Tomlinson DR, Sidenius P, Larsen JR: Slow component-a of axonal transport, nerve *myo*-inositol, and aldose reductase inhibition in diabetic rats. *Diabetes* 1986; 35:398–402.

116. Tomlinson DR, Townsend J, Fretten P: Prevention of defective axonal transport in streptozotocin-diabetic rats by treatment with "Statil" (ICI 128436), an aldose reductase inhibitor. *Diabetes* 1985; 34:970–972.

117. Tomlinson DR, Townsend S: Protection by the aldose reductase inhibitor "Statil" (ICI 128436) against loss of an axonally transported enzyme in nerve terminals of diabetic rats. *Diabetes* 1985; 34(suppl 1):202A.

118. Wells AM, Greene DA: A Sorbinil-responsive *myo*-inositol-related Na/K-ATPase defect in diabetic rat superior cervical ganglion. *Diabetes* 1985; 34(suppl 1):102A.

119. Sima AF, Lattimer SA, Yagihashi S, et al: Axo-glial dysjunction. A novel structural lesion that accounts for poorly reversible slowing of nerve conduction in the spontaneously diabetic Bio-Breeding rat. *J Clin Invest* 1986; 77:424–484.

120. Sima AAF, Bril V, Greene DA: A new characteristic ultrastructural abnormality, and morphologic evidence for pathogenetic heterogeneity in human diabetic neuropathy. *Clin Res* 1986; 34:688A.

121. Medori R, Autilio-Gambetti L, Monaco S, et al: Experimental diabetic neuropathy: Impairment of slow transport with changes in axon cross-sectional area. *Proc Natl Acad Sci USA* 1985; 82:7716–7720.

122. Greene DA, Lattimer SA, Sima AAF: Acute paranodal nerve fiber swelling and conduction slowing in the insulin-deficient BB rat reflects *myo*-inositol depletion and Na/K-ATPase deficiency rather than sorbitol accumulation. *Clin Res* 1986; 34:683A.

CHAPTER 5

Diabetic Nephropathy

For many years after identification of the polyol pathway and the implication that it participated in the pathogenesis of certain complications of diabetes, evidence that it might play a role in the development of diabetic nephropathy was largely inferential. Fundamental to the support of such a hypothesis would be the demonstration that aldose reductase activity and sorbitol content are increased in the characteristic tissue sites of the diabetic renal lesions. If there is a causal link between polyol accumulation and diabetic nephropathy, then aldose reductase activity should be demonstrable in glomerular tissue, and the glomerular polyol content should be elevated in diabetes.

Initial attempts to fulfill these criteria yielded negative experimental results. One early study found that neither of the sorbitol pathway intermediates, sorbitol and fructose, could be detected in glomeruli isolated from rats with streptozotocin diabetes left untreated for 14 days.[1] The same investigators reported that sorbitol and fructose did not accumulate in metabolically active glomeruli isolated from normal rats and incubated for 2 hours in media containing 590 mg% glucose.[1] Analysis by assay of enzyme

activity in frozen dried tissue showed no change in the amount of
sorbitol converted to glucose by glomeruli from rats with alloxan
diabetes of 14 days' duration compared to control.[2] However, sorbitol dehydrogenase activity, also measured by enzymatic assay, was
abundantly present in glomeruli and was increased in glomerular
samples from alloxan-diabetic rats.[2] A subsequent study identified
aldose reductase activity, measured as the conversion of sorbitol to
glucose, in glomeruli from nondiabetic and diabetic human
subjects[3]; aldose reductase activity was significantly elevated in
diabetic samples, but sorbitol dehydrogenase activity was reduced in
glomeruli from diabetic subjects (Table 5-1). Immunohistochemical
study of frozen sections with an antibody raised against canine renal
medullary aldose reductase demonstrated the presence of the
enzyme in a wide variety of tissues in the dog, including several loci
in the kidney, but not in renal glomeruli.[4] Several other studies
identified aldose reductase in the renal medullae, papillae, and
tubules[1,2,5] and in view of this it was proposed that sorbitol accumulation at such sites promoted osmotic swelling and thereby con-
tributed to the tubular nephropathy that may be associated with
uncontrolled diabetes.[6] Using specific antibodies to aldose reduc-

TABLE 5-1   Aldose Reductase and Sorbitol Dehydrogenase Activity in Human
Glomeruli

| Sample | Age (years) | Duration of Diabetes (years) | Activity (nmol/kg/hr) | |
			Aldose Reductase	Sorbitol Dehydrogenase
Nondiabetic	19		22.8	18.6
	45		8.8	7.2
	56		9.1	8.7
	57		1.3	8.8
	65		12.0	11.4
	Mean ± SD		10.8±7.8	10.9±4.5
Diabetic	19	0.5	31.9	2.4
	37	5	76.8	5.4
	52	16	48.4	1.8
	68	13	11.6	3.3
	84	7	89.4	5.5
	Mean ± SD		51.6±31.9	3.7±1.7

Data from Corder et al.[3]

tase that had been purified from rat seminal vesicles, Ludvigson and Sorenson localized aldose reductase immunohistochemically in several areas of the kidney.[7] The most intense staining was seen in the inner medulla, whereas the outer medulla and the cortex stained faintly and inconsistently. Within the cortex, however, aldose reductase staining was found in the convoluted portions of the distal tubule and in the glomerular epithelial cells.

More recently, actual measurement of the polyol content has conclusively demonstrated that sorbitol accumulates in renal cortical tissue in the two traditional experimental models in which increased polyols would be anticipated. First, the level of galactitol is increased in renal cortex obtained from galactosemic rats, and second, the sorbitol content of glomeruli isolated from streptozotocin-diabetic rats is dramatically increased compared to that in glomeruli isolated from control animals.[8,9] The experiments in the latter report were performed with animals that had untreated diabetes for 6 to 9 weeks, were severely hyperglycemic, and had renal hypertrophy. Interestingly, the glomerular polyol content was less in 9-week than in 6-week animals—a finding compatible with cell leakage as a consequence of chronic polyol accumulation (Figure 5-1).[10] Since the diabetic-induced increase in glomerular sorbitol and the galactose-induced increase in renal cortical galactitol were both prevented by oral administration of an aldose reductase inhibitor, there is little doubt that the polyol pathway is operative in the renal cortex, and that it has the capacity to expand greatly in the presence of hyperglycemia or galactosemia. It is presumed that, in the glomerulus, this activity largely resides in the epithelial cells (podocytes) since these are the only glomerular cells that exhibit immunohistochemical reactivity to aldose reductase antibody.[7] Additionally, monolayer cultures of monkey kidney epithelium cells accumulated sorbitol when incubated in a high-glucose medium.[11] In this context, it is interesting that enlargement of renal cortical podocytes, suggestive of intracellular edema, and abnormal cytoplasmic extensions of the epithelial cell membranes have been described in diabetic glomerulosclerosis, and that the proteinuria occurring in diabetes has been related to morphologic alterations present in the epithelial cell foot processes.[12-14] Epithelial cells participate in basement membrane synthesis, and it is possible that enhanced polyol pathway activity disturbs metabolic processes

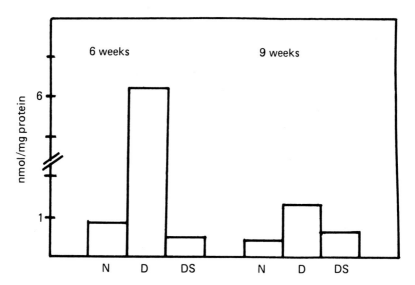

FIGURE 5-1   Polyol content of glomeruli isolated from control (N), diabetic (D) and Sorbinil-treated diabetic (DS) rats after 6 and 9 weeks of diabetes. Data from Beyer-Mears and Cohen.[9]

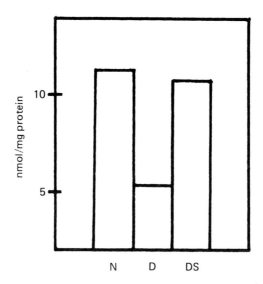

FIGURE 5-2   *Myo*-inositol content of glomeruli isolated from control (N), diabetic (D) and Sorbinil-treated diabetic (DS) rats after 9 weeks of diabetes. Data from Beyer-Mears and Cohen.[9]

involved with basement membrane production, although direct experimental evidence to support such a postulate is currently lacking. That the renal hypertrophy associated with galactosemia is reportedly diminished with aldose reductase inhibition[15] again suggests that the polyol pathway contributes in some way to renal cellular expansion.

Depletion of glomerular *myo*-inositol accompanies the sorbitol increase in streptozotocin diabetes (Figure 5-2). This change, as has been demonstrated in peripheral nerve, is prevented by treatment with an aldose reductase inhibitor,[9,16] indicating that the accumulation of polyol pathway intermediates in some way contributes to the fall in tissue *myo*-inositol content. The reduction in *myo*-inositol has been demonstrated by gas-liquid chromatographic analysis of homogenized, deproteinized isolated glomeruli, and by comparative in vitro radiolabeling experiments with [³H]-labeled *myo*-inositol of glomeruli isolated from control and streptozotocin-diabetic animals.[9,17] Incorporation of [³H]*myo*-inositol was significantly greater in glomeruli from diabetic rats compared to that in glomeruli from control animals at all incubational time periods examined (Figure 5-3). This increased radiolabeled *myo*-inositol incorporation in diabetic samples is compatible with a decrease in the amount of unlabeled (cold) *myo*-inositol in the cell, since the specific activity of the radiolabel would be increased when taken up by diabetic glomeruli in which there is depletion of (unlabeled) *myo*-inositol. A sodium-dependent, glucose-inhibited *myo*-inositol transport system has been demonstrated in isolated rat renal glomeruli, analogous to that identified in peripheral nerve.[18] Thus, reduced glomerular *myo*-inositol content in diabetes may reflect inhibition of *myo*-inositol uptake imposed by hyperglycemia, as has been proposed to explain similar findings in peripheral nerve. Glucose has also been shown to impair *myo*-inositol transport in isolated adipocytes and, presumably as a consequence, the formation of phosphatidylinositol in this tissue.[19]

Although the direct or indirect consequences of reduced *myo*-insotol and/or increased sorbitol on glomerular metabolism are not clear, the similarity of findings with respect to polyol and *myo*-inositol levels in glomeruli and peripheral nerve of animals with experimental diabetes suggested that other metabolic abnormalities might be common to both tissues. Indeed, examination of glomeru-

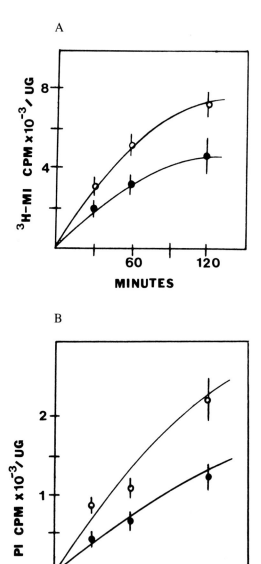

FIGURE 5-3 [³H]-*myo*-inositol (³H-MI) incorporation into glomerular phospholipids (A) and phosphatidylinositol (B) in control (●) and diabetic (○) samples. Reprinted with permission from Cohen MP et al: Effect of diabetes and sorbinil treatment on phospholipid metabolism in rat glomeruli. *Biochim Biophys Acta* 1986; 876:226–231.

lar sodium/potassium adenosine triphosphatase (Na/K-ATPase) revealed that activity was reduced in streptozotocin diabetes.[20] Again, this change was prevented by administration of an aldose reductase inhibitor, which has also been shown to correct decreased Na/K-ATPase activity in peripheral nerve in experimental diabetes.[21] It was also partially ameliorated by treatment with insulin, indicating that the decreased glomerular Na/K-ATPase activity derived from the abnormal metabolic milieu of diabetes rather than from a nephrotoxic effect of streptozotocin (Table 5-2). Although another communication reported that whole-kidney Na/K-ATPase was increased, rather than decreased, in streptozotocin-diabetic rats,[22] it appears that technical differences, choice of tissue sample, and duration of diabetes account for this dichotomy. For example, with increasing duration of untreated diabetes, superimposed hemodynamic and other factors may alter renal ATPase activity independently of the diabetic state. A rise in whole-kidney Na/K-ATPase activity may reflect a contribution from tubular components involved with compensatory hyperplasia and hypertrophy accompanying renal hyperfunction in diabetes.[23,24] Tubules and medulla contain large amounts of ATPase activity,[22,25] alterations in which could obscure more subtle changes in glomerular segments in response to specific conditions.

That inhibition of aldose reductase activity prevents both the fall in *myo*-inositiol levels and the reduction in Na/K-ATPase activity observed in glomeruli from diabetic animals suggests that these changes are linked not only to enhanced polyol pathway activity but also to each other. Among the proposed explanations for these findings is the postulate that the polyol pathway, or sorbitol accumulation, promotes *myo*-inositol efflux from the cell,[16] and that the

TABLE 5-2   Glomerular Na/K-ATPase Activity

Experimental Group	Activity (μmol Pi/mg/min)
Control	0.623 ± 0.054
Diabetic	0.425 ± 0.053
Sorbinil-treated diabetic	0.677 ± 0.107
Insulin-treated diabetic	0.542 ± 0.068

Data from Cohen et al.[20]

resulting reduction in *myo*-inositol limits the availability of this hexitol for important inositol-containing phospholipid cycles associated with cell membrane structures and enzyme complexes. In this construct, reduced Na/K-ATPase activity might be related to decreased phosphatidylinositol, a membrane phospholipid that is intimately associated with this enzyme.[26] However, actual quantification of phosphatidylinositol in crude glomerular membranes revealed no significant differences in preparations from diabetic rats compared to concentrations in tissue from control animals (Table 5-3).[17] Furthermore, only about 25% of the phosphatidylinositol in renal microsomes appears necessary for activation of Na/K-ATPase.[26] This combination of findings makes it unlikely that changes in phosphatidylinositol content, even if such were demonstrable, could account for the reduced glomerular Na/K-ATPase activity in acute experimental diabetes. On the other hand, phosphatidylinositol is a minor component, comprising less than 5% of total phospholipids in the kidney,[27] and it is both a precursor and a breakdown product of a cyclic series of reactions within the polyphosphoinositide response system.[28,29] Thus, modest changes in phosphatidylinositol, especially if confined to the "hormone-sensitive pool," might escape detection by quantitative analysis.

Another interesting postulate that could help explain the prevention of *myo*-inositol depletion, and perhaps the decrease in Na/K-ATPase activity, by inhibition of aldose reductase activity relates to the finding that at least one aldose reductase inhibitor can interact directly with cell membranes. Binding of [³H]Sorbinil to crude membranes prepared from isolated rat glomeruli was found to be dose dependent, saturable, and inhibited by increasing concentrations of the unlabeled compound,[30] suggesting that the drug may

TABLE 5-3 Glomerular Phosphatidylinositol Content in Experimental Diabetes

Experimental Group	Phosphatidylinositol (μg Pi/mg dry wt)
Control	0.16 ± 0.02
Diabetic	0.17 ± 0.03
Sorbinil-treated diabetic	0.16 ± 0.02

Data from Cohen et al.[17]

affect membrane-associated processes independent of, or in addition to, its aldose reductase-inhibiting properties.

A number of questions remain unresolved concerning the specific experimental findings cited above. For example, if one postulates that *myo*-inositol falls because it competes with the glucose transporter for cell entry,[31] how is the reduction in *myo*-inositol prevented by inhibition of aldose reductase in the face of persistent hyperglycemia? If decreased Na/K-ATPase activity relates to *myo*-inositol depletion, how does prevention of polyol accumulation by means of aldose reductase inhibition prevent the decrease in enzyme activity? More importantly, what, if any, is the role of the polyol pathway in the pathogenesis of diabetic nephropathy?

Among the biochemical changes believed to be pathogenetically linked to diabetic nephropathy are increased basement membrane collagen synthesis,[32-37] decreased basement membrane collagen turnover,[38-41] quantitative and/or qualitative abnormalities in basement membrane proteoglycans and particularly the glycosaminoglycan components,[42-49] and excess nonenzymatic glycosylation of basement membrane proteins.[50-55] These processes participate in the pathophysiology and structure/function changes manifest in the diabetic glomerulus as an accumulation of glomerular basement membrane in the peripheral capillary loops, an expansion of the mesangial matrix, a diminution in the anionic sites which regulate charge-selective permeability properties of the glomerular filtration barrier, and a disturbance in the organization, assembly, or interaction of macromolecules in the extracellular matrix. It remains to be established whether changes in the glomerular polyol and *myo*-inositol contents and in Na/K-ATPase activity influence basement membrane collagen and/or proteoglycan synthesis, or matrix organization, and if so, by what mechanisms.

The results of one early series of experiments offered promise toward uncovering a link between basement membrane synthesis and activation of the polyol pathway in diabetes. These experiments examined the effect of a quinoline derivative with aldose reductase-inhibiting properties on basement membrane collagen synthesis by the parietal yolk sac model system and by kidney glomeruli incubated in vitro.[56] This compound, GPA 1734, potently inhibited the formation of hydroxyproline and hydroxylysine, which reflects collagen production, in these tissues without having significant effect on total protein synthesis. The biochemical effect appeared to be at the level of the hydroxylating enzymes, since the compound inhibited the activity of prolyl hydroxylase partially purified from rat skin. Whether this effect is unique to that particular compound, and whether it is related to or independent of its aldose reductase-inhibiting property, are questions worth exploring.

Another recent study, reported in abstract form, examined the influence of treatment with Sorbinil on the gel electrophoretic patterns of urinary proteins in streptozotocin-diabetic rats.[57] Untreated diabetic rats excreted several proteins with molecular weights greater than albumin, in contrast to control animals, which excreted only albumin and low-molecular-weight proteins. Sorbinil treatment was reported to halt the progression of proteinuria and to restore the urinary protein pattern to normal. If these results are confirmed, the possibility that activation of the polyol pathway, or inhibition of aldose reductase, in glomerular epithelial cells affects the glomerular filtration barrier should certainly be examined. Similarly, the recent report that treatment with an aldose reductase inhibitor or dietary *myo*-inositol supplementation significantly reduced the increased glomerular filtration rate that is characteristically found in early, untreated experimental diabetes raises new questions concerning the relationships between glomerular polyol, *myo*-inositol, and hyperfiltration as well as their relative contributions to nephropathic processes.[58]

References

1. Hutton JC, Schofield PJ, Williams JF, et al: The localization of sorbitol pathway activity in the rat renal cortex and its relationship to the pathogenesis of the renal complications of diabetes mellitus. *Aust J Exp Biol Med Sci* 1975; 53:49–57.

2. Corder CN, Collins JG, Brannon TS, et al: Aldose reductase and sorbitol dehydrogenase distribution in rat kidney. *J Histochem Cytochem* 1977; 25:1–8.

3. Corder CN, Braughler JM, Culp PA: Quantitative histochemistry of the sorbitol pathway in glomeruli and small arteries of human diabetic kidney. *Folia Histochem Cytochem (Krakow)* 1979; 17:137–146.

4. Kern TS, Engerman RL: Immunohistochemical distribution of aldose reductase. *Histochem J* 1982; 14:507–515.

5. Gabbay KH, O'Sullivan JB: The sorbitol pathway in diabetes and galactosemia: Enzyme and substrate localization and changes in the kidney. *Diabetes* 1968; 17:300A.

6. Gabbay KH: The sorbitol pathway and complications of diabetes. *N Engl J Med* 1973; 288:831–836.

7. Ludvigson MA, Sorenson RL: Immunohistochemical localization of aldose reductase. *Diabetes* 1980; 29:450–459.

8. Beyer-Mears A, Nicolas-Alexandre J, Cruz E: Sorbinil inhibition of renal aldose reductase. *Fed Proc* 1983; 42:858.

9. Beyer-Mears A, Ku L, Cohen MP: Glomerular polyol accumulation in diabetes and its prevention by oral sorbinil. *Diabetes* 1984; 33:604–607.

10. Reddy VN, Schauss D, Chakrapani B, et al: Biochemical changes associated with the development and reversal of cataracts. *Exp Eye Res* 1976; 23: 483–493.

11. Hutton JC, Williams JF, Schofield PJ, et al: Polyol metabolism in monkey-kidney epithelial cell cultures. *Eur J Biochem* 1974; 49:347–353.

12. Cohen AH, Mampaso F, Zamboui L: Glomerular podocyte degeneration in human renal disease. *Lab Invest* 1977; 37:40–42.

13. Jones DB: Correlative scanning and transmission electron microscopy of glomeruli. *Lab Invest* 1977; 37:569–578.

14. Jones DB: SEM of human and experimental renal disease. *Scan Electron Microsc* 1979; 3:679–689.

15. Beyer-Mears A, Cruz E, Dillon P, et al: Diabetic renal hypertrophy diminished by aldose reductase inhibition. *Fed Proc* 1983; 42:505.

16. Finegold D, Lattimer SA, Nolle S, et al: Polyol pathway activity and *myo*-inositol metabolism. A suggested relationship in the pathogenesis of diabetic neuropathy. *Diabetes* 1983; 32:988–992.

17. Cohen MP, Klepser H, Cua E: Effect of diabetes and Sorbinil treatment on phospholipid metabolism in rat glomeruli. *Biochim Biophys Acta* 1986; 876:226–231.

18. Ulbrecht JS, Bensen JT, Greene DA: Sodium-dependent *myo*-inositol uptake in isolated renal glomeruli: Possible inhibition by glucose. *Diabetes* 1985; 34(suppl 1):13A.

19. Kaplan SA, Lee W-NP, Scott ML: Glucose inhibits *myo*-inositol transport and phosphatidylinositol formation in adipocytes. *Diabetes* 1985; 34(suppl 1): 183A.

20. Cohen MP, Dasmahapatra A, Shapiro E: Reduced glomerular sodium/potassium adenosine triphosphatase activity in acute streptozotocin diabetes. *Diabetes* 1985; 34:1071–1074.

21. Greene DA, Lattimer SA: Action of Sorbinil in diabetic peripheral nerve: Relationship of polyol (sorbitol) pathway inhibition to a *myo*-inositol-mediated defect in sodium-potassium ATPase activity. *Diabetes* 1984; 33:712–716.

22. Finegold DN, Nolle SS, Lattimer S, et al: Alterations in renal ouabain sensitive Na/K-ATPase activity in streptozotocin diabetes. *Clin Res* 1984; 32:395A.

23. Ku DD, Meezan E: Increased renal tubular sodium pump and Na, K-adenosine triphosphatase in streptozotocin-diabetic rats. *J Pharmacol Exp Ther* 1984; 229:664–670.

24. Seyer-Hansen K: Renal hypertrophy in experimental diabetes: Relation to severity of diabetes. *Diabetologia* 1977; 13:141–143.

25. Lo C-S, August TR, Liberman UA, et al: Dependence of renal (Na.K-ATPase)-adenosine triphosphatase activity on thyroid status. *J Biol Chem* 1976; 251:7826–7833.

26. Roelofsen B, Trip MVL-S: The fraction of phospatidylinositol that activates the (Na$^+$/K$^+$)-ATPase in rabbit kidney microsomes is closely associated with the enzyme protein. *Biochim Biophys Acta* 1981; 647:302–306.

27. Toback FG: Phosphatidylcholine metabolism during renal growth and regeneration. *Am J Physiol* 1984; 246:F249–F259.

28. Farese RV: Phosphoinositide metabolism and hormone action. *Endocr Rev* 1983; 4:78–95.

29. Nishizuka Y: Turnover of inositol phospholipids and signal transduction. *Science* 1984; 225:1365–1370.

30. Cohen MP, Klepser H: Binding of an aldose reductase inhibitor to renal glomeruli. *Biochem Biophys Res Commun* 1985; 129:530–535.

31. Greene DA, Lattimer SA: Sodium and energy-dependent uptake of *myo*-inositol by rabbit peripheral nerve: Competitive inhibition by glucose and lack of insulin effect. *J Clin Invest* 1982; 70:1009–1018.

32. Cohen MP, Khalifa A: Renal glomerular collagen synthesis in streptozotocin diabetes. Reversal of increased basement membrane synthesis with insulin therapy. *Biochim Biophys Acta* 1977; 500:395–404.

33. Cohen MP: Glomerular basement membrane synthesis in streptozotocin diabetes, in Podolsky S, Viswanatha M (eds): *Secondary Diabetes, the Spectrum of the Diabetic Syndromes*, pp 541–551. New York, Raven Press, 1980.

34. Cohen MP, Dasmahapatra A, Wu VY: Deposition of basement membrane in vitro by normal and diabetic renal glomeruli. *Nephron* 1981; 27:146–151.

35. Khalifa A, Cohen MP: Glomerular protocollagen lysyl hydroxylase activity in streptozotocin diabetes. *Biochim Biophys Acta* 1975; 386:332–339.

36. Ristelli J, Koivisto VA, Akerblom HK, et al: Intracellular enzymes of collagen biosynthesis in rat kidney with streptozotocin diabetes. *Diabetes* 1976; 25:1066–1070.

37. Spiro RG, Spiro MJ: Effect of diabetes on the biosynthesis of renal glomerular basement membrane. Studies on the glucosyltransferase. *Diabetes* 1971; 20:641–648.

38. Brownlee M, Spiro RG: Glomerular basement membrane metabolism in the diabetic rat. *In vivo* studies. *Diabetes* 1979; 28:121–125.

39. Cohen MP, Surma ML, Wu VY: In vivo biosynthesis and turnover of glomerular basement membrane in diabetic rats. *Am J Physiol* 1982; 242:F385–F389.

40. Romen W, Heck T, Rauscher G, et al: Glomerular basement membrane turnover in young, old, and streptozotocin-diabetic rats. *Renal Physiol* 1980; 3:324–329.

41. Romen W, Lange H-W, Hempel K, et al: Studies on collagen metabolism in rat. II. Turnover and amino acid composition of the collagen of glomerular basement membrane in diabetes mellitus. *Virchows Arch [Cell Pathol]* 1981; 36:313-320.

42. Martines-Hernandez A, Amenta P: The basement membrane in pathology. *Lab Invest* 1983; 48:656-677.

43. Cohen MP, Surma ML: [^{35}S]-Sulfate incorporation into glomerular basement membrane glycosaminoglycans is decreased in experimental diabetes. *J Lab Clin Med* 1981; 98:715-722.

44. Cohen MP, Surma ML: Effect of diabetes on in vivo metabolism of [^{35}S]-labeled glomerular basement membrane. *Diabetes* 1984; 33:8-12.

45. Kanwar YS, Rosenzweig LJ, Linker A, et al: Decreased de novo synthesis of glomerular proteoglycans in diabetes: Biochemical and autoradiographic evidence. *Proc Natl Acad Sci USA* 1983; 80:2272-2275.

46. Rohrbach DH, Wagner CW, Star VL, et al: Reduced synthesis of basement membrane heparan sulfate proteoglycan in streptozotocin-induced diabetic mice. *J Biol Chem* 1983; 258:11672-11677.

47. Parathasarathy N, Spiro RG: Effect of diabetes on the glycosaminoglycan component of the human glomerular basement membrane. *Diabetes* 1982; 31:738-741.

48. Rohrbach DH, Hassell JR, Kleinman HK, et al: Alterations in the basement membrane (heparan sulfate) proteoglycan in diabetic mice. *Diabetes* 1982; 31:185-188.

49. Wu VY, Cohen MP: Platelet factor 4 binding to glomerular microvascular matrix. *Biochim Biophys Acta* 1984; 797:76-82.

50. Vogt BW, Schleicher ED, Wieland OH: ϵ-Amino-lysine bound glucose in human tissues obtained at autopsy: Increase in diabetes mellitus. *Diabetes* 1983; 31:1123-1127.

51. Cohen MP, Urdanivia E, Surma M, et al: Increased glycosylation of glomerular basement membrane collagen in diabetes. *Biochem Biophys Res Commun* 1980; 95:765-769.

52. Cohen MP, Wu VY: Identification of specific amino acids in diabetic glomerular basement membrane subject to nonenzymatic glycosylation in vivo. *Biochem Biophys Res Commun* 1984; 100:1549-1554.

53. Perejda AJ, Uitto J: Nonenzymatic glycosylation of collagen and other proteins: Relationship to the development of diabetic complications. *Coll Rel Res* 1982; 2:81-88.

54. Trueb B, Fluckiger R, Winterhalter KH: Nonenzymatic glycosylation of basement membrane collagen in diabetes mellitus. *Coll Rel Res* 1984; 4:239-251.

55. Uitto J, Perejda AJ, Grant GA, et al: Glucosylation of human glomerular basement membrane collagen: Increased content of hexose in ketoamine linkage and unaltered hydroxylysine-o-glycosides in patients with diabetes. *Connect Tiss Res* 1982; 10:287-296.

56. Maragoudakis ME, Kelinsky H, Wasvary J, et al: Inhibition of basement membrane synthesis and aldose reductase activity by GPA 1734. *Fed Proc* 1976; 35:679.

57. Beyer-Mears A, Varagiannis E, Cruz E: Effect of Sorbinil on reversal of proteinuria. *Diabetes* 1985; 35(suppl 1):101A.

58. Goldfarb S, Simmons DA, Kern E: Amelioration of glomerular hyperfiltration in acute experimental diabetes by dietary *myo*-inositol and by an aldose reductase inhibitor. *Clin Res* 1986; 34:725A.

CHAPTER 6

Aldose Reductase and the Vascular System

Microvasculature

Using a model that they developed to study the influence of various manipulations on vascular permeability, Williams and co-workers have described some interesting effects of experimental diabetes, galactose feeding, and the aldose reductase inhibitor Sorbinil. This model uses new vessels formed by angiogenesis in granulation tissue induced by subcutaneous implantation of sterile polyester fabric, and measures the permeation of ^{125}I-labeled albumin in this tissue by comparing the ratios of radioactive albumin to ^{51}Cr-labeled erythrocytes in the tissue and in the blood at a fixed time after injection of both radioisotopes.[1-3] Vascular permeation of albumin in granulation tissue from female BB/W rats and from male streptozotocin-diabetic rats was significantly greater than that in granulation tissue induced by the same procedure in control animals.[2-4] Since such differences in albumin permeation were not observed in other tissues, such as skin, fat, or aorta, taken from control and diabetic rats, the investigators proposed that the functional integrity of the vasculature is more likely to be impaired in recently formed than in older vessels. Galactose feeding also produced increased ^{125}I-labeled albumin permeation in these angiogenic new vessels and in eyes, even though it had previously been found that albumin permeation was not increased in the eyes of diabetic rats.[5]

The finding that both diabetes and galactose feeding caused increased vascular permeability in this model suggested that polyol accumulation might be involved in the observed defect in albumin permeation in the newly formed vessels. In subsequent experiments, male diabetic rats were treated with Sorbinil, commencing the day of implantation, or were castrated 10 days before the polyester fabric was implanted.[6,7] Either manipulation was successful in preventing the diabetes-induced increase in vascular permeability, indicating that aldose reductase participated in the development of this abnormality and suggesting that sex steroids influence the activity or expression of this enzyme. Castration also markedly lessened the diabetes-associated increase in sorbitol levels and decrease in *myo*-inositol content in granulation tissue. It was further noted that granulation tissue from diabetic animals had increased collagen cross-linking, assessed by percent solubility in 0.5 M acetic acid, and that this change was prevented by castration of diabetic animals but was unaffected by Sorbinil treatment.[8]

Macrovasculature

Thoracic aorta produces increased amounts of sorbitol and fructose when incubated in media containing high glucose concentrations.[9,10] There is a progressive increase in tissue sorbitol content when segments of thoracic aorta are exposed to increasing concentrations of glucose (0 to 50 mM). Notably, aortic sorbitol content also increased when incubations were conducted in the presence of epinephrine (2 μg/mL), isoproterenol (4 μg/mL), dibutyryl-3′,5′-adenosine monophosphate (1×10^{-4} M), ouabain (1×10^{-5} M), or angiotensin II (1 μg/mL), although the mechanism by which these agents promote sorbitol accumulation is obscure. In analogy to the lens, it was initially believed that osmotic and ionic changes resulting from polyol accumulation and leading to fibrosis could help explain the high incidence of atherosclerosis in the diabetic population. Water content is, in fact, increased when rabbit thoracic aorta smooth muscle cells or aortic segments are incubated for 2 hours with a 20 to 50 mM glucose concentration, and this increased water content occurs without a significant increase in the tissue inulin space. Osmotic-induced tissue damage could occur, and the explanation may thus still pertain, at least in part. Glucose-induced polyol accumulation in aortic smooth muscle cells is associated with a reduction in the *myo*-inositol content, and inhibition of aldose reductase (with ibuprofen) restores *myo*-inositol levels even when glucose concentration in the incubational media is kept at 50 mM.[11] Thus, as in peripheral nerve and the renal glomerulus, changes resulting from *myo*-inositol depletion may exert a deleterious influence on aortic wall metabolism in diabetes, and the relationship between the polyol pathway and the development of macrovascular complications is probably as complex as it is in other tissues.

In this context, the metabolic changes that occur when the aorta is deprived of its normal extracellular *myo*-inositol concentrations are of interest.[12] When normal rabbit aortic intima-media preparations are incubated without *myo*-inositol, oxygen uptake falls concomitant with depletion of endogenous *myo*-inositol. Comparison of [^{14}C]glycerol incorporation into aortic phosphatidylinositol in the presence versus the absence of media *myo*-inositol unmasked a restricted pool of tissue phosphatidylinositol that has rapid turnover, reflecting basal phosphatidylinositol hydrolysis. Thus, maintenance of normal plasma levels of *myo*-inositol is required to prevent inhibition of a discrete component of basal de novo phosphatidylinositol synthesis. Additionally, normal levels of *myo*-inositol are required for maintenance of a specific component of resting energy utilization by aortic tissue. This energy utilization largely derives from oxygen consumption resulting from Na/K-ATPase activity, and the resting Na/K-ATPase activity falls when the tissue is depleted of *myo*-inositol. These results link tissue *myo*-inositol content, phosphatidylinositol metabolism, and Na/K-ATPase activity, and provide insight into the relationship between these metabolic changes that has not been readily afforded by examination of the effect of diabetes on phosphatidylinositol content or metabolism in other tissues (see Chapters 4 and 5).

Other metabolic effects associated with increased flux through the polyol pathway in the aortic wall as a result of increased intracellular glucose concentration include a reduced oxygen uptake, enhanced glycolysis, and an increase in the ratio of the concentrations of lactate to pyruvate.[10] These changes are similar to those observed in human erythrocytes exposed to high glucose concentration in vitro, and may reflect alterations in the redox states of the diphosphopyridine nucleotide cofactors.[13]

Erythrocytes

The intrinsic capability of normal red blood cells to undergo shape adaptation permits them to traverse capillaries with diameters smaller than their own. This property of erythrocyte deformability depends on compositional and elastic features of the membrane, and on the composition of intracellular and plasmatic fluids. The deformability of red cells from patients with diabetes mellitus is impaired, and alterations in the filtration properties of erythrocytes have been consistently demonstrated in diabetes.[14-22] In addition to other rheologic abnormalities associated with diabetes, such as increased plasma viscosity,[18,23] decreased membrane fluidity,[19] and exaggerated erythrocyte aggregability and adhesiveness,[17,24,25] decreased erythrocyte deformability has been implicated in the pathogenesis of diabetic microvascular complications. For example, one study found that deformability was significantly less in diabetic patients with widespread complications than in those with minimal or no complications.[23] A variety of factors, including ATP or calcium levels, plasma pH, and intracellular or plasma osmolarity, can influence deformability, and changes in this red cell property that occur in diabetes have been related to abnormal membrane fluidity,[16] altered composition or saturation of membrane lipids,[26-28] and intraerythrocytic aberrations due to sorbitol accumulation[29] or increased glycosylated hemoglobin content.[14,18] In fact, deformability has been reported to be reduced in proportion to the degree of intraerythrocytic sorbitol accumulation (Figure 6-1).[29]

Erythrocytes from patients with diabetes contain significantly higher levels of sorbitol than do cells from nondiabetic subjects.[30-32] The activity of aldose reductase, measured as NADPH-oxidizing activity, is reportedly higher in red cells from diabetic patients with retinopathy or cataracts than it is in erythrocytes from suitable control patients, and shows a positive correlation with Hb A_{1c} levels in

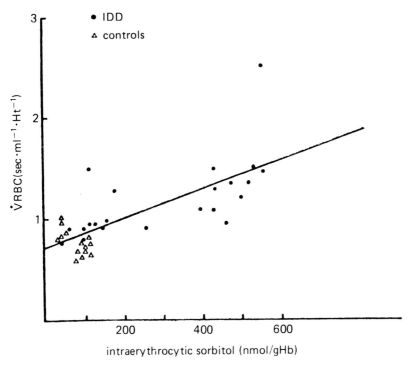

FIGURE 6-1   Correlation between red cell sorbitol and filtration index (VRBC) in control (△) and diabetic (●) subjects. Reprinted with permission from Caradente O et al: Role of red cell sorbitol as determinant of reduced erythrocyte filtrability in insulin defendant diabetes. *Acta Diabetol Lat* 1982; 19(4):359–369.

diabetic cataract patients.[33–35] Similarly, activity of the aldose reductase-like glyceraldehyde dehydrogenase is elevated in diabetic patients with retinopathy and cataract.[36] Sorbitol is also produced in normal red cells when they are incubated in a glucose-containing medium, and there is some evidence that red cells from diabetic subjects accumulate more sorbitol than do cells from normal individuals exposed in vitro to the same incubation system.[13,30,31,37] Inhibition of aldose reductase activity prevents erythrocyte accumulation of sorbitol in vitro,[38] and treatment of diabetic patients with an aldose reductase inhibitor normalizes the red cell sorbitol content.[32,39–42] However, inhibition of aldose reductase does not affect the concentration of 2,3-diphosphoglycerate (2,3-DPG) in erythrocytes or the oxygen affinity of hemoglobin.[40] This is of interest in view of the suggestion that increased polyol pathway activity decreases the ratio of NAD to NADH, thereby decreasing 2,3-DPG levels and, in turn, influencing oxyhemoglobin dissociation.[13,43] In any event, a relationship between 2,3-DPG concentration and red cell deformability has not been established. It remains to be determined whether there are other potentially deleterious metabolic effects within the erythrocyte that derive from changes in the oxidized and reduced forms of the NAD^+ and $NADP^+$ redox systems that may be initiated by enhanced polyol pathway activity.

Erythrocyte deformability is also significantly diminished in experimental diabetes.[44] Of considerable interest is the finding that oral administration of an aldose reductase inhibitor to rats with streptozotocin diabetes restores deformability, although not quite to normal levels[44,45] (Figure 6-2). This correction was seen despite comparable levels of hyperglycemia in untreated and Sorbinil-treated rats, indicating that the effect of the agent was not mediated through an influence on plasma viscosity. Further support for such

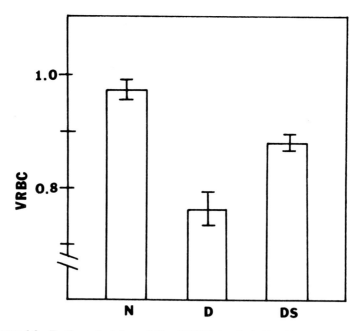

FIGURE 6-2   Erythrocyte deformability (VRBC) in whole blood from control (N), diabetic (D), and Sorbinil-treated diabetic (DS) rats. Data from Robey et al.[45]

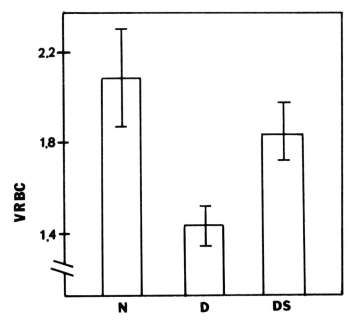

FIGURE 6-3   Deformability in washed erythrocytes from control (N), diabetic (D), and Sorbinil-treated diabetic (DS) rats. Data from Robey et al.[45]

an interpretation was offered with the finding that the defect in erythrocyte deformability in diabetes, and its correction with aldose reductase inhibition, persisted even when red cells were washed (to eliminate the hyperglycemic milieu and other plasma factors of potential influence) and resuspended before measuring their deformability (Figure 6-3). However, persistent hyperglycemia may explain the finding that erythrocyte deformability in whole blood remained less than that of control in red cells from Sorbinil-treated animals.

The mechanism by which the aldose reductase inhibitor Sorbinil prevents the decreased erythrocyte deformability associated with experimental diabetes is not clear. Sorbinil reduces the elevated red cell sorbitol levels in diabetes, and normalization of the intra-erythrocytic sorbitol content may in part explain the ability of Sorbinil to prevent reduced erythrocyte deformability. This explanation presumes that osmotic effects attendant to sorbitol accumulation contribute to the decreased deformability. However, there is some question whether absolute levels of sorbitol achieved in the red cell are sufficient to produce an osmotic effect. Intraerythrocytic sorbitol concentrations are in the micromolar range,[13,39] whereas those reported for peripheral nerve and lens are 10- to 100-fold higher, and it is therefore unlikely that polyol accumulation in the red cell is sufficient to be osmotically active. Further, the addition of Sorbinil in vitro to erythrocytes incubated with glucose (500 mg/dL) prevented the sorbitol accumulation but not the reduced deformability observed with exposure to high glucose concentration.[38] It appears that neither the reduced deformability associated with experimental diabetes nor its correction by aldose reductase inhibition can be fully explained by osmotic factors accompanying erythrocytic sorbitol accumulation, and other influences must be sought.

In contrast to findings in several other tissues (nerve, glomeruli, retinal vasculature), the elevated erythrocyte sorbitol content in diabetic samples is apparently not accompanied by a diminution in red cell *myo*-inositol levels, at least in human diabetes.[32] *myo*-Inositol levels in erythrocytes from streptozotocin-diabetic rats do not reflect changes in *myo*-inositol content in nerve or lens.[46] Although this finding suggests that *myo*-inositol depletion is not an obligatory concomitant of polyol accumulation in all cells, the reason for the relationship between these two changes in other tissues has not been clearly delineated.

References

1. Chang K, Uitto J, Rowold EA, et al: Increased collagen cross-linkages in experimental diabetes. *Diabetes* 1980; 29:778–781.

2. Williamson JR, Rowold E, Chang K, et al: Albumin permeation of new (granulation tissue) vessels is increased in diabetic rats. *Diabetes* 1984; 33(suppl 1): 3A.

3. Kilzer P, Chang K, Marvel J, et al: Albumin permeation of new vessels is increased in diabetic rats. *Diabetes* 1985; 34:333–336.

4. Williamson JR, Chang K, Rowold E, et al: Sorbinil prevents diabetes-induced increases in vascular permeability but does not alter collagen cross-linking. *Diabetes* 1985; 34:703–705.

5. Chang K, Rowold E, Marvel J, et al: Increased [^{125}I]-albumin permeation of vessels in rats fed galactose. *Diabetes* 1985; 34(suppl 1):40A.

6. Williamson JR, Chang K, Rowold F, et al: Diabetes-induced increases in vascular permeability are prevented by castration and by Sorbinil. *Diabetes* 1985; 34(suppl 1):108A.

7. Williamson JR, Chang C, Rowold E, et al: Diabetes-induced increases in vascular permeability and changes in granulation tissue levels of sorbitol, *myo*-inositol, *chiro*-inositol, and *scyllo*-inositol are prevented by Sorbinil. *Metabolism* 1986; 35(suppl 1):41–45.

8. Williamson JR, Rowold E, Chang K, et al: Sex steroid dependency of diabetes-induced changes in polyol metabolism, vascular permeability, and collagen cross-linking. *Diabetes* 1986; 35:20–27.

9. Clements RS, Morrison AD, Winegrad AI: Polyol pathway in aorta. Regulation by hormones. *Science* 1969; 166:1007–1008.

10. Morrison AD, Clements RS Jr, Winegrad AI: Effects of elevated glucose concentrations on the metabolism of the aortic wall. *J Clin Invest* 1972; 51:3114–3123.

11. Morrison AD: Linkage of polyol pathway activity and *myo*-inositol in aortic smooth muscle. *Diabetes* 1985; 34(suppl 1):12A.

12. Simmons DA, Kern EFO, Winegrad AI, et al: Basal phosphatidylinositol turnover controls aortic Na^+/K^+ ATPase activity. *J Clin Invest* 1986; 77:503–513.

13. Travis SF, Morrison AD, Clements RS Jr, et al: Metabolic alterations in the human erythrocyte produced by increases in glucose concentration. *J Clin Invest* 1971; 50:2104–2112.

14. Cataliotti R: Spectroscopic evidence of structural modifications in erythrocyte membranes of diabetic patients. *Stud Biophys* 1978; 73:199.

15. Hoare EM, Barnes AJ, Dormandy JA: Abnormal blood viscosity in diabetes mellitus and retinopathy. *Biorheology* 1978; 13:21.

16. Kamada T, Otsuji S: Low-levels of erythrocyte membrane fluidity in diabetic patients. A spin label study. *Diabetes* 1983; 32:585–591.

17. Schmid-Schonbein H, Volger E: Red cell aggregation and red cell deformability in diabetes. *Diabetes* 1976; 25:897–902.

18. McMillan DE, Utterback NG, La Puma J: Reduced erythrocyte deformability in diabetes. *Diabetes* 1978; 27:895–901.

19. Baba Y, Kai M, Kamada T, et al: Higher levels of erythrocyte membrane microviscosity in diabetes. *Diabetes* 1979; 28:1138–1140.

20. Dormandy JA, Hoare E, Colley U, et al: Clinical, haemodynamic, rheological and biochemical findings in 126 patients with intermittent claudication. *Br Med J* 1973; IV:576–581.

21. Dormandy JA, Hoare E, Dhatab AH, et al: Prognostic significance of rheological and biochemical findings in patients with intermittent claudication. *Br Med J* 1973; IV:581–583.

22. Pozza G, Cordaro C, Carandente O, et al: Study on relationship between erythrocyte filtration and other risk factors in diabetic angiopathy. *Ric Clin Lab* 1981; 11(suppl 1):317–326.

23. Barnes AJ, Locke P, Scudder PR, et al: Is hyperviscosity a treatable component of diabetic micro-circulatory disease? *Lancet* 1971; 2:789–791.

24. Satoh M, Imaizumi K, Bessho T, et al: Increased erythrocyte aggregation in diabetes and its relationship to glycosylated hemoglobin and retinopathy. *Diabetologia* 1984; 27:517–521.

25. Wautier JL, Paton RC, Wautier M-P, et al: Increased adhesion of erythrocytes to endothelial cells in diabetes mellitus and its relation to vascular complications. *N Engl J Med* 1981; 305:237–242.

26. Cooper RA: Abnormalities of cell membrane fluidity in the pathogenesis of disease. *N Engl J Med* 1977; 297:371–377.

27. Eck MG, Wynn JO, Carter WJ, et al: Fatty acid desaturation in experimental diabetes mellitus. *Diabetes* 1979; 28:479–485.

28. Clark DL, Harnel FG, Queener SF: Changes in renal phospholipid fatty acids in diabetes mellitus; correlation with changes in adenylate cyclase activity. *Lipids* 1983; 18:696–705.

29. Carandente O, Colombo R, Girardi AM, et al: Role of red cell sorbitol as determinant of reduced erythrocyte filtrability in insulin dependent diabetics. *Acta Diabetol Lat* 1982; 19(4):359–369.

30. Malone JI, Knox G, Harvey C: Sorbitol accumulation is altered in Type I (insulin-dependent) diabetes mellitus. *Diabetologia* 1984; 27:509–513.

31. Malone J, Knox G, Benford S, et al: Red cell sorbitol—an indicator of diabetic control. *Diabetes* 1980; 29:861–864.

32. Popp-Snijders C, Lomecky-Janousek MZ, Schouten JA, et al: *Myo*-inositol and sorbitol in erythrocytes from diabetic patients before and after Sorbinil treatment. *Diabetologia* 1984; 27:514–516.

33. Crabbe MJC, Basak Halder A: Affinity chromatography of bovine lens aldose reductase, and a comparison of some kinetic properties of the enzyme from lens and human erythrocyte. *Biochem Soc Trans* 1980; 8:194–195.

34. Basak Halder A, Wolff S, Ting H-H, et al: An aldose reductase from the human erythrocyte. *Biochem Soc Trans* 1980; 8:644–645.

35. Crabbe MJC, Brown AJ, Peckar CO, et al: NADPH-oxidizing activity in lens and erythrocytes in diabetic and nondiabetic patients with cataract. *Br J Ophthalmol* 1983; 67:696–699.

36. Crabbe MJC, Halder AB, Peckar CO, et al: Erythrocyte glyceraldehyde-reductase levels in diabetes with retinopathy and cataracts. *Lancet* 1980; 2:1268–1270.

37. Morrison AD, Clements RS Jr, Travis SB, et al: Glucose utilization by the polyol pathway in human erythrocytes. *Biochem Biophys Res Commun* 1970; 40:199–205.

38. Robey C, Dasmahapatra A, Cohen MP: In vitro effects of hyperglycemia and Sorbinil on erythrocyte (RBC) deformability. *Diabetes* 1986; 35:108A.

39. Malone JI, Leavengood H, Peterson MJ, et al: Red blood cell sorbitol as an indicator of polyol pathway activity. *Diabetes* 1984; 33:45–49.

40. Martyn CN, Matthews DM, Popp-Snijders C, et al: Effects of sorbinil treatment on erythrocytes and platelets of persons with diabetes. *Diabetes Care* 1986; 9:36–39.

41. Puhakainen E, Saamanen AM, Lehtinen J, et al: The effect of aldose reductase inhibitor (sorbinil) on erythrocyte sorbitol concentration in diabetic neuropathy. *Acta Endocrinol* 1983; 103(suppl 257):56.

42. Raskin P, Rosenstock J, Challis P, et al: Effect of tolrestat on RBC sorbitol levels in diabetic subjects. *Diabetes* 1985; 34(suppl 1):7A.

43. Huehns ER: Disorders of carbohydrate metabolism in the red blood corpuscle. *Clin Endocrinol Metab* 1976; 5:651–674.

44. Robey C, Dasmahapatra A, Cohen MP, et al: Sorbinil prevents decreased erythrocyte deformability in diabetes. *Diabetes* 1985; 34:161A.

45. Robey C, Dasmahapatra A, Cohen MP, et al: Sorbinil prevents decreased erythrocyte deformability in diabetes mellitus. Manuscript submitted, 1986.

46. Stockard C, Clements R: Usefulness of blood elements in the prediction of the fructose and *myo*-inositol content of nerve and lens. *Diabetes* 1984; 33(suppl 1):89A.

CHAPTER 7

Clinical Trials

Clinical studies examining the effect of aldose reductase inhibitors on symptoms and signs of diabetic neuropathy in human patients have been conducted for the past several years. To date, there are nine full reports published in the standard medical literature describing the results of these studies.[1-9] Several large-scale clinical trials, sponsored by pharmaceutical houses, to evaluate the safety and efficacy of their respective agents are either commencing, ongoing, nearing completion, or currently undergoing data analysis. However, aside from interim presentations, abstracts, and comments offered at various professional meetings or at special conferences sponsored by the involved pharmaceutical concern,[10-16] the coordinated findings of such multicenter, cooperative clinical trials are not yet available for review.

The earliest studies reported experience with alrestatin, an isoquinoline derivative developed by Ayerst Laboratories. Although this drug proved hepatotoxic, and Ayerst has replaced it with the less toxic tolrestat, it appeared to alleviate neuropathic symptoms in many of the 37 patients in whom it was used for which there is published information.[1-4] The first study gave alrestatin, 50 mg/kg of body weight per day IV in four divided doses to two patients with non-insulin-dependent diabetes, and 1 g four times per day orally for 30 days to four patients with adult-onset diabetes and severe peripheral neuropathy of 5 months' to 6 years' duration.[1] The patients receiving intravenous therapy reported marked improvement in clinical symptoms 2 days following the start of the infusions, with subjective improvement lasting up to 3 weeks after the infusions were discontinued. However, there were no significant changes in peripheral nerve conduction velocities and no objective improvements on neurologic examination in these patients. The four patients who received oral alrestatin experienced no beneficial symptomatic effect and had no objective improvements on neurologic examination or in peripheral nerve conduction velocities.

Subsequently, 10 patients between the ages of 43 and 67 years who had had diabetes for a mean duration of 14.4 years were given alrestatin, 50 mg/kg of body weight IV in four divided doses, daily for 5 days.[2] All of the patients had clinical manifestations of diabetic neuropathy, including paresthesias and muscle fatigability; seven claimed that symptoms were improved by the end of the treatment period, although there was no placebo control group. Motor nerve conduction velocities after treatment did not differ from baseline values, but posttreatment sensory conduction velocities increased substantially in four patients. The drug had no adverse effect on blood or urine chemistries.

Another study evaluated the effect of alrestatin, up to 8 g/day in divided oral doses for 12 weeks, on clinical and electrophysiologic parameters of nerve function in 14 patients, 6 of whom had insulin-dependent diabetes and 8 of whom had non-insulin-dependent diabetes.[3] The mean age of all patients receiving alrestatin was 55 years, and the mean duration of diabetes was 18.6 years. A second group of 16 patients, similarly composed and with comparable mean age and duration of diabetes, received placebo tablets for a 12-week period, and the study was conducted in a randomized, double-blind manner. Variables used to assess response included quantitative measurements of sensory thresholds for vibratory, tactile, and thermal stimuli; appreciation of warm-cold difference with a thermostimulator; motor and sensory conduction velocities; and galvanic skin response to a startle reaction. Of the 14 patients on alrestatin and the 14 patients given placebo who completed the study, all of whom had objective evidence of polyneuropathy, 7 out of 12 alrestatin-treated patients with subjective complaints at the time of entry reported improvement in symptoms, compared with 4 out of 13 placebo-treated patients reporting improvement after treatment. The mean scores for sensory impairment and discriminative sensation significantly improved in patients receiving the drug but not in those receiving placebo. Sensory thresholds, especially vibratory, improved on drug but not on placebo. Motor conduction velocities, especially in the ulnar nerve, also significantly improved with drug therapy. Galvanic skin response, a measure of autonomic function, improved with alrestatin, although not significantly. Using a summary of all the variables assessed in the evaluation of polyneuropathy in this study, the investigators concluded that signs of improvement occurred in 13 of the 14 patients treated with alrestatin, and suggested that treatment with an aldose reductase inhibitor might in the future be instituted early in the course of diabetes, "perhaps when the first clinical or even neurophysiological sign of polyneuropathy appears." Given the unknown effects of long-term inhibition of aldose reductase and the present uncertainty of the clinical benefits, such a prediction seems premature, if not ill advised.

A fourth study with alrestatin used the drug in a single-blind, non-randomized, placebo-controlled crossover trial over a 4-month period in nine patients with severe, painful diabetic neuropathy.[4] Eight patients reported subjective improvement after 3 weeks of the drug, and the five who completed 8 weeks of treatment continued to feel improved. Three of these five reported return of pretrial level of symptoms after the subsequent 8 weeks of placebo. Four patients could not complete the study because of drug toxicity (rash, nausea, change in hepatic or renal function). Treatment with alrestatin had no objective effect on motor or sensory nerve function, as assessed by conduction velocities, latency, and amplitude.

The other published clinical trials have used Sorbinil, a spirohydantoin derivative developed by Pfizer, for the treatment of symptomatic diabetic neuropathy.[5-9] Perhaps the most widely known and cited of these studies, and probably the most encouraging, was that conducted in two medical centers with 39 patients who received Sorbinil for 9 weeks in a randomized, double-blind crossover trial.[5] Nerve conduction velocities in the peroneal motor, median motor, and median sensory nerves were greater during treatment with

Sorbinil, 250 mg/day, than during the placebo period, and conduction velocities for all three nerves declined significantly within 3 weeks after the drug was discontinued. Although the magnitude of the Sorbinil effect on conduction velocities was small, the investigators pointed out that there may be both reversible and irreversible components to diabetic neuropathy, that only the former may be amenable to treatment with aldose reductase inhibitors, and that irreversibility may be a function of time.

A subsequently published double-blind, placebo-controlled crossover trial examined the effect of Sorbinil, 200 mg daily for 4 weeks, in 13 patients ranging in age from 42 to 72 years, with a mean duration of diabetes of 17.3 years.[6] Response was assessed by tests of motor, sensory, and autonomic nerve function and by patient evaluation of pain severity and sleep duration. None of the patients noted subjective improvement with Sorbinil treatment, and the drug had no significant effect on motor or sensory nerve conduction velocities, vibration perception thresholds, or beat-to-beat variation in the heart rate as a measure of autonomic function. One patient had a toxic reaction, which manifested as fever, rash, and oral ulceration, that necessitated withdrawal from the study and that resolved after discontinuing the drug. The investigators noted that their patients were older, had a longer duration of diabetes, and had more severe clinical symptoms than did the patients in whom improvement in motor conduction velocity was observed in the larger clinical trial conducted in the two centers.

A third study with Sorbinil, performed in a double-blind, randomized, placebo-controlled manner, gave the drug (200 mg daily in two doses) to 15 patients ranging in age from 35 to 68 years who had chronic painful diabetic neuropathy.[7] Treatment was evaluated by subjective assessment of change in pain severity; clinical examination of tendon reflexes and of response to touch, vibration, pain, and temperature; motor and sensory nerve electrophysiology; and cardiovascular reflex tests of autonomic nerve function. Of the 12 patients who received Sorbinil for 27 consecutive days, 10 reported symptomatic improvement while taking the drug; subjective improvement persisted in four of five patients who received placebo during the subsequent 4 weeks. Sensory impairment seemed to worsen on the drug, but tendon reflexes seemed to improve. Sensory potentials in the sural nerve were greater during drug treatment, but there was no improvement in motor nerve conduction, and sensory nerve conduction may have deteriorated. The investigators speculated that subjective response in the absence of objective electrophysiologic evidence of improvement may indicate that the pain of diabetic neuropathy reflects metabolic rather than structural neural damage. Four patients in this study experienced adverse side effects while taking Sorbinil, consisting of an erythematous maculopapular rash associated with oropharyngeal involvement in three patients, transient leukopenia in two patients, fever in one patient, and cervical lymphadenopathy in another. The rashes completely resolved within 10 days after the drug was discontinued. However, adverse reactions to Sorbinil appear to be a significant problem. In a group of 45 patients exposed to the drug, 16 patients were noted to have drug-related problems.[17] In 11 of these patients, such problems took the form of a febrile illness variably associated with myalgia, lymphadenopathy, a maculopapular rash, transient neutropenia, thrombocytopenia, mild derangement of liver function tests, and a worsening of glycemic control. Although symptomatic recovery occurred within 10 days after discontinuing the drug, abnormalities in tests of liver function persisted in some patients.

In another study, 11 patients with severely painful diabetic neuropathy were treated with a single daily dose of Sorbinil, 250 mg, for periods ranging from 10 days to 5 weeks.[8] Eight of the patients received placebo, in single-blind fashion, for 4 days to 3 weeks, before taking the drug. Response was assessed by subjective rating on a pain scale, measurement of motor and sensory nerve conduction velocities, and evaluation of autonomic function by electrocardiographic monitoring of expiration/inspiration ratios of the heart rate. Eight patients reported moderate to marked relief of symptoms, and four patients with diabetic amyotrophy experienced improvement in proximal muscle strength. Motor and sensory conduction velocities improved in these four patients. Autonomic nerve function improved in six of seven patients in whom it was tested. However, a letter to the editor regarding this study noted that the patients who improved most had forms of painful neuropathy known to undergo spontaneous remission, and that of the total of 21 estimates of nerve conduction in individual patients, 38% showed deterioration during treatment.[18] No toxic effects of the drug were noted in this group of 11 patients, although a twelfth patient had a macular-erythematous rash on the sixth day of treatment and was withdrawn from the study.

The most recent publication describing results of treatment with Sorbinil reports on symptomatic responses and electrophysiologic and neurophysiologic parameters in 37 patients with diabetic neuropathy, 18 of whom received 50 mg daily and 19 of whom received 200 mg daily for 4 weeks.[9] Although the drug produced no significant effect in vibratory perception thresholds or on nerve conduction velocities or amplitudes, nine of the patients receiving 200 mg/day reported subjective improvement. Five of the patients treated with 50 mg/day, believed to be an inadequate therapeutic dose, also reported an improved sense of well-being while taking the drug. Retinal function, evaluated by adaptation to darkness with nyctometry, did not change during treatment with Sorbinil. No change in blood chemistries was observed, and there were no reported clinical side effects of the drug. The investigators noted that their patients were older (mean age 54 years) and had a longer mean duration of diabetes (17 years) than did the group of patients in the two-center study who showed improvement in nerve conduction velocity after receiving Sorbinil. The mean age of that group was 48 years, and the mean duration of diabetes was 9.8 years.

It appears that Sorbinil produces inconsistent, if any, improvement in objective parameters of nerve dysfunction, but can result in symptomatic improvement, the reasons for which are not entirely clear. Alleviation of symptoms and modest improvement in tests of nerve function, if they occur, are most likely to be seen in younger diabetic patients in whom the duration of diabetes and of neuropathic symptoms has not been unduly long. The question of toxicity, particularly desquamative dermatitis, is of concern to Pfizer, the Food and Drug Administration, and the physicians and patients who have used this agent, while the question of efficacy has cast doubt on the ultimate therapeutic role of aldose reductase inhibitors in general. Nevertheless, it is clear from the number of pharmaceutical houses developing aldose reductase inhibitors, undertaking programs for their clinical testing, and competitively racing for their market launch that discussion of these drugs will continue in the medical and lay news for some time to come.

References

1. Gabbay KH, Spack N, Loo S, et al: Aldose reductase inhibitors: Studies with alrestatin. *Metabolism* 1979; 28(suppl 1):471–476.

2. Culebras A, Alio J, Herrara JL, et al: Effect of an aldose reductase inhibitor on diabetic peripheral neuropathy. *Arch Neurol* 1981; 38:133–134.

3. Fagius J, Jameson S: Effects of aldose reductase inhibitor treatment in diabetic polyneuropathy—a clinical and neurophysiological study. *J Neurol Neurosurg Psychiatry* 1981; 44:999–1001.

4. Handlesman DJ, Turtle JR: Clinical trial of an aldose reductase inhibitor in diabetic neuropathy. *Diabetes* 1981; 30:459–464.

5. Judzewitsch RG, Jaspan JB, Polonsky KS, et al: Aldose reductase inhibitor improves nerve conduction velocity in diabetic patients. *N Engl J Med* 1983; 308:119–125.

6. Lewin IG, O'Brien IAD, Morgan MH, et al: Clinical and neurophysiological studies with the aldose reductase inhibitor, Sorbinil, in symptomatic diabetic neuropathy. *Diabetologia* 1984; 26:445–448.

7. Young RJ, Ewing DJ, Clarke BF: A controlled trial of Sorbinil, an aldose reductase inhibitor, in chronic painful diabetic neuropathy. *Diabetes* 1983; 32:938–942.

8. Jaspan J, Herold K, Maselli R, et al: Treatment of severe painful diabetic neuropathy with an aldose reductase inhibitor: Relief of pain and improved somatic and autonomic nerve function. *Lancet* 1983; 2:758–762.

9. Christensen JEJ, Varnek L, Gregersen G: The effect of an aldose reductase inhibitor (Sorbinil) on diabetic neuropathy and neural function of the retina. *Acta Neurol Scand* 1985; 71:164–167.

10. Fagius J, Jameson S: Treatment of diabetic polyneuropathy with an aldose reductase inhibitor—a clinical and neurophysiological study. *Acta Neurol Scand* 1980; 62(suppl 6):125A.

11. Gonzalez ER: Can aldose reductase inhibition ameliorate diabetic neuropathy? *JAMA* 1981; 248:1169–1170.

12. Hotta N, Kakuta H, Kimura M, et al: Experimental and clinical trial of aldose reductase inhibitor in diabetic neuropathy. *Diabetes* 1983; 32(suppl 1):98A.

13. Lehtinen JM, Hjvonen SK, Uusitupa M, et al: The effect of an aldose reductase inhibitor (Sorbinil) on diabetic neuropathy. *Diabetologia* 1984; 27:303A.

14. Proceedings of Aldose Reductase Inhibitor Symposium, London, 1984. *Diabetic Medicine*, vol 2, 1985.

15. Proceedings of Puerto Rico Conference on Sorbinil and Diabetic Complications. *Metabolism* (suppl), April 1986.

16. Koglin L, Clark C, Ryder S, et al: The results of the long-term open-label administration of ALREASE™ in the treatment of diabetic neuropathy. *Diabetes* 1985; 34(suppl 1):202A.

17. Martyn CN, Matthews DM, Popp-Snijders C, et al: Effects of Sorbinil treatment on erythrocytes and platelets of persons with diabetes. *Diabetes Care* 1985; 9:36–39.

18. Young RJ, Matthews DM, Clarke BF, et al: Aldose reductase inhibition for diabetic neuropathy (letter to the editor). *Lancet* 1983; 2:969.

Bibliography

Addison DJ, Garner A, Ashton N: Degeneration of intramural pericytes in diabetic retinopathy. *Br Med J* 1970; 1:264–266.

Akagi Y, Kador PF, Kuwabara T, et al: Aldose reductase localization in human retinal mural cells. *Invest Ophthalmol Vis Sci* 1983; 24:1516–1519.

Akagi Y, Yajima Y, Kador PF, et al: Localization of aldose reductase in the human eye. *Diabetes* 1984; 33:562–566.

Asbury AK, Aldridge H, Hershberg R, et al: Oculomotor palsy in diabetes mellitus: A clinico-pathologic study. *Brain* 1970; 93:555–566.

Ashton N: The blood-retinal barrier and vaso-glial relationships in retinal disease. *Trans Ophthalmol Soc UK* 1965; 85:199–230.

Attwood MA, Doughty CC: Purification and properties of calf liver aldose reductase. *Biochim Biophys Acta* 1974; 370:358–368.

Baba Y, Kai M, Kamada T, et al: Higher levels of erythrocyte membrane microviscosity in diabetes. *Diabetes* 1979; 28:1138–1140.

Barbosa J: Plasma *myo*-inositol in diabetics including patients with renal allografts. *Acta Diabetol Lat* 1978; 15:95–101.

Barnett PA, Gonzalez RG, Chylack LT, et al: The effect of oxidation on sorbitol pathway kinetics. *Diabetes* 1986; 35:426–432.

Barnes AJ, Locke P, Scudder PR, et al: Is hyperviscosity a treatable component of diabetic microcirculatory disease? *Lancet* 1971; 2:789–791.

Basak Halder A, Wolff S, Ting H-H, et al: An aldose reductase from the human erythrocyte. *Biochem Soc Trans* 1980; 8:644–645.

Behse F, Buchthal F, Carlson FI: Nerve biopsy and conduction studies in diabetic neuropathy. *J Neurol Neurosurg Psychiatry* 1977; 40:1072–1082.

Bell ME, Peterson RG, Eichberg J: Metabolism of phospholipids in peripheral nerve from rats with chronic streptozotocin-induced diabetes: Increased turn-over of phosphatidyl-4,5-bisphosphate. *J Neurochem* 1982; 39:192–200.

Berti-Mattera L, Peterson R, Bell M, et al: Effect of hyperglycemia and its prevention by insulin treatment on the incorporation of [^{32}P] into polyphosphoinositides and other phospholipids in peripheral nerve of the streptozotocin diabetic rat. *J Neurochem* 1985; 45:1692–1698.

Beyer-Mears A, Cruz E: Reversal of diabetic cataract by Sorbinil, an aldose reductase inhibitor. *Diabetes* 1985; 34:15–21.

Beyer-Mears A, Cruz E, Dillon P, et al: Diabetic renal hypertrophy diminished by aldose reductase inhibition. *Fed Proc* 1983; 42:505.

Beyer-Mears A, Cruz E, Nicolas-Alexandre J, et al: Xanthone-2-carboxylic acid effect on lens growth, hydration and proteins during diabetic cataract development. *Arch Int Pharmacodyn* 1982; 259:166–176.

Beyer-Mears A, Cruz E, Nicholas-Alexandre J, et al: Sorbinil protection of lens protein components and cell hydration during diabetic cataract formation. *Pharmacology* 1982; 24:193–200.

Beyer-Mears A, Farnsworth PN: Diminished diabetic cataractogenesis by quercitin. *Exp Eye Res* 1979; 28:709–716.

Beyer-Mears A, Ku L, Cohen MP: Glomerular polyol accumulation in diabetes and its prevention by oral Sorbinil. *Diabetes* 1984; 33:604–607.

Beyer-Mears A, Nicolas-Alexandre J, Cruz E: Sorbinil inhibition of renal aldose reductase. *Fed Proc* 1983; 42:858.

Beyer-Mears A, Varagiannis E, Cruz E: Effect of Sorbinil on reversal of proteinuria. *Diabetes* 1985; 35(suppl 1):101A.

Bhuyan KC, Bhuyan DK, Katzin DM: Amizol-induced cataract and inhibition of lens catalase in rabbit. *Ophthalmic Res* 1973; 5:236–247.

Bischoff A: Morphology of diabetic neuropathy. *Horm Metab Res* 1980; 9(suppl):18–28.

Blankenship GW, Machemer R: Pars plana vitrectomy for the management of severe diabetic retinopathy: An analysis of results five years following surgery. *Ophthalmology (Rochester)* 1978; 85:553–559.

Boghosian RA, McGuiness ET: Affinity purification and properties of porcine brain aldose reductase. *Biochim Biophys Acta* 1979; 567:278–286.

Boghosian RA, McGuiness ET: Pig brain aldose reductase: A kinetic study using centrifugal fast analyzer. *Int J Biochem* 1981; 13:909–914.

Boot-Hanford R, Heath H: The effects of aldose reductase inhibitors on the metabolism of cultured monkey kidney epithelial cells. *Biochem Pharmacol* 1981; 30:3065–3069.

Bous F, Hockwin O, Ohrloff C, et al: Investigation on phosphofructokinase (EC 2.7.1.11) in bovine lens in dependence on age, topographic distribution and water soluble protein fractions. *Exp Eye Res* 1977; 24:383–389.

Branlant G: Properties of an aldose reductase from pig lens. *Eur J Biochem* 1982; 129:99–104.

Brightbill FS, Myers FL, Bresnick GN: Postvitrectomy keratopathy. *Am J Ophthalmol* 1978; 85:651–655.

Brismar T, Sima AAF: Changes in nodal function in nerve fibres of the spontaneously diabetic BB-Wistar rat: Potential clamp analysis. *Acta Physiol Scand* 1981; 113:499–506.

Broekhuyse RM: Changes in *myo*-inositol permeability in the lens due to cataractous conditions. *Biochem Biophys Acta* 1968; 163:269–272.

Brown MJ, Sumner AJ, Greene DA, et al: Distal neuropathy in experimental diabetes. *Ann Neurol* 1980; 8:168–178.

Brownlee M, Spiro RG: Glomerular basement membrane metabolism in the diabetic rat. *In vivo* studies. *Diabetes* 1979; 28:121–125.

Buzney SM, Frank RN, Varma SD, et al: Aldose reductase in retinal mural cells. *Invest Ophthalmol Vis Sci* 1977; 16:392–396.

Carandente O, Colombo R, Girardi AM, et al: Role of red cell sorbitol as determinant of reduced erythrocyte filtrability in insulin dependent diabetics. *Acta Diabetol Lat* 1982; 19(4):359–369.

Cataliotti R: Spectroscopic evidence of structural modifications in erythrocyte membranes of diabetic patients. *Stud Biophys* 1978; 73:199.

Chand D, El-Aguizy K, Richards RD, et al: Sugar cataracts in vitro: Implications of oxidative stress and aldose reductase I. *Exp Eye Res* 1982; 35:491–497.

Chang K, Rowold E, Marvel J, et al: Increased [^{125}I]-albumin permeation of vessels in rats fed galactose. *Diabetes* 1985; 34(suppl 1):40A.

Chang K, Uitto J, Rowold EA, et al: Increased collagen cross-linkages in experimental diabetes. *Diabetes* 1980; 29:778–781.

Chaudhry PS, Cabrera J, Juliani HR, et al: Inhibition of human lens aldose reductase by flavinoids, sulindac and indomethacin. *Biochem Pharmacol* 1983; 32:1995–1998.

Chen HM, Chylack LT Jr: Factors affecting the rate of lactate production in rat lens. *Ophthalmic Res* 1977; 9:381–387.

Chiou SH, Chylack LT, Bunn HF, et al: Role of nonenzymatic glycosylation in experimental cataract formation. *Biochem Biophys Res Commun* 1980; 95:894–901.

Chochinov RH, Ullyot LE, Moorhouse JA: Sensory perception thresholds in patients with juvenile diabetes and their close relatives. *N Engl J Med* 1972; 286:1233–1237.

Christensen JEJ, Varnek L, Gregersen G: The effect of an aldose reductase inhibitor (Sorbinil) on diabetic neuropathy and neural function of the retina. *Acta Neurol Scand* 1985; 71:164–167.

Chylack LT, Cheng H-M: Sugar metabolism in the crystalline lens. *Surv Ophthalmol* 1978; 23:26–34.

Chylack LT Jr, Henriques HF, Cheng H-M, et al: Efficacy of alrestatin, an aldose reductase inhibitor, in human diabetic and nondiabetic lenses. *Ophthalmology* 1978; 86:1579.

Chylack LT Jr, Henriques H, Tung W: Inhibition of sorbitol production in human lenses by an aldose reductase inhibitor. *Invest Ophthalmol vis Sci* 1978; 17(ARVO Suppl):300.

Chylack LT, Kinoshita JH: Biochemical evaluation of a cataract induced in high glucose medium. *Invest Ophthalmol Vis Sci* 1969; 8:401–412.

Clark DL, Harnel FG, Queener SF: Changes in renal phospholipid fatty acids in diabetes mellitus; correlation with changes in adenylate cyclase activity. *Lipids* 1983; 18:696–705.

Clements RS: Diabetic neuropathy—Newer concepts in etiology. *Diabetes* 1979; 28:604–611.

Clements RS, Bell DHS: Diagnostic, pathogenetic and therapeutic aspects of diabetic neuropathy. *Spec Topics Endocrinol Metab* 1982; 3:1–43.

Clements RS, Diethelm AG: The metabolism of *myo*-inositol by the human kidney. *J Lab Clin Med* 1979; 93:210–219.

Clements RS, Morrison AD, Winegrad AI: Polyol pathway in aorta. Regulation by hormones. *Science* 1969; 166:1007–1008.

Clements RS, Reynertson RH, Starnes WS: *Myo*-inositol metabolism in diabetes mellitus. *Diabetes* 1974; 23:348A.

Clements RS, Reynertson R: *Myo*-inositol metabolism in diabetes mellitus. Effect of insulin treatment. *Diabetes* 1977; 26:215–221.

Clements RS, Stockard CR: Abnormal sciatic nerve *myo*-inositol metabolism in the streptozotocin-diabetic rat. Effects of insulin treatment. *Diabetes* 1980; 29:227–235.

Clements R, Winegrad AI: Purification of alditol NADP oxidoreductase from human placenta. *Biochem Biophys Res Commun* 1972; 47:1473–1480.

Cogan DG, Kinoshita JH, Kador PF, et al: Aldose reductase and complications of diabetes. *Ann Intern Med* 1984; 101:82–91.

Cogan DG, Toussaint D, Kuwabara T: Retinal vascular patterns. IV. Diabetic retinopathy. *Arch Ophthalmol* 1976; 66:366–372.

Cohen AH, Mampaso F, Zamboui L: Glomerular podocyte degeneration in human renal disease. *Lab Invest* 1977; 37:40–42.

Cohen MP: Glomerular basement membrane synthesis in streptozotocin diabetes, in Podolsky S, Viswanathan M (eds): *Secondary Diabetes, the Spectrum of the Diabetic Syndromes*, pp 541–551. New York, Raven Press, 1980.

Cohen MP: *Diabetes and Protein Glycosylation: Measurement and Biologic Relevance*. New York, Springer-Verlag, 1986.

Cohen MP, Dasmahapatra A, Shapiro E: Reduced glomerular sodium/potassium adenosine triphosphatase activity in acute streptozotocin diabetes. *Diabetes* 1985; 34:1071–1074.

Cohen MP, Dasmahapatra A, Wu VY: Deposition of basement membrane in vitro by normal and diabetic renal glomeruli. *Nephron* 1981; 27:146–151.

Cohen MP, Khalifa A: Renal glomerular collagen synthesis in streptozotocin diabetes. Reversal of increased basement membrane synthesis with insulin therapy. *Biochim Biophys Acta* 1977; 500:395–404.

Cohen MP, Klepser H: Binding of an aldose reductase inhibitor to renal glomeruli. *Biochem Biophys Res Commun* 1985; 129:530–535.

Cohen MP, Klepser H, Cua E: Effect of diabetes and Sorbinil treatment on phospholipid metabolism in rat glomeruli. *Biochim Biophys Acta* 1986; 876:226–232.

Cohen MP, Surma ML: [^{35}S]-Sulfate incorporation into glomerular basement membrane glycosaminoglycans is decreased in experimental diabetes. *J Lab Clin Med* 1981; 98:715–722.

Cohen MP, Surma ML: Effect of diabetes on in vivo metabolism of [^{35}S]-labeled glomerular basement membrane. *Diabetes* 1984; 33:8–12.

Cohen MP, Surma ML, Wu VY: In vivo biosynthesis and turnover of glomerular basement membrane in diabetic rats. *Am J Physiol* 1982; 242:F385–F389.

Cohen MP, Urdanivia E, Surma M, et al: Increased glycosylation of glomerular basement membrane collagen in diabetes. *Biochem Biophys Res Commun* 1980; 95:765–769.

Cohen MP, Wu VY: Identification of specific amino acids in diabetic glomerular basement membrane subject to nonenzymatic glycosylation in vivo. *Biochem Biophys Res Commun* 1984; 100:1549–1554.

Conrad SM, Doughty CC: Comparative studies on aldose reductase from bovine rat and human lens. *Biochim Biophys Acta* 1982; 708:348–357.

Cooper RA: Abnormalities of cell membrane fluidity in the pathogenesis of disease. *N Engl J Med* 1977; 297:371–377.

Corder CN, Braughler JM, Culp PA: Quantitative histochemistry of the sorbitol pathway in glomeruli and small arteries of human diabetic kidney. *Folia Histochem Cytochem (Krakow)* 1979; 17:137–146.

Corder CN, Collins JG, Brannon TS, et al: Aldose reductase and sorbitol dehydrogenase distribution in rat kidney. *J Histochem Cytochem* 1977; 25:1–8.

Cotlier E: *Myo*-inositol active transport by the crystalline lens. *Invest Opthalmol* 1970; 9:681–691.

Cotlier E: Aspirin effect on cataract formation in patients with rheumatoid arthritis alone or combined with diabetes. *Int Ophthalmol* 1981; 3:173–179.

Cotlier E, Fagadau W, Cicchetti DV: Methods for evaluation of medical therapy of senile and diabetic cataracts. *Trans Ophthalmol Soc UK* 1982; 102:416–422.

Cotlier E, Sharma YR, Niven T, et al: Distribution of salicylate in lens and intraocular fluids and its effect on cataract formation. *Am J Med* 1983; 75(6A):83–90.

Crabbe MJC, Basak Halder A: Affinity chromatography of bovine lens aldose reductase, and a comparison of some kinetic properties of the enzyme from lens and human erythrocyte. *Biochem Soc Trans* 1980; 8:194–195.

Crabbe MJC, Brown AJ, Peckar CO, et al: NADPH-oxidizing activity in lens and erythrocytes in diabetic and nondiabetic patients with cataract. *Br J Ophthalmol* 1983; 67:696–699.

Crabbe MJC, Freeman G, Halder AB, et al: The inhibition of bovine lens aldose reductase by Clinoril, its absorption into the human red cell and its effect on human red cell aldose reductase activity. *Ophthalmic Res* 1985; 17:85–89.

Crabbe MJC, Halder AB: Kinetic behavior under defined assay conditions for bovine lens aldose reductase. *Clin Biochem* 1979; 12:281–283.

Crabbe MJC, Halder AB, Peckar CO, et al: Erythrocyte glyceraldehyde-reductase levels in diabetes with retinopathy and cataracts. *Lancet* 1980; 2:1268–1270.

Creighton MO, Trevithick JR: Cortical cataract formation prevented by vitamin E and glutathione. *Exp Eye Res* 1979; 29:689–693.

Cromlish JA, Flynn TG: Pig muscle aldehyde reductase. Identity of pig muscle aldehyde reductase with pig lens aldose reductase and with low Km aldehyde reductase of pig brain and pig kidney. *J Biol Chem* 1983; 258:3583–3586.

Cromlish JA, Flynn TG: Purification and characterization of two aldose reductase isoenzymes from rabbit muscle. *J Biol Chem* 1983; 256:3416–3424.

Culebras A, Alio J, Herrera JL, et al: Effect of an aldose reductase inhibitor on diabetic peripheral neuropathy. *Arch Neurol* 1981; 38:133–134.

Cunha-Vaz J, DeAbreau JRF, Campos AJ, et al: Early breakdown of the blood-retinal barrier in diabetes. *Br J Ophthalmol* 1975; 59:649–656.

Cunha-Vaz JG, Mota C, Leite E, et al: Effect of aldose reductase inhibitors on the blood retinal barrier in early diabetic retinopathy. *Diabetes* 1985; 34(suppl 1): 109A.

Cunha-Vaz JG, Mota CC, Leite EC, et al: Effect of sulindac on the permeability of the blood retinal barrier in early diabetic retinopathy. *Arch Ophthalmol* 1985; 103:1307–1311.

Cunha-Vaz JG, Mota CC, Leite EC, et al: Effect of Sorbinil on blood-retinal barrier in early diabetic retinopathy. *Diabetes* 1986; 35:574–578.

Das B, Hair GA, Srivastava SK: Activated and unactivated forms of aldose reductase and its role in diabetic complications. *Fed Proc* 1985; 44:1391(A).

Das B, Srivastava SK: Purification and properties of aldose reductase and aldehyde reductase II from human erythrocyte. *Arch Biochem Biophys* 1985; 238:670–679.

Das B, Srivastava SK: Activation of aldose reductase from tissues. *Diabetes* 1985; 34:1145–1151.

Datiles M, Fukui H, Kuwabara T, et al: Galactose cataract prevention with Sorbinil, an aldose reductase inhibitor: A light microscopic study. *Invest Ophthalmol Vis Sci* 1982; 22:174–179.

Datiles MD, Kador PF, Fukui HN, et al: Corneal re-epithelialization in galactosemic rats. *Invest Ophthalmol Vis Sci* 1983; 24:563–569.

Daughaday WH, Larner JL: The renal excretion of inositol in normal and diabetic human beings. *J Clin Invest* 1954; 33:326–332.

Davies PD, Duncan G, Pynsent PB, et al: Aqueous humor glucose concentration in cataract patients and its effect on the lens. *Exp Eye Res* 1984; 39:605–609.

Dische Z, Zil H: Studies on the oxidation of cysteine to cystine in lens protein during cataract formation. *Am J Ophthalmol* 1951; 34:104–113.

Dons RF, Doughty CC: Isolation and characterization of aldose reductase from calf brain. *Biochim Biophys Acta* 1976; 452:1–12.

Dormandy JA, Hoare E, Colley U, et al: Clinical, haemodynamic, rheological and biochemical findings in 126 patients with intermittent claudication. *Br Med J* 1973; IV:576–581.

Dormandy JA, Hoare E, Dhatab AH, et al: Prognostic significance of rheological and biochemical findings in patients with intermittent claudication. *Br Med J* 1973; IV:581–583.

Doughty CC, Lee S-M, Conrad S, et al: Kinetic mechanism and structural properties of lens aldose reductase, in Weiner H, Wermuth B (eds): *Enzymology of Carbonyl Metabolism: Aldehyde Dehydrogenase and Aldo/Keto Reductase*, pp 223–242. New York, Alan R. Liss, 1982.

Dreyfus PM, Hakim S, Adams RD: Diabetic ophthalmoplegia: Report of a case with postmortem study and comments on vascular supply of human oculomotor nerve. *Arch Neurol Psychiatry* 1957; 77:337–349.

Duke-Elder WS: Changes in refraction in diabetes mellitus. *Br J Ophthalmol* 1925; 9:167–187.

Dvornik D, Simard-Duquesne N, Kraml M, et al: Polyol accumulation in galactosemic and diabetic rats: Control by an aldose reductase inhibitor. *Science* 1973; 182:1146–1148.

Dyck PJ, Lamberg EH, Windebank AJ, et al: Acute hyperosmolar hyperglycemia causes axonal shrinkage and reduced nerve conduction velocity. *Exp Neurol* 1981; 71:507–514.

Dyck PJ, Sherman WR, Hallcher LM, et al: Human diabetic endoneurial sorbitol, fructose and *myo*-inositol related to sural nerve morphometry. *Ann Neurol* 1980; 8:590–596.

Eck MG, Wynn JO, Carter WJ, et al: Fatty acid desaturation in experimental diabetes mellitus. *Diabetes* 1979; 28:479–485.

El-Aguizy HK, Richards RD, Varma SD: Sugar cataracts in mongolian gerbil (*Meriones unguiculatus*). *Exp Eye Res* 1983; 36:839–844.

Engerman RL, Kern TS: Experimental galactosemia produces diabetic-like retinopathy. *Diabetes* 1984; 33:97–100.

Fagius J: Microneurographic findings in diabetic polyneuropathy with special reference to sympathetic nerve activity. *Diabetologia* 1982; 23:415–420.

Fagius J, Jameson S: Treatment of diabetic polyneuropathy with an aldose reductase inhibitor—a clinical neurophysiological study. *Acta Neurol Scand* 1980; 62(suppl 6):125.

Fagius J, Jameson S: Effects of aldose reductase inhibitor treatment in diabetic polyneuropathy—a clinical and neurophysiological study. *J Neurol Neurosurg Psychiatry* 1981; 44:999–1001.

Farese RV: Phosphoinositide metabolism and hormone action. *Endocr Rev* 1983; 4:78–95.

Faulborn J, Conway BP, Machemer R: Surgical complications of pars plana vitreous surgery. *Ophthalmology (Rochester)* 1978; 85:116–125.

Feldman HB, Szczepanik PA, Harne P, et al: Stereospecificity of the hydrogen transfer catalyzed by human placental aldose reductase. *Biochim Biophys Acta* 1977; 480:14–20.

Finegold D, Lattimer SA, Nolle S, et al: Polyol pathway activity and *myo*-inositol metabolism. A suggested relationship in the pathogenesis of diabetic neuropathy. *Diabetes* 1983; 32:988–992.

Finegold DN, Nolle SS, Lattimer S, et al: Alterations in renal ouabain sensitive Na/K-ATPase activity in streptozotocin diabetes. *Clin Res* 1984; 32:395A.

Foulks GN, Thoft RA, Perry HD, et al: Factors related to corneal epithelial complications after closed vitrectomy in diabetics. *Arch Ophthalmol* 1979; 97:1076–1078.

Friend J, Snip RC, Kiorpes TC, et al: Insulin insensitivity and sorbitol production of the normal rabbit corneal epithelium in vitro. *Invest Ophthalmol Vis Sci* 1980; 19:913–919.

Fukuma M, Carpentier J-L, Orci L, et al: An alteration in internodal myelin membrane structure in large sciatic nerve fibres in rats with acute streptozotocin diabetes and impaired nerve conduction velocity. *Diabetologia* 1978; 15:65–72.

Fukushi H, Merola L, Kinoshita JH: Altering the course of cataracts in diabetic rats. *Invest Ophthalmol Vis Sci* 1980; 19:313–315.

Fukushi H, Merola LO, Tanaka M, et al: Reepithelialization of denuded corneas in diabetic rats. *Exp Eye Res* 1980; 31:611–621.

Gabbay KH: Purification and immunological identification of bovine retinal aldose reductase. *Isr J Med Sci* 1972; 8:1626–1628.

Gabbay KH: The sorbitol pathway and complications of diabetes. *N Engl J Med* 1973; 288:831–836.

Gabbay KH: Hyperglycemia, polyol metabolism and complications of diabetes. *Annu Rev Med* 1975; 26:521–536.

Gabbay KH, Cathcart ES: Purification and immunologic identification of aldose reductases. *Diabetes* 1974; 23:460–468.

Gabbay KH, Kinoshita JH: Growth hormone, sorbitol, and diabetic capillary disease. *Lancet* 1971; 1:913.

Gabbay KH, Merola LO, Field RA: Sorbitol pathway: Presence in nerve and cord with substrate accumulation in diabetes. *Science* 1966; 151:209–210.

Gabbay KH, O'Sullivan JB: The sorbitol pathway in diabetes and galactosemia: Enzyme and substrate localization. *Diabetes* 1968; 17:239–243.

Gabbay KH, O'Sullivan JB: The sorbitol pathway in diabetes and galactosemia: Enzyme and substrate localization and changes in the kidney. *Diabetes* 1968; 17:300A.

Gabbay KH, Snider JJ: Nerve conduction defect in galactose-fed rats. *Diabetes* 1972; 21:295–300.

Gabbay KH, Spack N, Loo S, et al: Aldose reductase inhibitors: studies with alrestatin. *Metabolism* 1979; 28(suppl 1):471–476.

Garner MH, Spector A: Selective oxidation of cysteine and methionine in normal cataractous lens. *Proc Natl Acad Sci USA* 1980; 77:1274–1277.

Gillon KRW, Hawthorne JN: Sorbitol, inositol and nerve conduction in diabetes. *Life Sci* 1983; 32:1943–1947.

Gillon KRW, Hawthorne JN, Tomlinson DR: *Myo*-inositol and sorbitol metabolism in relation to peripheral nerve function in experimental diabetes in the rat: The effect of aldose reductase inhibition. *Diabetologia* 1983; 25:365–371.

Goil MM, Harpur RP: Aldose reductase and sorbitol dehydrogenase in the muscle of *Ascaris suum* (Nematoda). *Parasitology* 1978; 77:97–102.

Goldfarb SA, Simmons DA, Kern E: Amelioration of glomerular hyperfiltration in acute experimental diabetes by dietary *myo*-inositol and by an aldose reductase inhibitor. *Clin Res* 1986; 34:725A.

Gonzalez ER: Can aldose reductase inhibition ameliorate diabetic neuropathy? *JAMA* 1981; 246:1169–1170.

Gonzalez AM, Sochor M, McLean P: Effect of experimental diabetes on glycolytic intermediates and regulation of phosphofructokinase in rat lens. *Biochem Biophys Res Commun* 1980; 95:1173–1179.

Gonzalez AM, Sochor M, McLean P: The effect of an aldose reductase inhibitor (Sorbinil) on the level of metabolites in lenses of diabetic rats. *Diabetes* 1983; 32:482–485.

Gonzalez AM, Sochor M, Rowles PM, et al: Sequential biochemical and structural changes occurring in rat lens during cataract formation in experimental diabetes. *Diabetologia* 1981; 21:5.

Goosey JD, Zigler JS Jr, Kinoshita JH: Cross-linking of lens crystallins in a photodynamic system. A singlet oxygen mediated process. *Science* 1980; 208:1278–1279.

Grachetti A: Axoplasmol transport of noradenaline in the sciatic nerves of spontaneously diabetic mice. *Diabetologia* 1979; 16:191–199.

Graf RJ, Halter JB, Halar E, et al: Nerve conduction abnormalities in untreated maturity-onset diabetes: Relation to levels of fasting plasma glucose and glycosylated hemoglobin. *Ann Intern Med* 1979; 90:298–303.

Greene DA, DeJesus PV, Winegrad AI: Effects of insulin and dietary *myo*-inositol on impaired peripheral motor nerve conduction velocities in acute streptozotocin diabetes. *J Clin Invest* 1975; 55:1326–1336.

Greene D, Lattimer SA: Sodium and energy-dependent uptake of *myo*-inositol by rabbit peripheral nerve. *J Clin Invest* 1982; 70:1009–1018.

Greene DA, Lattimer SA: Impaired rat sciatic nerve sodium-potassium ATPase in acute streptozotocin diabetes and its correction by dietary *myo*-inositol supplementation. *J Clin Invest* 1983; 72:1058–1063.

Greene DA, Lattimer SA: Impaired energy utilization and sodium-potassium ATPase in diabetic peripheral nerve. *Am J Physiol* 1984; 246:E311–E318.

Greene DA, Lattimer SA: Action of sorbinil in diabetic peripheral nerve. Relationship of polyol (sorbitol) pathway inhibition to a *myo*-inositol mediated defect in sodium-potassium ATPase activity. *Diabetes* 1984; 33:712–716.

Greene DA, Lattimer SA: Protein kinase C agonists acutely normalize ouabain-inhibitable respiration in diabetic rabbit nerve. *Diabetes* 1986; 35:242–245.

Greene DA, Lattimer SA, Sima AAF: Acute paranodal nerve fiber swelling and conduction slowing in the insulin-deficient BB rat reflects *myo*-inositol depletion and Na/K-ATPase deficiency rather than sorbitol accumulation. *Clin Res* 1986; 34:683A.

Greene DA, Lewis RA, Lattimer SA, et al: Selective effects of *myo*-inositol administration on sciatic and tibial motor nerve conduction parameters in the streptozotocin-diabetic rat. *Diabetes* 1982; 31:573–578.

Greene DA, Winegrad AI: In vitro studies of the substrates for energy production and the effects of insulin on glucose utilization in the neural components of peripheral nerve. *Diabetes* 1979; 28:878–887.

Greene DA, Winegrad AI: Effects of acute experimental diabetes on composite energy metabolism in peripheral nerve axons and Schwann cells. *Diabetes* 1981; 30:967–974.

Halder AB, Crabbe MJCC: Inhibition of aldose reductase by phenylglyoxal, diethylpyrocarbonate and thiol modifiers. *Biochem Soc Trans* 1982; 10:401–403.

Halder AB, Crabbe MJC: Bovine lens aldehyde reductase (aldose reductase). Purification, kinetics and mechanism. *Biochem J* 1984; 219:33–39.

Halder AB, Wolff S, Ting H-H, et al: An aldose reductase from human erythrocyte. *Biochem Soc Trans* 1980; 8:644–645.

Hamlett YC, Heath H: The accumulation of fructose-1-phosphate in the diabetic rat retina. *IRCS Med Sci* 1977; 5:510.

Handlesman DJ, Turtle JR: Clinical trial of an aldose reductase inhibitor in diabetic neuropathy. *Diabetes* 1981; 30:459–464.

Hanker JS, Ambrose WW, Yates PE, et al: Peripheral neuropathy in mouse hereditary diabetes mellitus. I. Comparison of neurologic, histologic and morphometric parameters with dystonic mice. *Acta Neuropathol (Berl)* 1980; 51:145–153.

Hastein T, Velle W: Placental aldose reductase activity and foetal blood fructose during bovine pregnancy. *J Reprod Fertil* 1968; 15:47–52.

Hastein T, Velle W: Purification and properties of aldose reductase from the placenta and seminal vesicle of the sheep. *Biochim Biophys Acta* 1969; 178:1–10.

Hawthorne JN, Pickard MP, Griffin HD: Phosphatidylinositol, triphosphoinositide and synaptic transmission, in Wells WW, Eisenberg F (eds): *Cyclitols and Polyphosphoinositides*, pp 145-151. New York, Academic Press, 1978.

Hayman S, Kinoshita JH: Isolation and properties of lens aldose reductase. *J Biol Chem* 1965; 240:877-882.

Hayman S, Lou MF, Merola LO, et al: Aldose reductase activity in the lens and other tissues. *Biochim Biophys Acta* 1966; 128:474-482.

Heath H, Kang SS, Philippou D: Glucose, glucose-6-phosphate, lactate and pyruvate content of the retina, blood and liver of streptozotocin-diabetic rats fed sucrose- or starch-rich diets. *Diabetologia* 1975; 11:57-62.

Heath H, Hamlett YC: The sorbitol pathway: Effect of streptozotocin induced diabetes and the feeding of a sucrose-rich diet on glucose, sorbitol and fructose in the retina, blood and liver of rats. *Diabetologia* 1976; 12:43-46.

Henrickson HS, Reinertsen JL: Phosphoinositide interconversion: A model for control of Na^+ and K^+ permeability in the nerve axon. *Biochem Biophys Res Commun* 1971; 44:1258-1264.

Hermann RK, Kador PF, Kinoshita JH: Rat lens aldose reductase: Rapid purification and comparison with human placental aldose reductase. *Exp Eye Res* 1983; 37:467-474.

Hers HG: Le mécanisme de la formation du fructose séminal et du fructose foetal. *Biochim Biophys Acta* 1960; 37:127-138.

Hers HG: Le mécanisme de la transformation de glucose en fructose par les vésicules séminales. *Biochim Biophys Acta* 1956; 22:202-203.

Hoare EM, Barnes AJ, Dormandy JA: Abnormal blood viscosity in diabetes mellitus and retinopathy. *Biorheology* 1978; 13:21.

Hockwin O, Bergeder HD, Kaiser L: Über die Galaktosekatarakt junger Ratten nach Ganzkorperröntgenbestrahlung. *Ber Dtsch Ophthalmol Ges* 1967; 68:135-139.

Hockwin O, Bergeder HD, Ninnemann U, et al: Untersuchungen zur Latenzzeit der Galaktosekatarakt von Ratten. Einfluss von Röntgenbestrahlung und Diätbeginn bei verschieden alten Tieren. *Graefes Arch Klin Ophthalmol* 1974; 189:171-178.

Hoffman PL, Wermuth B, von Wartburg J-P: Human brain aldehyde reductases: Relationship to succinic semialdehyde reductase and aldose reductase. *J Neurochem* 1980; 35:354-366.

Hogan MJ, Feeney L: The ultrastructure of the retinal vessels. II. The small vessels. *J Ultrastruct Res* 1963; 9:29-46.

Hollows JC, Schofield PJ, Williams JF, et al: The effect of an unsaturated fat-diet on cataract formation in streptozotocin-induced diabetic rats. *Br J Nutr* 1976; 36:161-177.

Hothersall JS, McLean P: Effect of diabetes and insulin on phosphatidylinositol synthesis in rat sciatic nerve. *Biochem Biophys Res Commun* 1979; 88:477-484.

Hotta N, Kakuta H, Fukasawa H, et al: Aldose reductase inhibitor and fructose-rich diet: Its effect on the development of diabetic retinopathy. *Diabetes* 1984; 33(suppl 1):199A.

Hotta N, Kakuta H, Kimura M, et al: Experimental and clinical trial of aldose reductase inhibitor in diabetic neuropathy. *Diabetes* 1983; 32(suppl 1):98A.

Hu T-S, Datiles M, Kinoshita JH: Reversal of galactose cataract with Sorbinil in rats. *Invest Ophthalmol Vis Sci* 1983; 24:640–644.

Huehns ER: Disorders of carbohydrate metabolism in the red blood corpuscle. *Clin Endocrinol Metab* 1976; 5:651–674.

Hutton JC, Schofield PJ, Williams JF, et al: Sorbitol metabolism in the retina: Accumulation of pathway intermediates in streptozotocin induced diabetes in the rat. *Aust J Exp Biol Med Sci* 1974; 52:361–373.

Hutton JC, Schofield PJ, Williams JF, et al: The localization of sorbitol pathway activity in the rat renal cortex and its relationship to the pathogenesis of the renal complications of diabetes mellitus. *Aust J Exp Biol Med Sci* 1975; 53:49–57.

Hutton JC, Schofield PJ, Williams JF, et al: The failure of aldose reductase inhibitor 3,3′-tetramethylene glutaric acid to inhibit in vivo sorbitol accumulation in lens and retina in diabetes. *Biochem Pharmacol* 1974; 23:2991–2998.

Hutton JC, Williams JF, Schofield PJ, et al: Polyol metabolism in monkey-kidney epithelial-cell cultures. *Eur J Biochem* 1974; 49:347–353.

Hyndiuk RA, Kazarian EL, Schultz RO, et al: Neurotrophic corneal ulcers in diabetes mellitus. *Arch Ophthalmol* 1977; 95:2193–2196.

Inagaki K, Miwa I, Yashiro T, et al: Inhibition of aldose reductases from rat and bovine lenses by hydantoin derivatives. *Chem Pharmacol Bull* 1984; 30:3244–3254.

Inagaki K, Miwa I, Okuda J: Affinity purification and glucose specificity of aldose reductase in bovine lens. *Arch Biochem Biophys* 1979; 216:337–344.

Ishikawa T: Fine structure of retinal vessels in man and the macaque monkey. *Invest Ophthalmol* 1963; 2:1–15.

Jacobson M, Sharma YR, Cotlier E, et al: Diabetic complications in lens and nerve and their prevention by sulindac or Sorbinil: Two novel aldose reductase inhibitors. *Invest Ophthalmol Vis Sci* 1983; 24:1426–1429.

Jaspan J, Herold K, Maselli R, et al: Treatment of severe painful diabetic neuropathy with an aldose reductase inhibitor: Relief of pain and improved somatic and autonomic nerve function. *Lancet* 1983; 2:758–762.

Jakobsen J: Axon dwindling in early experimental diabetes. I. A study of cross-sectioned nerves. *Diabetologia* 1976; 12:539–546.

Jakobsen J: Peripheral nerves in early experimental diabetes. Expansion of the endoneurial space as a cause of increased water content. *Diabetologia* 1978; 14:113–119.

Jakobsen J: Early and preventable changes of peripheral nerve structure and function in insulin-deficient diabetic rat. *J Neurol Neurosurg Psychiatry* 1979; 42:509–518.

Jakobsen J, Sidenius P: Decreased axonal transport of structural proteins in streptozotocin-diabetic rats. *J Clin Invest* 1980; 66:292–297.

Jedziniak JA, Chylack LT, Chen H-M, et al: The sorbitol pathway in the human lens: Aldose reductase and polyol dehydrogenase. *Invest Ophthalmol Vis Sci* 1981; 20:314–326.

Jedziniak JA, Kinoshita JH: Activators and inhibitors of lens aldose reductase. *Invest Ophthalmol* 1971; 10:357–366.

Jeffreys JGR, Palmano KP, Sharma AK, et al: Influence of dietary *myo*-inositol on nerve conduction and inositol phospholipids in normal and diabetic rats. *J Neurol Neurosurg Psychiatry* 1978; 41:333–339.

Johnson PC: Thickening of the human dorsal root ganglion perineurial cell basement membrane in diabetes mellitus. *Muscle Nerve* 1983; 6:561–565.

Johnson PC, Brendel K, Meezan E: Human diabetic perineurial cell basement membrane thickening. *Lab Invest* 1981; 44:165–170.

Jones DB: Correlative scanning and transmission electron microscopy of glomeruli. *Lab Invest* 1977; 37:569–578.

Jones DB: SEM of human and experimental renal disease. *Scan Electron Microsc* 1979; 3:679–689.

Judzewitsch RG, Jaspan JB, Polonsky KS, et al: Aldose reductase inhibitor improves nerve conduction velocity in diabetic patients. *N Engl J Med* 1983; 308:119–125.

Kador PF, Carper D, Kinoshita JH: Rapid purification of human placental aldose reductase. *Anal Biochem* 1981; 114:53–58.

Kador PF, Goosey JD, Sharpless NE, et al: Stereospecific inhibition of aldose reductase. *Eur J Med Chem* 1981; 16:293–298.

Kador PF, Kinoshita JH, Tung WH, et al: Differences in the susceptibility of aldose reductase to inhibition. *Invest Ophthalmol Vis Sci* 1980; 19:980–982.

Kador PF, Merola LO, Kinoshita JH: Differences in the susceptibility of aldose reductase to inhibition. *Doc Ophthalmol Proc Ser* 1979; 18:117–124.

Kador PF, Sharpless NE: Pharmacophor requirements of the aldose reductase inhibitor site. *Mol Pharmacol* 1983; 24:521–531.

Kador PF, Sharpless NE: Structure-activity studies of aldose reductase inhibitors containing the 4-oxo-4H-chromen ring system. *Biophys Chem* 1978; 8:81–85.

Kador PF, Sharpless NE, Goosey JD: Aldose reductase inhibition by anti-allergy compounds, in Weiner H, Wermuth B (eds): *Enzymology of Carbonyl Metabolism: Aldehyde Dehydrogenase and Aldo/Keto Reductase*, pp 243–259. New York, Alan R. Liss, 1982.

Kador PF, Zigler S, Kinoshita JH: Alterations of lens protein synthesis in galactosemic rats. *Invest Ophthalmol Vis Sci* 1979; 18:696–702.

Kadoya K, Hashi H, Yui MNH, et al: Influence of aldose reductase inhibitor on peroxidation reaction in the lens of streptozotocin diabetic rats. *Nippon Ganka Kiyo* 1983; 34:2172–2176.

Kahn HA, Liebowitz HM, Ganley JP, et al: The Framingham eye study. II. Association of ophthalmic pathology with single variables previously measured in the Framingham study. *Am J Epidemiol* 1977; 106:33–41.

Kamada T, Otsuji S: Low-levels of erythrocyte membrane fluidity in diabetic patients. A spin label study. *Diabetes* 1983; 32:585–591.

Kanski JJ: Anterior segment complications of retinal photocoagulation. *Am J Ophthalmol* 1975; 79:424–427.

Kanwar YS, Rosenzweig LJ, Linker A, et al: Decreased de novo synthesis of glomerular proteoglycans in diabetes: Biochemical and autoradiographic evidence. *Proc Natl Acad Sci USA* 1983; 80:2272–2275.

Kaplan SA, Lee W-NP, Scott ML: Glucose inhibits *myo*-inositol transport and phosphatidylinositol formation in adipocytes. *Diabetes* 1985; 34(suppl 1):183A.

Keller H-W, Stinnesbeck TH, Hockwin O, et al: Investigations on the influence of whole body X-irradiation on the activity of rat lens aldose reductase (E.C.1.1.1.21). *Graefes Arch Klin Ophthalmol* 1981; 215:181–186.

Kennedy A, Frank RN, Varma SD: Aldose reductase activity in retinal and cerebral microvessels and cultured vascular cells. *Invest Ophthalmol Vis Sci* 1983; 24:1250–1258.

Kern TS, Engerman RL: Distribution of aldose reductase in ocular tissues. *Exp Eye Res* 1981; 33:175–182.

Kern TS, Engerman RL: Immunohistochemical distribution of aldose reductase. *Histochem J* 1982; 14:507–515.

Kern TS, Engerman RL: Hexitol production by canine retinal microvessels. *Invest Ophthalmol Vis Sci* 1985; 26:382–384.

Khalifa A, Cohen MP: Glomerular protocollagen lysyl hydroxylase activity in streptozotocin diabetes. *Biochim Biophys Acta* 1975; 386:332–339.

Kikkawa R, Hatanaka I, Yasuda H, et al: Effect of a new aldose reductase inhibitor, (E)-3-carboxymethyl-5[(2E)-methyl-3-phenylpropenylidene] rhodanine (ONO-2235) on peripheral nerve disorders in streptozotocin-diabetic rats. *Diabetologia* 1984; 24:290–292.

Kilzer P, Chang K, Marvel J, et al: Albumin permeation of new vessels is increased in diabetic rats. *Diabetes* 1985; 34:333–336.

Kinoshita JH: Cataracts in galactosemia. *Invest Ophthalmol* 1965; 4:786–799.

Kinoshita JH: Mechanisms initiating cataract formation. *Invest Ophthalmol* 1974; 13:713–724.

Kinoshita JH, Barber GW, Merola LD, et al: Changes in the levels of free amino acids and *myo*-inositol in the galactose-exposed lens. *Invest Ophthalmol* 1969; 8:625–632.

Kinoshita JH, Dvornik D, Kraml M, et al: The effect of an aldose reductase inhibitor on the galactose-exposed rabbit lens. *Biochim Biophys Acta* 1968; 158:472–475.

Kinoshita JH, Fukushi S, Kador P, et al: Aldose reductase in diabetic complications of the eye. *Metabolism* 1979; 28(suppl 1):462–469.

Kinoshita JH, Futterman S, Satoh K, et al: Factors affecting the formation of sugar alcohols in ocular lens. *Biochim Biophys Acta* 1963; 74:340–350.

Kinoshita JH, Merola LO: Hydration of the lens during the development of galactose cataract. *Invest Ophthalmol* 1964; 3:577–584.

Kinoshita JH, Merola LO, Dikmak E: The accumulation of dulcitol and water in rabbit lens incubated with galactose. *Biochim Biophys Acta* 1962; 62:176–178.

Kinoshita JH, Merola LO, Dikmak E: Osmotic changes in experimental galactose cataracts. *Exp Eye Res* 1962; 1:405–410.

Kinoshita JH, Merola LO, Hayman S: Osmotic effects on the amino acid-concentrating mechanism in the rabbit lens. *J Biol Chem* 1965; 240:313–315.

Kinoshita JH, Merola LO, Satoh K, et al: Osmotic changes caused by the accumulation of dulcitol in the lenses of rats fed with galactose. *Nature (Lond)* 1962; 194:1085–1087.

Kinoshita JH, Merola O, Tung B: Changes in cation permeability in the galactose-exposed rabbit lens. *Exp Eye Res* 1968; 7:80–90.

Koglin L, Clark C, Ryder S, et al: The result of the long-term open-label administration of ALREDASE™ in the treatment of diabetic neuropathy. *Diabetes* 1985; 34(suppl 1):202A.

Krupin T, Waltman SR, Oestrich C, et al: Vitreous fluorophotometry in juvenile-onset diabetes mellitus. *Arch Ophthalmol* 1978; 96:812–814.

Krupin T, Waltman SR, Szewczyk P, et al: Fluorometric studies on the blood retinal barrier in experimental animals. *Arch Ophthalmol* 1982; 100:631–634.

Ku DD, Meezan E: Increased renal tubular sodium pump and Na,K-adenosine triphosphatase in streptozotocin-diabetic rats. *J Pharmacol Exp Ther* 1984; 229:664–670.

Kuwabara T, Cogan DG: Retinal vascular patterns. VI. Mural cells of the retinal capillaries. *Arch Ophthalmol* 1963; 69:492–502.

Kuwabara T, Kinoshita JH, Cogan DC: Electron microscopic study of galactose-induced cataract. *Invest Ophthalmol* 1969; 8:133–149.

Lee SM, Schade SZ, Doughty CC: Aldose reductase, NADPH and NADP$^+$ in normal, galactose-fed and diabetic rat lens. *Biochim Biophys Acta* 1985; 841:247–253.

LeFevre PG, Davis R: Active transport into the human erythrocyte: Evidence from comparative kinetics and composition among monosaccharides. *J Gen Physiol* 1951; 34:515–524.

Lehtinen JM, Hjönen SK, Uusitupa M, et al: The effect of an aldose reductase inhibitor (Sorbinil) on diabetic neuropathy. *Diabetologia* 1984; 27:303A.

Lerner BC, Varma SD, Richards RD: Polyol pathway metabolites in human cataracts. *Arch Ophthalmol* 1984; 102:917–920.

Lewin IG, O'Brien IAD, Morgan MH, et al: Clinical and neurophysiological studies with the aldose reductase inhibitor, Sorbinil, in symptomatic diabetic neuropathy. *Diabetologia* 1984; 26:445–448.

Li W, Chan LS, Khatami M, et al: Inhibition of *myo*-inositol uptake in cultured bovine retinal capillary pericytes by D-glucose: Reversal by Sorbinil. *Invest Ophthalmol Vis Sci* 1985; 26(suppl):335.

Li W, Chan LS, Khatami M, et al: Characterization of glucose transport by bovine retinal capillary pericytes in culture. *Exp Eye Res* 1985; 41:191–199.

Li W, Khatami M, Rockey JH: The effects of glucose and an aldose reductase inhibitor on the sorbitol content and collagen synthesis of bovine retinal capillary pericytes in culture. *Exp Eye Res* 1985; 40:439–444.

Li W, Shen S, Khatami M, et al: Stimulation of retinal capillary pericyte protein and collagen synthesis in culture by high-glucose concentration. *Diabetes* 1984; 33:785–789.

Lo C-S, August TR, Liberman UA, et al: Dependence of renal (Na/K-ATPase)-adenosine triphosphatase activity on thyroid status. *J Biol Chem* 1976; 251: 7826–7833.

Low PA, Dyck PJ, Schmelzer JD: Mammalian peripheral nerve sheath has unique responses to chronic elevations of endoneurial fluid pressure. *Exp Neurol* 1980; 70:300–306.

Low PA, Dyck PJ, Schmelzer JD: Chronic elevation of endoneurial fluid pressure is associated with low-grade fiber pathology. *Muscle Nerve* 1982; 5:162–165.

Ludvigson MA, Sorenson RL: Immunohistochemical localization of aldose reductase. I. Enzyme purification and antibody preparation—localization in peripheral nerve, artery and testis. *Diabetes* 1980; 29:438–449.

Ludvigson MA, Sorenson RL: Immunohistochemical localization of aldose reductase. II. Rat eye and kidney. *Diabetes* 1980; 29:450–459.

MacGregor LC, Matschinsky FM: Treatment with aldose reductase inhibitor or with *myo*-inositol arrests deterioration of the electroretinogram of diabetic rats. *J Clin Invest* 1985; 76:887–889.

MacGregor LC, Matschinsky FM: Correlation of biochemical and electrophysiological abnormalities in retinas of experimentally diabetic animals. *Diabetes* 1985; 34(suppl 1):13A.

MacGregor LC, Rosecan LR, Laties AM, et al: Microanalysis of total lipid, glucose, sorbitol, and *myo*-inositol in individual retinal layers of normal and alloxan diabetic rabbits. *Diabetes* 1984; 33:89A.

McMillan DE, Utterback NG, La Puma J: Reduced erythrocyte deformability in diabetes. *Diabetes* 1978; 27:895–901.

Malone J, Knox G, Benford S, et al: Red cell sorbitol—an indicator of diabetic control. *Diabetes* 1980; 29:861–864.

Malone JI, Knox G, Harvey C: Sorbitol accumulation is altered in Type I (insulin-dependent) diabetes mellitus. *Diabetologia* 1984; 27:509–513.

Malone JI, Leavengood H, Peterson MJ, et al: Red blood cell sorbitol as an indicator of polyol pathway activity. *Diabetes* 1984; 33:45–49.

Maragoudakis ME, Kelinsky H, Wasvary J, et al: Inhibition of basement membrane synthesis and aldose reductase activity by GPA 1734. *Fed Proc* 1976; 35:679.

Maragoudakis ME, Wasvary J, Gaigiulo P, et al: Human placental aldose reductase: Sensitive and insensitive forms to inhibition by alrestatin. *Fed Proc* 1979; 30:255(A).

Markus HB, Raducha M, Harris H: Tissue distribution of mammalian aldose reductase and related enzymes. *Biochem Med* 1983; 29:31–45.

Martines-Hernandez A, Amenta P: The basement membrane in pathology. *Lab Invest* 1983; 48:656–677.

Martyn CN, Matthews DM, Popp-Snijders C, et al: Effects of Sorbinil treatment on erythrocytes and platelets of persons with diabetes. *Diabetes Care* 1985; 9:36–39.

Mayer JH, Herberg L, Tomlinson DR: Axonal transport and nerve conduction and their relation to nerve polyol and *myo*-inositol levels in spontaneously diabetic BB/D rats. *Neurochem Pathol* 1984; 2:285–293.

Mayer JH, Tomlinson DR: Prevention of defects of axonal transport and nerve conduction velocity by oral administration of *myo*-inositol or an aldose reductase inhibitor in streptozotocin-diabetic rats. *Diabetologia* 1983; 25:433–438.

Mayer JH, Tomlinson DR: Axonal transport of cholinergic transmitter enzymes in vagus and sciatic nerves of rats with acute experimental diabetes mellitus; correlation with motor nerve conduction velocity and effects of insulin. *Neuroscience* 1983; 9:951–957.

Mayer JH, Tomlinson Dr, McLean WG: Slow orthograde axonal transport of radio-labelled protein in sciatic motoneurones of rats with short-term experimental diabetes: Effects of treatment with an aldose reductase inhibitor or *myo*-inositol. *J Neurochem* 1984; 43:1265–1270.

Mayhew JA, Gillon KRW, Hawthorne JN: Free and lipid inositol and sugars in sciatic nerve obtained postmortem from diabetic patients and control subjects. *Diabetologia* 1983; 24:13–15.

Medori R, Autilio-Gambetti L, Monaco S, et al: Experimental diabetic neuropathy: Impairment of slow transport with changes in axon cross-sectional area. *Proc Natl Acad Sci USA* 1985; 82:7716–7720.

Michell RH: Inositol phospholipids and cell surface receptor function. *Biochim Biophys Acta* 1980; 415:81–147.

Monckton G, Pehoevich E: Autonomic neuropathy in the streptozotocin diabetic rat. *Can J Neurol Sci* 1980; 7:135–142.

Moonsammy GI, Stewart MA: Purification and properties of brain aldose reductase and L-hexonate dehydrogenase. *J Neurochem* 1967; 14:1187–1193.

Moore SA, Peterson RG, Felton DL, et al: Reduced sensory and motor conduction velocity in 25-week-old diabetic [C57BL/K$_s$ (db/db)] mice. *Exp Neurol* 1980; 70:548–555.

Morrison AD, Clements RS Jr, Winegrad AI: Effects of elevated glucose concentrations on the metabolism of the aortic wall. *J Clin Invest* 1972; 51:3114–3123.

Morrison AD, Clements RS Jr, Travis SB, et al: Glucose utilization by the polyol pathway in human erythrocytes. *Biochem Biophys Res Commun* 1970; 40:199–205.

Myers RR, Costello ML, Powell HC: Increased endoneural fluid pressure in galactose neuropathy. *Muscle Nerve* 1979; 2:229–303.

Morrison AD: Linkage of polyol pathway activity and *myo*-inositol in aortic smooth muscle. *Diabetes* 1985; 34(suppl 1):12A.

Natarajan V, Dyck PJ, Schmid HO: Alterations in inositol lipid metabolism of rat sciatic nerve in streptozotocin-induced diabetes. *J Neurochem* 1981; 36:413–419.

Nishizuka Y: Turnover of inositol phospholipids and signal transduction. *Science* 1984; 225:1365–1370.

Obazawa H, Merola LO, Kinoshita JH: The effects of xylose on the isolated lens. *Invest Ophthalmol Vis Sci* 1974; 13:204–209.

O'Brien MM, Schofield PJ: Polyol pathway enzymes of human brain. *Biochem J* 1980; 187:21–30.

O'Brien MM, Schofield PJ, Edwards MR: Inhibition of human brain aldose reductase and hexonate dehydrogenase by alrestatin and Sorbinil. *J Neurochem* 1982; 39:810–814.

Ohrloff C, Zierz S, Hockwin O: Investigations of the enzymes involved in the fructose breakdown in the cattle lens. *Ophthalmic Res* 1982; 14:221–229.

Okuda J, Miwa I, Inagaki K, et al: Inhibition of aldose reductases from rat and bovine lenses by flavinoids. *Biochem Pharmacol* 1982; 31:3807–3822.

Ono H, Hayano S: 2,2',4'4'-Tetrahydroxybenzophenone as a new aldose reductase inhibitor. *Nippon Ganka Gakkai Zasshi* 1982; 86:353–357.

Ono H, Nozawa Y, Hayano S: Effects of M-79,175, an aldose reductase inhibitor, on experimental sugar cataracts. *Nippon Ganka Gakkai Zasshi* 1982; 86:1343–1350.

Palamano KP, Whiting PH, Hawthorne JN: Free and lipid *myo*-inositol in tissues from rats with acute and less severe streptozotocin-induced diabetes. *Biochem J* 1977; 167:229–235.

Parathasarathy N, Spiro RG: Effect of diabetes on the glycosaminoglycan component of the human glomerular basement membrane. *Diabetes* 1982; 31:738–741.

Perejda AJ, Uitto J: Nonenzymatic glycosylation of collagen and other proteins: Relationship to the development of diabetic complications. *Coll Rel Res* 1982; 2:81–88.

Perry HD, Foulks GN, Thoft RA, et al: Corneal complications after closed vitrectomy through the pars plana. *Arch Ophthalmol* 1978; 96:1401–1403.

Peterson MJ, Sarges R, Aldinger CE, et al: CP-45,634: A novel aldose reductase inhibitor that inhibits polyol pathway activity in diabetic and galactosemic rats. *Metabolism* 1979; 28(suppl 1):456–461.

Peterson MJ, Sarges R, Aldinger CE, et al: Inhibition of polyol pathway activity in diabetic and galactosemic rats by the aldose reductase inhibitor CP-45,634. *Adv Exp Med Biol* 1979; 119:347–356.

Pfeifer MA, Weinberg CR, Cook DL, et al: Correlations among autonomic, sensory and motor neural function tests in untreated non-insulin-dependent diabetic individuals. *Diabetes Care* 1985; 8:576–584.

Pfister RR, Schepens CL, Lemp MA, et al: Photocoagulation keratopathy: Report of a case. *Arch Ophthalmol* 1971; 86:94–96.

Pfister JR, Wymann WE, Mahoney JM, et al: Synthesis and aldose reductase inhibitor activity of 7-sulfamoylxanthone-2-carboxylic acids. *J Med Chem* 1980; 23:1264–1267.

Pitkänen E: The serum polyol pattern and the urinary polyol excretion in diabetic and uremic patients. *Clin Chim Acta* 1972; 38:221–230.

Pitkänen E, Servo C: Cerebrospinal fluid polyols in patients with diabetes. *Clin Chim Acta* 1973; 44:437–442.

Popp-Snijders C, Lomecky-Janousek MZ, Schouten J, et al: *Myo*-inositol and sorbitol in erythrocytes from diabetic patients before and after Sorbinil treatment. *Diabetologia* 1984; 27:514–516.

Poulsom R, Boot-Hanford RP, Heath H: Some effects of aldose reductase inhibition upon the eyes of long-term streptozotocin-diabetic rats. *Curr Eye Res* 1982; 2:351–355.

Poulsom R, Heath H: Inhibition of aldose reductase in five tissues of the streptozotocin diabetic rat. *Biochem Pharmacol* 1983; 32:1495–1499.

Poulsom R, Mirrlees DJ, Earl DCN, et al: The effects of an aldose reductase inhibitor upon the sorbitol pathway, fructose-1-phosphate and lactate in the retina and nerve of streptozotocin diabetic rats. *Exp Eye Res* 1983; 36:751–760.

Powell HC: Pathology of diabetic neuropathy: New observations, new hypotheses. *Lab Invest* 1983; 49:515–518.

Powell HC, Costello ML, Myers RR: Endoneurial fluid pressure in experimental models of diabetic neuropathy. *J Neuropathol Exp Neurol* 1981; 40:613–634.

Powell H, Know D, Lee S, et al: Alloxan diabetic neuropathy: Electron microscopic studies. *Neurology* 1977; 27:60–66.

Powell HC, Myers RR: Schwann cell changes and demyelination in chronic galactose neuropathy. *Muscle Nerve* 1983; 6:218–227.

Pozza G, Cordaro C, Carandente O, et al: Study on relationship between erythrocyte filtration and other risk factors in diabetic angiopathy. *Ric Clin Lab* 1981; 11(suppl 1):317–326.

Proceedings of Puerto Rico Conference on Sorbinil and Diabetic Complications. *Metabolism* 35(suppl 1), April 1986.

Proceedings of Aldose Reductase Inhibitor Symposium, London, 1984. *Diabetic Medicine*, vol 2, 1985.

Puhakainen E, Saamanen AM, Lehtinen J, et al: The effect of aldose reductase inhibitor (Sorbinil®) on erythrocyte sorbitol concentration in diabetic neuropathy. *Acta Endocrinol* 1983; 103(suppl 257):56.

Raff MC, Asbury AK: Ischemic mononeuropathy and mononeuropathy multiplex in diabetes mellitus. *N Engl J Med* 1968; 279:17–22.

Raskin P, Rosenstock J, Challis P, et al: Effect of tolrestat on RBC sorbitol levels in diabetic subjects. *Diabetes* 1985; 34(suppl 1):7A.

Reddy DVN: Amino acid transport in the lens in relation to sugar cataracts. *Invest Ophthalmol* 1965; 4:700.

Reddy VN: Metabolism of glutathione in the lens. *Exp Eye Res* 1971; 11:310–328.

Reddy VN, Chakrapani B, Steen D: Sorbitol pathway in the ciliary body in relation to accumulation of amino acids in the aqueous humor of alloxan diabetic rabbits. *Invest Ophthalmol* 1971; 100:870–875.

Reddy DVN, Kinsey VE: Transport of amino acids into intraocular fluids and lens in diabetic rabbits. *Invest Ophthalmol* 1963; 2:237–242.

Reddy VN, Schauss D, Chakrapani B, et al: Biochemical changes associated with the development and reversal of galactose cataracts. *Exp Eye Res* 1976; 23:483–493.

Richon AB, Maragoudakis ME, Wasvary JS: Isoxazolidine-3,5-diones as lens aldose reductase inhibitors. *J Med Chem* 1982; 25:745–747.

Ris MM, von Wartbury J: Heterogeneity of NADPH-dependent aldehyde reductase from human and rat brain. *Eur J Biochem* 1973; 37:69–77.

Ristelli J, Koivisto VA, Akerblom HK, et al: Intracellular enzymes of collagen biosynthesis in rat kidney with streptozotocin diabetes. *Diabetes* 1976; 25:1066 1070.

Robey C, Dasmahapatra A, Cohen MP, et al: Sorbinil prevents decreased erythrocyte deformability in diabetes. *Diabetes* 1985; 34:161A.

Robey C, Dasmahapatra A, Cohen MP: In vitro effects of hyperglycemia and Sorbinil on erythrocyte (RBC) deformability. *Diabetes* 1986; 35:108A.

Robey C, Dasmahapatra A, Cohen MP, et al: Sorbinil prevents decreased erythrocyte deformability in diabetes mellitus. Manuscript submitted, 1986.

Robison WG, Kador PF, Kinoshita JH: Retinal capillaries: Basement membrane thickening by galactosemia prevented with aldose reductase inhibitor. *Science* 1983; 221:1177–1179.

Roelofsen B, Trip MVL-S: The fraction of phosphatidylinositol that activates the (Na^+/K^+)-ATPase in rabbit kidney microsomes is closely associated with the enzyme protein. *Biochim Biophys Acta* 1981; 647:302–306.

Rohrbach DH, Hassell JR, Kleinman HK, et al: Alterations in the basement membrane (heparan sulfate) proteoglycan in diabetic mice. *Diabetes* 1982; 31:185–188.

Rohrbach DH, Wagner CW, Star VL, et al: Reduced synthesis of basement membrane heparan sulfate proteoglycan in streptozotocin-induced diabetic mice. *J Biol Chem* 1983; 258:11672–11677.

Romen W, Heck T, Rauscher G, et al: Glomerular basement membrane turnover in young, old, and streptozotocin-diabetic rats. *Renal Physiol* 1980; 3:324–329.

Romen W, Lange H-W, Hempel K, et al: Studies on collagen metabolism in rats. II. Turnover and amino acid composition of the collagen of glomerular basement membrane in diabetes mellitus. *Virchows Arch (Cell Pathol)* 1981; 36:313–320.

Ross WM, Creighton MO, Stewart-DeHaan PJ, et al: Modelling cortical cataractogenesis: 3. In vivo effects of vitamin E on cataractogenesis in diabetic rats. *Can J Ophthalmol* 1982; 17:61–66.

Russell P, Merola LO, Yajima Y, et al: Aldose reductase activity in a cultured human retinal cell line. *Exp Eye Res* 1982; 35:331–336.

Satoh M, Imaizumi K, Bessho T, et al: Increased erythrocyte aggregation in diabetes and its relationship to glycosylated hemoglobin and retinopathy. *Diabetologia* 1984; 27:517–521.

Schlaepfer WW, Gerritsen GC, Dulin WE: Segmental demyelination in the distal peripheral nerves of chronically diabetic chinese hamsters. *Diabetologia* 1974; 10:541–548.

Schmidt RE, Matschinsky FM, Godfrey DA, et al: Fast and slow axoplasmic flow in sciatic nerve of diabetic rats. *Diabetes* 1975; 24:1081–1085.

Schmid-Schonbein H, Volger E: Red cell aggregation and red cell deformability in diabetes. *Diabetes* 1976; 25:897–902.

Schnur RC, Sarges R, Peterson MJ: Spiro oxazolidinedione aldose reductase inhibitors. *J Med Chem* 1982; 25:1451–1454.

Schultz RO, VanHorn DL, Peters MA, et al: Diabetic keratopathy. *Trans Am Ophthalmol Soc* 1981; 79:180–199.

Segelman AB, Segelman FP, Varma SD, et al: *Cannabis sativa L.* (Marijuana) IX: Lens aldose reductase inhibitory activity of marijuana flavone C-glycosides. *J Pharm Sci* 1977; 66:1358–1359.

Seneviratne KN: Permeability of blood nerve barriers in the diabetic rat. *J Neurol Neurosurg Psychiatry* 1972; 35:156–162.

Servo C: Sorbitol and *myo*-inositol in the cerebrospinal fluid of diabetic patients. *Acta Endocrinol* 1980; 94(suppl 238):133–138.

Servo C, Bergstrom L, Fogelholm R: Cerebrospinal fluid sorbitol and *myo*-inositol in diabetic polyneuropathy. *Acta Med Scand* 1977; 202:301–304.

Servo C, Pitkänen E: Variation in polyol levels in cerebrospinal fluid and serum in diabetic patients. *Diabetologia* 1975; 11:575–580.

Seyer-Hansen K: Renal hypertrophy in experimental diabetes: Relation to severity of diabetes. *Diabetologia* 1977; 13:141–143.

Sestanj K, Bellini F, Fung S, et al: N([5-(trifluoromethyl)-6-methoxy-1-naphthalenyl] thioxomethyl)-N-methylglycine (tolrestat), a potent orally active aldose reductase inhibitor. *J Med Chem* 1984; 27:255–256.

Shakib M, Cunha-Vaz JG: Studies on the permeability of the blood retinal barrier. IV. Junctional complexes of the retinal vessels and their role in the permeability of the blood retinal barrier. *Exp Eye Res* 1966; 5:229–234.

Sharma AK, Baker RWR, Thomas PK: Peripheral nerve abnormalities related to galactose administration in rats. *J Neurol Neuropathol Psychiatry* 1976; 39:794–802.

Sharma YR, Cotlier E: Inhibition of lens and cataract aldose reductase by protein-bound anti-rheumatic drugs: Salicylate, indomethacin, oxyphenbutazone, sulindac. *Exp Eye Res* 1982; 35:21–27.

Sheaf CM, Doughty CC: Physical and kinetic properties of homogenous bovine lens. *J Biol Chem* 1976; 251:2696–2702.

Sheys GH, Arnold WJ, Watson JA, et al: Aldose reductase from *Rhodotorula*. *J Biol Chem* 1971; 246:3824–3827.

Sheys GH, Doughty CC: The reaction mechanism of aldose reductase from *Rhodotorula*. *Biochim Biophys Acta* 1971; 242:523–531.

Sherman WR, Stewart MA: Identification of sorbitol in mammalian nerve. *Biochem Biophys Res Commun* 1966; 22:492–497.

Sidenius P: The axonapathy of diabetic neuropathy. *Diabetes* 1982; 31:356–363.

Siddiqui MA, Rahman MA: Effect of hyperglycemia on the enzyme activities of lenticular tissue of rats. *Exp Eye Res* 1980; 31:463–469.

Sima AA: Peripheral neuropathy in the spontaneously diabetic BB-Wistar rat. *Acta Neuropathol (Berl)* 1980; 51:223–227.

Sima AAF, Bril V, Greene DA: A new characteristic ultrastructural abnormality, and morphologic evidence for pathogenetic heterogeneity in human diabetic neuropathy. *Clin Res* 1986; 34:688A.

Sima AAF, Lattimer SA, Yagihashi S, et al: Biochemical, functional, and structural correction of diabetic neuropathy in the BB-rat after insulin treatment. *Fed Proc* 1984; 43:375A.

Sima AF, Lattimer SA, Yagihashi S, et al: Axo-glial dysfunction. A novel structural lesion that accounts for poorly reversible slowing of nerve conduction in the spontaneously diabetic Bio-Breeding rat. *J Clin Invest* 1986; 77:474–484.

Simard-Duquesne N, Greslin E, Dubuc J, et al: The effect of a new aldose reductase inhibitor (tolrestat) in galactosemic and diabetic rats. *Metabolism* 1985; 34:885–892.

Simard-Duquesne N, Greslin E, Gonzalez R, et al: Prevention of cataract development in severely galactosemic rats by the aldose reductase inhibitor, tolrestat. *Proc Soc Exp Biol Med* 1985; 178:599–605.

Simmons DA, Kern EFO, Winegrad AI, et al: Basal phosphatidylinositol turnover controls aortic Na^+/K^+ ATPase activity. *J Clin Invest* 1986; 77:503–513.

Simmons DA, Winegrad AI, Martin DB: Significance of tissue *myo*-inositol concentrations in metabolic regulation in nerve. *Science* 1982; 217:848–851.

Sippel TO: Changes in the water, protein and glutathione contents of the lens in the course of galactose cataract development in rats. *Invest Ophthalmol* 1960; 5:568–575.

Sohda T, Mizuno K, Imamiya E, et al: Studies on antidiabetic agents. 5-Arylthiazolidine-2,4-diones as potent aldose reductase inhibitors. *Chem Pharm Bull (Tokyo)* 1982; 30:3601–3616.

Speiser P, Gittelsohn AM, Patz A: Studies on diabetic retinopathy. III. Influence of diabetes on intramural pericytes. *Arch Ophthalmol* 1968; 80:332–337.

Spiro RG, Spiro MJ: Effect of diabetes on the biosynthesis of renal glomerular basement membrane. Studies on the glucosyltransferase. *Diabetes* 1971; 20:641–648.

Srivastava SK, Ansari NH, Hair GA, et al: Aldose and aldehyde reductase in human tissues. *Biochim Biophys Acta* 1984; 800:220–227.

Srivastava SK, Hair GA, Das B: Activated and unactivated forms of human erythrocyte aldose reductase. *Proc Natl Acad Sci USA* 1985; 82:7222–7226.

Srivastava SK, Petrash JM, Sadana IJ, et al: Susceptibility of aldehyde and aldose reductase of human tissues to aldose reductase inhibitors. *Curr Eye Res* 1982; 2:407–410.

Stewart MA, Passoneau JV: Identification of fructose in mammalian nerve. *Biochem Biophys Res Commun* 1964; 17:536–541.

Stewart MA, Sherman WR, Anthony S: Free sugars in alloxan diabetic rat nerve. *Biochem Biophys Res Commun* 1966; 22:488–491.

Stewart MA, Sherman WR, Kurien MM, et al: Polyol accumulation in nervous tissue of rats with experimental diabetes and galactosemia. *J Neurochem* 1977; 14:1057–1066.

Stockard C, Clements R: Usefulness of blood elements in the prediction of the fructose and *myo*-inositol content of nerve and lens. *Diabetes* 1984; 33(suppl 1): 89A.

Sugimura K, Windebank AJ, Natarajan V, et al: Interstitial hyperosmolarity may cause axis cylinder shrinkage in streptozotocin diabetic nerve. *J Neuropathol Exp Neurol* 1980; 39:710–721.

Tanimoto T, Fukuda H, Kawamura J: Purification and some properties of aldose reductase from rabbit lens. *Chem Pharm Bull (Tokyo)* 1983; 31:2395–2403.

Tetjak AG, Limarenko IM, Lossova GV, et al: Interrelation of phosphoinositide metabolism and ion transport in crab nerve fiber. *J Neurochem* 1977; 28:199–205.

Thomas PK, Lascelles RG: The pathology of diabetic neuropathy. *Q J Med* 1966; 24:489–509.

Thornally PJ, Wolff SP, Crabbe MJC, et al: Auto-oxidation of glyceraldehyde and other monosaccharides catalyzed by buffer ions. *Biochim Biophys Acta* 1984; 797:276–287.

Timperley WR: Vascular and coagulation abnormalities in diabetic neuropathy and encephalopathy. *Horm Metab Res* 1980; 9(suppl):43–49.

Timperley WR, Ward JD, Preston FE, et al: Clinical and histological studies in diabetic neuropathy: A reassessment of vascular factors in relation to vascular coagulation. *Diabetologia* 1976; 12:237–243.

Toback FG: Phosphatidylcholine metabolism during renal growth and regeneration. *Am J Physiol* 1984; 246:F249–F259.

Tomlinson DR, Holmes PR, Mayer JH: Reversal, by treatment with an aldose reductase inhibitor, of impaired axonal transport and motor nerve conduction velocity in experimental diabetes. *Neurosci Lett* 1982; 31:189–193.

Tomlinson DR, Mayer JH: Defects of axonal transport in diabetes mellitus—a possible contribution to the aetiology of diabetic neuropathy. *J Auton Pharmacol* 1984; 4:59–72.

Tomlinson DR, Moriarty RJ, Mayer JH: Prevention and reversal of defective axonal transport and motor nerve conduction velocity in rats with experimental diabetes by treatment with the aldose reductase inhibitor Sorbinil. *Diabetes* 1984; 33:470–476.

Tomlinson DR, Sidenius P, Larsen JR: Slow component-a of axonal transport, nerve *myo*-inositol, and aldose reductase inhibition in diabetic rats. *Diabetes* 1986; 35:398–402.

Tomlinson DR, Townsend J: Protection by the aldose reductase inhibitor "Statil" (ICI 128436) against loss of an axonally transported enzyme in nerve terminals of diabetic rats. *Diabetes* 1985; 34(suppl 1):202A.

Tomlinson DR, Townsend J, Fretten P: Prevention of defective axonal transport in streptozotocin-diabetic rats by treatment with "Statil" (ICI 128436), an aldose reductase inhibitor. *Diabetes* 1985; 34:970–972.

Travis SF, Morrison AD, Clements RS Jr, et al: Metabolic alterations in the human erythrocyte produced by increases in glucose concentration. *J Clin Invest* 1971; 50:2104–2112.

Trüeb B, Fluckiger R, Winterhalter KH: Nonenzymatic glycosylation of basement membrane collagen in diabetes mellitus. *Coll Rel Res* 1984; 4:239–251.

Turner AJ, Tipton KF: The characterization of two reduced nicotinamide adenine dinucleotide phosphate-linked aldehyde reductases from pig brain. *Biochem J* 1972; 130:765–772.

Uitto J, Perejda AJ, Grant GA, et al: Glucosylation of human glomerular basement membrane collagen: Increased content of hexose in ketoamine linkage and unaltered hydroxylysine-o-glycosides in patients with diabetes. *Connect Tiss Res* 1982; 10:287–296.

Ulbrecht JS, Bensen JT, Greene DA: Sodium-dependent *myo*-inositol uptake in isolated renal glomeruli: Possible inhibition by glucose. *Diabetes* 1985; 34 (suppl 1):13A.

Unakar NJ, Tsui JY: Inhibition of galactose-induced alterations in ocular lens with Sorbinil. *Exp Eye Res* 1983; 36:685–694.

Valbo AB, Hagbarth K-E, Torebjork HE, et al: Somatosensory, proprioceptive and sympathetic activity in human peripheral nerves. *Physiol Rev* 1979; 59:919–957.

Van Heyningen R: Formation of polyols by the lens of the rat with sugar cataracts. *Nature (Lond)* 1959; 184:194–195.

Van Heyningen R: Metabolism of xylose by the lens. Rat lens in vivo and in vitro. *Biochem J* 1959; 73:197–207.

Varma SD: Superoxide and lens of the eye. A new theory of cataractogenesis. *Int J Quantum Chem* 1981; 20:479–484.

Varma SD, El-Aguizy HK, Richards RD: Refractive changes in alloxan diabetic rabbits. Control by flavinoids. *Acta Ophthalmol* 1980; 58:748–759.

Varma SD, Kinoshita JH: The absence of cataracts in mice with congenital hyperglycemia. *Exp Eye Res* 1974; 19:577–582.

Varma SD, Kinoshita JH: Sorbitol pathway in diabetic galactosemic rat lens. *Biochim Biophys Acta* 1974; 338:632–640.

Varma SD, Kinoshita JH: Inhibition of lens aldose reductase by flavinoids. *Biochem Pharmacol* 1976; 25:2505–2513.

Varma SD, Kumar S, Richards RD: Protection by ascorbate against superoxide injury to the lens. *Invest Ophthalmol Vis Sci* 1979; 18(suppl):98.

Varma SD, Mikuni I, Kinoshita JH: Flavinoids as inhibitors of lens aldose reductase. *Science* 1975; 188:1215–1216.

Varma SD, Mizuno A, Kinoshita JH: Diabetic cataracts and flavinoids. *Science* 1977; 195:205–206.

Varma SD, Shockert SS, Richards RD: Implications of aldose reductase in cataracts in human diabetics. *Invest Ophthalmol Vis Sci* 1979; 18:237–241.

Vere DW, Verrel D: Relation between blood sugar level and the optical properties of the lens of the human eye. *Clin Sci* 1955; 14:183–196.

Vogt BW, Schleicher ED, Wieland OH: ϵ-Amino-lysine bound glucose in human tissues obtained at autopsy: Increase in diabetes mellitus. *Diabetes* 1983; 31:1123–1127.

Waltman S, Krupin T, Hanish S, et al: Alteration of the blood retinal barrier in experimental diabetes mellitus. *Arch Ophthalmol* 1978; 96:878–879.

Ward JD: The polyol pathway in the neuropathy of early diabetes, in Camerini-Davalos RA, Cole HS (eds): *Vascular and Neurologic Changes in Early Diabetes*, pp 525–532. New York, Academic Press, 1973.

Ward JD, Baker RWP, Davis BH: Effect of blood sugar control on the accumulation of sorbitol and fructose in nerve tissues. *Diabetes* 1972; 21:1173–1178.

Wautier JL, Paton RC, Wautier M-P, et al: Increased adhesion of erythrocytes to endothelial cells in diabetes mellitus and its relation to vascular complications. *N Engl J Med* 1981; 305:237–242.

Wells AM, Greene DA: A Sorbinil-responsive *myo*-inositol related Na/K-ATPase defect in diabetic rat superior cervical ganglion. *Diabetes* 1985; 34(suppl 1): 102A.

Wermuth B, Burgesser H, Bohren K, et al: Purification and characterization of human-brain aldose reductase. *Eur J Biochem* 1982; 127:297–284.

White GL, Larabee MG: Phosphoinositides and other phospholipids in sympathetic ganglia and nerve trunks of rats. *J Neurochem* 1973; 20:783–798.

White GL, Schellhase HU, Hawthorne JN: Phosphoinositide metabolism in rat superior cervical ganglion, vagus and phrenic nerve: Effects of electrical stimulation and various blocking agents. *J Neurochem* 1974; 28:149–158.

Whiting PH, Palmano KP, Hawthorne JN: Enzymes of *myo*-inositol and inositol lipid metabolism in rats with streptozotocin induced diabetes. *Biochem J* 1979; 179:549–553.

Williams E, Timperley WR, Ward JD, et al: Electron microscopic studies of vessels in diabetic peripheral neuropathy. *J Clin Pathol* 1980; 33:462–470.

Wick AN, Drury DR: Insulin and permeability of cells to sorbitol. *Am J Physiol* 1951; 166:421–423.

Williamson JR, Chang K, Rowold E, et al: Diabetes-induced increases in vascular permeability are prevented by castration and by Sorbinil. *Diabetes* 1985; 34(suppl 1):108A.

Williamson JR, Chang C, Rowold E, et al: Diabetes-induced increases in vascular permeability and changes in granulation tissue levels of sorbitol, *myo*-inositol, *chiro*-inositol, and *scyllo*-inositol are prevented by Sorbinil. *Metabolism* 1986; 35(suppl 1):41–45.

Williamson JR, Chang K, Rowold E, et al: Sorbinil prevents diabetes-induced increases in vascular permeability but does not alter collagen cross-linking. *Diabetes* 1985; 34:703–705.

Williamson JR, Rowold E, Chang K, et al: Albumin permeation of new (granulation tissue) vessels is increased in diabetic rats. *Diabetes* 1984; 33(suppl 1):3A.

Williamson JR, Rowold E, Chang K, et al: Sex steroid dependency of diabetes-induced changes in polyol metabolism, vascular permeability, and collagen cross-linking. *Diabetes* 1986; 35:20–27.

Winegrad AI, Greene DA: Diabetic polyneuropathy: The importance of insulin deficiency, hyperglycemia and alterations in *myo*-inositol metabolism in its pathogenesis. *N Engl J Med* 1976; 295:1416–1421.

Winegrad AI, Simmons DA, Martin DB: Has one diabetic complication been explained? *N Engl J Med* 1983; 308:152–154.

Wirth H-P, Wermuth B: Immunochemical characterization of aldo-keto reductases from human tissues. *FEBS Lett* 1985; 187:280–282.

Wise GN, Dollery GT, Henkind P: *The Retinal Circulation*, pp 290–324, 350–420. New York, Harper & Row, 1971.

Wolff SP, Crabbe MJC, Thornally PJ: Autoxidation of glyceraldehyde and other simple monosaccharides. *Experientia* 1984; 40:244–246.

Wu V-Y, Cohen MP: Platelet factor 4 binding to glomerular microvascular matrix. *Biochim Biophys Acta* 1984; 797:76–82.

Yagihashi S, Kudo K, Nishihira M: Peripheral nerve structures of experimental diabetes in rats and the effect of insulin treatment. *Tohuku J Exp Med* 1979; 127:35–44.

Yamani T: Effect of aldose reductase inhibitor on the oscillatory potential in ERG of streptozotocin diabetic rats. *Folia Ophthalmol Jpn* 1983; 34:2237–2244.

Yanoff M: Diabetic retinopathy. *N Engl J Med* 1966; 274:1344–1349.

Yoshida H: The characteristics of aldose reductase in human lens, placenta, and rat organs. *Nippon Ganka Gakkai Zasshi* 1981; 85:865–869.

Young RJ, Ewing DJ, Clarke BF: A controlled trial of Sorbinil, an aldose reductase inhibitor, in chronic painful diabetic neuropathy. *Diabetes* 1983; 32:938–942.

Young RJ, Matthews DM, Clarke BF, et al: Aldose reductase inhibition for diabetic neuropathy (letter to the editor). *Lancet* 1983; 2:969.

Yue DK, Hanwell MA, Satchell PM, et al: The effect of aldose reductase inhibition on motor nerve conduction velocity in diabetic rats. *Diabetes* 1982; 31:789–794.

Index